ELIZABETH VO

(1866-1941) was born Mary Annette Beauchamp in Sydney, Australia, and brought up in England. Travelling in Italy with her father in 1889, she met her first husband, Count Henning August von Arnim-Schlagenthin. They were married in London the following year and lived in Berlin. After five years of marriage the von Arnims moved to their family estate, Nassenheide, in Pomerania: Elizabeth's experience and deep love of Nassenheide were to be wittily encapsulated in her first and most famous novel, *Elizabeth and Her German Garden*, published anonymously in 1898. The twenty-one books she then went on to write were signed 'By the author of Elizabeth and Her German Garden', and later simply 'By Elizabeth'.

Elizabeth von Arnim gave birth to four daughters and a son, whose tutors at Nassenheide included E. M. Forster and Hugh Walpole. Her idyllic Prussian days were, however, to be abruptly ended when, in 1908, debt forced the von Arnims to sell the estate. They moved to England, and in 1910 Count von Arnim died. Buying a site in Switzerland, Elizabeth built the Château Soleil where she worked on her books and entertained such friends as H. G. Wells (with whom she had an affair), Katherine Mansfield (her cousin), John Middleton Murry and Frank Swinnerton. On the outbreak of war she managed to escape to England, but she was unable to rescue her daughter Felicitas, who died in Germany. In 1916 Elizabeth von Arnim married Francis, second Earl Russell, brother of Bertrand Russell, whom she had met three years previously. This proved to be a disastrous union: in the first year of marriage Elizabeth ran away to America, and in 1919 the couple finally separated.

A greatly admired literary figure of her time, described by Alice Meynell as 'one of the three finest wits of her day', Elizabeth spent her later years in Switzerland, London, and the French Riviera where she wrote her autobiography, *All the Dogs of My Life* (1936). On the outbreak of the Second World War she moved to America, where she died two years later at the age of seventy-five.

The Enchanted April has recently been filmed as a BBC 'Screen on 2' dramatisation. Virago also publishes nine other novels by Elizabeth von Arnim.

VIRAGO
MODERN
CLASSIC
NUMBER
391

Elizabeth von Arnim

MR
SKEFFINGTON

Published by VIRAGO PRESS Limited October 1993
42–43 Gloucester Crescent, Camden Town, London NW1 7PD

Reprinted 1994

First published in Great Britain by William Heinemann 1940

A CIP catalogue record for this book is available from the British Library

Printed in Great Britain by Cox & Wyman Ltd, Reading, Berks.

FANNY, who had married a Mr. Skeffington, and long ago, for reasons she considered compelling, divorced him, after not having given him a thought for years, began, to her surprise, to think of him a great deal. If she shut her eyes, she could see him behind the fish-dish at breakfast; and presently, even if she didn't shut her eyes, she could see him behind almost anything.

. What particularly disturbed her was that there was no fish. Only during Mr. Skeffington's not very long reign as a husband had there been any at breakfast, he having been a man tenacious of tradition, and liking to see what he had seen in his youth still continuing on his table. With his disappearance, the fish-dish, of solid silver, kept hot by electricity, disappeared too— not that he took it with him, for he was much too miserable to think of dishes, but because Fanny's breakfast, from the date of his departure to the time she had got to now, was half a grapefruit.

Naturally she was a good deal worried by seeing him and the dish so distinctly, while knowing that neither he nor it were really there. She very nearly went to a doctor about it; but never having been much disposed to go to doctors she thought she would wait a little first. For after all, reasoned Fanny, who considered herself a very sensible woman, she was soon going to have a fiftieth birthday, and on reaching so conspicuous, so sobering a landmark in one's life, what more natural than to hark back and rummage, and what more inevitable, directly one rummaged, than to come across Mr. Skeffington? He had played, for a time, a leading part in her life. He had been, she recognized, the keystone of her career. It was thanks to the settlements he had made on her, which were the settlements of an extremely rich and extremely loving man, that she was so well off, and it was thanks to his infidelities—but ought one to thank infidelities? Well, never mind—that she was free.

She had adored being free. Twenty-two years of enchanting freedom she had had, and adoring every minute of them—except the minutes at the end of a love affair, when things suddenly seemed unable to avoid being distressing, and except the minutes quite lately, when she was recovering from a terrible illness, and had nothing to do but think, and began thinking about Mr.

Skeffington. Perhaps it was the highly unpleasant birthday looming so close that set her off in these serious directions. Perhaps it was being so wretchedly weak after diphtheria. Perhaps it was the way her lovely hair had fallen out in handfuls. But set off she did, and he who had once been her husband appeared to respond to the treatment with an alacrity which startled her, and gradually became quite upsettingly vivid and real.

This, though, had only happened in the last few months, and she was sure would soon, when she was quite strong again, pass. Up to her illness, how unclouded her life had been! Really a quite radiant life, full of every sort of amusing and exciting things like would-be lovers—at one time the whole world appeared to want to be Fanny's lover—and all because Mr. Skeffington was never able to resist his younger typists.

How angry those typists had made her, till it dawned on her that what they really were were gates to freedom. When at last she saw them in their true light, as so many bolts shot back and doors flung open, she left off being angry, and began instead —strictly speaking, she didn't suppose she ought to have—to rejoice. No, she oughtn't to have rejoiced; but how difficult it was not to like being without Mr. Skeffington. At no time had she enjoyed her marriage. She was very sorry, but really she hadn't. Among other things, he was a Jew, and she wasn't. Not that that would have mattered, since she was without prejudices, if he hadn't happened to look so exactly like a Jew. It wasn't a bit necessary that he should. Lots of people she knew had married Jews, and none of them looked so exactly like one as Job (Mr. Skeffington's name was Job, a name, everybody agreed, impossible to regard as other than unfortunate). Still, he couldn't help that, and certainly he had been very kind. Being an upright girl, who believed in sticking to her vows and giving as good as she got, she too had been very kind. Her heart, however, hadn't been in it. A marriage, she found, with someone of a different breed is fruitful of small rubs; and she had had to change her religion too, which annoyed her, in spite of her not really having any. So that when he offered her those repeated chances of honourably getting rid of him, though she began by being outraged she ended by being pleased.

§

Fanny well knew that her reactions to Mr. Skeffington's in-

fidelities weren't at all the proper ones, but she couldn't help
that. She was perfectly aware she ought to have gone on growing
angrier and angrier, and more and more miserable; and instead,
things happened this way: Obliged to forgive the first typist,
such was his penitence and such his shame, the second one,
though humiliating, didn't distress her quite so acutely. Over
the third she was almost calm. The fourth made her merely
wonder there should be so many young persons liking him
enough for that sort of thing, but she supposed it must be his
money. The fifth she called on, earnestly inquiring of the
alarmed and shrinking creature what she saw in him. At the
sixth, she went out and bought some new hats; and after the
seventh, she left.

Left, and never came back. Left, and beheld him no more
till they faced each other in the Divorce Court. Since then she
hadn't set eyes on Mr. Skeffington, except once, not long after
the final kicking free, when her car—his car, really, if you
looked at it dispassionately—was held up in Pall Mall at the
very moment when he, walking to his club, chanced to be passing. There she sat, such a lovely thing, delicately fair in the
dark frame of the car, obviously someone everybody would
long to be allowed to love, the enormous hat of the early
summer of 1914 perched on hair whose soft abundance he had
often, in happier days, uxoriously stroked, and was so completely already uninterested in him that she hardly bothered to
turn her head. Wasn't this hard? Now, wasn't this terribly
hard? Mr. Skeffington asked himself, his whole being one impassioned protest. Hadn't he worshipped her, lived for her,
thought only of her—even, somehow, when he was thinking
of the pretty little girl in the office as well? And what, in the
long run, were the pretty little girls in the office to a man?
Nothing; nothing; less than nothing, compared to a darling,
exquisite, and, as he had supposed, permanent wife.

But Fanny, sideways through her eyelashes, did see him, saw
how he hesitated and half stopped, saw how red he grew,
thought: Poor Job, I believe he's still in love with me, and idly
mused, as she was driven on up St. James's Street in the direction of her attractive house—his attractive house really, if you
looked at it dispassionately—on the evident capacity of men to
be in love with several women at once. For she was sure there
were several women in Job's background at the very moment
he was hesitating on the pavement, and turning red for love of

her. He couldn't do, she now thoroughly well knew, without several—one in his home, and one in his office, and one God knew where else; perhaps at Brighton, whither he was so fond of going for a breath, he used to explain, of sea air.

Yet here he was half stopping when he saw her, and gazing at her with those opaque dog's eyes of his as though she were the single love of his life. And she, who was a believer in one thing at a time, fell to considering her patience, her positively angelic patience, over his lapses. Seven lapses, before she did anything about them. Why, she might have divorced him, completely justified even in her mother's eyes, who was all for wives sticking to their husbands, after the second lapse, and started on her delicious career of independence at twenty-three instead of twenty-eight. Then she would have had five whole years more of it, with everybody bent on making up for his shameful treatment of her, and for what it was imagined she must have suffered. Five years her patience had cost her; five years of happiness.

And she asked herself, as she went into her flower-filled library —the quantity of flowers that arrived for Fanny every day at this period had to be seen to be believed—and found Lord Conderley of Upswich, an elderly (she thought him old, but he was, in fact, under fifty) and impassioned admirer, waiting to take her out to lunch—she asked herself what other woman would have been such an angel of forbearance. Or was it, really, not so much forbearance as that she didn't care?

Yes, thought Fanny, who was an honest girl, and liked to see things straight, it wasn't being an angel; it was because, after the third lapse, she simply hadn't cared.

§

But that was a long while ago. It didn't seem long, but it was. Then she was twenty-eight. Now she would soon be fifty. A generation had passed, indeed had flashed by, since she saw Mr. Skeffington that morning on the pavement of Pall Mall, and the plovers' eggs with which, at the Berkeley, Conderley had afterwards ardently fed her—solid enough the hard-boiled things had seemed, as she cracked their shells—where were they now? Reappeared as flowers, perhaps, or grass and been eaten by sheep, and once more, in the form of mutton, eaten perhaps by her. Everything, looking back, had dispersed and vanished, to

reappear as something else. Life was certainly a queer business
—so brief, yet such a lot of it; so substantial, yet in a few years,
which behaved like minutes, all scattered and anyhow. If she
and Job had had children they too, by this time, would be all
scattered and anyhow. Grown up. Married. And of course
making a grandmother of her. Incredible, the things one could
be made by other people. Fancy being forced to be a grandmother, whether you liked it or not!

But—grandchildren. She turned the word over on her tongue
cautiously, as if to see what it really tasted like. A woman
might hide for years from people who didn't look her up in
Debrett that she had had a fiftieth birthday, but she couldn't
hide grandchildren, they would certainly insist on cropping up.
Just as well, then, that there weren't any. Who wanted to be
dated?

Yet—didn't they fill a gap? Didn't they come into one's life
when it was beginning, like one's hair, to thin out? Since she
had had that awful illness in the autumn, with her temperature
up in the skies for days on end, her hair, she knew and deeply
deplored, wasn't what it was. Nothing, since then, seemed quite
what it was. She had stayed in the country for several months,
slowly recovering, and when she got back London and the
people in it might almost have been a different place and race
—so apathetic; so dull. While as for the way one's friends had
lately taken to dying . . .

§

Fanny was reflecting on these things in bed. It was an icy,
foggy February morning outside, but inside, in her bedroom, all
was rosy and warm. Wrapped in a rose-coloured bedgown—
when she was younger her bed arrangements had been sea-green,
but it is curious, she herself noticed, how regularly the beds of
older women turn pink,—the shaded, rose-coloured lights doing
their best for her, and a most beautiful wood fire bathing the
room in a rosy glow, she ate, or tried to eat, her breakfast of
half a grapefruit.

Cold, sour stuff to begin a winter day on, she thought, giving
up and pushing the tray aside. The idea was to keep slender;
but suppose you did keep slender—and nobody, since her illness, could possibly be more slender—what was the good of it if
you had no hair? One went to Antoine's, of course, and bought

some, but to buy hair, to *buy* hair, when one had had such heaps of it till only a few months ago, did seem most dreadful. And it put a stop to so many things, too, once one had got something on one's head that didn't really belong. For instance, poor Dwight, the latest, and also the youngest of her adorers—for some time now they had kept on getting younger,—a Rhodes scholar fresh from Harvard, and worshipping her with transatlantic headlongness, wouldn't be able to touch it reverently any more, as she used sometimes to allow him when he had been extra sweet and patient. If he did, the most awful things might happen; the most awful things *must* happen, when a woman lets herself have adorers, while at the same time easily coming to bits.

The ghost of a giggle, the faintest little sound of rather wry mirth, rose to her lips at the pictures that flashed into her mind; though indeed all this was very serious for her. Adorers had played a highly important part in her life; the most important part by far, really, giving it colour, and warmth and poetry. How very arid it would be without them. True, they had also caused her a good deal of distress when, after a bit, they accused her of having led them on. Each time one of them said that, and each in his turn did say it, she was freshly astonished. Led them on? It seemed to her that, far from having to be led, they came; and came impetuously, while she, for her part, simply sat still and did nothing.

§

Apparently snug and enviable in her rosy, cosy cave, she lay thinking about those adorers, so as not to think of Mr. Skeffington. Outside the fog was thick yellow, and it was bitter cold; inside was the warm Fanny, so apparently enviable. But in fact she wasn't enviable. She was warm, and as carefully lit up as an Old Master, but far from being enviable she was a mass of twinging nerves after a wakeful and peculiarly unpleasant night, which the grapefruit, sour and comfortless inside her, did nothing to soothe. Perhaps, she said to herself, eyeing its remains with distaste, in winter, and while she still hadn't quite picked up after her illness, she ought to have something hot for breakfast, something more nourishing, like a little fish . . .

And instantly, at the word, there he was again: Mr. Skeffington. She had been fending him off so carefully, and now, at a single word, there he was; and she seemed no longer to be in her bedroom, but with him downstairs in the dining-room, he behind the silver fish-dish, she opposite him behind the coffee-pot; just as they had sat through so many boring breakfasts during the precious years of her lovely, very first youth. And he was looking at her adoringly between his mouthfuls, and saying, with the brimming possessive pride she used to find so trying, "And how is my little Fanny-Wanny this fine morning?"—even if it wasn't a fine morning, but pouring cats and dogs; even if, a few hours before, on his proposing to join her in her bedroom, she had vehemently assured him she would never, never be his little Fanny-Wanny again, because of those typists.

For he was of an undefeatably optimistic disposition when it came to women, and very affectionate.

§

Overcome, she lay back on her pillows, shut her eyes, and gave herself up to gloom. She had had a dreadful night; she had been doing her best to forget it; and this was the last straw.

Her maid slid silently into the room, observed her attitude, removed the tray without disturbing her, and slid silently out again. "So that's how we are this morning, is it," thought her maid, whose name was Manby.

"Not even," Fanny was saying to herself, her eyes tight shut, her head thrown back in the pillows, her face blindly upturned to the ceiling, "not even to be able to mention fish, in an entirely separate connection, without his at once thrusting himself forward!"

It did begin to look as if she would have to go to a doctor, who of course, the first thing, would ask her how old she was; and when she told him truthfully, for it was no use not being truthful with doctors, would start talking—odious phrase—of her time of life. Really, though, Job was getting past a joke. Its being February, the month she married him in, oughtn't to have stirred him up like this, for there had been many Februaries since she left him, and in none of them had he so much as crossed her mind. Tucked away he had lain, good and quiet, in what she had supposed was the finality of the past. Now, here he was at every turn.

He must, somehow, be put a stop to. She knew he was nothing but a figment of her brain, but it was precisely this that made his appearances so shattering. To go off one's head at fifty seemed a poor finish to a glorious career. And it wasn't as if she hadn't done what she could, and reasoned with herself, and tried to be sensible and detached. Everything she could think of she had done, even to ordering his chair in the dining-room to be removed, even to taking cold baths. She had soon found out, though, that these measures were no good. The cold baths made her shiver for the rest of the day, and as for the chair, being only a figment, not having one didn't stop Mr. Skeffington's sitting down. Figments were like that, she had to acknowledge. They could sit on anything, even if it wasn't there.

Well, something would have to be done about it. She couldn't go on much longer, without having a real breakdown. After the night she had just been through, which she was trying so hard to forget by thinking of Dwight, by thinking of the way her hair had practically all gone, by thinking of anything that came into her head that wasn't Mr. Skeffington, however much she disliked the idea of messing about with doctors she would certainly have to see one. For Mr. Skeffington, that night, had been quite unbearably lively. He might be nothing but a figment, but she must say he did her imagination great credit, so vivid he was, so actual, so much on the spot. Up to then, he had only molested her in the day-time, sat at meals with her, met her in the library, attended her in the drawing-room; but the evening before, the evening, that is, of the anniversary of the day thirty years ago on which she had married him, when she came in late from a party—not in very good spirits because everybody had been so dull—he was waiting for her in the hall, and had taken her hand, or she felt as if he had taken it, and gone upstairs with her just as he had gone thirty years ago, and stayed in the room the whole time while she undressed, and insisted on kneeling down and putting her slippers on for her, and had actually kissed her feet. Dreadful to have a figment kissing one's feet, thought Fanny, opening her eyes with a shudder, and jerking herself upright in the bed.

§

She stared into the glowing, reassuring fire. Such a lovely fire. Everything so lovely round her. Nothing in the world, really, to worry about. She must hold on to herself. And if she did feel rather cold inside, it was only the grapefruit.

Manby, who seemed able to see through walls, knew she had opened her eyes, and slid in. She came in sideways, taking up as little space as possible in the doorway, so as not to cause draughts, and carrying the morning letters on a tray.

"Will you wear your grey or your brown this morning m'lady? Or should I put out your black?" she inquired.

Fanny didn't answer. She turned her head and looked at the tray, her hands clasped round her drawn-up knees. A lot of letters, but they all looked dull. Queer how uninteresting her letters and telephone messages had been since she came back. What had happened to everybody? Hardly ever did a nice man's voice come through on the telephone now. Relations rang up, and women friends, but the men, like her hair, seemed to have dropped off. She oughtn't to have stayed away so long. One's tracks got very quickly covered up, if one did. In the general scramble, it appeared one easily was forgotten, though it was too fantastic to suppose that she, of all people——

"Will you wear your grey or your brown, m'lady? Or should I——"

Odd, though, thought Fanny, putting out her hand and picking up the letters, what a lot of dull people there seemed to be about lately. Dull men. Uninterested men. Uninterested, and therefore uninteresting. When first she began going out again after being in the country, she was struck by it. London suddenly seemed full of them. She couldn't think where they all came from. Wherever she went, there they were too. In fact, there was no doubt London had quite changed. People, even her own particular men friends, weren't nearly so much alive as they used to be, and not half as interesting. They were very kind to her, and solicitous about draughts and all that, but beyond patting her hand affectionately, and remarking, "Poor little Fanny—you must pick up, you know. Beef tea and that, eh?" they hadn't much to say. They seemed to be getting old, and there were no young ones to take their place, because of the breathless rush people lived in now—except, of course, Dwight; but he was sitting, or standing, or whatever it was they did, for examinations, and had only been able to get away from Oxford once to see her. Serious, everybody had become; absorbed. Instead of being eager, they were absent-minded. Instead of seizing every opportunity to whisper amusing things in her ear about—oh well, very silly things, really—they talked out loud of the European situation. Everyone might have heard what they said. It wasn't in the least her idea of a really interesting conversation, that everyone might hear what one said.

"Will you wear your grey or your——"

Certainly the European situation was enough to make anybody talk out loud, but ever since she could remember there had always been something the matter with it, and it hadn't in the slightest way interfered with amusing, silly things being whispered in one's ear. How long was it since someone had whispered in hers? Last night, at that boring dinner, there was a girl, a rather too healthy, red girl, the daughter of the house, just out; and the elderly man next to her had whispered something in her ear, and Fanny, chancing to look down the table, had seen him doing it, and it was this that had started her off wondering how long it was since her own had been whispered in. The girl wasn't even pretty, she was merely young and tight-skinned. Tight-skinned youth; all, apparently, that was needed these days, Fanny had said to herself, turning to her host again, and slightly and unpleasantly surprised by the acid edge to her thought. For never, yet, in her life had she been acid.

"Will you wear your——"

"Oh, *bother*," snapped Fanny, finally exasperated by the persistent current of interruption—adding instantly with quick penitence, "I'm sorry, Manby. I didn't mean to be cross."

"It's the weather," said Manby, placidly. "All these fogs."

"Do you think I'm crosser than I used to be?" Fanny asked, looking at her anxiously and dropping the letters she was holding on to the bed.

Manby had been with her so many years that she had witnessed all her stages, from the Really Young and Exquisite one, through the Lovely as Ever one, to the one she was now in, which was called, by her friends, Wonderful. "Darling, you really are *wonderful*——" that's what they said now, whenever she appeared; and she didn't like it one little bit.

"I wouldn't go as far as to say *crosser*, m'lady," said Manby, cautiously.

Then it was true. She *was* crosser. Else Manby wouldn't be so cautious. Ah, but how lamentable to get crosser as one got older! A person going to have a fiftieth birthday should know better than that. Such a person ought at least by then have learned how to behave herself, and not snap at servants. Serenity, not crossness, was what the years should bring—ripeness,

sweetness, flavour. Like an apricot in the sun, one should hang
on the afternoon wall of life; like a ripe and perfect plum.

> *Old age, serene, and calm, and bright,*
> *And lovely as a Lapland night . . .*

—that was the sort of finish-up poor Jim Conderley, who was
fond of quoting and knew an immense lot of things to quote,
had prophesied hers would be, one day when she was saying
how awful it must be to be old—he was the one who used to
feed her with plovers' eggs when they were still worth their
weight in gold.

Not that she had reached the Lapland night condition yet;
it was only quite lately that she had got into the Wonderful
class, and in it, she supposed, she would stay some time. Unpleasant as it was to be called Wonderful, and dripping with
horrid implications, it was better than being a Lapland night,
which, however serene and calm and even lovely it might be,
would be sure to be cold. Let her keep out of the cold as long
as she could, she thought, shivering a little. On the whole, perhaps, she ought to be thankful that her friends would probably
go on saying for some time yet, though a little more stoutly, of
course, each year, "Darling, you're a perfect *marvel*."

A marvel. Imagine, thought Fanny, getting out of bed and
putting her arms into the sleeves of the dressing-gown—also
rose-coloured,—Manby was holding ready, imagine having
reached the consolation prizes of life.

She crossed to the dressing-table, and stared at herself in the
same glass which only such a little while ago, so it seemed, had
shone with the triumphant reflection of her lovely youth. A
marvel. Wonderful. What did such words mean except, *Considering your age, my dear,* or, *In spite of everything, you
poor darling?*

Last week she had been to Windsor to see a godson of hers at
Eton who had just got into Pop, and was secretly so proud of
it that she knew he would burst if he couldn't let himself go
to somebody who wasn't another boy; and when she got back
to London, the afternoon being fine and dry, she walked most
of the way, across the Park.

Well, why shouldn't she? It was far, but not impossibly far.
Her feet ached, but most feet ached on pavements. There was
nothing out of the way, she considered, in what she had done.

Yet the various friends waiting for her in the drawing-room when she came in, with one accord exclaimed, on hearing of it, "But darling, you really are *too* wonderful!"

Tiresome, people were becoming; so tiresome.

"Will you wear your——"

"Oh, for God's *sake* leave me alone!" cried Fanny, suddenly flinging round on her chair, whereupon Manby, after one cautious glance, withdrew, carefully and sideways, into the bathroom, where she busied herself with taps.

§

Then Fanny was ashamed of herself; thoroughly ashamed, this time. Staring into her own eyes in the glass, eyes hollow and—it couldn't be true?—pouched after the sleeplessness which was that miserable Job's fault, she wondered how she could be as cross as all that, and fly at the kind, devoted Manby. She didn't remember ever having done a thing like that before; and presently, after a brief interval during which she reflected with deep concern on these developments in her character, while regarding with even deeper concern her face in the glass, she once more, in a rather small voice, and half turning her head towards the open bathroom door, said she was sorry. "Do forgive me, Manby," she said. "I'm shamefully irritable this morning."

"It's quite all right, m'lady," answered Manby from among her taps. "Will you wear your——"

"I've slept so badly—hardly at all," explained Fanny. "That's probably what is making me so unbearable."

"Don't mention it, m'lady," said Manby, emerging from the bathroom, now that the atmosphere seemed clearer. "But I'm sorry to hear your ladyship hasn't slept. Should I prepare an aspirin? And will you wear your grey or——"

"It's Mr. Skeffington," said Fanny, twisting round on the chair again, and looking at her with lamentable, wide eyes.

"Mr. Skeffington, m'lady?" echoed Manby, stopping dead. She was immensely startled.

"He's growing so *real*," said Fanny, her eyes very wide.

"Real, m'lady?" was all Manby could falter—for this was a name that hadn't been mentioned in that house, except below stairs, for nearly a quarter of a century. "Is—is Mr. Skeffington not well, m'lady?" she asked, very tentatively, very nervously.

"I don't know, but I don't think *I* can be," said Fanny, "or I wouldn't keep on imagining—keep on imagining——"

And to the astonished dismay of them both, staring at Manby, and pushing her hair back from her forehead with a quick, distracted movement, she suddenly began to cry.

"Oh, oh," wept Fanny, not attempting to hide her face, still with it turned to Manby, still keeping on pushing her hair back from her forehead, "oh, oh, *oh*——"

§

Except at the end of a love affair, when everything was so bleak and miserable, and no light anywhere, she never cried. What was there to cry about, in her happy life? Happy herself, except on the above occasions, till her illness and Mr. Skeffington's reappearance she had made everybody round her happy too. So that tears were as good as unknown to her. But this, now—this thrusting up of Job out of the decent quiet of a buried past, this kind of horrible regurgitation, preventing her sleeping, making her repulsive to look at and unbearable to be with, was enough to make anybody cry. And what could one do about it? How could one stop him? It was such a hopeless business, trying to stop somebody who wasn't there.

The sound of her own violent weeping appalled both herself and Manby. Neither of them had had an idea she had so much noise in her. Manby, who had brought water, who had brought an aspirin, who had poked the fire, telephoned down for brandy, and done all that mortal maid could do, was now completely nonplussed. Should she ring up a doctor? she asked at last, at her wits' end.

"No, no—I'll go to one," sobbed Fanny. "Yes—I will, I will. This very morning. I want a specialist—it's only a specialist can help. I'll get dressed and go at once——"

"Will you wear your grey or your——"

"Oh, Manby, *please* don't say that any more!" Fanny implored, seizing a handkerchief and pressing it on each swollen eye in turn. "It's that that set me off being so—so cross, and so—so sorry——"

"Then should I put out your black, m'lady?"

Never, she told the secretary, Miss Cartwright, later in the morning, when her poor lady had at last quietened sufficiently to be dressed and put in the car and sent out into the fog to

a doctor, never could she have believed she would give way
as she did, as she kept on doing. Relapses. Every time she,
Manby, said anything. And what was so alarming was that it
all seemed really to have something to do with—she put her
hand to her mouth, and looked round fearfully before saying
it, under her breath—Mr. Skeffington.

"Not——?" Miss Cartwright asked also under her breath.
She stared. She had only been in the house six weeks, but
a secretary can learn much in less time than that.

Manby nodded. "That's right," she said. " 'Im. The
'usband." For even now, in moments of emotion, her h's were
apt to fail her.

§

Fanny went first to Bond Street, to Madame Valèze, the
famous restorer of women's looks. The car groped its way
cautiously through the fog, while she held her furs over her nose
and mouth to prevent herself, she said, from choking, but really
to hide. She couldn't appear before anyone, not even a chance
passer-by, not even a doctor, till her face was put right—
indeed, least of all before a doctor, who would certainly, if
she went all swollen up from crying, suppose her further gone
in a breakdown than she was. And then that would depress
her, and Job would have more of a look-in than ever.

But under the deft hands of Hélène, Madame's head assistant
—even Madame, who was so conscientious, hadn't ventured
out this terrible morning, and that *miladi* should do so was
indeed a reproach to those who stayed at home, said the glib
Hélène—she spent a calming hour, lying back in an extremely
comfortable chair, her throbbing head bound round with iced
bandages, and on each burning eye a little cold bag that felt
like a blessing. Unguents were spread and re-spread over the
loose places of her skin; creams were patted in; beneath her chin
was specially attended to; and the last thing she heard before
going to sleep—for she did go to sleep, and stayed asleep
exhausted, till she was finished—was Hélène's suggestion that
she should take a special chin course, which would enormously
help it, and the last thing she thought was, "Imagine having reached the stage when one's chin needs enormously
helping."

Then she went off, soothed by the gentle movements, and

only woke up when Hélène, in a tone of triumph, asked her to look at her self in the glass.

Certainly she was more presentable, and the tear-stains, about which Hélène had been busily conjecturing, were gone. But she looked curiously like the other women who go to beauty parlours. Their faces all, after treatment, seemed to have on exactly the same mask.

Well, at least she wasn't a give-away any longer, she thought; and felt so much refreshed after the sleep that she wondered if it were really necessary to go to the nerve-man. Hadn't she better wait a little, for another day or two, and see how she got on? She did so deeply dislike beginning this doctor business; it was so difficult to shake off, once one had started it.

Hesitating even at his very door, she sat for a few minutes in the car before committing herself by getting out, her delicate eyebrows knitted in a frown of doubt—those eyebrows on whose behalf, in order adequately to praise them, Lord Conderley used to ransack literature from the Elizabethans to Mr. H. G. Wells.

The chauffeur stood patiently waiting for a sign.

"Oh well," she finally made up her mind, wrapping her furs closer round her and preparing to take the plunge: "I suppose, now that I'm here, I may as well see the old thing."

§

Sir Stilton Byles, however, the eminent nerve-and-women's-diseases specialist, wasn't an old thing at all, as Fanny would have known if she had listened more attentively to the conversations of her friends, when they talked about their ailments. He may not have been exactly a young thing, but he certainly wasn't an old one. He was an outspoken man of thirty-eight, without a shred of bedside manner, nor any of such nonsense as sympathy. He didn't sympathize. Why should he waste time sympathizing with all these idle women, and the self-indulgent ways by which they had come by their diseases? And why should he pretend he did? His business was to cure them, or anyhow to get them to believe they were cured. And every day, when his work was over, he would fling the window open to purge his consulting-room of scent, and exclaim: "God, these women!"

Fanny's friends, who all had nerves, and all were of the kind the eighteenth century called fine ladies, found his manner most refreshing. After the sleek, soft ways of the doctors they used to go to, he was infinitely bracing. They loved going to see him. They came away feeling incredibly brisked up, and ready for anything. As hard and taut as prize-fighters they felt, after a twenty minutes' scrap with Sir Stilton. Divine, they agreed, not to be mewed over, but given a clean, straight sock—their very language, after being with him, was virile—on the jaw. And they suggested to each other that he probably would be a marvellous lover, and they wondered whether there were a Lady Byles, and, if there weren't, couldn't he perhaps be asked to dinner?

In their hundreds they flocked to Sir Stilton. His consulting-room was fragrant—he called it reeking,—with them. "Oh, my God," he would mutter under his breath, when a specially scented one came in.

Because of the creatures, though, he was growing very rich, and it was worth putting up with their scents and their silliness to be well on the way to the top of his profession at thirty-eight. Lately, too, royalty had begun to find him refreshing; twice within a week had he been summoned to Princesses of the Blood; and Fanny, when she decided to go to a doctor, naturally went to the one everybody else went to. Without troubling to make an appointment she went, experience having taught her that she need never make appointments—and indeed it was true that, however long a waiting-list might be, she herself, arriving last, got in first.

Therefore the person dressed as a nurse, but not a nurse really, who opened the door, never having seen her before was surprised. So airy a non-recognition of barriers hadn't yet come her way. What? No appointment? What? When Sir Stilton was invariably booked up days, even weeks ahead? Impossible, she said loftily. Out of the question.

"Would you have me die?" asked Fanny, with the smile which for so many years had been an enchantment, and still was sweet.

"Oh well," said the apparent nurse, melting into something of the bedside manner her chief hadn't got, "we'll hope it isn't as bad as that."

"Give him this," said Fanny, walking past her into the hall, and scribbling on one of her cards.

"*I'm an urgent case,*" she scribbled; and since she was the daughter of a duke, and the extremely well-provided-for ex-wife of an extravagantly rich man, Sir Stilton, who had the peerage at his fingers' ends, besides such facts concerning famous financiers as might be useful, hardly kept her waiting five minutes.

"Well, there's nothing urgent about *you,*" he said, when, catching hold of her wrist, he had counted her pulse, while he glanced a second time at what she had scribbled on her card.

"Oh, but isn't there!" exclaimed Fanny; and began to tell him about Mr. Skeffington.

§

Ten minutes later she was out in the hall again, her cheeks flushed, her eyes shining, her head held high.

"Call my car, please," she commanded; as different a person as possible from the person who had smiled so charmingly at the nurse when she arrived.

"He's done it again," thought the nurse proudly, hurrying to open the door; and she couldn't help saying: "Wonderful, isn't he?"

"Oh, he's God's own wonder!" was the answer, flashed round at her; an answer which almost seemed—only this, of course, was impossible—angry.

It was, though, angry, and Fanny's eyes were shining, not with the fresh lease of life her friends acquired from Sir Stilton's bracing talk, but with rage. She hadn't been so angry since the discovery of Mr. Skeffington's first lapse. Odious doctor. Those friends of hers, who crowded to him, could be nothing but a lot of masochists.

"You should have stuck to him," had been the creature's comment—so useful after twenty-two years—when she had done describing Mr. Skeffington's conduct.

"Stuck to him? What, when he——?"

"How old are you?" was the abrupt interruption; and when she told him truthfully, it being merely foolish not to, he remarked: "You surprise me."

It was at this point that Fanny began feeling stung; for, from his expression, it seemed as if what surprised him wasn't, as for an instant she had naturally supposed, that she was as old as that, but that she was as young as that. So she was stung.

"It's because I haven't slept all night," she hastily explained, trying to hide that she minded.

"You see how important quiet nights are for women of your age," he said.

"And for everybody, I imagine," said Fanny haughtily.

"That is, if you don't want to be an eyesore."

An eyesore? Was he suggesting that she was an eyesore? She, Fanny Skeffington, for years almost the most beautiful person everywhere, and for about five glorious years quite the most beautiful person anywhere? She? When the faces of the very strangers she passed in the street lit up when they saw her coming? She, *Noble, lovely little Fanny,* as poor Jim Conderley used to say, gazing at her fondly—quoting, she supposed; and nobody quoted things like that to eyesores.

True, Jim had quoted a good while ago; and it was also true, now that she came to think of it—let her be honest—that people passing in the street had seemed to look at her lately with surprise rather than admiration. But anyhow, there was Dwight, and only last autumn, just before her illness, he was declaring he couldn't live away from her, that he would chuck everything and come and be her lodge-keeper, or pantry-boy, if he might only sometimes see her, for she was the most beautiful thing on God's earth. Young men didn't say things like that to eyesores. True, since then she had hardly set eyes on him, for almost immediately she fell ill. He had, however, been to London since she came back, and dined with her—once only, though, now that she came to think of it. Examinations keeping him in Oxford, he said. Or—her thoughts, before Sir Stilton's fixed and coldly appraising eye, hesitated—wasn't it really examinations?

She sat staring at the cold face before her without seeing it. In so short a time as less than six months, she reassured herself, it wasn't possible to change from the most beautiful thing on God's earth into an eyesore. Or—again she hesitated—was it?

Sir Stilton, however—detestable man—was going on talking. "Now that your love-days are over——" he was saying.

It was she this time who interrupted abruptly, stung too badly to remember discretion. "And how, pray," she inquired, flushing and lifting her chin—a gesture which instantly fixed his cold eye on those parts which Hélène had said could be enormously helped, "how, pray, do you know they are over? How do you know I'm not having what you call love-days at this very moment?" For after all, Dwight would come flying to London any moment, exams or no exams, if she simply lifted a finger. Or—once more her thoughts faltered before that steady eye—wouldn't he?

"Oh, my poor lady," was all Sir Stilton said to that.

Then there was silence, while they stared at each other, he with his clean-shaven lips sardonic, and his finger-tips neatly fitted together, she too badly stung to speak.

What men there were in the world, she was thinking, what *common* men. But also, thank God, what other men, who saw one quite differently, who adored one, and swore they couldn't live away from one. At least, that was what they swore last autumn, and last autumn was still only just round the corner; or wasn't it?

Outraged, she stared at this dreadful Byles who was daring to pity her, but even while she stared her doubts were beginning to grow more insistent, and crept, like the cold fog outside, into her heart. Suppose—now just let her for a moment *suppose,* she said to herself, trying to face things sensibly— that the man was right, and she was indeed simply a poor lady deluding herself. Suppose everything that had made life so warm and happy was soon going to be over for her, was perhaps already over; what then? What did a woman do then? What did she do with the second part of her time in this queer world, the elderly-to-old part, the part that came next, and started, say, on her fiftieth birthday? If the woman had no children, that is, and no special talents, and no particular interest beyond her friends and the beauty that had always unfailingly made everything so easy for her, and if, into the bargain, she had had, for the best of legitimate reasons, to get rid of her husband? People used to praise her for being so kind. They used to tell her she had a dear nature. But how easy to be kind and all that, how impossible not to be, when one had everything in the world. Kindness spilled over from her own happiness; and what she now wanted to know was whether, in the unfamiliar cold years that lay ahead of her, the years on the other side of fifty, bound, each one, to be colder than the last because each one stripped her more bare, she would be quite so kind, and generous, and uncritical and all the rest. She remembered her comment on the girl at the party last night—tight-skinned youth. Distinctly critical that was. And how long would she go on being what they called a dear, when there was nobody to care whether she was a dear or not? And wouldn't it be a most miserable thing if she couldn't get out of the habit of smilingly lifting that finger which used to bring everybody rushing to her feet, and, when she lifted it, no one moved?

Her eyes grew dark with something disagreeably like fear. She no longer saw anything at all of Sir Stilton. Staring at him, what she saw for some frightening moments was an old woman left more and more alone, gradually eating more and more, till at last she ate a great deal, and then, being upset inside, taking it out on her maid.

"But that," came the voice out of the darkness which for the last few moments had hidden Sir Stilton, as though answering her thoughts, "is just where husbands come in, and why it is such a mistake not to stick to them. Lovers, as no doubt you are aware, for you evidently must have been a pretty woman once, and probably had several——"

Once. He was saying once. The word brought her back to complete awareness of him again. Once. When, whatever might lie in front of her, it did remain true that less than six months ago Dwight—"Why," she interrupted herself, struck by a sudden painful thought, "how I'm clinging to Dwight! That *boy*. As if he were my only hope. That poor little *boy*——"

"Lovers," went on Sir Stilton, finishing his sentence, "as of course you must remember, invariably end by turning sour on the stomach."

Acutely aware of him now, she gazed at him icily. What an expression. What a way of describing those windings-up, sad, but with a charm of their own, and always ennobled by a real distress, which were so vivid in her memory. Poor Adrian Stacy, Dwight's predecessor, had been wound up less than a year ago; and she could repeat every word of the occasion, and not a word but did credit to them both. The winding-up of the one before that, Perry Lanks—or wasn't he the one before that? She couldn't quite remember—since become such a celebrity, hadn't been quite so good, because he was a lawyer, and wanted facts.

"Oh, Perry, there are no facts in love," she had told him, naturally not liking to be pinned down. Whereupon he had suggested, exactly as if he were cross-examining her, that she was being foolish.

"My dear, there are always facts," he had said, looking tired and patient.

Still, even so, there was nothing that actually could be called sour about their parting, in spite of her conviction—she hoped she didn't show it,—that when a lover begins to look tired and patient it is time he was wound up; and as for the others, they were thought of to that day with nothing but affection and tenderness.

Yet here was this man, this Byles man, whose every word was like a slap in the face, connecting them, her dear, kind lovers, with sour stomachs.

"I can't imagine——" she began.

"—why your friends come to me," he promptly finished for her.

"Exactly. How much do I——?" she added, stretching out for her gloves and bag.

"I haven't earned my fee yet," he said. Adding, "Sit down," for she had got up and was towering over him.

"Thank you, no," she said, opening her bag. "How much do I——"

"Well, don't sit down then, but listen."

"There's nothing I wish to hear. How much do I——"

"Listen, please, instead of wasting time," he said, sharply. "The only person in the long run, who is of any use to a woman whose run has also been long——"

"Is this right?" she cut him short, determined to hear no more, and laying pound-notes on the table.

"The only person in the world, I tell you, who will stick to such a woman, who will *bother* about her," he persisted, pushing the notes aside, "is her husband. He has got to, you see, poor devil, as a rule. And the sensible thing for you to do is to get into touch with Skeffington again as quickly as possible. Sound advice," he said, rapping the table with a paper-knife. "You'll live to be grateful for it, I assure you."

He threw down the paper-knife, and got up too. He was shorter than she was—a short-legged, thick man, and she continued to tower. Skeffington, indeed, she thought, looking down her still lovely nose at him; without any "Mr."; just Skeffington; as though they were friends.

"Why not call him Job, and have done with it?" she freezingly suggested—at least, she hoped she was freezing.

Nothing, however, froze Sir Stilton. "Certainly," he said. "Delighted. I like Jews. Get into touch with Job, then. Real touch, I mean, not just fancying he's there when he isn't. Lay him, in fact. If he haunts you, he must be laid. The only way—you had better listen," he broke off, for she had turned her back and was walking to the door—"the only way, I tell you, to rid the mind of dreams and illusions is bodily contacts. How do you suppose love affairs would ever come to an end, if it weren't for the bodily contacts? Make friends with Job. See him often. Ask him to dinner. Lay him, in fact."

She turned and looked at him, her hand on the door-knob. "I came to you," she said, "for help, and all I've got——"

"Is insults. That's what you were going to say. Well, I dare say, I dare say, from your point of view. You can't stand plain truth. None of you women can. But for all that you've got help from me all right, if you choose to accept it. I've given you the soundest possible advice. Act on it, and you'll be cured. Just one moment, please——" he went on, raising his hand. "Ask that unfortunate husband of yours to dinner, and you'll find that the minute he's with you in the flesh he'll leave off being with you in the spirit. And by the way," he said quickly, for she was opening the door, "if any of the others start bothering you, the ones who weren't your husbands, and you begin seeing them when they aren't there—quite a possible development, mind you,—ask them to dinner too. Ask the lot," he finished, grinning a little. "Ask the whole lot, and size them up. They would size you up too, and then you'd all see——"

But she was gone. Pulling the door open with such violence that the woman dressed as a nurse came hurrying into the hall, her face scarlet, her eyes shining, she demanded her car.

"He's wonderful, isn't he?" said the nurse proudly.

"Oh, he's God's own wonder!" exclaimed Fanny, proceeding with such haste across the hall that the nurse had difficulty in keeping up with her.

And Sir Stilton, waiting in his consulting-room for the next patient, walked to the window and flung it open.

II

§

OUTSIDE London, beyond the belt of fog that lay thick and black over Harley Street where Fanny had just been, and

Charles Street whence she had started, and Paddington whither she was going, it was a beautiful day—clear, frosty, with the bare branches of the wintry trees standing out, each a separate miracle of intricate grace, against a most delicate, blue sky. Larks quivered and trilled. In the little lanes, whose matted grass edges were ribbons of hoar-frost, carters, loading their horses, whistled cheerfully. Housewives sang as they banged mats against the door posts. And the world was so sparkling and so fairylike a place that nobody that morning, in the country, was cross.

Fanny, choking in London, scented what must be going on a few miles away, and felt that if she could get into the sun she might, in spite of everything, manage to calm down. So she had herself driven, on leaving Harley Street, to Paddington, deciding she would there take the first train to anywhere where she could breathe. Breathe, and think. Better, breathe and not think. But, anyhow, breathe.

Certainly she couldn't go home till she had recovered a little. She was much too angry at present to see anybody, or to be able to endure Miss Cartwright's carefully unnoticing face, or the anxious inquiries of Manby. She would send a message to Miss Cartwright to telephone cancelling her engagements for the day, and she would withdraw into solitude, and there sit quiet, and smooth out her ruffled feathers.

They were immensely ruffled. For the first time in her life she had been in the company of a common man, who said straight in her face things she had till then never imagined could be so much as thought about her, and she felt she deserved a little relaxation. Relaxation. Furious as she was, she couldn't help smiling at the word. Even in moments of distress and anger, she was often able to laugh at herself—an endearing trait, said her men friends; and her women friends, while admitting it was endearing and that Fanny was sweet, thought that though she might laugh at one crumpled rose-leaf in her bed, they doubted whether she would laugh much if the whole bed were full of crumpled rose-leaves. It was among the things that had been worrying her lately, the way this faculty of standing aside and watching herself, and being amused by what she saw, seemed to be deserting her. Surely she was taking everything that happened very heavily now? Without much pluck? And didn't this point to a serious deterioration in her character? This, and flying at servants;

this, and being so quick with acid adjectives to describe youth.

Job's fault, of course; really all Job's fault. But him she was going to leave behind in London. This one day she was determined to be free of him; and she would spend it in the country, not speaking to a soul, not being spoken to, rid of everybody and everything. Vague longings for pure, cold, solitary things like primroses, and moss, and little leafless coppices, came into her mind, and she wished it weren't still only the seventh of February, and that she could have sat in some earthy, damp-smelling wood, and tied cool primroses into bunches, quite still and quiet.

The trains were late because of the fog, and the first one, leaving forty minutes after it ought to have left, was for Oxford. Oxford would do very well, she thought, taking a ticket. No lonely copses there, but in its ancient gardens she would find silence. Also, she had nothing but pleasant associations connected with Oxford; it was, for instance, entirely free from Job. He wouldn't be there, because he never had been there or anywhere like it, his education—you could read about it in *Who's Who*—having been private. The man Byles wouldn't be there either, because the last thing that would remind her of him would be evidences of civilization. Dwight— yes, Dwight would be there, but he hadn't yet left off being a pleasant association, and perhaps, after a long day by herself, when it began to get dark she might go to his rooms, and ask to be given muffins—that is, if by that time she were feeling better.

However, she wasn't sure about going to Dwight. Remembering the way Byles had said: "Oh, my poor lady," she thought perhaps she would wait before seeing him, or rather before letting him see her. He had, she knew, the most romantic, poetic notions of her perfections, and possibly, beholding her at this unfavourable moment, might think she was always now going to look like that, and then—

Here Fanny gave herself a little shake, for she was ashamed. That boy. As though it mattered what he might think. No, she wouldn't see him. Let him come to Charles Street and see her. Was she then so really elderly that even an undergraduate at Oxford was of value to her? The next phase, if she didn't take care, would be going to Eton for her adorers; and there slid into her mind, apparently from nowhere, the words, *In sickness and in health*. . . .

How comfortable, how restful, how safe, she thought, considering them wistfully.

Yes, but what they were talking about was husbands. It was husbands who had to stick to one in sickness as well as in health, in one's wrinkled stages as well as in the tight-skinned ones. Lovers hadn't got to, and wouldn't dream of doing it either, especially not young lovers. They set so high a standard for one when first they fell in love that the exertion of keeping up to it wore one out, and brought on the very condition that frightened them off. Not that she ever had to exert herself yet—oh, well, just a little, perhaps, on Dwight's last visit, when he saw her again for the first time after her illness, and looked at her with such lamentable eyes. She had supposed it was deep, loving sympathy in his eyes. Now she wasn't quite so sure. It might, just as easily, have been another Oh, my poor lady.

§

Walking along the platform at Paddington, that place of so many happy departures, because Conderley, in the days she now thought of as the Conderley Era, much as geologists speak of the Reptilian Age, had been a Lord-in-Waiting, and when his waits were at Windsor she would sometimes go down and spend an afternoon with him, coming back in time for dinner with her arms full of flowers and her eyes all lit up (for say what you will, there's nothing like a lover for making a woman be all lit up)—walking, then, along this platform of memories that dark and foggy morning, she looked, among the other waiting passengers, as a bird of paradise might look who should have strayed into a flock of sparrows. Conspicuous, that is. Very. Her black, as Manby described the soberest of her suits, didn't seem sober at all set beside the clothes of the poor. Inevitably, seeing the House it came from, there was an air about it, and an air, too, about her small black hat, pulled at the precise right angle over one eye. This hat, a most rakish and provocative affair in the eyes of the humble women on the platform, was perfectly plain except for a single scarlet quill sticking out, gaily and brightly, in the gloom, and her eyes, though the reverse of gay, were bright, too, from her recent scrap with Sir Stilton, and her cheeks were still flushed with fury. So that altogether she was a conspicuous figure; and a knot of harassed women, drooping beneath bundles and babies, watched her, half envious and half shocked.

"One of them kept ones," they decided, the most harassed among them remarking to her grim-mouthed neighbour that there seemed a lot to be said for this being kept business.

"Shut up, Mrs. Tombs," rebuked the neighbour.

"Hullo, Fanny," said a man's pleasant voice behind her as the train drew in. "Where on earth are you off to in this beastly fog?" And as she turned, surprised and vexed, for she had no wish to meet anyone she knew, he added, his eyes twinkling all over her, "You're looking very fit this morning. Getting back into your stride, what?"

Instantly she began to revive. There it was at last, after weeks and weeks, the familiar note of admiration. It warmed her like wine; it braced her like a tonic; better than any medicine or advice doctors might give her, was this simple assurance in her cousin's voice and eyes that she was lovely. Bother birthdays, bother Byles, bother Job, thought Fanny, smiling up into the smiling eyes which were so flatteringly and openly taking in every detail of her appearance.

"I'm fresh from a beauty parlour and a doctor," she said, "so if I can't look fit now, when shall I?"

"A doctor, Fanny? My dear girl," said Pontyfridd, taking her arm and walking her across the platform to a suitable carriage—he was her first cousin, as well as her first love when she was still in the schoolroom, and they had always been the greatest friends,—"don't, for God's sake, get into the doctor habit. You've been dosed enough, all those months in the country. Just forget it now, and enjoy yourself. Niggs——" she was his wife,—"is never out of that fellow's house. That fellow in Harley Street. Styles, or some such name."

"Byles," said Fanny.

"Yes, Byles. My heaven, what a name. Do you know him?"

"Do I not?" said Fanny gaily, for suddenly Byles and his hateful talk seemed entirely negligible. Here she was, with her own sort, her own set, her own blood, and oh, it was cosy—so cosy and safe, after the desolation of Byles's presence. "That's why," she laughed up at Pontyfridd, bigger than ever in his fur-lined coat, "I'm off for a day in the country, to try and get over him."

"Splendid, darling. You'll come with me, and we'll get over him together. Wait till his bills begin coming in, though. He

needs a lot of getting over then. You'd think my poor small
Niggs had more the matter with her than her tiny body possibly
had room for. I'm going to Windsor. I've got to see the Office
of Works about something at the Castle. We'll lunch together,
and you shall tell me what you've got into your little head
that has started you off being doctored again. Yes, darling,
you're lunching with me to-day," he said as she opened her
mouth to speak. "Why it's simply years since we've had a
jaunt together."

He helped her into the carriage. "There they go," grumbled
Mrs. Tombs, nudging her neighbour. "Getting into a first-class
carriage while you and me, just because we're respectable, 'as
to go third like 'errings."

"Shut up, Mrs. Tombs," rebuked the neighbour.   .

Mrs. Tombs, however, declined to shut up. On the contrary,
she loudly commented on the rug the gentleman was carefully
tucking round the lady's knees. "See that there rug?" she
inquired of her embarrassed neighbour. "Solid fur, that is. Do
you and me get tucked up in solid fur? Not 'alf, and it's
because we're respectable. I tell you, Mrs. W., there's no
money in being respectable."

"Now just you 'ush," said the neighbour, shocked.

"Well, I ain't going to. I've 'ushed a lot too much, first
and last. 'Ushing don't get you far, no more than being
respectable. An' if we could look inside them two stomachs
in there, I don't mind betting they're both as full as they'll
'old of good fried bacon. You and me ain't got no bacon inside
us, 'ave we, an' d'you know why?"

"No, and don't want to," snapped her friend, trying to
pull her away.

"Want to or not, you're goin' to 'ear," persisted Mrs. Tombs.
"It's because we're respectable. I tell you there's no *money*
in it, and I'm fed up, and I'd chuck it to-morrow and go off
with 'im in there or anybody you like to name, if 'e'd give me
a good 'ot breakfast first."

"You're a sinful woman, an' I shall 'ave to pray for you,"
was all her scandalized neighbour could say, making another
attempt to pull her away.

"George darling," said Fanny, carefully not looking through
the window, and though she couldn't quite hear what the two
were saying, unable not to conjecture it was something about
herself and her cousin that wasn't quite nice, "do you think

that poor thing is——? Do you think she has been——?"

"I hope so," said Pontyfridd, who, being as quick at hearing as he was at seeing, hadn't missed a word. "Poor devil," he added. "This frightful morning is enough to make anyone want to. But I must say it seems a bit early." And on a sudden impulse—he was famous in the family for his sudden impulses,—he opened the door, jumped out, went up to the two women, who looked completely scared, and patted Mrs. Tombs reassuringly on the shoulder.

"You'll miss the train, now," he said pleasantly, "if you stand here gossiping. Both of you go and have a good hot meal in the restaurant car. My guests, you know. I'll tell the attendant. Hurry along—and have lots of bacon with the chicken," he finished, winking at Mrs. W., who, as she said afterwards, could have sunk, and gently pushing Mrs. Tombs, while Mrs. W. pulled, towards the rear of the train.

"Take your seats, please," shouted the guard, coming along with his green flag.

"Hold on a minute," called out Pontyfridd. "Let these ladies get to the restaurant car——" and going back into his compartment he slammed the door, re-arranged the rug round Fanny, and asked if she had heard what they said.

"No," said Fanny. "But I think it was rude. What was it?"

"I'll tell you at luncheon," laughed Pontyfridd, settling himself in his corner.

But presently he didn't laugh, and said, for the second time, "Poor devil." And, again presently, he leaned across to her, and asked, "Fanny, do you ever hate yourself?" and when she, smiling at such an odd question, and still being very much the adorable, desirable woman, answered, "No. Ought I to?" he looked at her a moment a little thoughtfully, and offering her his cigarette case said, "Well, well—what a time we take to grow up, don't we."

§

She hadn't an idea what he meant; but, as it didn't sound very promising, decided not to ask. Besides, there was an expression on his face as if for two pins he might start talking about the European situation—a serious, slightly abstracted expression.

She was a sensible woman—Fanny long had prided herself

on being sensible,—and she knew that men sometimes must be
serious; but let them, she held, be serious in their offices, or
their Cabinet meetings, or their cathedrals, or the House, and
not waste precious moments when they are alone with a pretty
woman. Everything had its appointed moment. Even the Bible
said there was a time for this, and a time for that; while as
for the phrase pretty woman, she very well knew it was an
under-statement. Always she had been most exquisite. She
was simply unable to remember a time when, if she came into
a room, there hadn't seemed to be a quick silence, a holding
of the breath.

So that naturally she was, till lately, very sure of herself,
and just now on the platform, when Pontyfridd's eyes examined
her with such obvious pleasure and appreciation, she had been
as sure of herself as ever, at once forgetting every one of her
recent worries and doubts, while as for Sir Stilton, with his
ridiculous, Oh, my poor lady, he might never have existed.
Therefore it seemed a pity that George, so generally cheerful
and on the spot on occasions like this, should choose suddenly
to go grave. It was those two drunks. They had upset him.
Which poet was it poor Jim Conderley used to quote, who
said he never could really let himself go to being happy because
of his dying day, and because women had cancer? Something
like that he had said; she couldn't remember the exact words.
But as though it helped, not being happy! George was rather
like that. The minute he saw anybody poor or cold, he left
off being cheerful. If she hadn't been there, he probably would
have presented the two women with his fur-lined coat. As it
was, he had presented them with a meal, she discovered, on
the attendant's appearing and wanting to know if the order was
correct.

"You're terribly sweet, George," she said, when the man
had gone, laying her hand affectionately for a moment on his
knee. "I wish I had thought of that. But I seem to think of
things too late always—that sort of thing, I mean."

"My lamb, you'd have created a terrific sensation if you
had tried to do anything, and those women would have run
like hares. Cold?" he added suddenly, looking at her more
attentively.

Now what did he see? wondered Fanny, at once getting
deeper into her collar.

§

By this time the train was well out of the black London fog, and had got into a white mist. An extremely unbecoming hard glare was filling the carriage, from which there seemed no escape except deep in the collar of her coat. Also, the wrath Byles had stirred in her had now died down and with it the brightness of her eyes. Then there had been those women, and George thinking about them instead of about her, and turning serious, which naturally had reacted on her. So that though she managed to go on smiling gaily for a little, her smiles grew fainter as the light grew stronger and he remained thoughtful, and after West Drayton they vanished altogether, because it was there that his eyes suddenly began searching her face, with the result that he asked her if she were cold.

That meant she must be looking pinched. Most unbecoming to look pinched. Flattened nostrils, and things like that.

"Oh no—not a bit," she said quickly, wriggling deeper into her collar.

"Don't you catch cold now, Fanny," he said, leaning across and taking the collar in both hands and drawing it closer round her throat.

So that was it. Those terribly observant eyes had caught sight of what Hélène had declared could be helped enormously; and immediately she made up her mind that nothing would induce her to lunch with him. What? Sit opposite him, probably facing a horrid big plate-glass window, and be obliged to unfasten her coat?

He, having fixed her up, as he imagined, all snug and warm, gave the fur an almost motherly final pat, and said, "You oughtn't to be out a day like this. It's much too freezing for a wispy thing like you. I know what," he went on quickly, "I've got some brandy. I'll give you some. Warm you up," he assured her, pulling out a small flask, and beginning to pour a little into a tiny glass.

"Do I look—so funny?" faltered Fanny.

"Not funny, darling. Never could you look anything but adorable——" well, that was better—"but a bit tired," he said, intent on not spilling the brandy.

Tired. Most unbecoming. Hollow eyes, and things like that. How much she disliked being told that she looked tired; how much she dreaded it. Only too well did she know what it meant when people, full of sympathy, exclaimed, "Fanny darling, *how* tired you're looking! Don't you think you ought to be in bed?"

"You told me at Paddington I was——" she began; and stopped.

"So you were, at Paddington," he agreed. "Pitch dark there, though, and anybody"—he smiled, as he offered her the little glass,—"can look fit if it's dark enough."

The brandy spilled. Either the train gave a lurch, or she took the glass clumsily, or both; but it was spilled.

"That's not kind," she said, pushing the glass away and leaning back in her corner. It was she herself now who pulled her collar as close as possible round her throat. "No, don't pour out any more. Besides, you've got to get out soon. George, that's the first unkind thing you've said to me in your life."

"Darling, I'd die sooner than hurt a single one of your extremely precious hairs——" had he noticed them too, then, and how thinned out they were?—"but we all know, don't we, that you've been very ill, and aren't nearly as strong yet as you're soon going to be—oh Lord, here's Slough. Come along. The other train's waiting."

But Fanny wouldn't come along. No, she was going to Oxford. No, she had never agreed to lunch. No, she had arranged to go to Oxford, and must stick to it. "You'll miss your train," she said, as he still stood outside the door, trying to persuade her.

"My sweet Fanny, don't be tiresome. Look how the sun's shining. And why on earth you should go to Oxford and waste your time on undergraduates——"

Waste her time? Could he mean that even undergraduates wouldn't now——?

Startled, she looked at him. Nothing after that would make her budge. So he had to go, and as his train moved out of the station and curved away round the Windsor bend, and hers presently went on its different way, she was for a while dejected again, and frightened.

Then she pulled herself together. "You're growing altogether too suspicious and touchy to live," she said aloud; and decided that what she probably needed was a good meal, and that the first thing she did in Oxford would be to go and have one.

§

Avoiding the bigger hotels, she went to a small one she came
across in an obscure street, where she lunched alone, except
for one old lady in a dark corner, attended by an ancient
waiter. There was a big bright fire, and a sideboard loaded
with shining electro-plated empty soup-tureens, and enormous
dish-covers which covered nothing, and she thought the food
much better than any she got at home.

"Why doesn't Mrs. Denton ever give me this?" she wondered, eating something she didn't know, and liking it very
much.

It turned out, on inquiry of the waiter, who seemed slightly
surprised at the question, to be part of a beef-steak pudding,
and the vegetable, he informed her, again with slight surprise
on her praising it too, was cabbage. "Savoy," said the waiter.
"Savoy," repeated Fanny, making a mental note, so as not to
forget to ask Mrs. Denton whether she knew about it.

After the pudding, there was apple-pie and custard, but that
wasn't so good; one would have to be really very hungry, she
thought, to like this kind of crust. The coffee, however, was
hot and not bad, and she drew her chair up to the fire to drink
it, and lit a cigarette, and, being satisfactorily fed, was inclined
to smile at herself, after the varied emotions of the night,
and of the day, too, as far as it had got, for being able to sit
warming her knees at a strange fire in Oxford, in a condition
hardly distinguishable from placid.

"It's the pudding," she decided presently. "I'm what
Edward would have called slabbed down, or plugged, or some
frightful word like that——" Edward having been the one next
after Lord Conderley in her life, and as great a contrast to him
as the Cainozoic Period was to the Reptilian Age preceding
it. Her feelings, she recognized, couldn't have free play while
they were entombed in pudding, hence their quiescence. How
useful. She mustn't forget to ask Mrs. Denton if she knew how
to make it. She might try it when Job began bothering. And
gazing into the fire, her thoughts wandered to Edward in his
hey-day.

Dear Edward. What fun he had been. So completely disrespectful of everything and everybody Conderley had taught
her to venerate. He never opened a book; he said poetry gave

him a stomach-ache. And once, in the early days, when the Conderley atmosphere still hung about her and she said something about the poet Wordsworth, he called him old Fish Face. This, clearly reprehensibly, had greatly refreshed her. Strange what virtue there is in just change. Darling Edward. He used to look so particularly charming in his grey top-hat at Ascot. Yet that, too, had ended in tears—not the top-hat, though she did briefly wonder how grey top-hats ended, but their happy days together. His tears, too, if you please, this time; Edward, of all people, actually crying. But by then she had got involved with Perry—he was the one who finished by looking patient—and the only decent thing was to say good-bye to Edward. She hoped he had kept well. She didn't mean kept *well*, though of course she hoped that too, but *kept* well. He had been so very good-looking. She would really grieve if she thought he had, perhaps, grown fat, and on those hot islands, where he was Governor or something, letting himself go to too much whisky.

§

Immersed in the past, she sat quietly smoking while the old lady, from her table in the dark corner, watched her with a hostile eye. Old ladies of the class which is regarded as the backbone of England, and all clergymen who didn't know who she was, viewed Fanny at this time with suspicion. She was so very striking, and also ravaged. No good woman is ever, held the clergymen and the old ladies, either striking or ravaged, but especially not ravaged. The truly good woman merely gradually fades, they held. She grows dimmer and dimmer, and more and more like what one's mother used to be.

Fanny, however, at fifty wasn't in the least like anybody's mother, but had become, to look at, the sort of woman from whom clergymen instinctively shrink, and seeing her in a train they would get into another carriage, or meeting her in the street they would gaze, carefully absorbed, at the nearest equivalent to a view. If, though, on the other hand, at a public meeting she was sitting on the platform among archbishops, and her name was on the list of supporters so that they could read and know who she was, their confidence and admiration at once knew no bounds.

"That very beautiful Lady Frances Skeffington was there— you know, the daughter of the Duke of St. Bildads, the unlucky duke whose estate was ruined by having to pay death duties three times within five years," they would tell their wives afterwards. "The Archbishop seemed to take great pleasure in having her sit next to him."

"Wasn't she divorced, or something?"

"My dear, we mustn't judge."

This, though, wasn't a public meeting; there was no list of names to guide anybody, and the old lady had to go by appearances. In that place and room they were against Fanny, who presently heard an extremely distinct voice coming out of the corner behind her saying, "I mind smoking."

She was startled, and turned round quickly. She had forgotten the old lady. "I'm so sorry," she said, throwing her cigarette into the fire.

"If you had asked me if I minded I would have told you I did," said the old lady, folding up her table napkin and putting it through a bone ring. "But as you didn't ask me, I must tell you, without being asked, that I do mind. I mind very much."

"I'm so sorry," said Fanny again.

Then there was silence, during which the old lady, from the cover of her corner, studied the sideways view of the small black hat, for Fanny, now aware of her, and feeling it rude to sit with her back turned, had pushed her chair round a little, the curve of the scarlet quill, the tip, if she had known it, of a celebrated nose, and an ear-ring made of a single jewel, which she judged sham.

"One excuses," she was thinking, "a pretty girl for being a pretty girl, because it is not her fault, but an elderly woman can only lay the blame on herself if she manages, by artifices of which she should be ashamed, to seem more or less good-looking. Having had her turn, she should blush to try to go on out of it. Probably this one is here, all painted and dolled up, to see if she can pick up innocent boys."

And she thanked heaven that she herself had no innocent boys liable to be picked up, nor that which must, or should, precede innocent boys, a husband; for husbands too, she understood, were liable to become entangled in predatory female activities.

"Perhaps she'll go now," thought Fanny, who had seen the napkin being put through a ring, and therefore deduced the old lady must be staying in the hotel and liked having the same napkin over again.

She had a great longing for a cigarette, and also a great
longing, having had the cigarette, to get out into the sun before
the really lovely winter day folded itself away into evening;
but as the old lady didn't move, she herself got up, smiled
vaguely over her shoulder at her, received no faintest movement
of a muscle in return, and went into the passage.

Opposite, there was a door which had *Smoking* written on
it. It opened into a small sitting-room, with another bright
fire burning, and going in and drawing up a comfortable chair
to the fire, she sat down and again lit a cigarette. But she hadn't
been there more than five minutes before the old lady came
in, and stood looking at her.

"Am I keeping the fire off you?" asked Fanny after a
moment, during which nothing was said, and moving her chair
to one side. "Oh, and——" she added with a smile, holding
it up, "do you mind my cigarette in here?"

"Certainly I mind it," said the old lady concisely.

"But," Fanny justified herself, "it *is* written on the door."

"You asked me if I minded, and I have told you."

"Oh, then, of course——"

And this one, too, was thrown into the fire.

The old lady stood in the middle of the room, leaning on
her stick. "If I've said it once to the management, I've said
it a hundred times," she said irritably, "that the notice on the
door ought to be covered up, and 'Private' put instead. This
is my sitting-room."

"I'm so sorry," said Fanny, hastily getting out of the chair.
"You do see, though, don't you, that it was impossible for
me to know?"

"Perhaps I should explain that the room is for my exclusive
use so long as no one else is staying in the hotel. Passers-by
are not eligible. I imagine you are a passer-by?"

"Yes, but I might take a room for the night and not stay
in it, and then become eligible for the sitting-room, couldn't I?"
asked Fanny.

"Certainly, if you care to fling money about," said the old
lady, looking her up and down as much as to say she wondered
whose money. "It seems a great deal to pay, though, for the
questionable pleasure of smoking one cigarette."

"I'd have to have several, to make up for it," smiled Fanny.

"Then I should be driven into my bedroom. Not that I am
not used to that. So many queer people come to Oxford in

term time, and all of them want to smoke in here. The management is most disobliging, and does nothing to stop them. Sometimes it is so disobliging that it almost seems as if it wanted me to go. Yet, as I live here most of the year, I presume I am of value to them. Then there's the repertory theatre, and the whole of that unpleasant gang. They come here too, and make a noise, and still the management does nothing. Much as I dislike cinemas, I must say there's something to be said for them in university cities. At least the absurd creatures, those so-called stars, are fixed to their screens, and can't get off them when the performance is over, and walk about the town obstructing and inciting.''

Fanny, during this, was gradually making for the door. She suspected that she was going to be buttonholed. The poor old thing evidently had no one to talk to, and was bursting with things she wanted to say. If she, Fanny, were a really nice, kind woman, she would stay and listen, but she didn't think she could really be nice and kind, so urgent was her wish to get away. Always she had dreaded buttonholers. There was an arch one in a poem Jim used to read aloud, and it was like a nightmare the way he went on and on, not letting the unhappy man he had got hold of, and who was very busy, if she remembered, and in a great hurry, go till he had said his say. This old lady showed signs of being his near relation. She was quite unlike a Lapland night. There was nothing serene and calm about her, and certainly nothing lovely. Something was wrong with that description of old age. The poet who wrote it must have been very young, and couldn't have seen many old ladies. The one before her, she felt uncomfortably, was much more the real thing. Was it possible that she herself would some day be like that? So old, that everybody who was fond of her was dead, and she dragging round hotels because her servants were dead too, and she didn't like new ones? Or, even worse, perhaps be in the clutches of a companion, and the companion, when she was bored and cross, bullying her? *Noble, lovely little Fanny*, whose life had ringed her round like a wreath of flowers, and all her flanks—odd how Conderley's quotations stuck,—with silken garlands drest; could it really be that to this complexion—his phrase again,—she would come at last?

The old lady, who now had assumed for Fanny the shape of things to come, was arranging herself in what was evidently

her special chair, which was also the one Fanny, decidedly
unlucky that day, had sat in, and was welling up in it form-
lessly. "Why doesn't she go?" she was thinking. "I want my
nap."

But Fanny, in spite of the fear of being buttonholed,
hesitated, because of the picture in her mind of what, if she
went away, she would be leaving behind the shut door—the
silence of the dingy hotel-room, empty except for that lonely
figure by the fire, and for weeks, for months, for several more
years perhaps, there the figure would be sitting in that same
silence, except during occasional brief incursions of the repertory
gang, and except from time to time for an argument, evidently
embittered, with the management. And she thought, "Some
day I shall be sitting too like that, when I've quarrelled with
the companion——" adding, her better nature getting the upper
hand, "I expect I ought to stay with the poor old thing really,
and let her talk. George would. Look how kind he was to those
women at Paddington. Why, he even patted them."

But her better nature, being as yet undeveloped—"What a
time we take to grow up," George had said in the train, struck
by something he missed in her,—didn't keep the upper hand
long. The sun out in the street was shining too brightly, the
room, facing north, with its dingy old contents, was too tomb-
like. Of course it was quite true that some day she herself
might be sitting alone in just such conditions, but meanwhile—

Meanwhile, she fled. "No good taking time and tombs by
the forelock," she thought, pulling open the door, and with
a quick good-bye going out into the passage.

Upon which the old lady said, "Thank goodness," settled
herself comfortably in her chair, and at once went to sleep.

§

How beautiful it was outside, in the frosty stillness of the
winter afternoon.

Fanny stood a moment on the edge of the pavement, drawing in deep breaths of clear, cold purity, and ridding her clothes
of what she felt was the smell of mortality. Here, in these
streets, there was nothing but youth, living, vital, energetic,
absurd, adorable youth, with all its extremes of happiness and
heartbreaks. Just as in that room she had left there had seemed

to hang a smell of mortality, so out here there seemed to be
a smell of new milk. How angry the young men would be,
she thought amused, if she told them they made her think
of milk. But they did. Pailfuls of frothing, sweet new milk
everywhere; everywhere groups of thick-haired—especially she
noticed the lovely thickness of their hair,—shining-faced, red-
with-the-cold, cheerful young men.

"This is marvellous," said Fanny to herself, forgetting Byles,
forgetting George, forgetting Job, and lifting her face up to
the sun. "Really I am very glad I came."

Some pailfuls of new milk passing on the pavement—she
begged their pardon, she meant young men—looked shyly at
her for a moment, instantly hiding, under the cloak of good
manners, their admiration and interest. It was certainly
interest, and she hoped it was admiration, but of that she
couldn't be quite sure, standing as she was with her face in the
full light of the sun. Nice, after all, to be admired by these
pleasant boys; so nice, that for her own satisfaction she would
decide that they did admire her, even if it wasn't true.

Her intention had been to walk in the garden of St. John's,
but this was rather far, and so long had she lingered over the
pudding and the old lady that in another hour the sun would
have set, and gates would begin to be shut. So she went to the
New College gardens instead, for she was only a few yards
off from the little curly street that leads to the main entrance.
She had no need to ask the way, because this was Dwight's
college, and sometimes she had lunched in his rooms, and knew
well the little street, the lovely garden, and the quiet path at
the end, with a high wall on one side and a screen of trees
on the other, up and down which, after luncheon, she and
Dwight would pace. He, in this seclusion, was able freely to
illustrate his worship by gesticulations suited to his words—
he was taking modern languages, and had a great choice of
words,—while she listened to the rooks, whose cawings from
a child had fascinated her, as they loved and quarrelled among
their nests in the ancient elms. And Dwight would say that her
lunching with him was an honour which would encircle his
rooms in a nimbus for ever, and that they would shine now
down the ages—"Oh Dwight, what a long time. Look at
that rook—do you think it is being angry or affectionate?"—
with her refulgence, or radiance, or something; probably
refulgence, for he preferred the bigger-mouthed words.

This was the great difficulty about Dwight—always, the minute she was with him, she became absent-minded. Couldn't fix her attention; simply *couldn't*. Why, even when he was practically on his knees in Charles Street, telling her she was the most beautiful thing on God's earth, though she liked it very much with one half of her, the other half was wondering if Miss Cartwright had remembered to ring up Harrods about cleaning the chair covers.

She knew this was hard on Dwight, who was really a very dear boy, and extremely good-looking, and whose devotion was just then particularly welcome and reassuring, but what could she do? Mend her ways? Yes, she would seriously try to do that; and meanwhile how pleasant it was walking along what he called their path, without him. She and the rooks were very good company; it was a perfect moment of the afternoon; and she could think of him boxed up and examined with wide-awake affection and sympathy, because she wasn't being lulled into absent-mindedness by his unceasing and curiously monotonous flow of eloquence.

Well, it was easy enough to like being alone in Oxford, she said to herself, going through the iron gates into the garden, for here the memories were all recent, and harmless and unhurtful. How different from the ones which would have wrung her heart if she had gone to Cambridge! But she couldn't have gone to Cambridge. She hadn't been there for years and years. For it was there that her dear only brother had been, the person on earth she had most loved; and during his few weeks at Trinity, before the war started and he joined up and was immediately killed, she had spent each Saturday and Sunday there, sleeping at the Bull and having all her meals, even breakfast, in his little nest of rooms at the top of a ladder-like wooden staircase in Neville's Court.

Vividly, as she went into the New College gardens, and for no reason that she could discover, the memory of that brief, acutely happy time came back to her. She was nearly ten years older than he was, and there was nothing she wouldn't have done for him. Indeed, there was nothing she didn't do, for it was because of him, though this she never breathed, that she had married Job.

The spectacularly rich Mr. Skeffington, who had an extraordinary gift for growing richer, was a wonderful *parti* for a penniless girl, she had always felt. Just as Bach could do what he liked with a collection of little black symbols, forming them as he chose into this or that immortal fugue, so could Job do what he liked with money. It came dancing into his pockets at a glance—a very different glance from the sort of dog-like glances she knew, for these other glances, familiar to his fellow-financiers, were hard as steel and alert and concentrated as a hawk's. He had an unerring instinct for attracting money, and, having attracted it, for manipulating it with the easy mastery of genius. Invariably he bought at the exact right moment, and sold at the exact right moment; and in private life he was generous, and kind, and affectionate, and devoted—an ideal son-in-law for a ruined duke, who, when he lost him as a relation through the divorce, grieved genuinely, and not merely because his wealth had been a godsend.

"Must you, Fanny my dear? Must you really?" the old man had asked. "Don't you think, if you tried very hard, you might perhaps——?"

Fanny shook her head. "Not seven," she answered. "Besides, it's a habit now, and after a bit there'll probably be seventy. Would you have me forgive seventy?"

No; the old man wouldn't have her forgive seventy.

§

Trippington was at a preparatory school when Fanny got engaged, and she went down to see him there and tell him herself, before anyone else knew.

"What—that Jew?" he exclaimed horrified. "But, Fan—you can't."

"Can't I? You'll see. He's a very nice man. Terribly kind. Much the kindest of anybody we know, and much the—the nicest, really."

"But—think of his nose."

"I do. I've thought of it a great deal. And I've come to the conclusion noses aren't everything."

"Aren't they, just. You wait till you have to start the day every morning with his wagging at you over the bacon."

"There won't be any bacon. I shall be a Jew too, and they don't have bacon."

"You a Jew too?" he exclaimed, this time completely overwhelmed. "Oh, but, Fan—you *can't*."

Then she put her arm round him, and began to kiss him, but

he pushed her away, and sat gripping his head in both hands.

"Now Trippy, little sweet," she said, leaning over him and giving him a butterfly-kiss with her eyelashes in the hope of making him smile, "don't be silly and throw cold water on my lovely plans. Be a good brother and give me your blessing—please, darling."

But Trippington, taking no notice of these blandishments, only said, "It's bloody,"—and immediately afterwards, looking suddenly distraught, announced that he must go out of the room a minute, because he was going to be sick.

And now he, for whose sake she had married Job, so that the thousands of acres her father had had to mortgage could be freed from debt and handed over to him, when he came to inherit, in the condition his ancestors knew, had long ago vanished out of her life, and Job, who freed the inheritance, had vanished too—Trippy for ever, behind the clanking gates of death, and Job for ever too, of course, but differently for ever. In his case she could still get at him if she wanted to, still invite him, if she wanted to, according to Sir Stilton's grotesque suggestion, to dinner; while Trippy—ah, but wasn't her darling Trippy, after all, lucky, never to have to grow old? Wasn't it a happy thing, in these days of apparently swiftly approaching horror, to know that he at least, her precious brother, was for ever safe?

§

Lost in these thoughts, she had by this time reached the secluded path, having walked, with the grace which made her movements so agreeable to watch, the length of the broad herbaceous border beneath the shelter of the great grey wall, and two dons, who were arguing about Pythagoras in an upper chamber overlooking the garden, paused to observe her progress.

"Who is that?" said one, hastily adjusting his spectacles.

"I don't know," said the other, hastily adjusting his. "But judging from what can be seen of the lady, I should say she was attractive."

"Well, we can't see much. And women seen from the back are often different from women seen from the front. I mean, more attractive."

"True, true. Which would you rather?"

"Both," said the other. "Now, about Pythagoras——"

Continuing along the path, Fanny came to the bend where it curved round behind the rook-filled trees, and gradually, much narrowed, returned on the south side of the garden to the iron gates again. At this bend there was a seat, and on the seat, in spite of the frostiness of the afternoon in that sunless spot, were a young man and a girl, absorbed in kissing each other; in fact, they were locked in each other's arms. Such honest kissing Fanny had never seen, so whole-hearted, so vigorous. The girl's cap had fallen off, and lay unnoticed on the ground. Her thick dark curls, wildly ruffled up, were the only bit of head to be seen. So much preoccupied were they, so dusky was the shrub-screened corner, and so light of foot the slender, not to say emaciated, Fanny, that she was upon them before either they or she knew it. Almost she tripped over their carelessly-flung-out and forgotten feet, and greatly startled and embarrassed, besides being really sorry to have disturbed what was, after all, one of the most interesting moments of life, she stammered something apologetic, and with bowed head and eyes discreetly lowered was hastening on, when the two made the mistake rabbits make, and instead of remaining motionless and interlocked, hurriedly disentangled themselves; and one of them was Dwight.

"Oh," he said, scrambling to his feet, instinctively pulling his scarf straight and passing his hand over his hair. His face was scarlet.

"Oh," said Fanny, pausing, for once in her life unable to deal with a social situation.

The girl, whose face too was scarlet—but that was from the violence of the kissing,—sat where she was, her curls in an immense disorder (enviable creature, thought Fanny even at this juncture, to have so much hair that when it was in disorder the disorder was immense), staring, half abashed and half defiant, at the obviously grand lady who seemed to know Dwight.

Could it be his mother? She had heard rich American ladies were terribly smart. And if it was his mother, wouldn't the fat be rather in the fire? But from both the lady's expression and Dwight's, it looked as if the fat were already in the fire—yet what had she done, except enjoy herself and help Dwight to enjoy himself? What was wrong with a little enjoyment?

She pulled Dwight's sleeve. "If it's your mother, you'd better introduce me," she said in a whisper; but they were all three so close together that whispering was no good as an instrument of tact.

"Do, Dwight," said Fanny, really very sorry for him.

Dwight mumbled something. Neither Fanny nor the girl was any the wiser. Miss Parker, Perkins, Parbury, Partington, it sounded like, something beginning with Par, and fizzling out in confusion; while the girl only caught the single monosyllable Skeff. But Skeff was enough to show her that it wasn't Dwight's mother, unless she had married again. Perhaps his aunt, then; though she really didn't know why, if it were only an aunt, he should look so much upset.

Then there was handshaking. The girl, getting up for this ceremony, showed herself as a dumpy little thing, very round in a yellow knitted jumper, tight-skinned indeed, thought Fanny, who, beholding her straightened out and unfolded, was sorrier than ever for Dwight. How much that poor boy must have suffered from her own exiguousness, and her marked avoidance of letting him come too close—no closer, in fact, than sometimes, before her illness, when there was still enough of it, being allowed to touch her hair. This little plump thing, bursting with young ripeness through her jumper, was real substantial flesh and blood, intensely alive, almost audibly crackling with vigour; and Fanny, looking at her, felt as if her own bones were hardly covered enough for decency, and that she was nothing but a pale ghost wandered from the rapidly cooling past, strayed into a richly warm generation to which she in no way belonged. Nor did she, confronted by the girl's abounding youth, even resent being taken for Dwight's mother. She easily might have been his mother. It would be the natural conclusion for that evidently lively young brain to come to. Besides, she was too completely sorry for him, standing there defenceless, all his fine words and eloquence silenced, to resent anything.

But she hadn't a notion what to do next. Dwight evidently hadn't a notion either. In the face of what she had seen, and they both knew she had seen, conversation on ordinary lines would be a mockery. Graciousness, too, on her part, could only further prostrate poor Dwight; while as for suggesting everyday things, such as their coming and having tea with her at the Mitre or somewhere, to sit having tea with him under the circumstances would be a mockery, and a most subtle torture for the unhappy young man.

It was the girl who solved the problem. Not liking the look

on either of their faces, and having no mind to be mixed up in
a row just when she had been enjoying herself so much, she
stooped quickly, snatched her cap, clapped it on her head with
the gay indifference of a child as to whether it were straight or
crooked, and said, "Well, so long. I must be trotting home to
get tea for mother——" and nodding a "Good afternoon, Mrs.
Skeff," to Fanny, and to Dwight a jaunty "See you this evening, p'raps——" with bounding little footsteps, buttoning her
jacket as she went, she hurried away.

Without her, though it couldn't be said there was relief, there
was at least change, the situation, however, still remaining in
the category of that which must be worse before it can be better.

"I'm so sorry, Dwight," was all Fanny could think of to say,
after a painful silence, as they walked slowly back the way she
had come. "I mean——"

But what did she mean? She meant, she supposed, for inter-
rupting, for blundering in on him.

Dwight, who such a few minutes before had been one enormous throb of very delicious and satisfactory love, now had only
a single wish, and that was never to feel, see, think of, or hear
about love again. "That's all right," he said, his hands in his
pockets, his eyes on the ground, his feet sulkily kicking up the
gravel at the edge of the path.

An inadequate reply. Still, was there any reply, she asked
herself, the unfortunate boy could make which would be
adequate?

"You needn't come with me, you know," she said, after
another painful silence. "Not if you'd rather—if there's anything else——"

But as everything she began to say at once landed her in fresh
difficulties, she stopped.

"That's all right," he said a second time; again inadequate,
and again sulkily kicking up the gravel.

Alas, poor Dwight—all his eloquent words gone dumb, at the
very moment when she, for the first time in his company, wasn't
absent-minded.

§

From their upper chamber the two dons, seeing her reappear-
ing on the path below, hastily adjusted their spectacles again.
This time she was coming towards them, and they were gratified

to observe that she was as attractive turned frontways as she had been turned the other way; or seemed to be, at that distance, to their short-sighted, Greek-strained eyes. Indeed, she seemed more than attractive—she seemed definitely beautiful, and very like their idea of Helen of Troy.

With alacrity they thrust Pythagoras out of their conversation, and concentrated on the approaching lady.

"I imagined she wouldn't be long without an escort," said the slightly older one of the two.

"It's that American—the Rhodes boy," said the slightly younger one, peering.

"What an odd place to go and fetch him out of—those bushes at the end of the garden."

"As if he were the infant Moses."

"And she a king's daughter."

"Which she easily might be—or a daughter of the gods."

"Curious, though, that our prize boy doesn't seem to be enjoying himself."

"No—does he. Slouching along."

"Yes. As though he were sulky."

"Yes, positively hang-dog. Amazing. *Si jeunesse savait—*"

"Ah. Yes, indeed. Ah. Well. Now about that theory of yours——"

For the couple having disappeared beneath the window, short of stretching themselves out of it to watch, which would have been unseemly, there was nothing for it but to get on with Pythagoras.

III

§

ALL Oxford, by the time Fanny got back to the inn where she had lunched, was having tea. She had said good-bye to Dwight at the foot of his staircase, alleging an engagement as she smiled a smile that couldn't but be bleak—it was indeed, she explained, because of this engagement, that she was there that day, and having thanked him for offering to see her to whatever door she was bound for, and said she could easily find her way alone and he wasn't to bother, and having done her best not to let this sound as if she were in any way minding anything, she walked away into the twilight, and out of his life.

She couldn't imagine herself in future anywhere in it. "He's the last," she thought, with chill conviction. "I feel in my bones he's the last, and my love-days, as Byles called them, are really and truly over.".

Just before they parted, holding out her hand in farewell, she said : "Don't worry, Dwight. These things might happen to anybody——" but that too had sounded all wrong; so repulsively magnanimous; or perhaps as though she were forgiving him, because she wanted him back; or perhaps as though she were indifferent, and wasn't caring.

No; there was nothing for it, really, but silence.

Going into a stationer's to buy a time-table, she found the next fast train for Paddington didn't start for over an hour. She would go back, then, to the inn, and wait there, where she knew there was only one old lady, rather than face the crowded tea-lounges of the bigger hotels. She no longer minded the old lady. On the contrary, she thought it would be tranquil to sit with her, and feel she was really sitting with herself in twenty years' time, when to-day was an old, old story, almost entirely forgotten, or, if not forgotten, only remembered with a smile.

But why, she thought, walking through the dusky streets to the inn, the time-table in her hand, wait till then to smile? Why not smile now? She who had so often in life laughed at herself, had she not better seize this unrivalled occasion for laughter?

"Don't be bitter, Fanny," one half of her admonished.

"I'm not bitter," the other half declared.

She was, though. She had been taken in. She had been made a fool of. She had been dragged in the most humiliating of all dusts, the dust reserved for older women who let themselves be approached, on amorous lines, by boys. Why, she hadn't even had the excuse some unfortunate middle-aged women have of being rent asunder by unseemly longings. It had all been pure vanity, all just a wish, in these waning days of hers, still to feel power, still to have the assurance of her beauty and its effects.

And what had Dwight got out of it? She hardly could face it, it was so extremely mortifying, but she couldn't help thinking that what Dwight had got out of it, being a youth perhaps developed in business instincts beyond his years but in harmony with his American parentage, was her social usefulness. In her house he had met everyone he would think most worth knowing. She had rewarded his devotion by introductions which would seem to him dazzling. He had become, helped by her, extremely smart and social; and in return, how hard the poor little thing had laboured at his fine phrases and far-fetched eloquence! She had absorbed them all. They had bored her, but she had believed every word. And when he said, sitting at her feet with his head in her lap, and she comforting him—comforting him!—with soft fingers in his hair, that he didn't know how he could live without her, she had absorbed that too. Wonderful, her capacity for absorbing. How often, and how much, he must have been entertained—

"Now Fanny, don't be bitter."

"I'm not bitter."

§

The old lady, who had reached what she regarded as the pleasantest point in her day, the point at which she played patience before going up to dress for dinner, which she did by putting a lace scarf on top of her day dress, was none too well pleased to see the door open, and the same person who had thrust herself forward earlier in the day appear again. True, having had her nap, and had her tea, and eaten all the quite good buttered toast the Blue Dog succeeded, most days, in producing, she was now in a different mood; for the tea, very black and strong, invariably enlivened her, and buttered toast had a lubricating effect on the joints of her mind, reducing her inner friction. So that if a moment did exist in the twenty-four hours when she could be described as approachable, that moment was this one.

Nevertheless, she wasn't pleased; and when Fanny, opening the door hesitatingly, said: "If I don't smoke, may I stay here a little while?" she answered, almost as grudgingly as she would have before she had had her nap, her tea, and her buttered toast, "The management would no doubt say you may," and went on with her game just as if nobody were there.

Fanny sat down on the other side of the fire, drew off her gloves, warmed her thin hands, and set herself to forgetting Dwight.

The old lady, observing her over the top of her spectacles in the intervals of laying down cards, decided she must have had a set-back. She looked more haggard than before; her

foraging expedition couldn't have been a success. And since
it came more easily to her to feel well-disposed to those who
had got what they deserved rather than to those who still hadn't,
she presently asked, being humanized into the bargain by
plenty of butter on her toast: "Are you not going to have any
tea?"

Fanny looked round at her absently. The tea-things hadn't
yet been cleared away, and gave a spurious air of comfort to
the shabby room. The lamps were lit, and the curtains drawn.
The fire had been made up, and in the warm light the old lady
didn't look nearly so dead as she had before; indeed, she didn't
look dead at all, but definitely alive, and enjoying her small
comforts with a kind of venerable gusto. Was it possible, then,
thought Fanny, to be content with so little? To be stripped
of everything that made life lovely, and not mind? But perhaps
she wasn't stripped, because there hadn't been anything to strip.
Therefore she wouldn't miss anything. Therefore, naturally,
she didn't mind.

"Yes," said Fanny, reaching across and ringing the bell
by the fireplace, "I think I will."

"There isn't much I can recommend here," said the old lady,
"but I can and do recommend the buttered toast."

"Then I'd better have some," said Fanny. And, thinking
that if she talked to someone neutral and indifferent it would
be better than sitting silent forgetting Dwight, she added: "Isn't
it rather tiresome living in hotels?"

"You ought to know," said the old lady.

"I? Why?"

"Are you not Repertory?"

"Repertory? Do you mean the theatre people you were
telling me about? No, I'm not."

"I took you for one of them. The colour of your hair——"

"It's quite natural," said Fanny quickly, the more quickly
because it wasn't.

"Indeed," said the old lady; and was pregnantly silent.

There is no doubt that Fanny that day had had a good many
blows, and a small extra one like this didn't very much matter;
so she only thought: "Poor old thing, she isn't contented after
all, or she wouldn't be sour." Must one be discontented,
though, when one was old, she wondered? Was it really
inevitable? The Lapland night lady wasn't. She was serene;
and a great success, evidently, when she was on her last legs.

But the drawback to her as a source of encouragement was her not being real. This other old lady, this one sitting laying her cards, her mouth all pursed up, was real, and in twenty years' time, or perhaps even sooner at the rate she appeared to be decomposing, Fanny's mouth might very well be all pursed up too, into a kind of cross little bag. The indignities of age! Impossible, really, to believe in the serene and calm and bright sort; and in that case had she not better be very kind to the poor old image of her own future, just as she hoped there would be someone to be very kind to her when she too was defenceless?

The old lady, however, wasn't at all defenceless, and would intensely have objected if she had known Fanny was preparing to be kind. "Then," she said, having given the pregnancy of her silence time to sink in, "since you say you are not Repertory, perhaps you will tell me what you are."

"Nearly fifty," was the unexpected answer.

At this the old lady took off her spectacles, laid them aside, and looked at Fanny curiously. Through the slits which were all that her shrivelled-up lids allowed to be seen of her eyes, she looked at her, interested in spite of herself. "How frank," she said. "May I ask why you tell me that?"

"Because it's on my mind. It's very much on my mind. And it's easy to tell things to a stranger, and perhaps be helped to be more sensible."

The waiter at that moment ambled in, in answer to the bell, and the old lady was spared having to comment on the notion that she might help. Why should she help? No one had ever helped her when she was fifty; no, nor when she was sixty either, nor seventy, nor eighty. People had to stand on their own feet. She hated floppers.

"I took you for sixty," she said—"since we are being frank," she added, observing that this was received with a certain shrinking.

"Sixty," repeated Fanny, forcing herself to say it. Sixty. If that were what she looked like, was it to be wondered at that Dwight——?

She stared at the old lady, drawing her rings up and down her fingers. "But why, then," she asked, after a moment, "did you think I belonged to the Repertory Theatre? Would they take me if I were——?" No, she couldn't say that word again.

"I supposed you might do the duchesses. The elderly, women-of-the-world duchesses. You could be got up quite well as one of them, except that they usually have large busts. In fact, if your clothes weren't so youthful and this room were a stage, you wouldn't be out of place at all. As it is——"

"Well, you yourself suggested I should have tea," said Fanny. "I can't go now till it has come. But while I'm waiting, won't we talk? Really talk? I'd so much like, for once, to talk quite simply and honestly. One can with strangers, I think. Do you mind? Who knows but what we each might say something that would help the other one? You're older than I am—that is," she interrupted herself, a horrid doubt seizing her, because she was no longer sure of anything, "are you?"

"Of course I am," snapped the old lady, thrusting the absurd idea of helping each other indignantly aside. "I'm eighty-three, and very glad too. No more nonsense about me. Not that there ever was much. None of that being pretty business, which you seem to have gone in for."

"I didn't go in for it. It went in for me. It began in my cradle, and has stuck to me ever since—I mean," added Fanny, noticing derision on the wrinkled face opposite, "till lately. Till quite lately. And do you know what I'm beginning to realize? That it's a very dreadful thing to have *been* beautiful."

"Tut, tut," said the old lady, greatly irritated by this.

"Well, it is," persisted Fanny. "It's a very *dreadful* thing."

"Tut, tut," said the old lady; and tartly advised her not to rate herself too highly.

"Well, I don't," persisted Fanny.

"Tut tut," said the old lady; and told her that the women in the history of the world who had had real beauty could be counted on the fingers of one hand.

"Well, I was one of them," persisted Fanny; and the old lady, incensed beyond speech, began drumming her fingers on the table.

"Is it possible you don't see *any* traces?" asked Fanny, leaning forward. "Not a *single* one?"

The old lady jerked her head aside with a movement of exasperation, refusing to look, and drummed harder than ever.

"But we're being frank," insisted Fanny. "You said we were being frank. Do let us get rid of parlour ways, and say straight out what each thinks. There's nobody I can talk to about this, except a stranger—somebody I'll never see again. I shall go away, and you'll die—well, of course you'll die," she added, seeing the old lady, in her turn, received this with a certain shrinking, "and so will I, and I might easily die first, and it seems a pity to waste a single minute of the few we shall ever have together being conventional and ordinary."

"But suppose I prefer being conventional and ordinary? *Greatly* prefer it?" rapped out the old lady.

"Have you so much time to waste?" asked Fanny, her eyes widening.

The old lady took a moment or two to get over this. "Ah— you are hitting back," she then said, liking it as little as Fanny had liked being taken for sixty; for the longer she lived the more did the idea of leaving off being alive annoy her— just as she had grown so thoroughly used to it, and just as, having survived the whole of her family, she was at last free from vexations. The security of undisturbed routine, the peace of repetition, were what she was now appreciating. Certainly her days were not eventful, but then she didn't want events; she had had them,—not many, but enough. Now all she wanted was warmth, food, sleep, and another day just like the one before.

These, she felt, were modest demands to make on life, and there could be no real reason why they shouldn't be granted for many years to come. She was perfectly sound in wind and limb; a little stout, perhaps, but nothing to speak of; and short of falling down in a bathroom, as older people seemed apt to do, and the possibility of which she had disposed of by not going into bathrooms, she saw no reason why she shouldn't live to be a hundred. Then why should this ill-bred person so uncivilly suggest that she hadn't much time to waste? Frankness became rudeness too easily for it ever to be of any real use in conversation.

The waiter came in with the tea. He seemed to linger longer than usual arranging it on a table by the fire, but the intruder, taking no more notice of him than if he had been a table himself, went on being frank, and said: "You don't understand. I'm not dreaming of hitting anybody. I'm just unhappy."

"Then you'd better have your tea while it's hot," tartly remarked the old lady, so that the waiter should know there was at least one sensible person in the room. She was irritated afresh by this ignoring of the waiter. What would he think?

He knew she had never met the woman before, and what in the world would he make of such confidences? *"I am just unhappy,* indeed," sniffed the old lady.

"If you are unhappy," she said, when he had gone, shutting the door very slowly behind him as though wanting to hear more, "I dare say you have only yourself to thank. And perhaps a little more of the conventionality and ordinariness you appear to think is waste of time might improve your general prospects."

"My general prospects! Heavens—my general prospects," repeated Fanny, with a wry smile.

"Now don't tell me about them, because I don't want to know," the old lady quickly intervened, holding up a prohibiting hand.

Fanny took off her hat, threw it on a sofa, and pushed her hair behind her ears. She had a headache. She felt she was being a fool—another fool, for had she not been one already, for months past, and an arch one, over Dwight? Now she was being a fool again, supposing in her need that she might be able to get the blood of comfort out of somebody who was probably just a stone. "You don't *begin* to understand," she said, turning to the tea-things and pouring herself out a cup of very black tea.

Without her hat, she seemed to the old lady a good deal less questionable. It was quite possible, with it off, after all to see traces of beauty; and there was a kind of undefeatable blamelessness about her forehead, however meretricious she might be lower down, with her darkened eyelashes and reddened mouth. Having had a sculptor for a father, a knighted sculptor of the Victorian age, the old lady in her youth had heard great talk of moulding and of bones, and was able to recognize that the bones and moulding she now saw were undoubtedly what her father and his friends would have thought highly of. The line of the brow, for instance; and a peculiar graciousness, almost innocence, about the temples.

Still, bones weren't everything, and didn't make up for her make-up—she dwelt a moment, pleased, on this sentence, glad to find she retained her early aptitude for turning a phrase. She had been the one of the family with a sense of humour. Her father used to say so. "Maud," he used to say, "you should send that to *Punch.*" So that, though she might be eighty-three in the years of her body, she was nothing like so much in those of her mind; and after all, it was minds—wasn't it?—which kept bodies alive.

"I understand perfectly," she said. "You're fifty, and you don't like being fifty. You've lost your looks, and you don't like having lost them. And you've got me penned in behind this table, and know that if I did try to struggle out and go up to my bedroom I should be cold, so that probably I'll stay here while you flood me with talk about yourself, whether I want to hear it or not. I should say you were own sister to the Ancient Mariner, and, like all egoists, a born detainer of unwilling listeners." And down she slapped another card.

"That's the man," said Fanny, pausing in her pouring out, teapot in hand. "That's the man I couldn't remember. After luncheon. When you complained so much."

"I? Complained?"

"That's the man—the Ancient Mariner. It's why I went away—because you were buttonholing me, just as he button-holed somebody."

"I? Doing what?" exclaimed the old lady, her small, pursed-up mouth opening into a circle of indignant repudiation.

"Well, detaining an unwilling listener, then," said Fanny with a smile.

"In my life I've never done such a thing," cried the old lady, stirred to her marrow. "And if you imagine I would dream of trying to detain a complete stranger, and a stranger, too, who——"

"It seems to me," said Fanny, filling her cup while the old lady's words failed her, "that far from being complete strangers we've grown extraordinarily intimate."

"If you mean by intimate, rude——"

"No. Frank."

"There isn't any difference."

"Yes, there is. Rude is personal. We're impersonal—impersonally truthful, because we're never going to see each other again."

"Then would it be frank or rude," smartly asked the old lady, "if my answer to that were, what a mercy?"

"Anyhow, I'm sure it would be truthful," said Fanny, smiling again.

Smiling again; she who less than an hour before——

She picked up a piece of toast, and began to eat it, staring into the fire. She forgot the old lady. She was back again in the garden of New College, all but stumbling over the two pairs of flung-out feet . . .

"Going?" said the old lady, hopefully, for with a sudden movement she had pushed her chair away from the fire.

"I'm hot," said Fanny; and so she was—tingling, smarting with heat, but not from the fire.

"Ah—I thought you couldn't really be going," said the old lady, who for a moment had perked up.

"I can't before the taxi comes. I ordered one to fetch me."

"And when will it?"

"Soon now, I think."

"Well, as I agree with you that we'll never see each other again, I'll tell you one thing before you go——"

"Is it rude?"

"No. Frank. At least, you may take it which way you please. Now pray listen. Though appearances are against you——"

"I wonder why you say that," interrupted Fanny. "Your and my appearances aren't the same, but I don't see that either of them is against us. We're in a different walk of life, that's all."

"A very different walk of life. Allow me to finish, please. Though appearances are undoubtedly against you, as any clergyman or other responsible person would tell you, you seem on the whole to have the makings of an interesting personality. Or let us say, if interesting is putting it too high, a personality."

"Yes," agreed Fanny, searching in her bag and finding and lighting a cigarette. "Oh, I forgot," she said, throwing it into the fire, as the old lady at once loudly choked. "Yes," she went on, her face serious. "I've often thought something could have been made of me if I had been taken in time."

"Your taxi is here, mum," said the waiter, opening the door.

"Well, perhaps not often," she corrected, reaching for her hat, "because in my sort of life one doesn't think. But sometimes."

"Your sort of life?" repeated the old lady, her suspicions roused afresh, and her compliment, she feared, premature. "Do you mean you really are——?"

"Yes. Fifty," said Fanny, getting up and putting on her hat in front of the glass over the fireplace with the minute care of habit, and just as if hats still mattered.

"Fifty, fifty. I know all about your being fifty by now," said the old lady pettishly.

"But I'm something else besides," said Fanny, tucking in a curl and examining the effect, just as if curls still mattered. "I'm a fool."

"Well, you needn't tell me that either," the old lady assured her.

Ready to go, Fanny picked up her gloves. "And this very afternoon," she finished, "since luncheon, actually since I last was in this room, I've discovered there's no fool so complete as an elderly one."

"Ah, I *thought* you'd had a set-back!" triumphed the old lady. "Now don't tell me about it," she added quickly, holding up her hand, "because you'd miss your train."

§

There was only one stop before Paddington, and all the way up to Slough, alone in her compartment, Fanny addressed herself to thought.

"I must think this out," she said to herself. "Everybody can't be wrong."

A highly unpleasant business, to have to think anything out. She had supposed herself full of courage and common sense, and had liked to take it for granted that if occasion arose she wouldn't act less heroically than her famous forebears; and now occasion, entirely absent till then from her fortunate and padded life, had arisen, and it was in so sordid and mean a form, and in other people's eyes so certainly silly, that it seemed almost absurd to bring heroism to bear on it. What could be sillier in other people's eyes than a woman kicking up a fuss because she, too, in her turn, had grown old, and her beauty was gone? Yet what could be more tragic for the woman who, having been used all her life to being beautiful, found that without her looks she had nothing left to fall back upon?

"That's what is wrong," she thought. "There *ought* to be something to fall back upon. Somebody ought to have told me about this in time."

But who? And would she have listened? Her friends, her relations, the whole world, had been bent on helping her to be a fool. Jim Conderley was perhaps the only one who might

have got her to be something better; as she had told the old
lady, she had often thought there were at least the makings
in her, if properly dealt with, of something better. But Jim
was so hopelessly infatuated. All he could do was to worship,
and quote poetry. Certainly she had picked up quite a lot of
poetry during his era, and from that she argued she might have
picked up other things, if they had been brought to her notice
in time. Nobody had brought anything to her notice, except
that she was beautiful; and she knew that.

"You've been seriously handicapped," she said, nodding at
her reflection in the window-pane.

Even her reflection looked old, she thought. Soon her very
shadow, she dared say, would begin to totter. When that
happened, she really would give in. Up to now, though, at least
there had been nothing wrong with her shadow, which
remained, she was glad to say, a most elegant, slender thing—
and she leaned her head back on the cushions, with a faint
laugh. Often she had laughed at herself when she was in any
sort of a quandary, but never so faintly as now; and the sight
of her hollow-cheeked reflection, which she could see out of
the corner of her eye in the window-pane, quickly stopped it.

There was every excuse, though, she reasoned, for the hollow
cheeks, after such a day of blows following on a tormented and
sleepless night. Still, five years ago, even perhaps only a single
year ago, no amount of blows and sleeplessness would have
prevented her reflection from shining back at her with very
nearly its usual loveliness. That horrid illness had done all
this. To be as ill as that on the verge of fifty was very different
from being as ill as that on the verge of thirty, and as she
would probably never now get back her beauty she had better
think out what had best be done with her boring, senseless
future.

Oh, so boring; oh, so senseless. Should she go in for good
works? Or attend lectures? Or learn languages? Or interest
herself in the European situation? Bleak, bleak. But wasn't
the alternative even more bleak, indeed grisly, to dribble idly
into old age by slow stages of increasing depression and dis-
content, punctuated—what fun!—by things like rheumatism
and being deaf?

And she pictured herself turning gradually into her own
caricature, an unkind caricature—more than unkind, a highly
malicious parody of what she used to be—still going to parties

because she couldn't bear to be alone, and when she got to them hardly able to keep her eyes open, still snatching at invitations and ordering new frocks; an old woman who would be explained to the indifferent young ones as somebody who once was much more beautiful than they could ever hope to be.

"Difficult as it is to imagine," she could hear the explainer saying, "that old lady over there in the corner, Lady Frances Skeffington—yes, the old lady with the stick, whose head won't keep still—used to be a celebrated beauty."

Beauty; beauty. What was the good of beauty, once it was over? It left nothing behind it but acid regrets, and no heart at all to start fresh. Nearly everything else left something. Husbands, for instance, left, or ought to leave children, and then one could be busy with them, and with their children. It was, she felt, one of her most just grievances against Job, that she was childless. At least, at that moment she felt it was one of her most just grievances. Only that morning she had felt the exact contrary—and been very glad, because of that little difficulty about being dated. But now that she was apparently dated anyhow by her face, now that she seemed to be stamped all over with dates, while common little girls bursting out of yellow jumpers——

"Please, Fanny, don't be bitter."

§

Here the train, by slowing down, interrupted her reflections, and supposing it to be a non-stop express, she thought she had reached Paddington, and got up and opened the window.

There, on the platform, waiting to get in, a sheaf of papers under his arm, was Pontyfridd, and since nothing escaped him, he at once saw her standing at the door of her carriage, and hurried towards it, waving his stick.

"What luck!" he exclaimed a little breathlessly, when he arrived at the door.

"But I'm getting out," said Fanny, trying to.

"No, darling—I'm getting in," he said, stopping her.

"But it's Paddington."

"No, it's Slough."

Fanny was annoyed. Having had enough of everything for that day, she had had quite particularly enough of George.

Only with an effort had she managed to recover from the things he had said or suggested on the journey down, and now that she was exhausted by all that had been happening to her, and was looking, she was very sure, worse than ever, the last thing she wished to face were his twinkling, all-observing eyes. Suppose, now that she was defenceless from fatigue, they should bore through her face and see into her mind? And suppose what they saw in it was Dwight? She could well imagine what George would think of her, if he were to find out about Dwight.

She sat down, leaned back, and said briefly, "Oh."

"Tired?" he asked, putting up the window and settling himself opposite her. George was the sort of man, thought Fanny, one should only be with when one was at one's best. Then he wouldn't keep on saying, Tired? Cold?—all the things with unpleasant implications.

"Yes. I am, rather," she answered, shutting her eyes. She couldn't be bothered any more to cope with George. Let him look at her if he wanted to. At least nothing obliged her to look at him.

The next thing she knew was that he had sat down beside her, and was putting his arm round her shoulders. "There, there," he said commiseratingly, drawing her close. "Poor little thing. Didn't enjoy yourself much at Oxford, did you? Rest your little head on Cousin George, and forget it."

This was nice. This was just what she had always longed for—to be able to nestle up to a kind, protecting man, who wanted nothing of her but to hold her close and safe against his heart.

She gave a small sigh of relief as she snuggled into his coat. Oxford. No, she hadn't enjoyed Oxford—unless, she thought, able to smile a little, so great was the comfort of his coat, it was that beefsteak pudding. Everything that had happened after that had been so many blows in the face. Perhaps what she really wanted, now that she was fifty and so tired, was a cradle and a nurse—to come back comfortingly, at the end, to what she had had at the beginning. Safety; protection; gentle love; oh—sweet, sweet. And if the nurse could be a man, and the cradle his strong, careful arms, so much the better.

"What you need is a husband, my lamb," said George, bending his head to the small ear with the big jewel.

"No, no," protested Fanny into the coat. "Dreadful."

But it gratified her anxious, humiliated heart, her heart aching for reassurance, to know there was at least one man who thought marriage quite natural for her.

"I mean a husband you've had for years, darling, and got quite used to," said George, spoiling it. And he went on, spoiling it beyond repair: "There's nothing like a husband, you know, at the tail-end of life."

Fanny was mute. George too, now, joining up with the others. Again she told herself that everybody couldn't be wrong. The people she had seen that day didn't know each other, had never met and discussed her together, yet each made exactly the same sort of remark. Really was there anything to be done, except hide her finished face against George's coat, and let desolation wash over her?

"You might be Byles," she murmured forlornly, after a moment.

"I might be who?" asked George, bending lower to catch what she was saying, for it was difficult to hear a murmur in the rattling, rushing train.

"Byles. The nerve man. This morning he said almost quite that. About husbands, and—tail-ends."

"Do you mean Niggs's doctor? Then he's more sensible than I supposed. Of course a husband is what little creatures like you need. By the way, have you heard anything lately of the one you started with? The fellow with the Biblical name—Esau, wasn't it? Or was it Israel?"

"It was Job," said Fanny, and pushed herself upright, out of his arm.

The mere name electrified her. She sat up straight and stiff and looked at him, the cheek that had been pressing against his coat reddened, her curl on that side disarranged.

Job, again. Job, even got into the train. Job, even issuing forth from her kind cousin's lips.

"Job. Yes. So it was. What a name. Do you know anything about him?"

"What should I know?"

"He hasn't been cutting down your allowance, has he?"

"My allowance? I haven't got an allowance. He made settlements. But if I had, why should he cut it down?"

"Well, I heard rumours that he's been under the weather a long time now. Lost money. Kept on losing money."

She stared at him.

"Job losing money?" she asked, the pupils of her eyes quite

dark with astonishment. That Job should ever lose money, he who had so great a gift for finding it, seemed miraculous.

"Oh, well—rumours, rumours. Mexico, or somewhere," said George vaguely, not sure of his facts, leaning back with his hands in his pockets, now that Fanny had withdrawn from his arm, and crossing his long legs. "You know how rumours float round. And naturally I at once began wondering if you, my love, were in any way affected."

"Nothing has happened to me. Nothing could."

"Oh, I dare say it's just talk. He seems to be back in England. After years abroad. Well, darling, it's a relief, anyway, to know you're safe. Never bothered you, has he, since you got rid of him? Played the game decently, eh? He was very much in love with you, poor devil—God, how much in love!" grinned George, as long-forgotten visions of Job, the hardest-headed man of money in Europe, abject with adoration following Fanny about at parties, never taking his eyes off her, flushing if she threw him half a look, trembling when she came near him, emerged again through the swamp of years. And he went on, after a moment: "Pity you couldn't have forgiven him. He was a good chap, really. What do a few little odds and ends of girls matter in a man's life in the long run? And now you'd have had him to take care of you."

Fanny was incensed. "Thank you," she said, stiff as stone, "I can take care of myself perfectly. And I'm *sick*," she added vehemently, "oh, sick, *sick* of this talk of long runs."

Her hands gripped the bag lying in her lap, her eyes were bright with indignation and revolt. What things she had had to listen to that day, and was still having to listen to! The train, having lurched through Ealing Broadway, was beginning to slow down, and Paddington was only a few minutes away. George might well have left Job out of the talk for this brief time together, and not thrust him back violently into her mind just as she was getting home and hoping he wouldn't be there. All day she had kept that wretched figment off, trying to believe that if she didn't think of him he might let her alone when she got home, and now here was George—George, of all people, who had been as much shocked at her marriage as poor little Tripp—pushing him forward, telling her he was a good chap, and ought to have been forgiven.

"Darling——" said George, surprised by her vehemence, and laying his hand placatingly on hers.

But Fanny was too indignant to be placated. "There's not a pin to choose between you and Byles," she cried, pulling her hand away; and the train having drawn in to Paddington, before he could uncross his legs and snatch his papers together, she had beckoned a porter to open the door and was gone— had disappeared into the crowd, and wound her way among the hindering groups on the platform with the quick light steps of someone who is both thin and determined.

"Well, well," said George; and collected his papers at leisure.

§

Going home in the taxi, Fanny, her head held as high and her eyes as shining as they had been that morning when she left Sir Stilton's consulting-room, defiantly decided that she wouldn't be browbeaten by anybody into being sorry she hadn't forgiven Job, and that she wasn't going to put up with his haunting pranks any longer. In Mexico, had he been? He should have stayed there. She supposed he wouldn't or couldn't, and persisted in hanging about her in Charles Street. If she found him there when she got home, then she would simply turn round and go to an hotel.

She did find him there, and she did immediately turn round and go to an hotel. Behind the footman who opened the door, behind the butler presiding over the footman who opened the door, behind the curious figure of Miss Cartwright hurrying out of her sitting-room, there he was, lurking.

"Oh," she exclaimed, stopping dead, blinking as she came out of the darkness into the bright light, "oh"—and stood a moment staring past the others.

"Very well, then," she suddenly said, as though making up her mind, "that settles it. I'll go to Claridge's. Miss Cartwright, will you please tell Manby to bring round my things?"

And the taxi-driver who brought her from Paddington had hardly done pocketing his money when there she was again, and he was taking her somewhere else.

The footman, the butler, and Miss Cartwright looked at each other. Miss Cartwright was not one, normally, to look at butlers and footmen, but on this occasion a common perplexity levelled social distinctions.

Very well, then, that settles it. What, precisely, had these

c

words meant? And to which of the three had they been
addressed? They none of them had an idea.

"Strange," said Miss Cartwright.

The butler shook his head.

"Peculiar, I call it," said the footman, thinking to curry
favour with the butler.

And when, an hour later, Manby arrived at Claridge's, bear-
ing the whole elaborate paraphernalia without which Fanny
couldn't be undressed at night or dressed again in the morning,
she found her flung down, just as she was except for her hat,
dead asleep across the bed.

IV

§

AT Upswich, Lord Conderley's place in Suffolk, whither, on
laying down his various offices, he had retired with his rather
young wife and quite young children, the following week was
blest by the sort of sunny February weather which makes
crocuses come out. A few days of frost, with a great red sun
dropping behind the low range of western hills each late afternoon, and then a sudden veering of the wind to the south, and
out rushed the crocuses, and up rushed the larks.

Upswich was situated not far from Ipswich, which sometimes
caused confusion. It was, however, quite unlike Ipswich, being
a single, beautiful old house, in a spacious, beautiful old park;
and Lord Conderley, when the King raised him to the peerage,
and he might choose what name he liked, could think of nothing
that pleased him better than the one he had already, and therefore remained Conderley, while adding Upswich.

Here at Upswich, being by now over seventy, he wrote
his memoirs, pottered in his rock-garden, observed the habits
of birds, fished, and rejoiced in a well-found library. He never
knew a dull moment, because directly moments threatened to
be dull he went and talked to his rather young, and entirely
satisfactory, wife. And they talked pleasantly together about
their children, and their children's future; or he read aloud to
her, while she knitted.

The only drawback to marrying late in life—otherwise, he
considered, so wholly admirable a thing for a man to do—was

that by the time one's children were grown up one would be
too old to be of much, if any, use to them. Of the age of grand-
fathers, not fathers, one would be; or even of great-grandfathers.
When his boy, who was also his youngest child, came of age,
he himself, if still alive, would be over ninety—an age for
chimney-corners and a stick, rather than for guiding a possibly
impetuous young man by precept and example. Precepts, felt
Lord Conderley, when delivered in a voice that quavered,
wouldn't be very impressive, while as for example, how could
a man be anything except virtuous and a conscientious doer
of his duty, when age had completely freed him from temptation
to be or do anything else?

Of these things, however, he said no word to his wife. They
were the single fly in his happy home ointment, and he wasn't
going to trouble her by letting her know how much, sometimes,
he minded them.

She, a country-bred girl, of obscure but pleasant parentage,
with four brothers and two sisters, all most reliable, was of
the very stuff, in his opinion, good wives are made of—healthy,
sweet-tempered, sensible, simple, ready to learn, enjoying
looking up to him, interesting herself in all he did, not knowing
any of his former friends, and liking to be read aloud to. It
was a great thing that she should like to be read aloud to,
because he so much liked reading aloud; and only sometimes
on a hot summer afternoon, if he read aloud in the garden,
she would miss a sentence or two because of having gone to
sleep, or on a winter evening by the fire, after an active day.
Usually, however, she stayed awake.

They had been married nearly ten years, and he was medi-
tating what affectionate little surprise he could prepare for her
for the anniversary, when Fanny's letter arrived at breakfast.
His wife didn't know about Fanny. That frantic episode—
frantic on his side, for never had he so deeply loved, and not
frantic at all on Fanny's, though highly enjoyable and happy—
had been over and done with for years by the time he married,
and he had seen no reason why it should be gone into, or
even mentioned. Fanny was enshrined in his memory as
the nearest thing to perfect loveliness he had ever known. She
was also enshrined there as a great promoter of ups and downs.
During the three years she had been his darling friend, he had
become intimately acquainted with contrasts of rapture and
despair which he, a quiet man, of the gentle, court-official type

who in leisure moments reads the classics and is never without a little volume of Horace in his pocket, hadn't supposed existed. The exquisite creature, delightfully interested in the things he told her were interesting, so eager to hear about them, so appreciative, when he had pointed it out, of their beauty, had been the most enchanting of companions besides the most adorable of beloved. For three years no man could have been happier, nor any man more miserable—miserable, because that very adaptability which had made her walk into his life, his interests, and his heart with such ease, and curl herself up in them so snugly, had kept him on tenterhooks lest she should ever adapt herself equally easily to someone else. And so she did, after a while, and of all people to that flashy fellow Edward Montmorency, the last sort of man he would have imagined she could endure. With the utmost sympathy and tenderness, and crying so much that he found himself comforting her and wiping away her tears, she had delicately shelved him; and he had been so seriously ill of it that he had had to go away for six months on sick leave, and for years afterwards wouldn't go anywhere, except to Court functions he couldn't avoid, for fear, positively, that if by accident he were so close to her that he had to say something and hear her speak, he might drop dead at her feet.

These are not things one tells one's wife, of whom one is very fond, and to whom one is very grateful, and with whom one is very happy. At his wife's feet he had never even remotely considered the possibility of dropping dead. He hardly knew she had any feet. She was that best sort of woman for permanent purposes, the sort one stays comfortably alive with. Affection and kindness were the basis of their pleasant partnership. The short courtship had been affectionate, and the honeymoon kind. Their life since then had been unchangingly affectionate and kind. He had wanted a cheerful companion in his home, and had got her. He had wanted children, and had got them. She wasn't, it is true, particularly pretty, but being even now still only in the thirties had, in his elderly eyes, the attractiveness of youth. And what elderly man wants the bother of a very pretty wife? If she is very pretty, it only leads to other men eyeing her with concupiscence.

Audrey provided no such danger; not only because she was pleasant and healthy-looking rather than pretty, with her firm little round pink cheeks and bright, small eyes, but also because

of her quiet country bringing-up and honest, solid character.
Sure-footed and content, he could trustfully enter on the last
lap of his life; and when at breakfast, about a week after
Fanny's day in Oxford, he saw her well-known handwriting
among his letters—that handwriting which used to make his
heart beat with a violence that threatened to choke him—he
had so long been tranquilly happy in the state to which it
had finally pleased God to call him, that positively he felt
nothing but a mild surprise.

Fanny. What could she want? How odd that she should
write.

Having read the letter, he wasn't perhaps quite so tranquilly
happy. Yet, what had changed? There, round his table, still
sat his clean and shining children—little Jim fastened into a
high chair, with his nurse next to him shovelling him up with
porridge, and on the other side of the table little Audrey his
eldest, and little Joan, the middle one; while at the end, opposite
him, freshly soaped, and neat in her morning frock, was his
glossy wife, looking after everybody, joking with the children,
reading her letters, all at one and the same time.

The sun poured in, the room smelt good of breakfast, the
lawn beyond the windows was lively with crocuses, and everywhere in England, at that moment, were breakfast-tables just
like this one. No; not just like this one, for only on Conderley's
table lay a letter from Fanny, and it did somehow seem to give
his table, after he had read it, a different aspect from the one
it had before. No longer, somehow, was it so familiar and
so safely settled and jog-trot as breakfast yesterday had been,
and the day before that, and so on back to the first breakfast
of his married life. A query lay across it, like a small shadow;
several queries. And desiring not to think of them for a
moment, he put the letter down and fixed his attention on his
surroundings.

What an untidy eater little Jim still was, he thought, noticing
how much of his porridge stayed outside his mouth instead
of going inside it. And then he noticed that his two daughters,
who had a high-spirited habit of asking riddles at meals, were
laughing over them rather more noisily than perhaps they
should. And after that he noticed, with just the slightest of
starts, that his wife was looking at him.

"Anything wrong, Jim?" she asked brightly, having caught
his eye.

"Wrong, dear?"

"I thought the letter you were reading seemed to worry you."

"Oh, that. Well, no—not worry, exactly. But it does rather bore me."

"Nurse, *none* of that went down. Yes, Jim? Children, I wish you would learn to laugh in your sleeves—think how nice and muffled it would be. Yes, Jim?"

"Perhaps after breakfast," said Conderley vaguely, turning over his other letters.

But after breakfast it wasn't any easier. They went arm in arm together into the library, where she lit a cigarette and he a pipe, and then he suggested, having pulled at it in silence, that they should take a turn in the garden.

They took a turn. By this time his wife was definitely curious. "Well, Jim?" she said at last as, still arm in arm, they paced the sunny terrace beneath the south wall of the house, and still he said nothing.

He cleared his throat. She became every minute more curious.

"You remember hearing me speak of Fanny Skeffington?" he said, though well knowing she couldn't remember, because he never had spoken of her—such being the minor duplicities which sometimes entangle husbands.

"No," said Audrey. "I don't. Who is she?"

"Well, it's a long time ago, and I dare say you've forgotten. But as she was one of my—of our set years ago, I'm fairly certain I must have talked to you about her."

"No," said Audrey, positively. "You didn't."

"Well, it doesn't matter. But she wants to come here next week-end."

"What for?"

"To pay us a visit, dear, and to make friends, she says, with you."

"With me? Why?"

"My dear child, it would be as reasonable to ask why people ever want to make friends with anybody."

"Do you want her to come?"

"No."

"Well then, say she can't."

"Wouldn't that be rather brutal?"

"I can think of a thousand excuses you could make, not

one of them the tiniest bit brutal. If you like, I'll write."

"I don't think that would be a good plan. She doesn't know you yet, and though I hope she soon will——"

"Then you *do* want her to come," Audrey interrupted.

"Did I not tell you that I do not?" he answered, his natural gentleness a little ruffled.

"Then why do you say you hope she'll soon know me?"

"My dear, why does one ever say anything?" Conderley retorted, more ruffled.

In silence they paced the length of the terrace. It was a good and pleasant thing, he knew, to have a downright wife, and no wife could be more appreciated than his, but there were occasions, or rather, say, moments, so brief and fleeting were they, when a little more grasp, a shade more imagination . . . And she was thinking: "It's that Yorkshire pudding. I oughtn't to have let him eat it at dinner last night."

Recovering, he presently said: "I haven't seen poor Fanny for years."

"Is she poor?"

"Not in the financial sense."

"In what sense, then?"

"I suppose in the sense in which we speak of all people getting older as poor."

"Is she getting older?"

"My dear, what a question."

Yes; it was the Yorkshire pudding. He sounded quite cross, and that, she knew, couldn't possibly be just Jim.

"I mean," she said cheerfully, for nobody can mind what is really something one's husband has eaten, "is she quite old?"

"Well, it must be twenty years, or more, since last I saw her."

"Oh, then she must be *quite* old," said Audrey, reassured and appeased. She had somehow been supposing . . . "Used you to call her Fanny?" she went on.

"If you hadn't lived so entirely buried in your woods and fields, you would have known that we all, in the sort of set I lived in, called each other by our Christian names," he said; and again that pudding seemed to be welling up into his voice.

"But, Jim, did you actually call the——?" breathed Audrey, too much awestruck, however, to pronounce the august word.

"My dear child—really," protested Conderley; this time plainly altogether pudding.

In silence they paced the return length of the terrace. She
was telling herself she would never in future give him the
indigestible stuff later in the day than lunch; he was thinking,
Why does she make everything so difficult for me?

Then she said: "Did this Fanny somebody——"

"Skeffington. Fanny Skeffington. Lady Frances Skeffington,"
he interposed, speaking quite loud, and with great distinctness.

"——Skeffington, then. Did she call you Jim?"

"My dear, haven't I just told you that we all called each
other by our Christian names? But now tell me, Audrey," he
went on more gently, himself at this point noticing how cross he
sounded, and unpleasantly surprised that merely a letter from
Fanny should produce what amounted to their first—well, not
quarrel, but their not being as nice as usual to each other—
"tell me, Audrey, seeing that she is, as you say, quite old"—
for a moment he tried to picture Fanny quite old, but didn't
succeed—"and says in her letter——"

"May I see it?" Audrey interrupted, holding out her hand.

He wasn't prepared for this. It hadn't occurred to him that
she might ask to see the letter.

Embarrassed, he pretended to search his pockets. "I must
have left it in the library," he said, while, at the bottom of one
of them, he was holding it tight.

Now why did he do that? he wondered. There was nothing
to hide, really, in the letter. A few affectionate words, perhaps,
which could easily have been explained. What impulse, then,
made him pretend he hadn't got it?

He told himself he hadn't an idea; but he had, and he knew
he had, and the idea included the word desecration.

This took him aback. His wife, desecrating another woman's
letter by reading it—dear me, thought Conderley; dear me.
And he began to think that perhaps Fanny had better be put off.

"Tell me what she says, then," said Audrey.

"Something about having been ill, and that she has a great
wish to see her old friends once more——"

"Before she dies," put in Audrey; shocking him for the first
time in their life together.

There was a pause, during which he was mastering his real
anger. He wasn't cross this time, he was coldly angry. To talk
with such levity, such heartlessness, of Fanny's death, *Fanny's*
death, who had been all that he had ever known of life—
flaming, throbbing, torturing, exquisite life, compared to which   .

his and Audrey's existences were nothing but the sleep of slugs
. . . Certainly, then she should come. Certainly he wasn't
going to put off the visit of one who had once been so dear
to him for the sake of someone who wasn't dear to him at all.
No; positively for a moment his wife, the good and devoted
Audrey, mother of his children, faithful companion of his leisure,
tireless minister to his comfort, wasn't dear to him at all.

"There's really no question about the answer," he said,
directly he was able to speak quietly. "I shall write and say we
shall both be delighted."

"Which of course won't be in the least true," said Audrey,
going on being annoyingly honest. "I shan't be delighted at
all—that is," she said, taking his arm again, which he had
withdrawn, "unless you are. Shall you be? I can't quite make
out."

She looked up at him affectionately. She hadn't an idea she
had angered him. She was very much at home with the image
of him she had built up in her heart, encouraged by his gentle
friendliness.

"My dear Audrey," he said, still very cold, his limp arm
giving no sort of encouragement to the warm pressure of hers,
"there's such a thing as kindness and courtesy to one's old
friends."

"Yes, I know," she said, holding his arm close to her side,
"and you shall do whatever you think right, and I promise
to be the perfect hostess. But you'll have to explain her
thoroughly before she comes, or I shan't know where I am."

"There'll be plenty of time for that," said Conderley,
releasing himself and looking at his watch. "I have an appointment at ten with Jackson," he added suddenly; and without
another word, filling his pipe as he went, walked off in the
direction of the greenhouses.

§

By the time Fanny arrived on the following Saturday afternoon—it was to be the shortest form of week-end—Audrey
knew everything about her that she was to know; not all that
there was to know, but all that she was to know; and Conderley,
calm again, and much surprised that he should have been so
angry, had amply reflected on the extent to which the wife of

one's bosom is really shut out of it. She knew who Fanny's father was, she knew her only brother had been killed in the war, she knew she had married a Jew—"How could she?" inquired Audrey—she knew she had been divorced——

"No, *she* divorced him," Conderley corrected.

"It's the same thing."

"Indeed, no. You must really get it right."

—and finally she knew, having looked it up in Debrett, that she would be fifty next month, on the twelfth of March; she knew no more. Lady Frances had never married again, Conderley told her, who, without the least intending it, gave the impression that since parting from her husband Fanny had lived an austere single life, suggesting vestal virgins to Audrey, in Charles Street, taken care of by a devoted maid, who would no doubt end in the columns of *The Times*, under the heading Faithful Service.

"Poor thing," said Audrey with a happy little sigh, slipping her hand in his. "And no children, either. It all sounds so miserable."

What interested her most, though, was the divorce. She couldn't leave off talking about it. She harped. And when at last he remonstrated with her for this persistence, she explained she had never yet consciously met a *divorcée*, let alone had to entertain one, and felt as if it were going to be rather a landmark in her life.

"*He* was the *divorcé*," corrected Conderley, patiently.

"It's the same thing," said Audrey, who seemed incapable of discriminating between guilty and innocent parties. "Divorce, after all, is divorce, you know, Jim." And she would look at him as though inviting him to deny it if he could, and he would take up *The Times*, and bury himself.

Presently, still harping, she would say: "The Queen——" by whom she meant Victoria—"refused to receive people at Court, mother said, whichever party they were, guilty or innocent."

And again, a little later, he meanwhile remaining buried: "There's no smoke without fire, you know, Jim."

And again, after a further interval, during which he stayed steadily buried: "You can't touch pitch without being defiled, you know, Jim."

"Oh, *God*," Conderley said to himself, in sudden stress of spirit. It was many years since he had said Oh, God.

§

They were both on the doorstep when Fanny arrived. Audrey had taken great pains with the rooms, filling them with country flowers like crocuses and snowdrops, and the best linen, and the sorts of books she thought someone lately ill and regaining strength might find invigorating, like *Walks in Rome*. Bright fires were everywhere. Tea was ready in the hall. Up to the last moment Conderley buried himself in *The Times*, and only when the car could be heard actually stopping did he hastily throw it down, and go out with his wife on to the steps.

He quite painfully minded, now that the moment had come, meeting Fanny, and resented that Audrey, as they stood together on the steps, should put her arm through his. He did belong to her. Nobody disputed it. So why this open possessiveness?

But he was doing her an injustice, for she was merely very shy, and instinctively clung to him. Also, Manby, who got out first, was mistaken by her for Fanny. "Why, Jim—how *old*," she whispered. "What a *bad* fifty"—and this made her more shy, when she discovered her mistake, besides annoying him, he felt, quite disproportionately.

But here was Fanny herself, bending her head so as not to knock it against the frame of the door. He went to help her, and holding her hand as she emerged, they saw each other close for the first time since the heart-breaking afternoon twenty years before, when he had assisted in wiping away her good-bye tears.

"Oh, *poor* Jim," thought Fanny—hesitating, not quite sure, yet only too sure, and distressed for him that he should be so stooping and so grey.

"My God, poor Fanny," thought Conderley, shocked. For she was much made up. No woman will go to a meeting with one who has long and deeply loved her without taking pains to look her best. Fanny had taken pains, and to Conderley, used now for years to living in the country among weather-beaten, tweed-skirted women, with a wife who did nothing to her face beyond washing it, she looked definitely improper. Her thinness made it worse. To have hollow cheeks was sad enough, but to paint them was to turn sadness into tragedy.

Noble, lovely, little Fanny . . .

Faintly down the years, like a small, wheezy tune on an old musical-box, drifted the words. He bent over her hand so as to hide what he was feeling, and she, seeing him from this angle, couldn't but notice how very scanty his hair was on the top. In fact, hardly there at all.

"Alas, poor Jim,". she thought, wishing she hadn't come.

"Alas, poor Fanny," he thought, wishing to goodness that he hadn't let her. And what was so curious was that neither had any real idea how each appeared to the other.

She was the first to say something. "This is wonderful, meeting again. Dear Jim, I can't tell you how glad I am," she said, trying to persuade herself that she knew this strange old man really very well.

But he, helping her up the steps, his hand under her elbow—it felt the thinnest little pointed thing, in his palm—still for a moment didn't speak. Then he said, breathing rather hard, for it had long been difficult for him to go up steps and talk at the same time, "I only wish you had had such a good idea sooner."

Did he mean before she left off being young, or before he grew so old? No, he was simply polite. She could see that, by the courteous bend of his head towards her, and the kindliness of his tired eyes.

"Poor Jim—dreadful to have such tired eyes," she thought, quickly looking away and forgetting that she had them herself.

"What a marvellous old house," she exclaimed, gazing up with great appreciation at its mellowness. "Oh—and is this Audrey?"

Audrey, coming forward with welcoming smiles, at once decided, in spite of never having seen one, that Fanny was every inch a *divorcée*, and was glad there weren't any other visitors. This was no guest, she felt, to show a bishop. She wondered what mother would have said. But she did realize, she who knew nothing about so-called smart women except from pictures, very queer ones, sometimes, in the *Tatler*, that probably other smart women would have noticed nothing out of the way. Jim hadn't mentioned this aspect of their guest. In spite of that, however, she immediately recognized the type, and became shyer than ever.

"I'm sure you are longing for tea," was all she could think of to say, in return for Fanny's affectionate greeting and kiss.

"I might easily have been your mother, you know," Fanny smiled, explaining the kiss.

Conderley thought the remark unfortunate.

"Shall we go in and have tea?" said Audrey, still unable to think of something to say, and therefore harping, said Conderley to himself, annoyed, since apparently harp she must, on tea this time. And here he realized, with a shock, that the minute Fanny appeared on the scene, whether actually, or in a letter, or in conversation, he became annoyed with Audrey.

She led the way, but sideways, into the hall. Not only did she suddenly feel extremely young—on the whole rather pleasant, that—but having absorbed in one lightning, all-comprehending glance everything Fanny had on, she was aware that she, Audrey, didn't know how to dress. This depressed her, because she had always so firmly supposed she did; and it was why she went into the hall sideways, hoping Fanny wouldn't, perhaps, that way see quite so much of her at once.

Now where, though, was the difference? she puzzled. They were both in country clothes. Difficult to say in what way hers were different from Fanny's, but different they were—as different as their faces, thought Audrey, who had also immediately recognized that underneath her guest's make-up, and in spite of hollows, there still were the lovely lines of something she herself had never had. She herself had never been anything more than a nice, fresh little thing—oh, she knew it, and had always thought it so wonderful of her Jim to want to marry her; so that what with the difference in their clothes and the difference in their faces, she became entangled in an inferiority complex, and found it almost impossible to utter a word.

Fanny, however, was just the right person to deal with shyness. Herself completely unselfconscious, because of never having had to trouble about the impression she might be making, she was free to throw herself into the feelings of others, and it was one of her chief charms, as well as one of the chief dangers for those others, the whole-hearted way she did it. One would have thought, watching her talk to somebody, that the person she was talking to was the single person in the world she wanted to be with. Audrey had no need to do more than pour out the tea; Fanny, who knew embarrassment when she saw it as well as any woman, did all the rest, till such time as her small hostess should have recovered. Had Jim, she wondered, thought it

necessary to tell his wife about her? If he had, then all the
more reason for quickly making friends. But anyhow, the little
primrosy effect of Audrey appealed to her, and from her heart
she, who never in her life had been jealous or possessive,
but always eager that people she cared for should know and like
other people she cared for and be happy with them, was glad
poor Jim should have found such a snug haven to come to
anchor in.

> *And so from year to year their little boat*
> *Lies in its harbour, rocking peacefully——*

"Jim," she said, turning to him, who sat silent, his bony
fingers clasped round his cup as though to warm them, "the
minute I see you I think of lovely things like poetry."

"Do you, Fanny?" he said, flushing. "How very charming
of you."

"And just then, seeing you and Audrey so cosy and happy
together"—Audrey's pink cheeks turned pinker, she liked this
so much—"something you used to quote——"

"Did he quote even in those days?" asked Audrey, peeping
out, as it were, for an instant round the door of her shyness.

"I believe he came into the world quoting," smiled Fanny,
as she stretched across to the sandwiches and took one—nice not
to have to bother about offering things, thought Audrey. "But
seeing you and Audrey reminded me of that bit about the little
boat and the harbour. Wordsworth, wasn't it?" And she remembered, with a kind of shocked inward laughter, being now
with Jim again, the irreverent Edward's name for the great
man. Fish Face, Edward had called him. Old Fish Face.
Dreadful. Yet, even now, it made her want to giggle.

The tactful Fanny knew she had only to start on poetry to
make Jim happy—unless, that is, his poor dear mind had gone
bald as his poor dear head. Evidently, though, it hadn't, for he
left off nursing his cup, got up with an alacrity he hadn't yet
shown, went out of the room, and came back immediately—
"Thank goodness," thought Audrey, who had been appalled
by his departure—with a fat volume. "Here it is," he said,
finding the place and pointing. His finger, very knuckly and
discoloured, shook.

"Do read it aloud," said Fanny, lighting a cigarette—nice,
thought Audrey, not to have to bother about suggesting things.

She leaned back in her chair. Audrey relaxed enough to be able to lean back in hers. Jim had an attractive voice, and read well. What a resource it was, Fanny thought, this reading aloud. No need to say a word; no need to do anything with one's weary, worried mind except let it idly wander. In that way, reading aloud was much better than chess, she decided, because not only had you to concentrate when you played chess, but compared to being read aloud to it was quite chatty, with its checks and its mates. Perry—she was thinking of Sir Peregrine Lanks, K.C., who was the one who came after Edward and ended by being tired and patient—had taught her chess, had insisted on teaching her chess, not being interested in this other resource of those who no longer have much to say to each other; and she had learned, though unwillingly, because after the first week or two of his devotion, she had somehow got the idea that though he obviously violently adored her he yet was inclined to suspect she was a goose. If she could play chess well, admittedly a game for the intelligent, mightn't he perhaps think she had brains? Accordingly, she secretly went to a chess-expert—a Russian her secretary had somehow discovered for her —and took lessons. Every morning off she went with Manby in attendance, and for a time Lanks was astounded by the progress she made. She seemed to pick it up by instinct, he said. He was positively excited and said he had never known such aptitude. "There's nothing you can't do, you adorable Fanny," he cried one day, enchanted when she had managed to nip off his queen.

Then the expert took to helping her move her knights in the way they should go by laying his hand over hers, and also whenever he had occasion, which was frequently, to say Mate, he began to coo. "Mate," he would coo rather than say, looking at her with melting meaning. "Ah—mate," he would coo again, sighing; while Manby, very genteel and self-effacing in a corner, appeared to be studying a Russian newspaper.

She gave up the lessons; her progress came to a dead stop; and Lanks, after a period of increasingly impatient surprise, returned, she was afraid, to his original suspicion.

All this Fanny idly remembered as with her ears, but not her mind, she listened to Conderley's attractive voice. She didn't look at him, as she easily might have done now that his eyes were on the book, because she had much rather not. It seemed almost indecent to look at somebody whom age had so much uncovered. Let her listen to his voice, which, like his hand-writing, was still unchanged. And the wood fire leaped and crackled, and the room smelt sweet of spring flowers, and out in the garden, where thrushes were singing in the dusk, some children presently ran by, chattering and laughing, and by the way Audrey half got up and then sat down again, and by the quick transformation on her face from respectful attention to real interest, Fanny knew they must be his and hers.

Had she done well, she asked herself in doubt, her heart sinking a little, to come here? Could it really help her to see all the things she had missed, to see how happy everybody else was, how secure, and safely, as it were, tucked up for the night? The night couldn't be very far from poor Jim now, that night on which she had lately, since her illness, begun to ponder in regard to herself; but there was nothing for him to mind about it, with this devoted little wife to see him through.

She, Fanny, when it came to be her turn, would have to look to Manby.

§

It wasn't till the evening, after dinner, that she found herself for a few minutes alone with Conderley. Audrey had gone to kiss the children in their cots, a rite she performed regularly, and in the library Conderley and Fanny were for the first time by themselves.

At once they both began to feel uncomfortable. Was this, then, thought Fanny, the way friendship ended, in feeling uncomfortable? It oughtn't to. It mustn't. She was sure it was all wrong that it should. But the real difficulty was that she couldn't believe this strange old man, drooping against the chimney-piece while he filled his pipe, was anybody she had ever known intimately.

"Do you mind a pipe?" he asked, pausing in its filling.

"You know I don't," she said; for how often, liking the smell, had she not encouraged that pipe?

But he didn't know. He had forgotten small things like that. He only remembered that there had been anguish. She remembered all the small things. Besides, for her there had been no anguish.

Her voice, though, thought Conderley, was still exactly the same. If he didn't look at her, it was just as though his lost Fanny were there, close to him again, in the low chair by the little table with violets on it. Audrey's little table; Audrey's violets; but, when he didn't look at her, his Fanny. He had better, then, look at her. There was neither honour nor profit to be got from shutting his eyes and listening to that darling—no, that once darling—voice.

She, for her part, was meanwhile saying to herself, "This is nonsense, two such old friends being shy of each other. I, anyhow, intend to be natural——" and immediately began being natural by saying, "Jim, have I changed much?"

He was startled enough to drop his tobacco-pouch. "Changed, Fanny? In what way?" he asked, rather laboriously picking it up again. For a long time now he hadn't been able to pick up things very easily.

"You know in what way. Is it—please tell me honestly, Jim—is it *much*?" And she went on, fighting against the contagiousness of his embarrassment, and trying hard to be perfectly comfortable and easy with him, "You've no idea how difficult it is really to see oneself as other people see one. One gets used to one's face, looking at it so often in the glass. If I could just get an occasional surprise view of it——"

"Well, but you mustn't forget you were still almost a girl when I—when we were friends," he said. "Of course since then you've grown up."

"George Pontyfridd told me the other day that I hadn't. At least, he said I was taking a long time over it. But he didn't mean physically. At first I thought he did, but on thinking it over I believe he meant my mind, or my imagination, or sympathy, or something."

"Well, but women do seem to retain a certain childlike quality——" began Conderley sententiously, wishing Audrey would come back.

"You mean, they go on being idiots," smiled Fanny. And as he made no answer beyond a deprecating shake of the head, she added, "If I had said that to Perry——"

"Perry?"

"Peregrine Lanks. You know."

Conderley gravely nodded. He did know. He knew that after that fellow Montmorency—well, what did it matter now?

"If I had said that to Perry," she went on, "about women going on being idiots, he would have told me that I took the words out of his mouth. But you are kinder, Jim, and——" she had been going to say "less quick", but stopped.

"Lanks has had a remarkable career," said Conderley, lighting his pipe and doing his best to keep the conversation off personalities. "He refused the Home Secretaryship because he didn't want to give up the enormous fortune he was making at the Bar."

"I know. Wonderful. But do we want to talk about him? You'll be talking about Hitler next."

"And why not? He is rather terrifyingly important at this moment."

Fanny sighed. "Oh, my dear Jim—the European situation. Even you," she said. "All right. Go on, then." And she too wished Audrey would come back.

"But it is, without any doubt, the most interesting subject just now that there is," said Conderley, doing something to his pipe, which wouldn't draw.

"Then you *do* think I've changed?" she said quickly.

He looked at her a moment, not seeing the connection. "Please, Fanny——" he then begged, adding, "haven't I changed too?"

"Oh—men. And you used to say——"

"Please, Fanny," he begged again.

"Well, but you did," she persisted. "When I told you all you cared about was my being so pretty, you used to say that it was my soul you loved. Did you love it? Because I've still got that self-same soul, you know, whatever I may look like outside."

"Perhaps we shouldn't remind each other of what we used to say," he suggested, uncomfortably.

"I don't think *I* said much, did I?"

"Perhaps because you didn't feel much."

"Oh, Jim—and I who was so devoted to you, and for such years!" she protested.

"Shall I tell you what I really think?" he said, earnestly desiring to steer the conversation away from whatever it was heading for.

"I wish you would," she answered, bracing herself.

"That you are, always were, and always will be, the most charming woman in the world." And he made her a ceremonious, quite Buckingham Palace and Windsor bow.

She dropped back into the cushions again. It put continents between them, centuries, this speech and bow.

"That sounds very hollow," she said at last, mournfully. "I didn't realize that we're nothing but acquaintances now."

"Before we go into that," he said, looking at her, "you must tell me what you mean by acquaintances."

He must look at her. Indeed, he went and turned on more lights, all the lights, till the room blazed. If he didn't see her and just heard her voice, it made him get too near aching. He hadn't supposed he would ever ache again, ache with longing after even the very miseries of his younger years; but then Fanny had always had a voice that twisted his heart, and unfortunately she still had it. Therefore let him look at her—look at at her, and be shocked. Better, any day, for a married man to be shocked than to ache. And why on earth didn't Audrey come back?

"Oh, just that," she said listlessly. "Acquaintances. Paying compliments. Making pretty speeches. All the things that people begin with. I didn't know they ended with them too."

"Please, Fanny——" he begged once more.

And then they were silent; and both wished Audrey would come back.

§

When at last she did, wondering, as she opened the door, at the bright light, she thought at first there was nobody in the room, it was so quiet. Then seeing them still there, each buried in an enormous chair and neither saying a word, she couldn't make it out.

They seemed, however, genuinely pleased to see her. Fanny sat up quite briskly, smiled affectionately, and asked her about the children. Jim brought her a chair, brought her a cushion, was assiduous—actually fetching her work-bag with her knitting.

She was much surprised. Usually it was she who was assiduous, not the other way round; and very rightly too, thought Audrey stoutly, who never for a moment had doubted that her Jim was yards above her in every way, and had done a most kind act, marrying her.

It is a useful conviction for a wife to have; it considerably encourages harmony in the home. Conderley, aware of it, for it was made evident in a thousand ways every day, found it touching and rather unaccountable, seeing how much older he was than she, and how enormously much older he was going to be, compared to her, in ten years' time. In ten years' time he would be an old dodderer of over eighty, and she would still be only in the forties—that most vigorous time of life, as he well remembered. Therefore, aware of how soon she was going to find herself married to a very old man, he did his best to be kind to the good little thing while he still had some vitality in him, and knowing that the last few days he had been cross and inclined to snap, and all, somehow, because of Fanny, he now began to perform actions symbolic of penitence, and fetched her work-bag.

"Aren't you well, Jim?" she asked after a moment, anxiously. Fetching things for her. Besides, the silence of the room when she came in. . . .

"Perfectly, dear. Why?"

"I thought—oh, I don't know, I just thought," said Audrey, bending her head over her work-bag, and relapsing into shyness.

§

On Sunday they went to church. Fanny didn't go, because of being a Jew.

"But she isn't a Jew," protested Audrey to her husband, while at the same time feeling rather relieved that the Vicar wouldn't see her.

"In religion she is," said Conderley, briefly. He didn't want to talk about Fanny. Audrey, on the other hand, wanted to talk about her all the time.

In religion Fanny certainly still was a Jew, not having bothered to change back again on divorcing Job. True, she hadn't liked being turned into a Jew just so as to be able to marry a rich man, but when she had the chance of returning to the faith of her fathers she didn't take it. What was the good of once more embracing—she believed that was the proper word —a faith that had never been particularly—she believed this was the proper word—lively? Such faith as she had was very easy-going; it was the simple faith of the outstandingly fortunate. We are all God's children, and there you are—this, if Fanny had been pressed, would have been her probable declaration.

Conderley, a strict observer of the rites of his Church, even at his most infatuated moments suspected her of being, really, a pagan, and Perry Lanks was convinced, and told her so, that she was nothing but an irresponsible hedonist.

She didn't mind what they said. She only laughed. In those days she was too busy being beautiful ever to think. Life rushed her along at breathless speed from one excitement to another, the War, and her work during it in France, being the greatest excitement of them all.

"You'd be incredibly perfect, if only you *knew* something—or at least could imagine," Perry Lanks had said one day, exasperated by constant mental frustration.

"I've got no time."

"Time, indeed! You've got all the time there is—the same time as the rest of us. But the trouble with you, Fanny, is that you don't know and aren't able to imagine *anything.*"

"Then teach me."

"I can't, because you don't even begin to guess that there's anything to know. While as for imagination——"

And he flung up his hands.

On six days, then, Fanny laboured and did all that she had to do, never giving her religious status a thought, but on the seventh she remembered it, and rested comfortably in bed. Not for her, that being gathered beneath a hostess's wing and gently shoo'd, in procession, to the family pew in a musty village church. Pleasantly she would loiter in her bedroom till luncheon; or, should there be anybody particularly attractive in the party, would meet him by arrangement made the evening before, and explore the gardens and greenhouses, in spite of knowing she would have to explore them all over again later in the day with her host—but then, as she told herself, setting off gaily on the first of these rounds, you can't have everything.

Now, however, perhaps for the first time in her life during a week-end in the country, there was no party, and from the look of things she didn't think the Conderleys ever had one. If she had married Jim—how often had he implored her to; fancy; poor old Jim—she supposed the beautiful William and Mary house would have rocked with parties, for in those days they seemed to collect about her. Wherever she went, there at once sprang up a party. How much happier for poor Jim was it to have married Audrey; how infinitely lucky he was to have got Audrey instead of herself—that nice, smooth little wife, years younger than he was, yet content to live the life liked by a man years older. And Audrey too was lucky, for marrying him she had been rescued from some clergyman. Everything about Audrey suggested, to Fanny, pews. She could see her being

devout in pews, and attentive at the feet of pulpits. Besides,
passion, Fanny was sure, was a thoroughly bad basis for
marriage. Jim, married to her, would have been a frazzle of
nerves, and intolerably jealous and suspicious.

No, she was best by herself. She was glad she hadn't married
any of them. But it was going to be lonely, it was going to be
difficult to bear the increasing loneliness. She ought really, she
supposed, to get into touch with old women, and find out what
they did with themselves at the tail-end, as George had said, of
their lives, but the thought of other old women filled her with
nausea. Besides, she had been in touch with one the week before
at Oxford, and had merely got rapped over the knuckles.

Well, anyhow, she had had a wonderful time, she told herself,
trying to be grateful, and now, she supposed, must start paying
for it. After fifty, the bills were bound to begin coming in. But
in an empty present, how difficult to be grateful for even the
fullest, most delightful past. It was like, when you were hungry,
trying to get satisfaction out of all your past good dinners; and
that Sunday at Upswich, Fanny, whose spirits usually rose on
fine mornings, was quite surprised, and almost hurt, to find
this image of eaten-and-done-with good dinners should afflict her
to the point of depression.

She would go out, and walk in the sun. She would be sensible,
and shake herself free of melancholy; or, if she couldn't shake
herself free of it, at least rejoice that being an unattached
woman she could be as melancholy as she liked in peace, without involving a husband or children in her ill humour—helpless
persons who couldn't get away, and were bound to suffer when
the wife or mother had a fit of the glooms. Yes, she would go
for a brisk walk, and plan what to say to Jim next time she got
him, as she was determined to get him, alone. Last night their
talk had been a wretched business; the talk she was going to
have before the day was over should be really natural, really
sensible, really helpful. She needed a true friend's advice so
badly. Who could give it better than one of her oldest, and
certainly for three years quite one of her dearest, friends?

Therefore, when she judged the church-goers to be well embarked on their prayers, she called for her thick shoes and
knitted cap, and set out across the crocuses to have a look at
those gardens and that park which might, for so many years
now, if she had chosen, have been hers; and walking through
them under the mild February sun, in the peculiar quiet of

English country on a Sunday morning, she soon, not yet having got out of the habit of happiness, felt better. By nature a quick rejoicer, it needed many and continuous blows to down Fanny. A prolonged succession of them had not yet been her fate—the day she went to Oxford, perhaps, having provided the nearest approach to it she had, up to then, been called on to endure; and she appeared at luncheon restored and cheerful, and very glad to find the children, whom she had not yet seen, were to lunch with them too.

These children were all quite plain, and infinitely lively. She wondered what sorts of faces they would have had if she had been their mother. That, of course, she thought, looking round at them, and at Audrey's pleased, purring expression, and at Jim's obvious pride in his boy, was the real solid foundation and promise of happiness in marriage—the children. And this was why it should be entered upon in the spirit recommended in the Prayer Book, not lightly or wantonly, but reverently, discreetly, advisedly, soberly, and in the fear of God—the very opposite of the spirit in which love affairs were embarked upon.

Evidently, she said to herself, the Conderleylets were brought up to be entirely fearless, for little Audrey, sitting opposite her, asked her father in a loud whisper whether he didn't think the beautiful lady was the beautifullest he had ever seen, and just like pantomimes; and little Joan, on her other side, invited her, with high-spirited irrelevance—at least Fanny, who had kept on her knitted cap, hoped it was irrelevance—to tell her the difference between a young maid and an old one, triumphantly explaining—

"Yes, I know that. I was brought up on it," Fanny tried to interrupt.

—triumphantly explaining, and refusing to be put out of her stride, that one was happy and careless, and the other cappy and hairless; and little Jim, catching at these suggestions, pointed his spoon at her head and cried—"Cappy!"—at which his sisters rocked with laughter, and he, encouraged, pointed his spoon again, and cried "Crocus hair!" and then laughed loudest of anybody, bouncing up and down in his high chair.

"I think, dear," Conderley mildly addressed his wife, as soon as he could be heard, "we are perhaps allowing the children to get a little out of hand."

"It's because of having been to church," explained Audrey,

embarrassed yet proud—for surely it was highly intelligent of
them, the way they were saying what the Bishop and her
mother, if they had been there, would, roughly, have been
thinking?

Fanny was delighted by her explanation. What fun if everybody came out of church in such tearing spirits. She instantly
had visions of vergers turning Catherine-wheels down the path,
headed by high-stepping curates, followed by a congregation
intoxicated by reaction. And never having had cause in her life
to be afraid of personal remarks, she took what the children
said as so many compliments, except that she rather wished
they would keep off her hair. She was sensitive about that since
her illness, and not quite sure whether Antoine had got the
colour right. He *said* it was exactly the original colour; but if
it was, it didn't seem to go quite so well with her face as it used
to. Certainly if it made little Jim think of the yellow crocuses on
the lawn, Antoine had got it seriously wrong. She would see
him about it the first thing, when she got back on Monday.

"I expect you would like to rest a little in our room," said
Audrey, after coffee had been drunk and the children had gone
off with their nurse. She still was shy, but not nearly so shy.
It wasn't really possible to be shy for long with Fanny. "I
usually"—she turned pinker—"read with the children for an
hour after lunch on Sundays."

"Does it have the same effect on them as church?" asked
Fanny hopefully. "Because if it does, please may I come and
listen?"

"They weren't very good to-day, I'm afraid," apologized
Audrey.

"I think, perhaps, dear, they need a little more training,"
said Conderley mildly.

"I do try," said Audrey; and something in the way she said
this, something simple and humble, made Fanny stoop quickly
and kiss her.

"Darling," she said.

Audrey blushed her pinkest. She liked Fanny so much, yet
felt it was somehow not quite right to like her. Also, in her
family they didn't say darling. Dear was as far as they got in
expressions of affection; and she and Jim, who certainly loved
each other as much as two people could, said dear too. Only
once had he called her dearest—the day little Jim was born;
but of course that was a special occasion. So that, though she

was pleased when Fanny said darling, she was uncomfortable as well, for ought someone who was really quite a stranger to use such a strong word?

As for Conderley, he looked on in silence, filling his pipe, and what his thoughts were he would have been hard put to it to tell. Perhaps one of them was relief that next day would be Monday, and perhaps another was that old age had much to be said for it. In a few years now he would hardly feel anything any more, or mind anything any more, or want anything any more. Very like death? Maybe, thought Conderley, pressing down the tobacco with his thumb; but what peace.

Peace, however, was still a good way off really for him, because the moment was at hand, as he well knew, when the host proposes a little walk, and takes the guest round the greenhouses. Fanny hadn't said anything to Audrey's suggestion about going up to her room and resting a little, so there was nothing for it but at least to offer her the greenhouses.

He fervently hoped she would refuse them. That ten minutes alone together after dinner the evening before had been patently distressing to them both, and she couldn't possibly wish for a longer repetition of it. If she went upstairs like a good girl, and didn't appear again till tea, three-quarters of the visit would be then safely over, and he had a plan for avoiding the ten minutes alone that night while Audrey went to kiss the children in their cots. It was a simple plan: they would all go and kiss the children in their cots.

But Fanny didn't refuse. Audrey, Conderley considered, made it impossible for her to.

"Would you like to come and have a look round the greenhouses, Fanny?" he forced himself to ask; and before she could answer, Audrey exclaimed with misplaced enthusiasm: "Oh yes, Jim—do. That'll just fill up the time till tea."

Confronted by this zeal in disposing of her, Fanny would have had to go, even if she didn't want to. But here was exactly what she did want; and presently, suitably shod and skirted, and armed with a stick—not the ebony, ivory-handled, rubber-tipped stick of her future, leaning on which she would totter into rooms at parties, but a stout one with an iron point —she started off in Conderley's company on the prescribed rounds, Audrey watching them from the window, and thinking that her Jim was beginning to stoop rather, and that Fanny's figure was really remarkable for her age. "From behind she is perfect," thought Audrey, who had herself never been, either from behind or before, anything but tubby.

"Shall we take the dogs?" inquired Conderley, pausing as they passed the stables. A dog or two are very useful, he said to himself, for filling up gaps in a conversation, or for deflecting its course should it begin to be undesirable.

Fanny said she would like the dogs, and Conderley whistled.

"Come on, Emily—come on, Spunks old boy," he called; and out they rushed—two fox-terriers, liveliest of their race.

They jumped up. "Down, down," said Conderley; but they wouldn't down.

Fanny patted their heads, and didn't flinch when they jumped up on her, too, and dirtied her coat, because she never minded things that Manby had to set right; and after an interval of admonishment and exhortation on Conderley's part, and a good deal of noise on theirs, having at last succeeded in wading through them she remarked, as they walked on and the dogs ran round and round in immense, enraptured circles, "They're just what we want."

"Who are?" said Conderley, breathless after his exertions.

"Emily and—Spunks, did you say? When we don't know what to talk about next, we can whistle and give them orders."

"But we do know what to talk about next," he said, disconcerted by her perspicacity. She was altogether most disconcerting. The evening before, during that awkward ten minutes alone in the library, who could have been more so? She oughtn't, of course, to have come. He oughtn't, of course, to have let her come. But having come, and he having let her come, seeing how difficult the situation was she should most carefully keep within the proper bounds. What the proper bounds were he didn't quite know, and anyhow couldn't, just then, consider, engaged as he was in whistling to the dogs, who had helter-skeltered off after a cat.

Conderley loved cats. He really couldn't allow those dogs— "Spunks! Emily!" he shouted breathlessly between violent whistles, hurrying his steps almost to a run—which must be very bad for him, Fanny thought. "Good dogs!" called Conderley. "Come here, good dogs! Poor little pussy—it's all right, pussy—good dogs!"

The cat ran up a tree. The dogs, baffled, and caring nothing that they were deemed good, leaped up and down at the bottom, frantically barking.

"Perhaps we had better take them back to the stables," he said, after further fruitless efforts, panting for breath."

"Perhaps we had," said Fanny. "And start fresh."

Nevertheless, he was reluctant to part from them. So long as they were there, he would at least be able to whistle; he might even pursue.

"Only, if we take them back," said Fanny, "we shan't be chaperoned."

"My dear——" began Conderley.

Really her perspicacity was disconcerting. And it was, like a child's, so outspoken and unexpected. A child; yet fifty. What a combination, he thought.

"This," he said, opening a door, "is the kitchen garden."

"Lovely," said Fanny. "Such mellow walls."

"And this," he said, leading the way to a greenhouse, "is where we cool off our primulas."

"Lovely," said Fanny. "Such a lot of them."

"I am very fond of primulas," said Conderley, gently fingering their petals. "Don't you agree they are sweet little things?"

"Yes. And very like Audrey."

"I have often thought so," he said, pleased.

"May I smoke in here?" she asked, taking out her cigarette-case. "It won't be bad for the primulas? By the way, Jim," she went on, lighting a cigarette with her lighter, "you've not wanted to know yet what I've come for."

He was glad he hadn't got to hold a match for her. His hand, lately, was so very shaky that it would have been embarrassing for them both, because she might have imagined——

"But you told me in your letter," he said. "You told me you wished to see your old friend again, and get to know his wife. I was much touched."

"There's more in it than that, though."

"Is there, Fanny?" he asked uneasily; and looked round for the dogs.

They were busily engaged in a distant corner of the kitchen garden scratching up the celery, and took no notice of him when he went out and whistled.

"In here," he said, coming back, feeling a little foolish, for she seemed to be watching him with something rather like a smile—"in here," he said, going towards a further door, "are

our arums. Audrey likes to have a good supply ready by
Easter."

"For the church," nodded Fanny, staying where she was.

"For the church," agreed Conderley. "And beyond
them——"

"I've been thinking a great deal lately," she interrupted,
leaning against the door, and not bothering about the arums
or what might be beyond them.

"Have you, Fanny?" he asked, uneasily again—why, he
didn't quite know; and no good, either, whistling to the dogs.

"Yes. Shut up at Claridge's."

"It seems a curious place either to be shut up at or to think
in. Our carnations are in there," he continued, hopefully
pointing to the third door. "Perhaps you noticed them last
night on the dinner-table."

"It did very well," said Fanny, ignoring the carnations. "I
stayed in my room, and never saw a soul—except Martha. You
remember Martha?"

"Lady Tintagel? Of course. The most charming of your
cousins."

"She and Tintagel happened to be passing through London,
and she met Manby in a passage."

"I'm glad to see Manby is still with you."

"You remember her, then. You didn't remember about
the pipe."

"About the pipe?"

"Oh—details, details," she said, waving this aside with a
movement of her cigarette.

"Have you left Charles Street?" he asked. "I saw your
letter was from Claridge's, but I thought——"

"Job is in Charles Street."

"Job?"

He stared. For a moment he really didn't know whom she
meant. Nearly a quarter of a century had passed since last she
mentioned Job.

"I've been seeing a good deal of him lately," she went on,
doing her best to sound sensible and unconcerned. "So I
thought I would clear out."

Conderley stared, his bushy white eyebrows drawn together.
They had always been bushy, and now were white as well.

"But Fanny," he said, "I don't understand."

"Neither do I," she answered, with a faint grimace. "And

I can't tell you how much I should dislike"—she caught her
breath a little—"dislike to be *conquered*. I've never yet been
conquered, you know, Jim. Imagine going down before just
one's own silly nerves! Not even with one's flag flying——"

She broke off. He stared in silence. What was this strange
talk? In his home the talk was never strange; it was all as
orderly, and comprehensible, and pleasant as these rows of
tidy, sweet primulas.

"It would be humiliating, wouldn't it," she said after a
pause, during which she was searching his face for traces of
him who was once such a close friend; for if she could find him
wouldn't he comfort? And mightn't he, perhaps, help?

"Humiliating, wouldn't it be," she said again, as he still
was silent, her voice gone small and tired, "to go down before
something that wasn't really there?"

But was Jim really there, either? she began to ask herself,
as he stood and stared and said nothing. Wasn't she telling
things the judicious keep only for their doctor to a quite strange
old man? Looks, after all, were symbols. He looked different,
because he was different. He had atrophied, petrified, gone
dim and quiet and slow, and only wanting, she decided with
impulsive unfairness, to avoid trouble. Extremely sensible of
course, and some day she too would no doubt reach that state.

But Conderley, though he might look different, and had
certainly slowed down, wasn't different. All he needed, in
these his latter years, was to be given a little more time than
before to get under way. No use pouncing a new idea on him.
It had to be insinuated, as it were, slowly into his mind.

"Do you mean Skeffington?" he asked at last.

"Yes. I do mean Skeffington," she said. "He was a
husband I had once—as perhaps you don't remember," she
finished, unable, for an instant, not to be a little bitter.

"But, my dear—you say he isn't really there."

"I know. Idiotic, isn't it. Sheer imagination on my part.
But you've no idea how troublesome it, in fact, is——" And
her eyes filled with tears of mortification, of helplessness, of
exasperation, too; and she pretended, so as to hide them, to
bend over and smell the primulas.

He was much concerned. He didn't understand what on
earth she was talking about, but he did see that her eyes were
filled with tears, and he took her hand. "I'm afraid you're in
trouble, Fanny," he said, very kindly.

"Worried," she answered, looking round at him over her shoulder, and trying to smile the brimming tears away.

He drew her hand through his arm, and patted it.

"If you're in trouble——" he began.

Then, suddenly determined, he said: "Come along—come along for a walk, and tell me all about it."

And leading her out of the greenhouse he forgot to whistle for the dogs, forgot even to shut the door on his precious primulas, and started off with her across the park and through the fields, towards those distant woods behind which the sun would presently be setting.

§

An hour later they were walking slowly back, hand in hand. There was comfort in being hand in hand; besides, they were both tired, having gone further, in the absorption of their talk, than they realized. Once, they rested on a fallen tree-trunk beside the path, but not for long, because it was so hard. Everything that Fanny sat on these days seemed hard, so thin had she become; while as for Conderley, he found it difficult enough to let himself down so low, and almost impossible to get up again.

"We two poor old things," smiled Fanny, as he shakily, having somehow struggled on to his own, helped her to her feet; for by this time she had told him all about her illness, and Job, and her visit to Byles, and her fears for the future, and was as natural as it is possible to be with somebody whom one still, when one looks at him, doesn't seem to know very well. But this could be circumvented by not looking at him; she could be altogether natural when she simply listened to his kind voice. And he felt almost exactly the same about her, the difference being that when she looked at him she was sorry, and when he looked at her he was shocked.

"Poor Fanny," he thought, unable, whenever his eyes rested on this wraith-like parody of the past, to prevent a slight shrinking away, "she is like a painted ghost."

"Poor darling Jim," she thought, "so this is what he was like underneath the whole time, only now it has worked its way through. Dreadful, the exposures of time."

Nevertheless, when he helped her up so shakily off the tree-trunk, and she said, We two poor old things, he protested that it was ridiculous to talk like that about herself, and assured her she had years and years before her, of——

"Usefulness," provided Fanny, as he seemed to be searching for a word.

"Well, why not?" he said, taking her hand again as they continued on their way. "One has got to do something. One can't go on always being——"

"Ornamental," provided Fanny again.

"That isn't what I was going to say."

"Isn't it, darling?"

She was calling him darling now, just as she used to, so natural had she become, and he wondered whether Audrey——

"Never mind. Go on. If one can't be—whatever it is you weren't going to say, one can at least be useful. Will you tell me exactly how, if you were me, you would set about it? Being useful, I mean. At the eleventh hour of my life managing to prevent its being a failure. Because that's really what I came here to find out from you."

He hesitated. "Well, for instance," he said after a moment, diffidently, "this business about poor Skeffington."

"Why 'poor'?"

"I expect by now it might fairly describe him. He can't be anything but lonely at his age, and having lost you."

"But he lost me so long ago. And for all we know he has married again. Besides, don't forget I kept on forgiving him. Not perhaps unto seventy times seven——" here part of the wreckage of a clergyman called Hyslup, who for a short time was an intimate friend (chronologically he came somewhere between Lanks and Dwight, though she never could remember exactly where, and represented her sole excursion into the preserves of clerics), floated to the surface of her mind—"because he hadn't worked through as many as seventy-seven typists then, but I forgave him at least six of them. And I hope you're not going to suggest——"

"I'm not going to suggest anything about Skeffington. My concern is only for you. It's all wrong that you should be seeing him in this way."

"It's dreadfully wrong, and most upsetting."

"It shows your nerves are in a very bad state."

"Yes, Jim. Just what I've been suspecting myself."

"And perhaps a complete change of scene——"

"Well, I did go to Claridge's."

"Fanny, you must be serious."

"Good heavens, do you suppose I'm not?"

"Then will you listen while I tell you what I really think?"

"Yes, if it isn't another pretty speech, winding up with a bow."

"I'm sorry if that hurt you. It was because I was nervous."

"Oh, darling Jim, I didn't mind really. And anyhow you're not nervous now. We're cosy now, aren't we? Tell me what you were going to say."

Cosy. Poor Fanny's favourite word. He had hardly ever heard anyone else use it. Even in the heyday of her beauty she would talk wistfully of cosiness, she seemed to long to be just cosy, to curl up, to be taken care of, not to have to respond to any violence of love. If ever a woman was adrift, he was afraid poor Fanny was. And she had always been adrift, he now saw, refusing to have anything to do with the innumerable anchors offered her, including—and with what entreaties!—his own. But there came a moment when an anchor was essential to a woman's comfort; he wouldn't say happiness, because he wasn't sure happiness existed except for children, but comfort. So long as she was young, she might toss about gaily enough on the crest of her popularity. By the time she was forty, she should have a husband and children. By the time she was fifty, she should have had them twenty years.

"Well, Jim?" said Fanny. "What were you going to say?"

"That you should go off and travel for six months."

"What? Be put to flight by Job? Never."

"It seems to me he has put you to flight already. Ousted you from your home."

"Claridge's isn't flight. I can go back at any minute."

"Then if you dislike that idea, I'm rather inclined to agree with——"

"Not with Byles? Don't tell me you agree with Byles?" she exclaimed, standing still and facing him.

"If Skeffington is behaving like a ghost, he should be laid," Conderley said with decision.

"Laid?" she repeated. "But that's what Byles said."

"Well, he wasn't far out, I think, when he suggested you should invite him to dinner," said Conderley, his voice chilling because she was facing him, and he had to look at her. Really she shouldn't, he thought; really she should *not* paint so much.

"But, Jim——" she protested. And staring at him, and at his white eyebrows, and changed sunken face, she asked herself what right this stranger had to give her advice; any advice; and especially fantastically silly advice. Byles. George. Jim. The pack of them being idiotic about that wretched Job.

"Things like that are simply not done," she said.

"My dear, after a certain age everything is done," he answered.

Whereupon she was suddenly humble, and said, "Yes, I forgot. I keep on forgetting how old I am"—and putting her arm through his as they walked on, clinging to him, indeed, as to a support in a world grown suddenly difficult and strange, she thought how very disturbing it was if being older, besides its many other drawbacks, included freedom to do what one used to be protected from by the proprieties. She could, then, if she liked, go off alone now with anybody who wanted her to, to Paris or the other places one went off to, and nobody would say a word. Why, what a cold, naked world, with no fences left. How *miserable* everything was.

Conderley, who couldn't bear Fanny, of all people, to be humble, held her arm very close to him the rest of the way home—no, not the rest of the way, but most of the way, for he gently disengaged himself when they arrived within sight of the house.

"Audrey?" inquired Fanny as he loosed her, looking at him with a smile.

"My dear, of course," he said; for he was a man of the strictest honour, besides having no mind to drop the solid little substance of Audrey for this thin shadow.

§

But wives always know. Nothing escapes their concentrated vigilance. He had hardly got as far into the hall as the tea-table before Audrey, looking at him with the attentive eyes of devotion, thought he seemed different, and when Fanny, who had gone upstairs to change her muddy shoes, came down and joined them, she was sure he was. Quite different. Much more at home with Fanny. As if—the phrase slipped into her mind—they had had it out.

But what had they had out? What could there possibly be

for them to have out? And she began thinking of last night
again, and the dead silence in the library when she came in,
and of the unusual attentiveness to her comfort.

A distant cousin, who had married a business man in
Liverpool and was of the opinion that only those know life
who live in ports, once warned her to be on her guard if ever
Jim should become particularly attentive. She remembered
this now. She hadn't thought of it since, no such occasion
having arisen. And if, added the cousin, he were to take to
giving her presents, she should keep her eyes well open; and
if these presents were to become obviously valuable, such as,
say, pearl necklaces, she shouldn't lose a minute in inferring
the worst.

"The gift of jewels *always* means there's love-making going
on somewhere," said the cousin, "and never is it legitimate.
Sometimes a husband whose wife has just presented him with
a long-wanted heir will give her gems, and these, perhaps,
needn't be open to suspicion, but short of that, on receiving
such a present she should immediately secure the services of a
detective."

Well, Jim had never given her pearls or other gems, so that
was all right. His presents, made only at Christmas and on
birthdays, were either copies of the poets—nicely bound, but
not in Russia-leather, which might, she supposed, have been
suspicious, or fountain-pens—not gold ones, which again might
have been suspicious, but decent, plain black. Once he gave
her a trowel. That was the low-water mark of his presents,
and, if her cousin was right, the high-water mark of his single-
minded devotion. He must have been completely faithful, in
every nook and cranny of his slightest thought, to give her
a trowel; and she had received it with an enthusiasm which
surprised him.

No; the presents didn't make her uneasy, she said to herself
pouring out tea, but his sudden particular attentiveness
perhaps might, if she thought about it much. So unlike him
to fetch her work-bag, and bring her a cushion. A pity mother
lived so far away. It would be nice to be able to talk to her,
and ask her—without mentioning Jim, of course, who was
much too sacred to be discussed—whether father had ever been
suddenly all over her like that, and, if he had been, whether
it meant his thoughts were straying where they shouldn't.

And it was just as she was wishing that mother could come

over oftener, and that Fanny had stayed in her own home, and that Jim had never known anybody except herself, and just as she was in the act of pouring cups of tea for the pair—it seemed a mockery to have to—that she heard Fanny say, refusing muffins Jim was offering her: "No, darling, thank you."

Darling? Audrey nearly dropped the teapot. Was this Lady Frances, of whom till a week ago she had never heard, actually calling her Jim, her very own, only Jim, darling? What terms were they on, then? What terms used they to be on?

Immensely and painfully startled, she looked from her to him and met his eye, and his eye too, she thought, seemed startled. Anyhow he at once turned away, and pretended to be busy with his bread and butter—which was quite unlike him, and deepened her uneasiness. He never ate bread and butter. Now he was almost hiding his face in it.

Fanny, however, who from long practice had acquired a sort of sixth sense when it came to the feelings of wives, picked up both these looks, thought what an old goose Jim was to let himself appear embarrassed, and turning to Audrey remarked that everybody in her day—she emphasized the distance in time between herself and Audrey—used to call each other darling. "Just like," she said, "the way French people, you know, when they talk, keep on saying Monsieur and Madame."

"Then I wish you would call him Monsieur," said Audrey, unexpectedly.

Fanny was confounded. So was Conderley. This sudden valiance, like the desperate valiance of a partridge protecting its young, confounded them both And Conderley's mind at once began to dwell on the advantages to a husband if his wife had been brought up to conceal, should she have one, her primitive side; and it dwelt still more earnestly on these advantages when, Fanny having begun saying appeasingly—no wife who has been properly brought up, thought Conderley, should need in public to be appeased—"But, *darling*——" was immediately cut short by Audrey putting the teapot down on the tray again quite noisily, and saying with the devastating downrightness of the shy once they are thoroughly roused, "I suppose you mean Madame?"

He was seriously put out. He wasn't prepared for primitiveness. Not in the hall. If there had to be primitiveness, and he saw no reason at all why there should ever be any, there were less conspicuous places in the house than the hall. His and Audrey's bedroom, for instance. Behind closed doors. After everybody had retired for the night. But to display it at the tea-table, and to a guest, and that guest Fanny, awoke in Conderley a curious desire to seek out her parents at once, and discuss with them their educational methods.

Angry with Fanny for being so foolish as to call him darling—he hadn't called her darling once, having taken the greatest care not to drop back into old habits—angry with Audrey for being such a rough little diamond, such a hedgehog, such a porcupine, such an everything that was ill-mannered and with spikes, he was also aggrieved on his own behalf, who had, since Fanny's arrival, been so specially glad whenever Audrey was in the room. Nothing could be more blameless, more creditable, than both his conduct and his feelings; and if he did, on their walk, take Fanny's hand and draw it through his arm out of pure pity and old friendship, hadn't he dropped it at once, on getting within eye-shot of the house?

"My dear Audrey——" he began; but was at a loss how to go on. All he could think of to say, and did finally say was, "Really."

"Well, Jim, it's quite natural," cried Audrey, continuing primitive, and defending herself with spirit, "I'm sure it's quite natural. Nobody likes somebody to call her husband darling, and then her husband look—look——" she was going to say guilty, but just managed not to. "I'm sorry if I seem rude," she finished up with a defiance that contradicted her words, "but I'm sure it's quite natural, and I know mother would think so too." And feverishly and noisily she arranged the cups and saucers on the tea-tray—to keep herself in countenance? To stop herself from crying? Fanny wondered.

Dreadful if she were to cry, poor little thing. Fanny, who was already confounded, the rarest state for her to be in, felt she would be confounded beyond hope of recovery if Audrey were to begin to cry. "Listen, children," she said, "there are two things people can do when they start quarrelling——"

"I'm not quarrelling," protested Audrey indignantly, positively banging the cups about.

"Bickering, then."

"I'm not. It's not true." And she knocked over, but this was by accident, the milk-jug.

"Really, Audrey," said Conderley, helplessly staring at the mess.

"Doing, then, whatever it is we're doing," said Fanny. "First, the bone of contention—that's me—can go home at once, or secondly it can stay out its appointed time, and undertake meanwhile to call Jim Monsieur."

"Now you're mocking me," cried Audrey, violently mopping up the milk with her handkerchief.

"I swear I'm not," said Fanny.

And Conderley, who had again absorbed himself in bread and butter, thought, "This is really a great pity——" which was the courtly man's equivalent for what, in a coarser mouth, would have been Damn the women.

§

But he was saved, the three of them were saved, or thought they were, though they weren't really, by the sudden irruption into the hall, first of cheerful voices merrily approaching, and then of the cheerful bodies from which the voices issued.

Four of them. The Cookhams. Audrey's relations. Father, mother, and two unmarried daughters. Come really by a miracle, living as they did a hundred miles away; and their car being old and constantly on the verge of a breakdown, and petrol being dear, they never dropped in just for an hour or two, but at stated intervals, about three times a year, brought their suit-cases and stayed a week.

Their winter week had been at Christmas, and they were not due again till at least Easter. Wonderful, then, that they should appear, as though sent from heaven, when Audrey most wanted them. She flew into her mother's arms, she hugged her almost hysterically, while the family explained, in one joyous chorus, that the day being so delicious they hadn't been able to resist going for a picnic, and the picnic being in the Upswich direction they thought they would for once be reckless, and not care about a few more gallons of petrol, but come on and take Jim and Audrey by surprise, and go back by moonlight, and make a regular day of it.

A united, affectionate family, eagerly appreciative of each other and of small joys like a fine day and a picnic; and they had so many exclamations to make, and so many to listen to

from Audrey, that it was several minutes before they became
aware of Fanny.

When, having finished hugging and being hugged by Audrey,
who was almost too demonstrative, her mother thought, and
wondered whether the dear child could be quite well, they
turned to greet their excellent son and brother-in-law and
saw the guest, they were surprised. Their immediate sub-
conscious reaction as they beheld her—on their top layers they
were as cordial as ever—was to give her the benefit of the
doubt; and Mrs. Cookham, the kindest-hearted, least suspicious
of women, added without knowing she was adding it, "Poor
thing," and the girls wondered what sort of extraordinary
person Audrey had got hold of, and only the father went so
far as to think, rather definitely, Come, come.

"Oh," said Audrey, who for a blissful moment had forgotten
Fanny, and was reminded of her by seeing where their eyes
had concentrated, "oh, yes—this is Jim's friend. Staying with
him for the week-end."

Could introduction be clumsier, be more unfortunate?
Conderley sincerely hoped it wasn't done on purpose. He held
it for really impossible that Audrey, besides suddenly becoming
primitive, should also suddenly become malicious. No, she was
merely flustered; though of course even to be flustered seemed
to him, a man of Courts, yet another great pity.

He at once came forward, and took the introductions in hand
himself. Each Cookham was properly presented to Fanny,
their names, and her name, being pronounced with distinctness,
and such explanatory comment added as my mother-in-law,
my father-in-law, my sisters-in-law, as seemed useful, though
no elucidation was offered after Fanny's name; and then the
hall, which for an instant had gone quiet, recovered its breath,
and began to resound once more with cheerful chirpings.

It was as if a company of lively sparrows had got loose
in it. The Cookhams, out for a spree, weren't going to let it
be interfered with by the unexpected apparition of Fanny, and
got over her almost at once. They talked, they laughed, they
ate cakes and drank cups of tea without stopping. Healthy,
and hungry after only sandwiches since breakfast, the girls
soon cleared up everything there was to eat, and even Fanny,
sitting down beside Audrey's mother—she thought it wise, under
the circumstances, at once to make friends with Audrey's
mother—found herself infected by the prevailing high spirits

and started having tea all over again herself, while Audrey, in this general atmosphere of almost Christmas goodwill, couldn't help cheering up a little, and thinking she had perhaps been silly. Or hadn't she?

Anyhow, she was quite sure that it was heavenly to have mother again so unexpectedly; and how dear she looked, thought Audrey fondly, with her weather-beaten, wrinkled face, and wisp of grey hair coming untidily out from under her old picnic hat, next to the glass-smooth, red-and-white Fanny, each of whose crocus hairs—clever of little Jim—was so perfectly curled and placed exactly where it ought to be that it made one's back ache in sympathy with the maid, who must have stood on her poor feet at least an hour getting them to go like that.

The girls chattered and ate; Audrey busily plied them with her good things; her mother and Fanny were friends from the first; and only Major Cookham, a retired officer, who in his youth had been quartered at Hounslow, well within reach of London gossip, seemed to be turning things over in his mind.

Conderley, observing this, resented it. By now, smarting as he was from Fanny's lapse and from Audrey's misbehaviour, he resented everything, but especially thoughtfulness in a person who was looking at Fanny. No Cookham was naturally thoughtful; therefore when the head of the family, usually as chatty a man as you will meet anywhere, and as uninquiringly ready to accept whoever came his way as the rest of them, having looked at Fanny became thoughtful, Conderley didn't like it.

"Tea, father?" he said abruptly, to distract his parent's attention.

It had amused him, when he married Audrey, to be able to call a man younger than himself father, and Major Cookham had been equally amused to be able to call a man older than himself son, and since both were people of regular habits, used to a life of punctual repetitions, they didn't easily tire of a joke once they had got accustomed to it, and had gone on smiling at this one ever since. Conderley, however, didn't smile now. He said, "Tea, father?" as abruptly as a challenge, and without the smallest sign of the customary appreciation that here was a joke.

"If you please," said Major Cookham; at once adding,

before his son-in-law could turn away to fetch it, "I am much interested, Jim, in meeting your friend."

"Audrey's friend, too," said Conderley, irritably.

"Oh, of course, my dear boy. Naturally. Tell me——"

But Conderley had gone after the tea.

Directly he came back Major Cookham began again.

"Tell me, Jim," he said, "usedn't she to be a great——"

"Yes," said Conderley. "Cake, father?"

"Ah, I thought it was the same lady," said his father-in-law. "I remember, as a young chap at Hounslow—tell me, wasn't she——? Wasn't there some——?"

"No," said Conderley, his bushy eyebrows drawn ominously together, "there wasn't. And in any case *she* wasn't. *He* was."

"Ah—conundrums, conundrums," said Major Cookham, taking a piece of cake. "But I think I understand. And it makes a difference, certainly."

"It makes all the difference."

"Indeed, yes. Yet you know, in Queen Victoria's time——"

"Confound Queen Victoria's time," said Conderley, turning on his heel.

Major Cookham was amazed. He paused in the stirring of his tea to stare after him incredulously. That his son-in-law, so long connected with the Court, should confound anything royal, even if it was only time, quite took his breath away. Nor had he ever heard him use the word confound before. He could only watch him departing, and, more thoughtful than ever, slowly stir his tea.

Presently, however, Conderley came back. He had to come back, because there was nowhere else for him to go. Impossible for him to join the group of Audrey and her sisters, because he was too angry with Audrey, and he wouldn't join Fanny and his mother-in-law because it was Fanny who had brought all the trouble on him, with her thoughtlessly familiar ways. So he went back to his father-in-law, and sat down beside him on the sofa.

He, having assimilated the outburst about Queen Victoria's time by the simple method of ascribing it to something Audrey had given the poor chap for lunch, was free now to go on talking about Fanny, which he at once did. "And Audrey likes her," he said, still thoughtfully, while he stirred his tea.

The implication of this remark deeply annoyed Conderley.

"My mother-in-law appears to like her too," he pointed out with unnecessary emphasis, looking at the two by the window, who were plainly much interested in whatever it was they were talking about.

Major Cookham looked, and agreed. The ladies might even be described as cheek by jowl. And what cheeks he thought, and what jowls. Never were there greater contrasts.

"They set each other off," he observed, still slowly stirring his tea; upon which Conderley, who wasn't very quick at suspecting people, glanced at him rather in detail.

Then there was a movement by the window, and Mrs. Cookham turned her head, smiled, got up, and came across to them.

"Ted, go and talk to Lady Frances," she said. "I want to see something of my son-in-law——" for she was very fond of Conderley, and he, usually, was very fond of her. Only not at that moment. At that moment he wasn't fond of any-body. And when her husband had gone, and with a little bow, as if asking for permission, had sat down beside Fanny, and Mrs. Cookham, putting her hand affectionately on Conderley's said, "Well, Jim?" he answered, "Well, mother?" as stiff as a ramrod, and with no slightest movement of response to her caress.

"I like your Fanny," said Mrs. Cookham, settling herself next to him on the sofa.

"She isn't my Fanny any more than she is Audrey's," said Conderley, irritably.

"Then I like both your Fannies—only that doesn't sound as if it were grammar. She has been telling me all about everything."

"Indeed."

"She seems to have had a sad life."

"Indeed."

"Didn't you know?" Mrs. Cookham asked, in some surprise.

"How should I?"

"But she's your friend—oh yes, Audrey's friend too, of course. Don't be so bristly, Jim. Are you a little cross to-day, dear?" And she gave his hand a small stroke, but still find-ing no response put her own back in her lap, where it belonged; for she was a woman who cheerfully adapted herself to the moods of men.

"Not that she complained," she went on, after a silence,

during which she was wondering what Audrey could have been giving the dear man for lunch, ascribing, as the charitable Cookhams invariably ascribed any behaviour that infringed the laws of sweetness and light, to something wrong with the behaver's stomach. "She is very gallant, I think. But never to have had a home life, or children, and to have lost her husband so young——"

"Poor *thing*," said Conderley, himself astonished that he should say it so acidly. But hadn't he had enough to try him this week-end? Hadn't he? And really the continual talk of Fanny, first by Audrey, then by his father-in-law, and now by his mother-in-law—was there no other subject in the world, then?

Mrs. Cookham looked at him, again surprised. "Don't you like her?" she asked.

"Like her?" repeated Conderley, his annoyance arrested by the strangeness of such a question. Vivid pictures of the past floated before his eyes, and he wondered what his mother-in-law, if she could see them too, would make of her own question. But of course she would find it impossible to believe they were real.

"Would she be here if I didn't?" he answered; whereupon she said, with cheerful mischievousness, "Oh, but Audrey might have invited her. You said she was her friend too, you know——" and he could only reflect that both his parents-in-laws were showing themselves, that day, in very tiresome lights.

He was silent. Therefore she too said nothing, adapting herself as usual, and together they watched the group at the tea-table, and the two in the window. Major Cookham seemed to be half alarmed and half happy. He was so close to Fanny that her make-up couldn't but be alarming to him, and he was no doubt being happy, thought Conderley, continuing acid, against his better judgment. Anyhow, he had lost every shred of thoughtfulness, and from his chattiness it was evident he was being encouraged to talk about himself. Fanny was good at that, thought Conderley, remembering many things. In her hands a man became a trumpet, his own trumpet, through which he blew away to his heart's content, while she, with the most charming attentiveness, listened, applauded, exclaimed, sympathized, and drew him out.

At that distance, the hall being big and the lamps now lit,

from where Conderley sat details of Fanny's decay weren't noticeable, but only the lovely line of her little head and profile, thrown into relief by the dark curtains. Also, she had on a high-necked jumper that came up to her ears and hid the doubtful part of her throat, so that nothing was visible at that distance, and in that light, except lines of beauty. Against the background of her distinction, how unattractive the three at the tea-table looked, and how ordinary. Worse than ordinary—common, he thought; for no man can stop his thoughts. The sisters were certainly common, and so—why shouldn't he be honest?—was Audrey, in spite of many good and endearing qualities. She was good, she was kind, she was straight, she was devoted, she was healthy, she was the mother of his children, but she was common. What could be more common than her outburst half an hour ago? And how would it have ended if it hadn't been cut short by the arrival of her relations? Perhaps seeing from what a painful scene they had probably saved him, it would be decent to be a little less ill-humoured with his in-laws; and turning to Mrs. Cookham with the intention of trying to make amends, he was just going to say something amiable when she startled him by suddenly exclaiming, "I really don't understand how men can bring themselves to do such dreadful things."

He stared. "What things?" he asked, not without uneasiness. If she had said *think* such dreadful things, he would have been thoroughly uneasy, for certainly that which he had just been thinking was dreadful. It might be true, but there are many true thoughts which a decent husband should most sternly suppress, and he knew that this was one of them. Ashamed, he put it all on to Fanny. Never, until she came on the scene, had his thoughts of Audrey been anything but appreciative and affectionate. Fanny oughtn't to have come. He oughtn't to have let her come.

"Why, go off with another woman," said Mrs. Cookham.

Well, he hadn't done that, he thought, relieved; he hadn't gone off with another woman, the expression implying a wife at home. In fact, he hadn't gone off at all, either with another woman or just a woman. The only woman he had ever wanted to go off with had been Fanny, and she wouldn't go.

"So sad, too, when one remembers all the vows they make at their marriage service," continued Mrs. Cookham.

Well, he had kept all his vows, every one of them; not once

had he had the faintest wish to break them. His conscience there was pellucid, so that he was able to say amiably, "Of what are you thinking, mother?"

"Why, of that poor thing's husband—Lady Frances's. She didn't tell me what he had done, she just said when I asked her where he was, that she had lost him. A quarter of a century ago, she said. Imagine it—all that time for the poor thing to be alone. So pretty too, she must have been, and still would be if she would wash her face. Look at her now—if one is far enough away it is extraordinary how pretty she seems. And when I said that as a young widow she ought to have remarried, she said she hadn't been a widow. So then of course I guessed, and would have liked to comfort her, but it's difficult for a happily married woman to comfort an unhappily married one without sounding smug."

"Probably by now she has got over it," suggested Conderley. "After all, there's been a good deal of time." And he meditated on what Fanny had done with all that time, and the crowded excitements and radiance of it, and how impossible it would be for his simple mother-in-law, who had always been plain, and always been poor, and never moved farther from her remote country home than the nearest Cathedral city, to imagine it.

"Oh, I know, I know. And she didn't in the very least ask for sympathy. It's only when I think of what I would feel myself, if Ted were ever to——"

She broke off. Conderley, unable as a son-in-law to go into that, said nothing.

"But I did tell her," she went on presently, "that I thought forgiveness a good thing, especially after such a long while. I was actually courageous enough to suggest her taking him back. Smug again, you see, but then it's so easy to preach forgiveness to somebody else. And I wonder, I wonder, if I'd be able to take Ted back, supposing he——"

She broke off again; and again, on grounds of seemliness, Conderley wasn't able to go into it.

"I've been giving her much the same advice myself," he said, after a moment.

"Did you dear? Do you think she will act on it?"

"No."

"I don't either. The bare idea seemed to upset her so much, poor thing, that I thought I had better run away, and let Ted take his turn. It was very impertinent of me, of course, to suggest it, but we somehow at once seemed to become so extremely intimate——''

"I can well believe it. Fanny is like that. Intimate friends in the first five minutes," said Conderley, remembering many things.

"It's a delightful quality," approved Mrs. Cookham, the more warmly that he seemed to be criticizing it. "So time-saving."

"No doubt. But it cuts both ways. The start may be wonderful, but the next thing is you find yourself on the doorstep."

He sounded suddenly resentful. She looked at him a little curiously.

"And the door," he went on, after a pause during which he was remembering some more things, "shut."

Strange, Jim was to-day, thought Mrs. Cookham. With the best will in the world to regard him as perfect, she couldn't help noticing it. Then, too, there were Audrey's cheeks, such a hot, burning red, and her excessive joy, now that her mother came to think of it, when her relations unexpectedly came in. She had flung herself into her mother's arms almost as if she were running for safety. Not quite normal, such behaviour. Of course, if the child were going to have a baby—everything could always be accounted for by a baby; but short of that she was decidedly, to-day, unusual. And here was Jim being most unusual too. And he, anyhow, couldn't be going to have a baby.

"Shut," he said again, as though he had forgotten her and were talking to himself, lifting, at the same time, his hand, and letting it drop heavily on his knee again.

She could only look at him. She hadn't an idea what to do with a remark like that. It certainly sounded as if he had a grievance, and she was perfectly ready to sympathize with the dear man if she knew what about, but she didn't know what about.

Nonplussed, she took refuge in cheerful encouragement. "Oh no, dear," she said comfortingly, giving his hand a series of motherly little pats. "Oh no, no, dear. I really can't have you looking at it like that."

§

They stayed to dinner. Conderley pressed them to stay with almost as much warmth as Audrey. Here was a way, he felt, of passing the evening without further incidents, and Audrey looked forward to getting her mother for a few moments alone and finding out, without mentioning Jim, whether she had ever heard another woman calling father darling, and if so what she had done about it.

People who come to tea and stay to dinner seem, towards half-past six, to have been in the house a long while, and it was about then that Fanny began to feel her age. Major Cookham was a very nice man, and a very kind man, and a very good man, she was sure, but by half-past six she was sorry he was going to stay any longer. Dinner wasn't till half-past eight, and nobody was to dress because of course the Cookhams couldn't, so there they were, and Fanny's smiles, as Major Cookham went on telling her about himself, which had at first been spontaneous, at last became fixed. On the other hand, her attention became less fixed, so that she went on smiling even when he got, in his life, to Vimy Ridge. "What *fun*," she said, smiling as resolutely as ever; then, suddenly realizing what he was talking about, tried to cough it off.

Fortunately he was so much absorbed in autobiography that he didn't notice. Coughs were wasted on Major Cookham, she decided after a minute, putting away her handkerchief. So were fidgetings; so were looking round at the others; so were taking the words out of his mouth to help him along quicker— all of which she presently practised. No one came to her rescue. She had to drink Major Cookham single-handed to his dregs, she said to herself desperately, for Audrey went off with her mother and didn't come back, and the sisters, settling down next to Jim on his sofa on either side of him, each with an arm warm-heartedly through one of his, took a fresh lease of talk and laughter, telling him, with cheerful confidence in his interest, everything they had been doing since they saw him last.

Cheerful confidence. That, evidently, thought Fanny, looking from them to their autobiographical parent, was the Cookham keynote. With what cheerful confidence in her interest was not her companion spreading out his whole life before her; with what cheerful confidence, again, had not his wife counselled her to forgive Job, and take him back. Imagine it—just because you were confident yourself, giving advice like that. Overwhelming, such an attitude was, to anybody who felt as old and tired as she did. After an hour of unadulterated Major Cookham her eyelids were drooping, not only with fatigue but with feeling more like fifty than she had ever yet felt. Never had she felt so exactly like fifty, and she knew she must, by now, be looking perfectly ghastly, every line and hollow accentuated by weariness, and this knowledge made her feel even more deeply pessimistic.. Nothing, nothing at that moment inspired the exhausted Fanny with confidence, still less with cheerful confidence. Life was a game in which everybody was ultimately a loser, she told herself. You might win and win and win for a time, as she had won and won and won, and then you lost and lost and lost, in exact proportion, probably, to what you had won. Up you went; down you went; but once down you didn't go up again—you stayed down, and were done for.

Thus gloomy were her thoughts while Major Cookham continued to narrate, and it didn't enter his head that she mightn't be enjoying herself as much as he was. She had observed this in men before, this simple faith in the equal happiness of their listener, and had thought there was something rather sweet about it, something appealing to the maternal instincts, as there is about all artlessness. But Major Cookham's artlessness had gone on too long. The reactions of Fanny's maternal instincts were limited, and their limit was reached during his account of his sufferings the night Audrey was born, and how, positively, he suffered even more the day she married.

"Oh, come," said Fanny, still trying to smile, in spite of an almost overwhelming desire to lay her head on the window-ledge and go to sleep. What was this that Jim was letting her in for, at the end of a trying and chequered day? How could he leave her alone with his father-in-law so endlessly, when he must know what he was like?

"I give you my word of honour, Lady Frances, it's true. I knew well into what good hands I was giving her, but a father's feelings go very deep, very deep—perhaps even deeper than a mother's, when he sees the first of his fledgelings preparing to abandon the nest."

Here, however, she became aware that she had reached the

end of her tether. Quite suddenly she knew she could bear no more. She declined even to try to bear more. Why should she? And she got up, held out her hand to Major Cookham, who, surprised, struggled to his feet, and said good-bye to him with the sweetness she had long been famous for, explaining she was motoring up to London that evening, and must go and get ready.

It had come upon her in a flash, the way of escape. She knew perfectly well what Audrey and her mother were talking about, and felt quite unable to cope, during a whole long dinner and evening, with a suspicious mother-in-law as well as an incensed wife. Also, Major Cookham would certainly be put next to her, and he indeed was the last straw. Jim must know the sort of talker he was. Was he punishing her for calling him darling in front of Audrey? If that were so, then he certainly wasn't the Jim she had known, and the sooner she left his house the better. Family circles weren't for her. Let her get back to London, and deal with her troubles as best she could alone. Besides, when the host is annoyed, and the hostess upset, and the hostess's mother suspicious, and the hostess's father an autobiographer, it is time for a guest to go. She would use her last bit of strength carrying off the necessary fibs with a proper air of innocence. She was sure she could manage it, practised as she was in social duplicities. And having said good-bye to Major Cookham, and given him the last smile he would ever get, she crossed the hall to Conderley.

He, getting up as she approached, was glad to disentangle himself from his warm-hearted sisters-in-law, but was surprised that she should suddenly leave his father-in-law by himself. He was still more surprised, indeed astonished, when she said, with every appearance of being in a hurry, "Jim, I *must* go and see if Manby is ready."

"Ready?" he repeated. "What for? We're not going to dress, you know."

"But my dear—have you forgotten I've got to get up to London? And isn't it almost time for me to start? You did tell my chauffeur, didn't you?"

Conderley was completely taken aback. His father-in-law, who was evidently taken aback too by finding himself suddenly deserted, had sauntered into the middle of the room and was turning over books and papers on the tables, obviously without any real interest, and looking almost cross. No man likes to be cut short in his flow of narrative by the abrupt departure of the audience, especially not if he connects the departure with the narrative. Major Cookham didn't exactly do that, having too great a share of the cheerful family confidence, yet he couldn't help remembering that when Audrey introduced him to Lady Frances she said she was staying over the week-end. The week-end wasn't over. It wouldn't be over till to-morrow after breakfast, and he hadn't nearly finished all he had to say. So that he felt baulked and thwarted, he to whom an entirely new listener was a godsend in his quiet retired life with only the Rector to talk to, and he turned over the books and papers on the tables as near to sulkiness as a Cookham ever got.

He was the first one to be upset.

Then came Conderley, who couldn't make it out at all, being positive the arrangement had been from Saturday to Monday. On the other hand, here was Fanny, wide-eyed with surprise that he should have thought so.

"But Jim—surely I told you I had to get back, because I've promised to dine with the Tintagels to-night? I shall be dreadfully late, I'm afraid, as it is," she said.

It seemed rude to disbelieve her, though disbelieve her he did, and the situation rather reminded him in miniature, very much in miniature, of the one twenty years ago, when she so delicately, and also so deftly, ushered him out on to the doorstep.

He was the second person to be upset.

Then came Audrey, who, after a heart-to-heart talk with Mrs. Cookham, was sure she had been made a cat's-paw of by both Jim and Fanny, and whose life, she told her mother, was ruined. But if she was indignant that Fanny should be in the house, she was even more indignant when Conderley came up and told her she was going out of it. Flatly she refused to believe there had been any such Saturday-to-Sunday-evening arrangement. The invitation had been given and accepted for the week-end—unless, of course, Jim, who wrote the letter and didn't show it to her, had made a mistake.

She was the third person to be upset.

"My dear child, of course I must have made a muddle, or perhaps I hadn't read Fanny's answer very attentively," said Conderley, irritably.

"You didn't show me that letter either," cried Audrey. "He

hasn't shown me *any* of the letters," she explained, violently turning to her mother.

"Hush, dear—hush, now," soothed Mrs. Cookham, who would have been the fourth person to be upset if she had had a less sweet nature.

"And now, please," Conderley went on, exasperated but dignified, "will you kindly behave yourself, and go to Fanny? She is very much distressed there should have been this misunderstanding——"

"Oh, I like that!" cried Audrey.

"Hush, dear—hush, now," soothed her mother, taking her hand.

"She says if it weren't for her dinner engagement, she certainly wouldn't leave us——"

"Oh, go and tell that to the marines!" cried Audrey.

"Hush, dear—hush, now," soothed her mother, putting her arm round her.

"I repeat, it is entirely my fault," said Conderley. "I cannot do more. And I really must ask you, Audrey, to remember you're supposed to be a lady."

These were harsh words to fall from those kind lips. Audrey had never heard any like them before. They sobered her. Being a lady, she had sometimes suspected, was rather her weak point. To be asked to remember she was supposed to be one was just the same as if he had told her straight out she wasn't one. It reduced her to silence as nothing else could have. She almost hung her head.

As for Mrs. Cookham, she inquired of herself whether a man with anything on his conscience would be either so severe or so stately. Always slow to believe evil, and proud of, as well as devoted to, her son-in-law, she thought not. And how much better to think not and to go on being happy, than to spoil everything, as her poor little daughter seemed set on doing, by suspicions. Nobody, she felt, would ever know what Jim's relations with Lady Frances had really been. Probably they were entirely innocent, for why, else, didn't they marry? They could have married. There was nothing to stop them. He was a bachelor, and though she was divorced—Mrs. Cookham had been shocked at first when Audrey told her this, but only for an instant, for she got over shocks, thanks to her cheerful nature, quicker almost than anybody—she could have married him, if not with the blessing of the Church yet perfectly

legitimately in a registrar's office. They hadn't married. Jim
had remained free, and married Audrey. Then why, she had
asked her daughter, worry?

Her daughter, however, had insisted on worrying. "There
are worse things than marriage, mother," she had said
obscurely, sobbing, and apparently bent on shattering her
present peace by something that might, or might not, have
happened in the distant past.

Mrs. Cookham shook her head. Poor child, poor child. "Are
you going to have a baby, dear?" was all she could think
of to say; and it was while Audrey was indignantly asking if
one couldn't be angry without going to have a baby, that
Conderley came in to announce Fanny's departure, and being
in a temper she let that part of her which wasn't a lady emerge,
and manifest itself in such lamentable language as the bit about
the marines.

Would her Jim ever forgive her, he who was so punctilious
in courtesy, so mild-mannered, so complete a gentleman? He
might forgive, but could he ever forget? Wouldn't those
marines stand up between them, so many insuperable obstacles
to happy confidence, for the rest of their lives? Lady Conderley
of Upswich, wife of the present and mother of the future lord,
rudely doubting her husband's words, and inviting him to go
and tell them to the marines. And she didn't even know
who the marines were, or why one should go and tell them
anything.

Slowly she began moving towards him, her eyes round with
penitence and fright. "Jim——" she began. "Jim——"

"I suggest, Audrey," he said, taking no notice of her timid
approach, "that you go at once to Fanny's room and say and
do the right thing."

"Oh, Jim, what is the right thing? I only seem to know the
wrong ones," piteously cried Audrey, reduced as completely
to humbleness as before she had been roused to rage. But she
loved him so much, she loved him so much; and having crept
quite close to the stiff man, she ventured to lay her small solid
cheek, red-hot still with the varied emotions of the afternoon,
against his sleeve.

"Come now, Audrey," said Conderley, more kindly.

"*I* think she's going to have a baby," announced her mother.

He stared at Mrs. Cookham, and then looked down at the
glossy dark head against his sleeve. "Are you, my dear? Are

you, Audrey, my dear?'' he asked, putting his arm round her,
and suddenly altogether kind. "Audrey—is it true?''

"There's nothing like babies,'' thought Mrs. Cookham, as
she tactfully prepared to leave the room. "Really, I don't know
where we'd be without them.''

V

§

AFTER staying with friends, it is sometimes a comfort to go
home. Fanny, having said her last words, and smiled her last
smile, and kissed and been kissed by the penitent Audrey, and
having also, in that desire for a good curtain which so
frequently overtakes those who part, warmly invited nearly
everybody to come and stay with her in Charles Street, felt this
comfort acutely. Even though she weren't going home really.
Even though she were only going to Claridge's. The great thing
was to get away.

Accordingly, no sooner had the steps, and the lights, and the
waving Conderleys and Cookhams slipped behind into darkness, than she fell back on the cushions, shut her eyes, and
gave thanks. How precious were the negations—the not seeing,
not hearing, not talking, not being with anybody. Even Manby
couldn't get at her. Sitting next to the chauffeur, safely
separated by the glass partition, she couldn't even ask her
whether her feet were warm, and would she like another rug.
Oh, blessed, blessed, thought Fanny, to be alone, to be in the
dark, to be out of reach, not to be in Upswich any more.

But when a guest departs feeling like this, and when the hosts
are left with a distinct sensation of smarting, the visit can't
really be called a success. Nobody, however, dreamed of calling it that. Audrey had been sure it wouldn't be one, Conderley
had had the gravest doubts, all now justified, and Fanny saw
clearly, and roundly told herself, that she was a fool. A fool
to imagine that poor Jim, twenty years older, hopelessly settled
down, and she a mere ghost in his memory, could be any sort
of refuge for her. Old men weren't refuges. They needed
refuge themselves, for they were timid, and shrank from
responsibility, and advised one to be friends with one's
husband, and let go one's arm when they got near the house.

There was, in fact, no *love* in them. Not that one wished love to be in them, except that without it, without, anyhow, the capacity for it, people didn't seem to be much good. Dry as bones, cold as stones, they seemed to become, when love was done; inhuman, indifferent, self-absorbed, numb.

This line of exceedingly unjust thought, however, which though unjust at least was vigorous and kept her warm, didn't last much beyond Ipswich. Soon after that she began to wonder at herself for having behaved so badly in having cut short her visit like that, and a few miles farther on had arrived at the stage of being thoroughly ashamed. By the time the car passed through Colchester she was quite overwhelmed by compunction, and decided that never in her life had she heard of conduct more disgraceful. Talk of being inhuman and numb! It was she who had been inhuman, and utterly numb to the feelings of others, only intent on getting away and not caring how many lies she told. Just because she was bored and tired; just because, having stupidly said something bound to rouse Audrey, she felt she couldn't go through any resulting scene. And wasn't everybody, nearly, by the Sunday evening of a week-end party, bored and tired? And hadn't most of the guests by that time said something bound to rouse somebody? But other guests, more decent than herself, didn't go away and ruin their hostess's dinner plans; other guests didn't go off, simply because they were afraid they would have to sit next to Major Cookham.

Spoilt, selfish, unforgivable behaviour. What could she do to make up? Nothing, she well knew; and she well knew that she had seen the last of Conderley. She didn't like to face this, but at the back of her mind she was sure it was true. His book was closed for ever. The odd, short epilogue to the story, twenty years later, that had just taken place at Upswich, was finished, and now indeed it was the end. Sad, this was; one more bit of emptiness added to her life. And the glow having ebbed out of her, the first glow of successfully getting away, and the succeeding glow of anger at her own conduct, she now felt most uncomfortably flat, cold, and miserable.

Staring out of the window at the hedges flashing past, hedges lit up for a second and then gone black—very like her own life, thought the dejected Fanny—she tried to rally herself by considering the absurdity of feeling such desolate sensations because of Jim, without whom she had done very well for so long. He was nothing now but a kind, fumbling old man, doing his uninteresting best according to lights growing every day dimmer. But in spite of recognizing this, of knowing this was true, she couldn't get rid of the notion that if it were possible to unwind him, to strip off one by one the layers of the years, there he would still be, the man who used to fill her arms with flowers, and feed her, with reckless passion, on plovers' eggs when they were practically priceless.

Also, she might have added, but preferred not to, the man who lived only for her, and who all but died because of her. Instinctively she shut out these more piteous aspects. Besides, how foolish they seemed now. Who would imagine, looking at poor old Jim, that he ever had had enough life in him nearly to die? Just as well that she couldn't unwind him, that he must stay bound up tight as a mummy in his further twenty years. One didn't really want repetitions, however lonely and empty life gradually became. And she fell to thinking of another of her adorers—she hadn't been able to endure him for long, this one, because the moment he left off talking love she couldn't understand a word he said,—who used obstinately to assert that the past is really as present as the present, and that if only she were to approach it from the proper angle she would find she was still doing everything she had ever done; still, she supposed the tiresome man would have insisted, holding those flowers, still, awful thought, eating those plovers' eggs, and poor Jim still going through the dismal process of all but dying.

How miserable. One would be terrified to do anything if one believed things like that, for fear of being caught in endless repetition. No; repetitions were bad things. And it was when Jim began to be a repetition himself, going round and round in the same circle of overpowering devotion, that she had felt forced, if she wished not to suffocate, to pass on to the fresh woods and pastures new of Edward; and she mustn't now, just because it was dark, and she was tired and elderly, forget these facts and begin to be sentimental about him. Her proper attitude, and she insisted on adopting it, was to rejoice that he was freed from the encumbrance of emotion, and smug and content with his Audrey. Also, that he was never going to be lonely, and never would have to make the acquaintance of that frightening condition. It was she, Fanny, who was going to be the lonely one. In her life was no loving spouse to make her feel

important and wonderful. On the contrary, after having been
very important and most wonderful for so long to so many
people she was rapidly becoming just poor Fanny. She felt it;
she knew it; and it was awful. But never mind that now—let her
think for a moment longer of Jim, long enough to bless him
and bid him good-bye, and then finally, and for ever, forget him.

"Good-bye, Jim," she whispered, at once proceeding to perform, with bowed head, this last rite. "Good-bye, dear darling
Jim I used to know. Thank you for everything, and bless you."

He, in the warmly lit dining-room at Upswich, eating the
particularly good dinner intended for Fanny, his table covered
with fresh carnations and coloured candles and the family silver
and the beautiful old Conderley glass, all set out to do her
honour—he, sitting there wrapped in the atmosphere of restored
harmony and affection produced by the baby Audrey wasn't, as
it afterwards turned out, going to have, had of course no idea
that he was being blessed, thanked, and parted from in a cold
dark car, somewhere between Colchester and Chelmsford,
by her who had once been his whole life. Yet, in the act of
raising his glass privately to his wife, at a moment when the
Cookhams chanced to be engaged in eagerly telling each other
things they all knew already—the kind gesture would have
made Audrey happier if she had been more sure about that baby
—he suddenly hesitated, put it down again, and looked troubled.

"Oh, Lord—what have I done now?" Audrey hastily asked
herself; but as she couldn't remember having been anything but
as good as gold since the reconciliation in the bedroom, she
picked up her own glass, smiled hopefully, and said, "Well,
Jim?"

"I was only thinking——" he began; but again he hesitated, and looked troubled.

He never finished the sentence. He didn't, after all, drink any
health. For what he was thinking, and thinking with, perhaps,
his last ache of all because of her, was, "Poor Fanny."

VI

§

IN Bethnal Green that evening, a place Fanny was bound to
pass through, the clergyman called Hyslup, in whom she had

once been interested because he loved her so much and had a golden voice, was holding a mission service; it being Lent, and he being zealous.

He was holding the service in Bunbury Mews, a small side-street off the main road; and having a great natural gift of speech, besides a burning belief that what he preached was the one way of salvation, he easily collected a devout crowd. Issuing forth from his little tin mission-room after the evening service on those Lenten Sundays, dressed in a cassock and pre-ceded by a gleaming cross, he would get on a chair provided and held steady by a follower, and at once proceed, very beauti-fully, to pour into the anxious ears of the poor, comfort, encouragement and hope. There was a policeman on duty, but he did nothing to interfere with the continually growing crowd beyond checking it when it threatened to overflow into the main street, because he too wanted to listen; for the preacher's were the words that go straight to every heart, and most men would like, if possible, to be saved.

Fanny, feeling humble, and in the precise mood which wel-comes being saved, arrived at the corner of Bunbury Mews just as the tram in front of her car stopped and held it up; and idly looking out of the window she perceived with astonishment, a few yards away on a chair and engaged in impassioned gesture, him she still occasionally thought of as sweet little Miles. At the same moment Manby, from her seat in front, saw him too, and was equally astonished.

"Why, there's that 'Yslup,'" she said, almost with excite-ment to the chauffeur. "You know—'im who used to be about her ladyship so much." Adding, for she connected him only with luncheon-parties in Charles Street and flowers he kept on sending, and assiduous calls, "Well, I never."

Here was one of those coincidences life does sometimes pro-vide. Greatly astonished by it, at once reading into it something probably extremely significant, Fanny put down the window to see if she could hear.

She couldn't, but it was evident that her one-time worshipper was being eloquent. The look on the listeners' faces told her that; and it surprised her, for she remembered him chiefly as tongue-tied, as one who gazed rather than conversed. Yet, when he did speak, how golden had been his voice, how richly had it reverberated down her spine! It used to make her think of ripe apricots, of bursting figs. The first time he came out of his lovelorn silence sufficiently to ask if he might call her Fanny, she thought she had never heard a name more beautiful; and when a few days later he confessed, after a struggle which for all its speechlessness was obvious, that he worshipped her, the brief words set the room quivering with music.

Sitting in the car, she watched him with deep interest. Here was somebody who might help her. If he had the words of Eternal Life, as she suspected from the rapt attentiveness of his hearers, why shouldn't he spill some of them over on her? Perhaps religion was, after all, what she really needed, though she must say she didn't think much of the idea of being beaten to one's knees. Still, if it would make her less forlorn, if it would distract her attention from the way the years were letting her down, it might be worth trying. Only a few minutes before, when her chauffeur in his passion for speed had almost dashed into a ditch, and her impulse had been to tap on the glass and immediately dismiss him and set about finding somebody safer, she had been stopped by a gloomy wonder why she should bother any more about being safe. What for? What did a woman in her sort of shoes, worn-out shoes fifty years old, want still to save herself up for? And if religion would protect her from this kind of defeatist thinking, and succeed in hoodwinking her—persuading her, she meant—that her soul, if she tried hard enough, might presently take on all the beauty, if of a different kind, her body used to have, and all its delight, of a different kind too, in living and doing and looking forward, she would be willing at least to try it.

With Miles's help. Rather sweet, thought Fanny, beginning to smile again, to revive her relationship with Miles on a higher, a spiritual plane. She hadn't yet, owing to circumstances, ever been on a religious spiritual plane. With Jim she had climbed on to the plane of poetry, though only staying on it as long as he held her there; but that was a lower plane than the religious one—or wasn't it? Anyhow she would talk to Miles, and see what he had to suggest. And a happy facility for cheering up being one of Fanny's characteristics, she at once, at the prospect of possible help, began to feel better, shook off her gloom, and became alertly attentive to what was going on on the chair.

So this was Miles, now; this vehement figure, doing what he liked with a crowd. He had found his tongue, then, since leaving her—or was it she who had left him? Well, anyhow he was the one who went out of the door,—and the tongue he had found appeared to be the very tongue of angels. Watch those intent faces round him. See how thirstily they drank in every word. All this must have been in him when she knew him, and she had never suspected it. Perhaps he had been handicapped by loving her so much. Perhaps she hadn't taken enough pains to help him to self-expression, he being very much outside her usual circle, an obscure young clergyman from Kensington, met at a bazaar, and only invited to her house because of his manifest, touching devotion, and the really lovely way he said How do you do and Good-bye.

As far as she could remember, he wasn't a great success. Her friends used to take her aside and say, "Darling, *what* a little sweet—but why do you make him so speechlessly happy?"

Chronologically he came between Perry Lanks and the man who said the past was the present, and at first she had liked him because, after the clever Lanks, he had seemed so restful. There was, or seemed to be, a childlike simplicity about him in those days, an almost dewiness. Later he bored her for this very reason. Brains, she found, judging him to be without them, were what, after all, she preferred; for by that time she was very much used to the company of more or less able men, from each of whom, as they passed impetuously through her life, she picked up bits of knowledge and shreds of ideas.

From Miles she picked up nothing. He merely sat silent and gazed; and after a while this bored her. Still, she had cried at the parting. He had blessed her on saying good-bye for the last time, and she remembered thinking how dear it was of him to bless her, poor Miles, and she had cried.

§

Now here he was, changed beyond belief, into somebody positively exciting. How long was it since he sat silent and just gazed? Five years? Seven years? No, it must be more. He was thirty then—the sort of age at that time beginning to interest her, and he now looked as if he might be forty, worn by his own fire, and probably also by fasting. Clergymen who wore cassocks were apt to fast. She didn't know why one thing should involve the other, but it seemed to. She had an aunt who married a clergyman, and he wore cassocks too, and on Fridays and in Lent would hardly eat a thing, and then was so cross nobody could stay in the same room. She wondered what

Miles was like about the house—whether, half starved, and shattered by his own eloquence, he didn't go home and be rather short with his wife. Or perhaps he hadn't a wife? There was a kind of fierce fleshlessness about him that suggested thoroughness in doing without things. It suited him to be fleshless. Dear Miles, how nice he looked now. She felt so warmly always to those who had loved her, so ready, when she had had time to get over them, to be friends; and now, seeing Miles again, how much she would like to know if life had treated him nicely since that sad day when they parted. What was he saying, she wondered, with all that emphasis? Why shouldn't she get out, and go close enough to hear? There was no reason why she should hurry back to Claridge's, and seeing how chance had thrown him in her way, it seemed a pity not to make the most of it.

So she tapped on the glass, and signed to the chauffeur to come round and open the door.

Just at that moment the tram in front went on again, and the cars behind wanted to go on too, and there was some confusion. The chauffeur, unable to hurry her because of having to be respectful, felt his situation acutely, with a policeman shouting at him in front, held-up cars bellowing at him behind, while his lady, incapable of being flustered, and used to doing what she chose and how she chose and when she chose, with her customary grace and dignity took her time.

"What is this place?" she paused on the running-board to inquire, looking round her.

He was hard put to it to make the words Bethnal Green sound polite.

"Bethnal Green, is it?" repeated Fanny, still looking round her, while the hootings became frantic. "You go on, Griffiths——" as if he could help going on—"and wait for me farther down the road." And closely followed by Manby, she walked into the crowd with the air of one expecting it to make room for her; which, impressed by her being sure it would, it did.

§

Miles was watching her. He had been watching the main road ever since the uproar of horn-blowing drew his attention to it, and had seen her get out of her car and stand a moment above the crowd.

Fanny. Come back, just as he had at last realized, after long bitterness, what he really owed her. Everything, he owed her. With gratitude he recognized what she had done for him, in breaking his heart. From the most miserable creature on earth, a clergyman enthralled by a woman not his wife, she had set him on his feet, restored him to what he had always known was his special gift, the power to move multitudes, and been the real cause, strange though it might seem, that he could now, single-mindedly, devote himself to God.

He was glad that she had come, so that he could say Thank you. He was glad, too, to find he had no shred of his former feeling left, and could watch her approach with a detachment so complete that even while he watched he continued, uninterruptedly, to be eloquent. His sister. His greatly changed, and, he was afraid, from her appearance as she drew closer and he saw her more plainly, definitely sinful sister. Well, so much the better. He could help her. His work didn't lie among the good, but among the bad. Just as she had once helped him by casting him forth, so could he now help her, repaying the debt he owed her by presenting her, at what appeared to be, so much had she aged, almost the eleventh hour, with the prospect of salvation.

Her unexpected presence seemed to inspire him. He had never, he felt, spoken so well. He prayed that some at least of his words might wing their way into the hidden, and he was sure arid, recesses of her soul. And indeed Fanny was listening very attentively. It gave her the greatest pleasure, having got near enough, to hear what wonderful things were coming out of Miles's mouth. How delightful, she thought, immensely pleased that he should have turned out so well. Close up, too, he was really rather beautiful. Fasting became him; and the inner flames by which he seemed consumed were evidently doing him nothing but good.

Interested, she watched and listened. He used to be a little fat. Well, not fat perhaps, but chubby; which was why, when he sat silent and didn't say "Fanny", or things like that in his heart-shaking voice, she hadn't been able to feel as if he were particularly attractive. Most unfair, of course, that a silly thing like chubbiness should put a lover at a disadvantage, but it did; and for this one, whose great gift was his delicious voice and, as she now saw, his power over words, to be speechless with adoration, as well as chubby, was a disaster. She was so glad

he had fasted it away, and got over being speechless, and got
over everything, and was finally landed, triumphant and inspired, on that chair—helped up on to it, she clearly saw, really
by her.

These men owed her a great deal, reflected Fanny, full of an
almost personal pride in the eloquence proceeding from the
chair. They made a tremendous fuss at the time of their several
departures out of her life, wringing her heart-strings and giving
her a painful feeling of having perhaps been unkind, but in fact
each departure was the beginning of better and happier things
for them. Look at Jim, so smug and contented with his Audrey.
Look, now, at Miles. Impulsively, she tore a leaf out of her
engagement book, and scribbled, *Miles, you are marvellous.
You must let me see you. Can't I come and help you eat your
supper when you've finished being such a wonder? Where do
you have it?*

> *Fanny.*

She gave it, with a shilling, to a boy near her, and asked him
to get it, somehow, to Mr. Hyslup.

"Father 'Yslup?" queried the boy.

"I dare say," agreed Fanny.

" 'Im on the chair?"

"That's the man."

With the practised hand of one used to having notes sent him
while he was speaking, Miles took it from the boy, glanced at
it without the least break in what he was saying, and looking
straight at Fanny, where she stood wedged in among his intent
flock, raised his hand and briefly made the sign of the cross.
His flock, though a little surprised that this should be done in
the middle of the address, took it as being of general application
and bowed its heads, but Fanny knew it was for her, and said
to herself, gratified, "Darling Miles."

But what did he mean? That she was to wait? That he
would speak to her afterwards? That she was being dismissed?
He had made this same gesture over her at the miserable parting last time she saw him, when it was she who was dismissing
him. No, he wasn't dismissing her now, she decided, he was
blessing her, just as he had blessed her then; and it made her
feel as if she were framed in blessings, the one then and the one
now, and this gave her the agreeable sensation, frequent in old
days but rare indeed lately, of being safe and taken care of.

So she waited, and felt warmly towards him. And as she was so soon going to be with him her first thought, naturally, was what she looked like, and she wondered if it would be unseemly, or wrong, to open her bag, and attend to her face a little. Only powder, she would use; nothing scarlet or black. After all, this was an open-air meeting, it wasn't as if it were church. She could move behind the big man in front of her, and bend her head.

But Miles seemed to have developed quite extraordinarily in every way, and nothing, apparently, escaped him. For, having edged behind the man in front, and seen in her little glass how urgent it was at once to do something, no sooner had she started most carefully, and as she imagined invisibly, applying the powder, than he, in his sermon, or discourse, or address, or whatever one would call it, began to talk of harlots.

Not that this would have mattered, because sooner or later all clergymen get to harlots, but what seemed rather to under-line his remarks was that with one accord the people round her turned their heads and looked at her. Pure coincidence, of course; though it appeared to make Manby very angry, who glared about her and said in subdued but distinct tones—sub-dued, because she felt she was very nearly in church, and distinct because she wished for no possible misunderstanding, "Your ladyship shouldn't condescend to such places as this."

"Be quiet," rebuked Fanny, who was used to being looked at, and knew she wasn't a harlot; so what did it matter? "I want to listen." And she continued, having begun—for it is impossible only half to powder one's face—to arrange herself as nicely as possible, while at the same time attending to what Miles had to say.

It was wonderful, what he had to say. Everything that lovely voice touched at once became important and beautiful. And such passion, and such conviction! His body positively vibrated. Sinners of every sort, harlots, publicans, women taken in adultery—all were transmuted, at his touch, into purest gold. They turned, she thought, into the most fascinating figures, dealt with by this artist. His publicans were full of atmosphere. His women taken in adultery sheer music. When he came to them, Fanny's immediate neighbours showed a tendency to look round at her again, but were intimidated by Manby's glares, who was now well on the watch.

Fanny didn't mind their looking, nor what they thought.

Let them look, she said to herself, busily powdering, let them think. She had never been taken in adultery, so what did it matter? Manby was silly. Servants were very silly about that sort of thing, always terrified lest they and their belongings should be suspected of not being respectable. Poor things, they missed a lot of fun; and not only fun, but very lovely happinesses like poetry, and shining illusions. How pleasant it would be for them if they could understand a little of the angel-simplicity of just dear, kind love, of love without any fuss of lawfulness and hard-and-fast bargaining first in a church, of sweetly secret love, of love which, even if it ended in tears, had meanwhile been the warmest, friendliest thing in life. Indeed, in spite of her own experiences, she had sometimes doubted whether one could ever be friends, real, comfortable, easy friends with anybody, unless one had begun by being lovers. But she supposed Manby couldn't be expected to grasp that.

And having finished her face she put the powder away, shut her bag, and was ready to join in the final hymn; which she did with great pleasure, for she used to sing it when she was a child, and both words and tune brought back sunny memories of before she grew up, and knew what being so beautiful was going ultimately to do to her.

In fact, Fanny enjoyed herself. She spent a very pleasant and, for her, unusual half-hour; and now, after the blessing had dismissed, or tried to dismiss, the crowd which seemed reluctant to go away, with an instinctive little pat of her fur, and an instinctive little pull of her hat, she prepared for the further interest of supper with a purified, developed, and immensely improved Miles.

§

Their greeting was brief—warm on her side, and hurried on his, and he at once led her away in the direction of his lodgings.

Manby followed. Fanny hadn't told her to, but she wasn't going to lose sight of her lady in such a place. Besides, she distrusted 'Yslup, as she thought of him, there being no h's, and very few Mr.'s, in Manby's thoughts. He couldn't, she felt, be a real gentleman, or he wouldn't, having sat at table in Charles Street, stand on a chair in Bethnal Green. It was a come-down, and Manby had no use for come-downs, and was worried by seeing her lady going off, all friendly and chatty, with this one. She followed, saying to herself, What next? while the people they met stood aside respectfully and with a marked discretion, to let them, including Manby, pass.

"Do you know what they are thinking, Fanny?" Miles asked, having gravely returned several sets of grave greetings.

"No. Do you?"

"Of course I do. My people are open books to me. They are thinking, and hoping, that I am saving you."

"Is that why they look down their noses?"

"It has nothing to do with the way they may look," he said shortly.

"Well, my sweet——" he frowned at words which used to unlock heaven—"it would be very charming if it were true."

"There is nothing charming about being saved, Fanny," he rebuked.

Already, in the short distance they had walked, she had said several things which, needing rebuke, prevented the conversation from developing—things that broke up rather than helped build. How little, he thought, she had changed. Except in appearance, and there the right word was havoc, she hadn't changed at all, and appeared to have profited nothing from the usually chastening passage of time. There was the same easy assurance, the same certitude that if she praised he was bound to be delighted, the same incapacity for remaining serious, which he remembered in Charles Street, and which had been characteristic of every one of the foolish women he met at her house. She was, in fact, still Charles Street, while he for years, and he thanked God for it, had been pure Bethnal Green.

"Well, if you don't like charming, I'll say wonderful," she said, looking at him with a smile. Poor woman, she shouldn't smile, he thought, for each time she did she merely brought out a different set of wrinkles. "It would be wonderful if you saved me, dear Miles. Do try. I wouldn't be a bit surprised if you succeeded. You could talk anybody round, I'm certain."

"It has nothing to do with talking round, Fanny," he again rebuked. "A priest doesn't talk round. He prays, and grace is given."

She apologized, but quite cheerfully, as though rebukes were nothing to her. "My words are all the wrong ones this evening," she said, not looking at all, he noted, as if she really thought so. And for her part she wondered whether, though outwardly grown so thin, he wasn't still perhaps a little chubby inside. His mind, she meant. Padded.

He accepted her apology with an inclination of his head. "Unless you have greatly progressed," he said, "in matters of religion, since I used to call on you——" what an odd way of putting it, thought Fanny—"you are probably still abecedarian, and accordingly bound to blunder."

"Do you mind telling me what abecedarian means?" she said, apparently meekly; but he dared say she wasn't at all meek really. She never used to be. Kind, yes; too kind, as it tragically turned out, for how had it not led him on. But never meek.

He explained that it meant pertaining to the A B C.

She inquired whether he thought, then, she was still, spiritually, in the nursery.

He replied, "In God's nursery, Fanny——" whereupon, for a space, she was silent.

It gave him satisfaction to keep on calling her Fanny, the name he used hardly dare utter; it made him feel how completely the tables were turned. Indeed, there is no doubt that Miles, as they walked side by side, and each succeeding lamppost gave him another glimpse of her face, had some difficulty in not congratulating himself. He wouldn't have been human otherwise. Her age, too; he had had no idea, when he used to call on her, how much older she was than himself. It hadn't been noticeable then. Now it hit him in the eyes that he himself was at the beginning of the best years of a man's life, while she was certainly well on in the worst years of a woman's. And what a difference there was in their positions; he, become a conscious instrument of God's grace, while she—really, though, he wouldn't care to say what she had become, except that it was something manifestly in need of a very great deal of forgiveness. If, in God's mercy, he were to be chosen as the instrument for bringing this once proud beauty, humbled, to the throne of pardon, it would be, he felt, without any doubt the most wonderful moment of his career.

§

Meanwhile, however, he couldn't but notice that she seemed far, as yet, from being humbled. She had looked at him and smiled when he told her she was in God's nursery—merely smiled, without saying anything; almost as people smile, only it was impossible to credit this, when they are making allowances. Was she, then, entirely unaware of the immense change in their relative positions? The light assurance of her behaviour suggested she still imagined he was her slave. Strange that the vanity which accompanies beauty—excusable, perhaps, when there is such great beauty, or at any rate understandable—should persist after the beauty was gone. Poor woman; left without ballast, and ageing so rapidly. He felt very sorry for her, not even able to smile now without looking older than ever. But in spite of being sorry he must, nevertheless, before the evening was over, make it clear how matters really stood. He would do this by thanking her, with proper solemnity, and indeed with all his heart, for the service she had done him, years ago, in releasing him from his shameful bonds, and the mere dwelling on the shamefulness of the bonds, and the mere insistence on his joy of being quit of them, must certainly, he judged, clear things up for her.

"Don't walk so fast," she here interrupted, these reflections having invigorated his steps.

"I beg your pardon," he said, slowing down, but not at all liking the way she had almost issued a command.

The proud beauty again, he thought, unable not to feel a human resentment. In the old days she used to tell him to do this and do that, and with what abject eagerness had he not rushed off to obey her. But those days were for ever gone, and the time in her life arrived when she should at least, he considered, say Please.

"I forget you can no longer be very active, Fanny," he therefore said.

She didn't, however, mind this; she still only smiled at him. "No," she answered, "I'm not several other of the nice things I used to be, either, I'm sorry to say. But there's one thing I'm *much* more than I ever was before, and that is glad to see you, Miles darling."

Darling. Another endearment. And so warmly declaring that she was much more pleased to see him than she used to be.

He thought it wisest to behave as if he hadn't heard. Often it is best, as well as safest, he knew, to pretend not to have heard, not to have seen, not to have known; and he began telling her with deliberate distinctness of his vows of celibacy, of his dedi-

cation to the religious life, with all that it implied of poverty
and austerity, and how his household arrangements were pre-
sided over by his sister, who was also vowed—perhaps unnecessarily vowed, he had sometimes privately thought, looking at
her—to celibacy. "My real sister," he said, "though you,
Fanny, are my sister too."

"Am I? I like being that," she answered. "It's a friendly,
comfortable relationship. An immense improvement on our old
one—I mean," she added, seeing his frown, "on when you
used to call on me." And she told herself that perhaps Miles,
as a brother, might be quite useful in helping her with Job.
Being a priest, he might come to Charles Street and lay him.

"I have so many of them," sighed Miles—immediately
strangling the sigh.

"Many what?"

"Sisters."

"Were your parents so fruitful?"

"All poor and suffering women are my sisters," he said
coldly; for though he continually urged fruitfulness on such of
his flock as were married, for some reason the word annoyed
him applied to his own parents.

"Are they?" said Fanny, more doubtfully; for to be one of
a crowd of miserables, each thinking he was the very man to
help her with her particular Job, and taking up his time, didn't
seem so good. "But, darling——" he frowned—"*I'm* not poor
and suffering, and I'm quite well off."

At this he paused. Beneath a lamp-post he paused in order
to face her, while a group of people approaching made room for
them, respectfully stepping off the pavement.

"Well off, Fanny?" he inquired. "You think yourself well
off? Let me tell you," he solemnly assured her, "that you are
positively poverty-stricken."

But even this only pleased her. How very understanding of
him, she was thinking. He wasn't, after all, completely padded
inside. By poverty-stricken he meant her starving soul, and her
uneasy, groping mind, and her heart that was well on the way
to becoming a skeleton now that even Dwight had gone—all the
parts of one that begin, evidently, to give trouble after fifty.
He had guessed this. He knew it instinctively. Living sexlessly,
she reflected, he had probably developed feminine intuitions. It
was what happened, so she understood, even in the animal
world. Anyhow, Manby had a tom-cat once that she had had

to have turned into a neuter, and the first thing it did afterwards
was to produce kittens.

Pleased, she smiled at him, the light from the lamp overhead
glaring down pitilessly on her face. "I'm so glad," she said.

"Glad?" he repeated, surprised. "Do you in the least know
what I mean?"

"Yes. That I'm a poor, drifting, more or less lost soul"—
curious, he thought, how much women liked to be told their
souls are poor and lost—"and so you're going to help me. You
can, you know, Miles. I don't mean so much about religion,
though. It's Job. He's worrying me to death. He badly needs
something done about him."

§

Miles stared at her. Who was Job? Searching in his memory,
he found no Job. Her marriage had been so long before his
time, and he so much outside Fanny's world, that he had never
heard of Job. Not, that is, as Job. There had been, he knew,
a Skeffington in her life, for how else would she have come by
the name? And he knew, too, that Skeffington was a sinful
man, from whom she had been obliged to part; but he didn't
connect him with anyone called Job.

"Who is Job?" he therefore asked, watching the face so
cruelly slashed by the strong top-light. And he thought, as he
stared at it, and remembered how lovely it used to be, that she
was indeed a poor, lost, drifting soul, for all her grand clothes
and glistening car—a trivial poor soul, too, wasting her time trying to cover up the ruin left by her departed youth with this
lamentable façade of paint and plaster. Yes, undoubtedly
trivial. Trivial, flippant, soaked in worldliness. Before doing
anything for her, in the way of helping her to God's feet, he
sternly decided, she must wash her face.

"Darling," she said, amused by his question—how much
he disliked being called darling—"it's refreshing to find somebody who doesn't know. Job was a husband I used to have.
But I can't very well explain him under a lamp-post. He's
more an indoor subject. Come along, and I'll tell you when
we get to your lodgings."

A husband I used to have. Incurably flippant. And, Come
along—as though he were a little boy, or a dog.

Miles went along, because there was nothing else he could

do, but he went resentfully. She didn't appear to have the
remotest idea of his present position and—he said it in all
humility, ascribing it entirely to God's mercy—importance. Yet
she had stood in the crowd, and been flooded, with the rest of
them, by words one doesn't, he well knew, hear every day.
He couldn't not be aware that God had raised him very high
among orators, so high that, had he chosen to take his gift into
politics there was no position he might not have aspired to. And
would she then, he wondered, have told a Prime Minister, as
arrogantly as she told the really far nobler priest, to come along?

Fanny, with a most annoying serenity, was going along herself, taking for granted that he would follow. Used for years
now to veneration, to deference, to his own people stopping
when he stopped, and remaining motionless till he himself chose
to move, he watched her with an irritation unbecoming, he
recognized with real pain, in a priest, but impossible for the
moment to subdue. True, his own people only knew him as their
father in God, their guide and leader up the steep ascent to
heaven, and had never seen him abject with infatuation at a
woman's feet. Fanny, alas, had frequently thus seen him.
Every time he paid his increasingly agonizing calls, she had
seen him more abject and more infatuated, a slave craving to
give proofs of his abasement, an eager dog panting for a kind
word; and with bitter shame he acknowledged that, from her
point of view, there was some small justification for her present
blindness. Before the evening was over, however, she should
cease to be blind. His sister would help him remove the scales,
for she, at least, being its daily witness, exactly knew his standing. And meanwhile, there was nothing for it but to do, for
the last time, the deluded, arrogant woman's bidding, and go
along.

Inwardly exasperated, but outwardly composed, he therefore followed; and so did Manby, who had been waiting under
a different lamp-post, and asking herself at intervals, as she
had so often asked herself during her years in Fanny's service,
What next?

§

She, Manby, became a difficulty when they arrived at his
lodgings. He hadn't known she was there till he turned to
Fanny, at the top of the steep, oil-clothed stairs, to warn her
she must take his rooms, and his sister, and supper as she found

them—she wondered how else she could take them—and saw a
figure below in the little passage.

It was a sober, fat figure in black, and evidently attendant
on Fanny. Her maid, no doubt. One of those pampered para-
sites a spoilt rich woman is infested with. Like ticks on a dog.
Swollen with what they feed on.

Once more he was annoyed; and strange and mortifying was
it to Miles, who so much hoped he had conquered his baser
sides and could now no longer, by God's grace, be shaken out
of his serenity, how frequently he had allowed himself to be
annoyed during the last quarter of an hour. Indeed, continually. Ever since, that is, he began to walk with Fanny. But
really now, this maid—what was one to do with somebody's
grand lady's maid in such lodgings as his, where the cooking was
done on a gas-stove in a corner of the living room, and there
was no kitchen in which a servant might sit and wait? Fanny
was obviously a sinner, and as such would be welcomed by his
sister, whose business it was to welcome sinners, but all over the
maid, plainly to be seen even at that distance, was written that
she led a blameless life.

He had no time for, nor interest in, blameless lives, and
neither had his sister, for they both lived to bring light into
darkness, and if there were no darkness why waste light? Besides, the maid, as he had at once noticed, was fat, and therefore not a person who fasted, and if she came up and had to
sit with them in their little living room, they would be bound
to offer her a share of the supper, and she would no doubt accept
it. He knew exactly what there was for supper. Every Sunday
night in winter it was the same: a dish of potatoes in their
jackets, beetroot salad, and a tin of sardines—ample for two,
especially as his sister didn't eat sardines, hardly enough for
three, now that there was Fanny, and impossible for four. Somebody would have to be sacrificed, and since it was true that
noblesse oblige, it wouldn't be the maid.

Vainly Miles tried to stop his thoughts from running thus
sensually, but he was so hungry, and so tired, and so much in
need of nourishment, that the thought of anybody taking most
of his supper from him was hardly to be borne. All the week
he had strictly fasted, and to-day, Sunday, was the day he had
been trying not to look forward to, when there would be a little
more to eat. Lamentable, he recognized, to be such a weak and
inferior faster. It might, of course, be because he didn't fast

enough. He had been told that if one ate nothing at all, and only sipped water, one presently reached the stage when food no longer mattered. Ought he, then, to try to reach that stage? Was it required of him to begin to practise an austerity so great that it left nothing whatever in his life to comfort him except, three times a day, a little water?

His exhausted flesh shrank from so depressing an undertaking. That night, at least, it could bear no further trial. He must have his supper. Whatever happened in the week following, he must, this once more, have his supper. Yet he couldn't leave that maid down there in the cold passage while he ate it; and he couldn't leave her, either, on the tiny landing, where there wasn't room to turn round, and nothing to sit on. He was faced, therefore, by having to ask her in. He would have to look on while she probably ate most of everything. And it was with a sinking heart, though he well knew that a priest's heart should not thus sink, that he said to Fanny, as he took out his latch-key, "I believe your maid is downstairs."

"What—Manby?" exclaimed Fanny, peering over the stair-rail into the darkness below.

"Did your ladyship call?" immediately replied Manby's voice, respectful but determined.

§

Manby. The name struck Miles's ears as though they had been boxed. He forgot how hungry he was. He forgot about his supper. Manby. That woman. Still with Fanny.

Vivid was his recollection of her, and tinglingly painful the knowledge that she must equally vividly recollect him. He had never spoken to her, but well did he know her. On several occasions during the shameful period of his enthralment he had seen her—sent for by Fanny to bring her something, a handkerchief or something, always at the most bitterly disappointing moment for him, or coming out of the dining-room where she had been arranging flowers for one of the frequent dinner-parties. But on the last dreadful day of all—the recollection positively skinned him—she came out of it just as he was stumbling down the stairs, his face wet with tears, and in his heart only one prayer left, that he might get out of the house without being seen. And there she was standing and looking at him. And the recollection of the terrible moment, he was shocked to find, still was able to pull all his skin off.

Out of the past it surged up again, hot and flaying, when he heard her name. There was to be a dinner-party that evening, and Manby, whose gift for arranging flowers had long been discovered and made use of, had just finished setting out the results of her work on the dining-room table, and she came out into the hall at the very moment when he was stumbling down the stairs.

Astonished at the spectacle of a clergyman in such headlong descent, she had stood and stared. She knew what must have happened, and she oughtn't really, she told herself, to have been astonished, but he was the first clergyman she had seen in this, to her, familiar situation, and perhaps it was the contrast between his collar and his plight which transfixed her.

As for him, a sudden light flooded his brain when he saw her expression, revealing in a ghastly flash that she had witnessed this sort of departure before. And he couldn't find his hat, because of being blinded by tears, and his humiliation was complete when she came forward and found it for him, and when his shaking fingers dropped it she picked it up, and actually put it on his head for him.

No; he had hoped never to see Manby again.

§

"You'd much better go and wait in the car," called down Fanny.

"Much better indeed," sternly reverberated Miles's ripe, resounding voice.

"I couldn't find my way if I tried, m'lady," Manby, respectful but determined, explained from below, for at sight of the dark stairs, which didn't even smell as they should, she had made up her mind not to budge from that house till her lady came out of it with her.

It was at this point that Miss Hyslup, hearing talk, opened the door a slip and put her gaunt grey head out. "What is it, Miles?" she asked, opening the door wider when she saw him.

He turned to Fanny. "This is my real sister," he explained, introducing them. "And this, Muriel," he went on, taking Fanny's hand, "is my sister in the Lord."

"Oh," said Muriel.

"What next?" thought Manby.

§

Being shortsighted, Miss Hyslup could see none of Fanny's details in the bad light, but only an effect of great good looks and slender smartness. Furs. Fair hair. A gleam of pearls. A smell of violets.

She stood peering at her in uncertainty. The sisters in the Lord usually brought home by Miles weren't at all like this one; they were poor, miserable creatures whose one need was, quickly, food, and next a good warm and dry by the fire, and then words of advice, and finally a ticket, along with her blessing, for the dispensary. With these she was quite at home, and knew just what to say and do; but how deal, she wondered, with anybody who seemed so overwhelmingly not in need as the person on the landing?

"But you're a fine lady," she said, shy and doubtful, as she peered at her. "How do you come to be one of my brother's sisters in the Lord?"

"It seemed to happen very suddenly," smiled Fanny. "Down in the street."

"Oh, I see. In the street," said Miss Hyslup, to whom everything at once became clear. Well, she must do her best. It was her first experience of the successful kind, and she wondered what such a one was doing in the streets of Bethnal Green; but that was none of her business, and whoever Miles brought home for help should get it.

Pulling herself together as much as she could, for she was a good deal frightened, she advanced upon her duty as hostess-rescuer, and took Fanny by the hand. It was part of her job to take these poor things, she told herself, by the hand—you could wear a fur coat and still be a poor thing, couldn't you? Just as you could wear a coronet, and still have a kind heart— in a welcome which should at least have the appearance of warmth. So, though nervously, she pressed the hand she held, and Fanny, never one not to meet kindness half-way, cordially returned the pressure.

This made Miss Hyslup still more nervous. She, she knew, was the one to press, not the one to be pressed. Sometimes, at the end of an interview, she would even bestow a kiss on a pale cheek, on a sorry cheek, on a cheek accepting but never—she would have been immensely taken aback if it had been—a cheek responding. Still, having a fur coat probably made a difference to one's behaviour; it was not for her to judge. And with an effort to stand up squarely to her duty she said, shy but determined, "I am very glad to see you," drew her visitor into the room, pulled a third chair up to the table, asked her to take off her things, and expressed, in a timid but resolutely hospitable voice, the hope that she was hungry—"Because," she said, "we are just going to have supper."

So far, so good. This was how she treated the poor ones, and it seemed to work all right now, for her visitor was quite obedient, and did take off her things, the movements she made pulling off her fur coat appearing to let loose a thousand violets in the room. Fresh violets. Violets of sin, Miss Hyslup was afraid, trying to prevent their deliciousness from giving her too much pleasure by turning her head away, but how sweet. Sad, she thought—oh, sad, *sad*—that God's lovely creations should be used in payment of conduct she had never yet allowed herself to imagine clearly. And in Lent, too.

"I can't offer you much, I'm afraid. A few sardines," she said, made still more nervous by these scents of sin. Sin, she felt, oughtn't to smell nice. It didn't, either, as a rule, as no one knew better than herself.

"I love sardines," said Fanny, who had a feeling that she must somehow make up, by being extra pleasant and extra appreciative, for the dismal conditions these two lived in.

Miss Hyslup couldn't help wishing she didn't love sardines, for there are limits to what a tin of them can do in the way of going round, and on Sunday nights Miles seemed to need as many as he could get. The word love, too, in that particular mouth, even if used only in connection with sardines, surely was out of place? It was a holy word. It represented a holy thing. Ought these poor women, grand and shabby ones alike, to use it? She must say she hadn't yet heard the shabby ones using it. This was the first of Miles's sisters from whose lips— faintly Miss Hyslup shivered at the thought of Fanny's lips—it had fallen.

Perhaps having a fur coat emboldened its wearer. Anyhow, it was not for her to judge. And rousing herself to the proper pitch of kindness, she said, "I'm glad."

"There's a maid," here put in Miles, who had shut the door, and was standing holding his biretta in his hand, too uncertain about what was to happen next to hang it on its usual hook.

"A maid?" repeated his sister, pausing in the act of lifting the cover from the dish in which the twelve sardines were neatly arranged in a circle, each one's shoulder on the next one's tail. For a moment she supposed he thus chose to describe someone neither married nor a widow. She was aware her brother had unusual gifts of oratory and used them freely. She never knew what words he might say next. "Where?" she asked, looking round nervously.

"Oh yes—mine. Downstairs," said Fanny, remembering Manby.

"Do you mean a lady's maid?" said Miss Hyslup, her heart sinking further than ever. "Then," she added bravely—for was not a lady's maid, if brought in by Miles, her duty too?—"she must come up as well." And she cast a look of unhappy good-bye at the sardines.

The maid perhaps upset her more than anything. Violets and fur coats were intimidating enough, but here was something much worse to face. Should the lady's maid of one of these poor women be regarded as a poor woman too? Did she come under the heading of Miles's sister?

She looked round the little room, already so much crowded that it seemed on the verge of bursting. Could it hold any more? Yes, it would have to, she said to herself, squaring her shoulders; it would have to hold a lady's maid. Never in her life had she yet met one; and everything she had heard of them was intimidating.

She made a movement towards the door.

"But you can't—there isn't room," protested Fanny, catching at her sleeve and holding her back—a familiarity which only just failed to give the nervous creature a fit. "You go," she said, turning to Miles. "Tell her she'll get pneumonia standing there in the cold, silly old obstinate thing, and she's to go back to the car at once, and if she won't go alone you take her."

At this speech, Miss Hyslup felt as if she were struggling on a slippery slope to keep her feet. A fur coat, a lady's maid, a car, and now, still more surprising, orders. Yes, orders; orders to Miles, who was the very fountain-head in that house, in that district, of orders himself. What they must *earn*, the grand ones, to be so confident and high-handed! And she found time to wonder, in the middle of much confusion of mind, whether one of Miles's sisters, while in the full blast of her prosperity, would be likely to accept either his ministrations or her own help. It was her particular job to help bad but sorry women. This one must be bad, or Miles wouldn't have brought her home, but she didn't seem sorry. And why should she be sorry, Miss Hyslup, visited for a moment by insight, asked herself, if she were, as she appeared to be, on the very crest of her—well, engagements? The sorry, she hadn't been able to help observing, though she didn't mention it to her brother, seemed always to be those who couldn't go on because of no longer being attractive. If they were still attractive, they waited to be sorry till they had lost their looks. And sometimes, in moments of more extreme lassitude—for she was, like most unloved women, in most things at bottom listless and half-hearted—she wondered what the Kingdom of Heaven, if one did manage to get there after all the trouble, could possibly be like, crowded up with the battered.

§

Miles had flushed deeply. Orders again, and orders given him in front of Muriel, which made them so much worse. Such orders, too; involving a *tête-à-tête* walk with Manby, which he, faint for want of food, worn out after his long day's preaching, was to take in the cold. Through the raw February night he was to walk with Manby, with almost the one person in the world he could never forgive. Well did he know she had done nothing, that she had merely been a chance spectator, but he could never forgive her for having seen him in the moment of humiliation. Fanny, who was the humiliator, he could and did forgive, for she was a sinner and he was going to save her, but the maid needed no saving. Patently blameless, she was just a virtuous parasite. And again he thought of her—though he tried not to, for, after all, he was a priest and it was Lent—as a tick.

At once aware of the clouds on his brow, his sister looked at him anxiously. She knew he was feeling having been given orders, poor Miles, and it was really too bad that he should have to go out again that cold night. But, on the other hand they couldn't allow the lady's maid to perish, could they, seeing that they were in Bethnal Green precisely to prevent occurrences of that kind. And willingly as she would have gone herself, if only to clear her brother's brow of clouds—for no domestic circle can have peace so long as it contains even a single clouded brow—

she couldn't, because of the way the newcomer was holding on to her sleeve.

"I do think," she therefore said, hesitating, deprecating, apologetic, as those are who feel they are between the devil and the deep sea, "that perhaps she oughtn't to be left down there in the cold."

Muriel now, thought Miles bitterly, his brow darkening alarmingly. Even Muriel. Backing the other one up.

This was women all over, he said to himself: they hung together. Put one man with two women, and immediately they were banded against him. Separately, it was easy to manage them. Separately, he had managed Muriel perfectly, who, with hardly anyone of her own class in Bethnal Green to egg her on to criticism, had done very well as a devoted sister and fellow-worker. Health-and-comfort orders she had given him, such as to put on thick clothes under his cassock when he was to address meetings out of doors, or to take a hot drink at night if he felt a cold coming on; but apart from these, which were well within her legitimate sphere, he in everything was her guide and superior—far more than he could ever have been to a wife, who would have seen him in moments when, if she chose, she could make him beg.

Miss Hyslup, really alarmed by his expression, made a more determined effort to free her arm and get away to the door. "I'll go, dear," she said hastily.

But Fanny held on tight. "No, no," she protested. "Let him. He'll be back in a minute, won't you," she added, turning to the outraged Miles. And to his sister she said, "I believe you spoil him."

Miss Hyslup could only look, in frightened bewilderment, from one to the other.

§

There was nothing for it, Miles saw, but at least to pretend to go.

Quietly he opened the door, followed by his sister's anxious, deprecating eyes, and went out, shutting it noiselessly behind him. That Muriel should allow this to happen to him was unheard of, she who well knew, if Fanny were unable to imagine it, how profoundly he needed rest and food on Sunday evenings. Nothing, though, would induce him to do anything about Manby. They might send him after her, and he might pretend to go, but he wouldn't, really. And having shut the door so slowly and carefully that it didn't make a sound, he stood on the little landing without moving, and listened to the clearings of the throat below that showed him she was still there.

She should remain there; and he would remain where he was —long enough, that is, to make it plausible for him to go back into the room again and say he had seen no sign of her. By not looking over the stair-rail, this would be true. Jesuitical? Perhaps. But the picture of him escorting Manby through the streets, Manby who, last time they met, put his hat on for him and would, he had no doubt, have wiped his tears away into the bargain if he hadn't rushed out of the house in time, was too hotly humiliating for him to care. When a man is thrust into such a position, he must use what weapons he can to get out of it. It wasn't his fault that he was in it; it was Fanny's. Fanny had thrust him in, with her orders and her high-handed interference. From the first day he met her to the day she cast him forth she had caused nothing but trouble; and now, after ten years of working out his salvation in Bethnal Green and slowly forgetting her, here she was again, and here again, immediately, was trouble.

Miles, at odds with himself, miserable that he should be forced into duplicity, hungry and tired out, leant against the wall and tried to raise himself above his situation by lifting up his heart in prayer, while Manby, below, cleared her throat. But presently he discovered with a shock that when she didn't clear her throat, and, after all, she couldn't be expected to go on clearing it without stopping, he could hear what his sister and Fanny were saying on the other side of the shoddy door, as distinctly as if he were in the room.

Hating eavesdropping, just as he hated all underhand ways— though it might fairly, he knew, be said that his own ways at that moment were underhand—he did his best to shut out what was being said by putting his fingers in his ears; but after a moment, finding the position too tiring, he felt in the pocket of his cassock for something he could use instead of his fingers, so that he needn't hold up his arms, and found Fanny's note.

The very thing. Yet—was it?

He hesitated. After all, that handwriting had once been cherished, and to use it for putting in his ears did seem rather discreditable. But something being said in the room overcame his sentimental scruples—it was Fanny asking Muriel how she came to have such a small brother, just as if some of the greatest men hadn't been small: Napoleon, for instance; and the poet Keats; and even, though he said it with all reverence, from measurements taken in Joseph of Arimathea's tomb, our Blessed Saviour Himself.

Always sensitive about being small, to hear it being mentioned by Fanny decided him, and slowly and noiselessly he tore the note in half, rolled the halves into two neat cylinders, and put one in each ear; and immediately a curious satisfaction filled him, wholly unworthy, he knew, but nevertheless having the quality of balm, for by this action he was secretly degrading her, getting even with her, though she didn't know it, paying her out.

Yes, but wasn't this very like spite? It startled him. He who preached love, understanding, pity, forgiveness, wanting to pay somebody out! How far, then, must he still be from grace, how earth-bound in bitter uncharitableness.

And he sought to comfort himself by questioning if such a thought could have been his own—for was it not his earnest intention to do what he could to save the woman?—and, so seeking, he fell into the sin of heresy. For if, he reasoned before he could stop himself, it was not his own thought, while at the same time it was evil, it must have been inserted into his mind by some strange and awful influence existing side by side with, and getting the upper hand of, God.

Before he knew what he was about, he had fallen into the sin of heresy.

Appalled, he tried hastily to lift up his heart again in prayer. But it remained inert. Nothing happened.

"I must fast more," the unhappy man decided.

§

Left alone with Fanny, Miss Hyslup stood a moment uncertain, remembered Miles's injunction frequently laid down— "It is essential," enjoined Miles at regularly recurring intervals, "to show affection to these poor women,"—was alarmed almost to petrifaction by having to show it to somebody so grand, tried, as a beginning to smile, only succeeded in making what she was sure must be an awful face, and finished by saying, in a voice she did her best to keep steady, "Won't you sit down?"

Fanny sat down.

Miss Hyslup then searched for her spectacles. To gain time she searched, and not only, though this was most important, so as to be able to see. In her capacious pockets, in the drawer of the table, on the sideboard crowded with tins of Ovaltine, of Sanatogen, of Oxo, of Benger's Food, of the many different preparations with which she plied her gifted brother to keep his strength up, she searched. Important in the highest degree, she felt, that she should see plainly this most recent sister of Miles. She must know what she was up against; for that she was up against something outside her experience seemed certain.

Wretchedly short-sighted, without her glasses she was helpless, and a prey to the oddest delusions. For instance, it appeared to her, without them, that she was shut up alone with beauty, and she couldn't quite believe that. She wasn't used to beauty. It never, except perhaps in the shape of an occasional child, came her way, and that it should actually have walked into her room and be taking, at her own request, a seat, seemed profoundly unlikely. Yet this, as far as she could make out in her blindness, was apparently what it was doing; accompanied by that lovely smell, so different from the smells she was accustomed to, and behaving with an easy-going familiarity to both her brother and herself which took her breath away.

"Are you looking for something?" asked Fanny, ready, if she knew what it was, to help. The question, she recognized, wasn't very intelligent, for nothing could be more evident.

"My spectacles," said Miss Hyslup distractedly.

No; Fanny wouldn't help her look for spectacles. Lately she had been altogether against people putting such things on.

Miss Hyslup went on searching. If she gained time, Miles would come back and explain. He oughtn't to have brought anyone like this home without a word of explanation. Used to being kind and patient for a long while with his other sisters before they would come out of their shells, she couldn't but see that this one hadn't got a shell at all. Composed and at home she sat, as if, (a)—Miss Hyslup, conscious her brain was liable to confusion, had a little private trick of getting her thoughts under headings—they had known each other from infancy, and (b) as if she had nothing to be ashamed of. This not only gave Miss Hyslup a congested feeling of being left with her entire stock of kindness and patience bottled up unneeded inside her, but also a sensation of topsy-turviness, of being herself the one who was to be subjected to comforting—in fact, of being herself the sinner.

She paused a moment in her search to stare down sideways at as much as she could see, without her spectacles, of the problem Miles had left her, and, as her custom was when in perplexity, cracked, one by one, the joints of her hard-worked fingers.

"*Don't* do that!" Fanny, wincing, wanted to cry out.

Aloud she said, in her turn, hoping to divert her hostess's attention from her fingers, "Won't you sit down?"

But it can never be the turn of a guest-penitent to invite a hostess-succourer to sit down, and Miss Hyslup, aware of this, more than ever wished Miles would come back, and cracked her finger-joints yet harder.

"*Please* don't do that!" Fanny wanted to beg.

She didn't, because of manners; but smiling up at her told her, again hoping to divert her attention, that she was so tall that her, Fanny's, neck would break if she, Miss Hyslup, didn't sit down, and asked her how she came to have such a small brother—thus deciding Miles, on the other side of the door, to divide her note in two and put it in his ears.

How does one ever come to have brothers, small or big? Miss Hyslup, even now, didn't quite know. Accustomed to regard questions as things needing conscientious answers—she was of those who painstakingly give the facts on being asked, How do you do,—this one disconcerted her extremely. Children reverenced their parents, particularly once they were dead. Children instinctively averted their gaze from considering any aspect of their parents which wasn't fully dressed. She herself instinctively, indeed with a kind of terror, averted her gaze from anything and everything which might be said not to have all its clothes on.

However, her visitor didn't seem to expect an answer. She merely again invited her to sit down, and Miss Hyslup found herself obeying, found herself struggling with a most inappropriate impulse to say Thank you.

With an effort, she managed to stop herself in time, dropped into the chair next her visitor, immediately felt something unusual beneath her, and found she was sitting on her spectacles.

"Oh, there they are!" she exclaimed, getting up again.

"Who?" asked Fanny, turning her head to the door.

Luckily they were in their case.

§

She put them on, her hands shaking a little.

"Now I can see," she said.

"It's often better not to," said Fanny.

But she didn't really mind the poor old thing seeing, she didn't shrink back, as she had taken to doing lately, from a close stare. This was because she was too much filled with pity for Miles's sister, who had to live in such miserable lodgings and only got cold sardines to eat on a winter's night, to bother about herself. "Poor thing," she thought, looking at the gaunt face so close to her own—"poor simple, half-starved, probably put upon by Miles, *good* poor thing"; while Miss Hyslup, for her part, shocked at the difference strong spectacles could make to what one was looking at, thought Poor thing too—poor painted, haggard, smiling, but she dared say crying all right inside, poor thing. Indeed, she went further than Fanny in pity, picturing the day when there would be no fur coat, violets, lady's maid and car any more, the day so terribly much nearer than it had seemed without her glasses, when the last sixpence was spent, when the ditch Miles said these women, if unrepentant, finished in, had been reached.

That way, picturing the inevitable end, she felt much less nervous, and able to be affectionate. For the doomed, one could always feel affection; one could feel affection for everybody, for positively everybody, she had discovered, simply by realizing they were doomed. When, as sometimes happened, and was happening now, she came across prosperity, and it seemed to flaunt, she had only to think of the day, near or distant but certain, when it would be stretched out beneath its last sheet with pennies on its eyes, at once not only to forgive it but to feel quite fond.

They sat looking at each other, each filled with sympathy and a desire to help. Fanny was thinking she must get Miles to let her arrange that he and his sister shouldn't be so poor. Miss Hyslup was thinking that the first step towards better things would be to persuade this at present lost soul to wash her face. The impressive clothes, now that she saw clearly how hollow their wearer's cheeks were, and how desperately tired her eyes, fell into their place quite naturally as just so much Death. They were the wages of Sin, and those, taught St. Paul, were Death.

How could one feel anything but tenderness towards a poor thing who was dressed from head to foot in Death?

"Tell me your name, dear," she said, quite at ease now, and all affection. "My brother forgot to."

Fanny said it was Fanny, and was so much touched by being called dear by someone in far greater need of kind words than herself, that she laid her hand on the big, bony one in the next lap.

"Poor thing," she thought, feeling the hand so rough.

"Poor thing," Miss Hyslup thought, feeling the hand so smooth.

A hand of sin, thought Miss Hyslup, looking down at the two in her lap, and a hand of—well, no, she couldn't say hers was a hand of virtue, because of the way she sometimes didn't like Miles as much as she ought to. And what, too, about those secret cups of cocoa she made for herself occasionally in Lent, when fasting had become really past a joke? Cups of guilt, Miles would have called them if he had known; and from the way she kept her eye on the door and her ears pricked till they were safely swallowed and the traces cleaned up, one might really have supposed that they were. Yet, were they? Didn't the Bible say, *By their fruits ye shall know them?* And weren't the fruits of the cocoa an ability to fast twice as well after it as before?

Miss Hyslup brought her thoughts back to the two hands. Certainly her own was a hand of effort and hard work, if that could be accounted virtue, and this other one had never, she was afraid, made an effort in its life—except, she supposed, hold itself out in the direction of money. Painted finger-tips, it had too; each tip a separate advertisement of vice. She couldn't help recoiling a little from the finger-tips, though after a moment's reflection she was able not to mind them either because, unless rescue arrived in time, they too merely represented so much Death. Quite pleasantly, therefore, she asked—odd how pleasant it was possible to be by merely calling up a picture of someone else's death—"Anything else besides Fanny?"

"Yes," said Fanny, smiling; but smiling tenderly, as at a sick child who is going to be helped to get well. "Skeffington."

Miss Hyslup was glad that she answered at once. Usually they didn't. When it came to giving their surnames, none of them ever wanted to, preferring to be known, she supposed in an attempt to protect their parents from association with their shame, only as Daisy, or Peggy, or even, she remembered one last week, as Kitty-Poo. But fur coats probably kept out other things besides the cold—sensitiveness, for instance; regard for one's family; while she could see for herself that they kept out any sort of decent shyness.

"Skeffington," she repeated, as though turning over all the Skeffingtons she had met, but really to think out how to make her next sentence affectionate enough. There was that little recoil from the finger-tips on the one hand, and on the other, fighting against it, the picture, so touching, so pitiful, at once able to melt her, of the sheet and pennies.

"I shall call you Fanny," she said with decision, over-coming the recoil.

"Do," said Fanny warmly. "And I'll call you Muriel."

But at this there was recoil again. "Oh," said Miss Hyslup taken aback. "Oh, well——"

She wasn't prepared for such a suggestion. Never yet had any of them dreamed of calling her Muriel. "Oh, well——" she said again, with an involuntary withdrawal of her hand from beneath Fanny's, "I don't quite know——" And she looked round the room nervously, as if seeking guidance.

There was no guidance. Miles wasn't there, and her mother —who certainly would have told this Fanny straight out, "You can't call my daughter by her Christian name, a woman like you,"—was dead.

"But are you going to suggest you should say Fanny while I say Miss Hyslup?" asked Fanny, amused but also rather pleased, for here, she felt, was a tribute. Miles's sister evidently thought herself immeasurably older. So she was, of course. Perhaps not immeasurably, amended Fanny, mindful of her fifty years, but certainly older.

"They all say Miss Hyslup."

"Who?"

"My brother's sisters in the Lord. I must tell you, though," Miss Hyslup went on hastily, anxious not to take up any attitude that might break a bruised reed or quench smoking flax, "that they're quite unlike you."

"Yes, I gathered that," said Fanny, remembering Miles's description of them. Miles's Miserables, she had already labelled them to herself.

"So that perhaps—in your case——" hesitated Miss Hyslup.

What would her dear mother think of her, giving in? What would even Miles think?

"You know," encouraged Fanny, patting her hand, "I don't suppose you're very *much* older than I am. Anyhow, nothing like venerable enough to justify my being so extremely respectful."

"I'm forty-eight," said Miss Hyslup.

"Oh," said Fanny.

§

For a moment she couldn't speak. Forty-eight. Incredible. Almost, really, impossible. This old, worn-out woman two years younger than herself. How Miles must have banged her about. Not physically, of course, but there were lots of ways of banging a woman about without touching her. She could be overworked. She could be underfed. She could be out-talked, out-argued, preached at, set an example to, and finally, as a reward on Sunday nights—Fanny glanced indignantly at the table—given a sardine.

"Muriel," she said, taking the big hand in both hers, and speaking very earnestly, "you must let me help you."

"That's funny," thought Miss Hyslup. It did seem very funny, that one of them should want to help her whose business it was to help them. Topsy-turvy.

"You're being killed," went on Fanny. "I can see it's killing you, being so poor."

"But we've taken vows of poverty," said Miss Hyslup.

"You have? What, vowed to be poor? Did you want to?" Fanny asked incredulously; and at once suspected coercion from Miles.

"A house mustn't be divided against itself," said Miss Hyslup.

Vows of chastity they had taken as well, but no need, luckily, to mention these. The fewer things one mentioned, the better one got on, she found. Besides, those particular vows were, anyhow, unmentionable. She knew they were, because the minute one approached the subject, in thought or speech, one felt hot. She did, anyway. So confusing, too, renouncing temptations one had never had and didn't really know about. The nearest she ever got to a fleshly temptation was her hot-water bottle. She supposed it must be a fleshly temptation,

because of the extreme pleasure she felt whenever she gave way
to it. Sometimes, in moments which Miles, she shamefacedly
was sure, would call, if he knew about them, wanton—after a
better meal than usual, or when she wasn't quite so tired—her
thoughts would run away with her, and she would imagine that
a husband might perhaps be like a glorified hot-water bottle;
a hot-water bottle enlarged to life-size; deliciously pervading
and warming one's cold, lonely bed. And sometimes, when she
really ached with longing for what she was never going to have,
she would fish the smooth india-rubber thing up from her feet,
and hold it with both arms close to her breast, and pretend it
was a baby—her very own, darling, sweet, cuddly, gurgly little
baby. After such thoughts, however, and after such actions,
she was, for days, wretched with repentance.

"I *knew* it must be Miles," exclaimed Fanny, all indignant
concern for Muriel. If Miles wanted to be poor, and fast himself into a skeleton, let him be it and do it alone, without dragging in his sister and turning her into an old woman before her
time. "You really *must* stand up to him," she urged. "It's
dreadful to let him have his own way to the point of starving
you. Shall I talk to him about it when he comes in? Would
it be a help?"

But Miss Hyslup didn't hear anything after that first
sentence. Miles, she was repeating to herself; Miles; the lady
off the street had called her brother Miles. Wasn't this something very strange, and unusual? Didn't it suggest either
effrontery, or intimacy? No, no, not intimacy of course. But
then—what effrontery!

"Do you," she asked, trying not to stiffen, for there are
moments when the meekest stiffen, no matter how hard they
try to think of sheets and pennies, "call my brother by his
Christian name to his face?"

"Oh, always," Fanny assured her. "Shall I talk to him?
Shall I tell him how wrong it is to——"

But again Miss Hyslup didn't hear. She was swallowing
quickly. The effrontery of that *always* was like a blow.

"Did you," she said after a moment, across what Fanny
was saying, taking refuge from that awful *always* in not
believing it, and accordingly being, as well as she knew how,
sarcastic, "did you begin doing so in the street?"

"Down in the street?" echoed Fanny, looking at her in
surprise. "Why, but I've known Miles for years," she said.

§

For years. Miss Hyslup was overwhelmed. That Miles should have concealed his knowledge of this woman for years seemed quite terrible. The only way, she instinctively knew, to deal with her kind was to be absolutely open and above-board. She, who was certain of so few things, was certain of this, that for a clergyman to be seeing one of them privately, for him never to mention her to his sister and co-worker in that sad field, was a very great mistake.

For an appreciable moment she sat unable to speak. Then she said, getting it out with difficulty, for a suspicion she really couldn't bear to have anything to do with, had begun to wriggle itself like a snake into her mind, "How many?" and Fanny, having reflected, said she thought it must be about ten.

"Ten?" repeated Miss Hyslup, speaking with still greater difficulty, for now the snake seemed to be getting her by the throat.

It was ten years ago that Miles went out one afternoon a clergyman, and came back a priest. She could only describe in this way the swift, complete change in him. A bitter priest, too, bent on taking the Kingdom of Heaven by violence, and dragging her along with him. Flight, panic-stricken flight from whatever it was that had happened to him, flight into austerity, into a frantic concentration on saving and being saved, was what he was suddenly set on. He gave up his nice, comfortable curacy in Kensington, took vows and made her take them, turned his back and made her turn hers, for ever on everything except self-denial, and settled in the poorest part of Bethnal Green, using its sordidness as if it were a hair shirt. Why?

For ten years she had puzzled miserably over this question, never daring to ask him the reason, because the look on his face, if she tried to approach the subject, shut her mouth; and now——

She drew her hands away from between Fanny's, and sat staring at her, her eyes big with horror, and couldn't and wouldn't believe it. It wasn't possible. No, it couldn't be possible really that Miles, already at that time in Holy Orders, and without his sister knowing anything about it, and after saying family prayers before breakfast, and after taking the Morning Service in his vicar's church, and after eating his mid-

day meal and invoking God's blessing on it, should have sallied
out and sinned.

In the afternoon too. Evidently it was in the afternoon he
sinned, for he was always back in time for dinner; and it made
the terrible a hundred times more terrible, somehow, that it
should have been perpetrated, indulged in—oh, she couldn't
think of words any more—by daylight. Night was the time,
wasn't it, she tremblingly said to herself, when people did their
deeds of darkness? It must be, or all the married couples,
who after all, having been blessed by the Church, were free
to choose their own time, wouldn't be up and about and fully
dressed for everyone to see, till late in the evening. Such a
ghastly extra tinge of wickedness it gave Miles's sinning, that
he should have committed it with God's sun shining in on him.
Like gilding the lily, confusedly occurred to her.

She bowed her head. She felt sick with betrayal. Out-
rageously bamboozled she had been, and left high and dry
alone with those vows of chastity. Hers had been real vows;
but how could anybody who hadn't *been* chaste, ever *be*
chaste? she asked herself. What was the use of locking the
stable door after the hideous horse had fled? And worst of
all, rankling most piercingly of all, was that he should have
dared be so severe when he found out about her hot-water
bottle.

Without looking up, she said, her voice trembling and her
hands, in spite of her clutching them so tight together,
trembling too, "It is about ten years ago that my brother
suddenly became religious."

"Oh, but he was religious before that," Fanny assured her.

"Suddenly religious," repeated Muriel, apparently addressing the tightly-clutched hands in her lap.

"Well, but all the time I knew him he was religious,"
insisted Fanny. "Very. He used to bless me."

"He used to bless you?"

She raised her head at this and stared, bewildered, at the
whitened and reddened sepulchre before her. Did people, then,
on these occasions bless each other as well? Oh, how little she
knew, how little she knew! But that her brother, her brother
dedicated to God, should have added blasphemy to——

"Yes. So sweet of him, poor Miles," said Fanny, remembering, with the tender smile which accompanies thoughts of past
adorations, that raised hand, that beautiful voice. *The blessing*

of God Almighty remain with you always, Miles used to say
in his beautiful voice, instead of the conventional good-bye.
It had thrilled her. It was because of it that she had endured
him as long as she did.

Then Miss Hyslup, ashamed to death of everybody and
everything, besides having to fight an overpowering desire to
burst into tears, got as near a taunt as she was ever to get.
"You'll tell me next," she said, barricading herself from the
threatening tears behind derision, "that he wished to marry
you."

"Yes, poor Miles—he did," said Fanny. "But I never marry
anybody."

At this Miss Hyslup did burst into tears. Now indeed her
universe had crumbled beneath her feet, and all her beliefs,
and all her trusts. That Miles, having sinned with one of them,
should actually have wished to marry her and actually been
refused, completely crushed her. Where, in the whole world,
was there anything or anybody left for her to be proud of?

"How wise, how wise——" she sobbed, a welter of bitterness and humiliation, while Fanny, astonished at this sudden
collapse, gazed speechlessly. "One can't help being a—a sister,
but one can help being a—a wife. Oh," she sobbed, flinging
her arms out on the table, and laying her grey head on them
in an abandonment of wretchedness, "life is too awful, too
awful. I c-can't go on. I don't want to be a s-sister any more.
I d-don't want to be anything any more. I want t-t- go—
go away and hide—and hide——"

"Muriel—*please,*" begged Fanny helplessly.

She couldn't think what had happened. Miles was evidently
worse to his unfortunate sister than she had suspected; but why,
all of a sudden, burst out into what seemed to be hysterics? Was
it anything she had said? Was it perhaps that, all these years
afterwards, Miles's poor sister was taking it to heart that she
hadn't married him?

Fanny got up and bent over her.

At once she was pushed violently away. Those violets . . .
that *stink* of violets . . . the woman daring to come close and
choke her with her vile sweetness. . . .

Never in her life having been pushed away before, let alone
violently, Fanny stood for a moment, surprised beyond speech.
But the sight of poor Muriel's tragic face, streaming wet with
tears as she struggled to her feet, made her not mind any-

thing that she did and only want to be allowed to comfort and soothe. Poor thing. Poor, distraught thing. If it hadn't been for the unwiped tears, she would have put her arms round her and kissed her—probably to be pushed away again; but who cared?

"Muriel, you *must* tell me what the matter is," she said, opening her bag and taking out a clean handkerchief. "Look— I haven't used it," she said, holding it out.

This was too much for Miss Hyslup. With a great sweep of her arm she knocked the hand and handkerchief aside, made a kind of passionate plunge at the door, and gasping incoherently: "I'll go and find him—I'll confront you both— he'll have to tell me the truth—I can't—I won't——" she pulled it open.

"Miles! Miles!" she cried, prepared to rush, thus calling, into the streets, and search the whole of Bethnal Green till she found him.

Fortunately, however, for everybody's good name, she found him at once.

§

Down in the passage, Manby, between those throat-clearings which increased in frequency the longer she stood in the cold, had been listening quite as attentively as Miles, on the landing, was listening before he stuffed up his ears, and had gradually come to the conclusion that she wasn't alone. Somebody was up there. Listening, too. And listening to her.

This gave her the creeps. What could be happening on the other side of the door through which her mistress had gone? The door had opened, and then shut on her; and after a few moments it had opened again, and then shut again. But no one came down the stairs; and gradually Manby grew certain someone was there, outside the door, standing motionless and listening. Listening to her.

Very unpleasant, thought Manby. She had never been listened to, when she wasn't saying anything, before. And by somebody invisible, too—invisible and motionless, hiding at the top of a flight of almost dark, and none too clean, stairs.

"One needs to be fond of her ladyship, the dance she leads one," she said to herself, intensely objecting to her position, and hardly even liking now to clear her throat, so uncanny was the sort of watchful silence that succeeded each of her homely noises.

Ought she to go up and face whatever was there? Had somebody been placed as sentinel outside the door, while inside her ladyship was being used for an unlawful purpose? Only the recollection of Miles's priestly garments gave her a little confidence. Gentlemen in cassocks and those queer-shaped things on their heads were usually reliable, she assured herself, and on the side of the law. Still, such confidence as she got out of this reflection cooled as time passed and the fog, creeping in through the badly-fitting street-door, obliged her to clear her throat more and more continuously; so that besides her fears for her mistress she began to have fears for herself, for her own chest, if she stayed in the damp down there much longer; and where would she be without her health?

Driven by these double fears, she had almost got enough courage together to go up and see for herself who was hiding on the landing, when in the brief interval of recovering from one bout of throat-clearing and preparing to start on another, she heard what she could only describe as a to-do burst out in the room overhead. A great to-do. The sort of thing her ladyship ought never to be exposed to.

At once defying fear, she set off climbing the stairs. With as much haste as her bulky body allowed, she panted up them to find out what was happening and to stop it, while Miles, feeling the vibration of her approach, had just decided that the only course left for him to take was to go down and meet her, lead her into his lodgings, and make the best of a thoroughly deplorable job, when the door behind him was pulled open, and his sister, crying his name, came rushing out as one demented.

Almost she fell on top of him, so close was he to the door, and so violent her exit. Only by seizing her by the arm did he prevent their both falling over in an unspeakably ignominious confusion; and as he had never seen her demented before or anything approaching it, he at once put it down to Fanny—how or why he was unable to imagine, but Fanny was somehow at the bottom of this disgraceful frenzy. Didn't he know Muriel for a completely colourless personality, as unemotional, because as empty of wishes or initiative, as a machine? Only a trouble-maker like Fanny could possibly stir her up to such a pitch. The whole house would hear her, if she didn't stop making such a noise. The whole of Bethnal Green would ring with the scandal of this exhibition, if he wasn't able to make her keep quiet.

"Go back, go back," he sternly commanded between his teeth, with his free hand trying, behind her, to find the handle of the door, and with his other, in an iron grip round her wrist, pushing her towards it.

"Yes—and you come with me," cried Muriel, incredibly dragging at him quite as hard as he was pushing her—why, the Communist on the floor above would hear her, and deride them both on platforms if she didn't stop—"and just tell the truth for once—before her and before me, and me seeing that you do——"

It was here that Manby arrived, out of breath, at the top of the stairs. In the dim light she saw, as she described the scene afterwards to Miss Cartwright, the 'Yslups behaving in a way she couldn't have believed. A clergyman, too; and one that had lunched in Charles Street.

"May I speak to her ladyship, please sir?" she asked respectfully, directly she had a little left off panting.

Her presence, her respectfulness, acted like oil on troubled waters. The Hyslups ceased, simultaneously, to struggle. That someone should be addressing them respectfully at once restored them to a proper pride and dignity.

"Who is that?" asked Muriel, almost in her normal voice, still, however, clutching at Miles's coat.

"Lady Fanny's maid," he said, letting go her wrist.

"Yes, ma'am. May I speak to her ladyship, please, ma'am?" said Manby turning to her, as quietly respectful as if what she had seen happening a minute before were the behaviour natural to clerics and their relations. "It's getting late, and the chauffeur thinks——"

§

There was no doubt that Manby saved the situation. Before such respectfulness, good manners were put on their mettle; before such calm, anything except more calm would have been impossible.

Muriel's calm was petrified, for no maid so respectable could be in the service of someone not respectable, and how had she not been behaving to her mistress? A ladyship, too. Muriel

knew no ladyships, but had a firm faith in the virtue of the
female aristocracy. Still, in the depths of her heart, in spite
of this firm faith, and on levels below her petrifaction stirred
rebellion. Why, if she isn't one, does she look like one?
questioned Muriel's heart, in its rebellious depths.

As for Miles, his calm was the calm of thankfulness. He
never would have supposed he could be thankful for Manby,
but he was. She was removing Fanny. In her presence scenes,
such as Muriel had evidently been on the verge of making, were
impossible. And he stood watching her taking charge, going
about her duties as quietly as if she were in Fanny's own
bedroom, with grateful recognition of her qualities.

"Your coat, m'lady," said Manby, composedly removing it
from the hook Muriel had hung it on, and without more ado
putting Fanny into it.

"Your bag, m'lady," she said, retrieving it from its perilous
position nearly in the oil of the sardine-dish.

"Your handkerchief, m'lady," she said, stooping, not without a wheeze, and picking it up from the floor where it had been
lying since it was swept, by Muriel, out of Fanny's hand.

And even when she went on to say, imperturbably, "Griffiths
has just sent word, m'lady, that he thinks the fog is coming
up thicker, and your ladyship should be getting home," Miles,
who presumed Griffiths was the chauffeur, and knew he
couldn't have sent word because he didn't know where they
were, found himself unable to condemn the falsehood in his
gratitude for its effect.

For it took Fanny away. He didn't want to save her any
more; at least, not till he had had his supper. Perhaps he didn't
want to save her at all, now. There were some people who
were best left in—no, no, what was he thinking? What terrible
word had he just been within an ace of saying?

She went at once—affectionately, he was surprised to see,
as far as Muriel was concerned, but almost silently. Naturally,
in front of Manby, Fanny had to go almost silently, for with
the old innocent standing there, there could be no explaining
that she wasn't what Muriel imagined. Clear was it now to
Fanny that Muriel imagined she was of the same profession
as Miles's other sisters in the Lord, and not merely of the same
profession, but also that she had seduced him. It astonished
her that she hadn't tumbled to it sooner, she who usually was
so quick at tumbling to the suspicions of sisters, wives, mothers

and daughters. But how, she had been asking herself, slammed
into the room alone while Muriel was hysterically calling out
on the landing, did one prove one wasn't a prostitute, and
hadn't seduced somebody's brother? Surely, very difficult.
Just saying, "I'm not," and "I didn't," wouldn't do it.
Then Manby appeared, and by her mere respectable presence
proved it at once. Difficult—oh, difficult, not to laugh, felt
Fanny, struggling to keep her face straight.

It kept quite straight, though, directly she looked at Muriel.
Who would laugh then?

"Let's be friends," she said, going to her quickly, and kissing her. "Let's see each other sometimes. I'd like to so much."

But all Muriel managed to answer, making an effort to get
back to the hostess level and standing very still, was, "Won't
you have something to eat?"

And Fanny said, putting both hands for a moment on her
shoulders, that she thought she ought to go home because of
the fog.

And Manby, respectful at the door, agreed.

And Miles, speaking most beautifully, turning every syllable
into a clear-cut gem, remarked that the fogs between Bethnal
Green and London proper were sometimes very bad at that
time of the year, and perhaps it might be a good thing to start.

Then Fanny, looking into Muriel's exhausted eyes, enlarged
to enormousness by her spectacles, bent forward and whispered
close to her ear, between two kisses, that she wasn't to mind.
"Don't mind," she whispered. "It doesn't matter. Please
don't mind. I don't a bit. So please don't either."

Which shocked Muriel all over again, shook her to her very
foundations. For oughtn't one to mind being taken for a
prostitute? And mind very much?

§

In silence Fanny walked back to the car, followed, a lamp-
post behind, by Manby, and accompanied by Miles. He, kept
once again from his supper by the exigencies of manners, said
nothing either.

She didn't want him to. She had had enough of his golden
voice, which left her completely cold now that she had seen
poor Muriel, and knew how he made her live, and knew about
the vow he had made her take. She must see what she could

do to help her—take her away somewhere for a holiday, get her out of those surroundings, even if only for a few weeks. How glad she was she wasn't tied up to a fanatical clergyman. How glad she was she wasn't tied up to anybody. She felt she was finishing with Miles, and it occurred to her, as she walked beside him, holding her fur over her mouth because of the fog, that she was finishing one after the other with those who used to be her devoted friends at a great rate. Jim, earlier in the evening; now Miles; and a week ago Dwight. Tidying them up. Clearing them out finally. Or was it that they, absorbed in their own lives and no longer the least interested in her, had cleared her out?

This, though, was a chilling thought. It didn't seem possible that she, Fanny, to these men who once were her worshippers, was now only a museum piece, rousing in them the sort of curiosity the crowd felt when Lazarus turned up again, while people like Muriel, who had never met her before, at once took her for a lost soul. Perhaps she was a lost soul. Perhaps that was how one ended—alone, and lost.

Chilling indeed were these thoughts. Raw and penetrating was the fog. Damp the dirty pavement. No wonder she was silent.

"Yes, Miles?" she said. turning to him and removing the fur for a moment from before her mouth; for he seemed at last to be saying something, and she thought she must have missed the first part.

He was, and she had; but he repeated it for her benefit.

"It is not to be wondered at, Fanny," he repeated, having been roused, by seeing the car quite close, to the duty of accounting for his sister's behaviour, and at the same time driving a much-needed lesson home, "that Muriel, judging from your appearance, should have mistaken you for what I prefer to believe you are not. The fact that Manby is still with you encourages me in this belief."

For a moment she said nothing. Then, looking at him sideways, with a faint smile, she asked, "Disappointed?"

"Disappointed, Fanny?" he echoed.

"That there's no saving to be done?" she said, continuing disconcerting and troublesome to the end.

VII

§

GRIFFITHS was one of those chauffeurs who don't like waiting
in the cold, and especially not in the cold of a place like
Bethnal Green. Therefore, when Fanny, getting into the car,
mechanically said, "Home," he took her home; he took her,
that is, to Charles Street, though well knowing she really meant
Claridge's. And he did this because he was cross.

This simple action had unforeseen consequences. They
began immediately Charles Street was reached, and went on
unfolding themselves, in highly unexpected ways, during the
weeks that followed; for arrived in Charles Street, Fanny, looking out of the window inquiringly, since it didn't feel at all
like the entrance to Claridge's, was about to ask Griffiths why
he had brought her there and tell him to go on, when in the
silence of the Sunday evening street she heard sounds of music,
and with astonishment realized that they were coming out of
her own house.

Manby heard them too. From her seat in front she half
turned to her mistress in a movement of surprise. Griffiths too
heard them and was surprised, looking inquisitively at the
shrouded windows. But Griffiths, unlike Manby, was pleased
as well as surprised, for he hated the butler, and scented trouble
for him.

"Why——" said Fanny uncertainly, staring up at the first
floor, where the drawing-room was, and also, apparently, the
music. No light, however, showed anywhere. All was dark and
shrouded.

Manby came round to the door. "Does your ladyship wish
to get out?" she asked.

"Yes, I think so," said Fanny; and did get out, and having
found her latchkey opened the front door, and switched on the
lights.

"*Well*," she said, standing still and staring round her.

The hall was full of coats, and jackets, and scarves, and
hats, and galoshes. Evidently there was a party, and equally
evidently, as she could see from the sort of garments piled on
the chairs, it was a servants' party. Having heard she was out
of London for the week-end, and anyhow knowing she was

established at Claridge's, her servants were seizing the opportunity to misbehave—her servants, whom she had taken for
granted were devoted to her, and wouldn't dream of doing
anything behind her back which they wouldn't do openly.

She was shocked. She would have supposed the elderly ones
were too elderly for this sort of thing, and would keep the
younger ones in order. She didn't know how young the girl
was the butler, till then a widower, had married lately. It was
this girl, itching for a bit of fun, who had corrupted her doting
husband.

The party was necessarily rather cramped, because the front
of the house had to continue dark, and only the back rooms
could be used—the library downstairs, and upstairs the hinder
part of the drawing-room. Also it was Sunday, and in spite
of the example of their betters, most of them wouldn't dance
that day. But for all that it could be a lively party. There
could, for instance, be music. Nobody found fault with music.
And it was arranged that before supper, which was laid in the
library—none of your basements and servants' halls when there
was a chance of being upstairs—there should be sacred music
in the back drawing-room where the piano was, and after
supper more music, but less sacred, because after supper, as the
butler knew from lifelong attendance on the suppers of the
rich, and his young wife with the sparkling eyes knew too,
from instinct rather than experience, it wasn't natural to be
sacred.

So just at the moment when Fanny came and stood
astonished in the hall, the rich sounds of an enormous bass
voice singing a song called *Nazareth*, which treated of a suitably pre-supper subject, came rolling down the stairs, accompanied not only by her piano but by a clarinet and a
happy-sounding chorus of other voices, women's as well.

> *Though poor be the chamber,*
> *Come ye, come and adore—*

roared the bass, dominating, almost drowning the other voices.

"How much they're enjoying themselves," thought Fanny,
unable not to smile at such gusto, and for a moment envying
the glorious refreshment it must be to let oneself go so
thoroughly.

Still, glorious and refreshing as it might be, it was an outrage, and showed how the best servants, servants who had

been with one for years, couldn't in the long run do without
a man over them. If Job had been there, they never would
have dared give a party without permission, even if they knew
he were at Claridge's, even if they knew he were much farther
away, out of the country, at the end of the world. In her
drawing-room too. Unforgivable, that was. All her pretty
cushions. They took advantage of a woman. They banked on
her kindness. But one had to be friends with one's servants,
Fanny said to herself, frowning and perplexed. One couldn't
live in a house with other human beings and not be friends.
Besides, they were always so nice to one, so really charming;
how could one not be nice and charming in return?

She stood looking round uncertainly, while Griffiths, without being given orders but determined the butler shouldn't
escape what was coming to him, cut off her retreat as much
as he could by bringing in the luggage, and immediately driving
off to the garage. What Job would have done, she knew,
would be at once to go upstairs, fling the drawing-room door
open, and thunder, "Get out." But it wasn't in her to thunder,
and she hadn't the heart—or was it that she hadn't the courage?
—to spoil their party by the dreadful shock of her sudden
appearance. She could see herself standing in the door,
Nazareth shrivelling away into silence, and all the eyes and
mouths round O's of horror.

No, not for her these dramatic interruptions. Besides, her
own embarrassment would be too acute. What she did might
be weak, but it was at any rate sensible, for seeing through the
open library door tables loaded with food, she went in, signing
to Manby to follow her, sat down, and began hungrily, for she
was half starved, to help herself to her own oysters.

Shirker, shirker, whispered her conscience; but how much
better be a shirker and have some food than, with nothing
inside her, go up and put poor Soames to really agonizing
shame before his guests. To-morrow would be time enough to
do what there was to be done; to-morrow, if only she could
think in the night what the proper steps were, she would take
them. And meanwhile what a comfort it was to get something
to eat.

> *Though poor be the chamber,*
> *Come ye—*

roared the bass above her head.

"Come along, Manby," she called, seeing her still standing in the hall. "Now's your chance."

Manby did go in, but only to say she would lock her lady-ship safely in the room, while she went upstairs to put a stop to the shame and disgrace going on there.

"You'll do nothing of the sort," said Fanny. "Sit down and eat something. You must be nearly dead."

And stretching out her arm she caught hold of Manby's, pulled her on to the next chair, and told her she couldn't believe she wanted to be a kill-joy.

"Kill-joy, m'lady?" repeated Manby, boiling over with just indignation at the goings-on over her head.

"It's much better to eat oysters," said Fanny, pushing a plate of them towards her.

"Now then, which of you's been doing the dirty on us and got in here first?" the butler, who didn't yet feel guilty because he didn't yet know he was found out, inquired of his crowding guests an hour later, when they trooped into the library and saw the used plates and emptied champagne glasses.

By that time Fanny, who had gone up the back way piloted by Manby, was in bed. "Do you think," she had paused to whisper on the way up, turning to look down doubtfully at Manby on the stair below, all her confidence in her servants shattered, "any of them will be there, too?"

"Where, m'lady?"

"In my bed."

"Oh, m'*lady!*" murmured Manby, scandalized; but not at all sure in her heart of hearts, seeing how much had happened already, that it mightn't turn out to be true.

§

It wasn't, however, true. No one was there; not even Job. Her mind, busy with what was happening downstairs, had no time to think of him, and unthought of he was powerless to worry her.

She stood watching Manby going round deftly twitching the dust-sheets off the furniture, putting a match to the fire, fetching her special bed-linen from the wardrobe-room next door and making the bed—trying to decide as the sounds of revelry from the library reached even up to her bedroom, whether she weren't a weak skulker not to go down and put a stop to it, or an unusually kind, nice woman. Probably a skulker. She didn't know. But what she did know was that the poor things were going to have an extremely unpleasant time next morning, and might as well enjoy themselves while they could.

For the entire staff, except Manby and Griffiths, would have, she supposed, to be dismissed. They were all in it, and all would have to go. All, too, probably had widowed mothers or paralysed fathers to support, which was what made it difficult and dreadful. Where would they go? How would they pick up a livelihood, when the reason for their going was known?

Poor things. Still—that supper. And the new cushions in the drawing-room, with the lovely, rare Chinese silk on them, spoilt by the grease she knew her menservants put on their heads.

Indignation flamed within her when she thought of the supper and the cushions. It flickered and went out when she remembered the comfort she had got out of the supper, while as for the cushions, Soames would probably see that they weren't used. But how awkward it was, first to flame up and then so quickly to flicker out. If that was what her indignation was going to do to-morrow, how would she be able to administer justice? Suppose somebody began to cry, for instance, would she still go on fiercely flaming? And if she didn't, if she simply let them all off, what would it be like, living on with a houseful of servants she didn't any longer trust?

Manby put a nightgown and slippers to warm in front of the fire. Fanny watched her, some lines a German suitor used to insist on bringing to her notice, passing through her mind:

Denn die Frau bedarf der Leitung
Und der männlichen Begleitung.

Could they be true? She had laughed at them then, and he had told her quite threateningly, for he regarded being turned down as an insult and if she had been a man would have called her out, that she would live to remember his words, and acknowledge he was right.

Well, she had lived to remember them, and did acknowledge there were occasions—he had meant permanences, and that was where he was wrong—unprecedented occasions like this one, when there really was something in them. A woman did sometimes need help; not guidance, not constant company, but

help. And not so much help, either, as trouble taken off her
hands. Job, now, would have been the very man for this—
directly her thought went in his direction, he seemed to leap
to her side, as if she had called him—but as he was out of the
question she must think over her friends, and see which would
be best for taking the wretched business on his shoulders.

George Pontyfridd? Perhaps. But he was never back in
London till Tuesdays, and even if he were, would probably
advise letting off all round. That was all very well, but he
hadn't got to live with a lot of sinning servants. If she did
let them off, how difficult afterwards not to distrust them, and
how difficult for them, having been let off, not to cringe.

Poor things. No; it would be too painful for everybody.
George wouldn't do. She needed somebody more sensible than
George. Who, among the men she knew now, would think
it a privilege to be asked to help her? Not one of them, she
felt in her bones. The present generation of men friends weren't
friends at all, but rather just acquaintances, and she must go
back into the past to find somebody who, because of the past,
would be glad to do something for her. Perry Lanks, perhaps?

Of course. The moment Lanks occurred to her, she knew
he was the very man. She hadn't seen him for years, but that
didn't matter—she felt just as affectionately towards him as
she used to in the days of the secret chess lessons. And he
would be rested by now, have had time to get over that tired,
patient feeling which appeared to overcome him towards the
end. Besides, he was a lawyer, and would know the ins and
outs of everything—rather a grand lawyer, perhaps, for this
sort of thing, but being her friend he wouldn't mind, for once,
condescending a little.

She could think of no one more exactly right. She would
ring him up the first thing in the morning, and tell his butler
to ask him to come round the minute he got back from the
country. For he too would be in the country over the week-
end, though, being so busy, he would be sure to come up very
early on Monday.

Yes; Perry was the man, she thought. Dear Perry. She
hadn't properly appreciated him in those days, but she was
wiser now.

And having arrived at this decision, she let Manby undress
her and tuck her up in bed, where, comforted, she at once went
to sleep.

§

But much water had flowed beneath the bridges of Lanks's life since he used to frequent Fanny. He wasn't the same man. Up and up he had gone in his profession, till he was now almost spectacularly eminent, earning so much that he had merely smiled when they offered him the Home Secretaryship. A dry, calculating man, roused only once from reality into seeing visions and dreaming dreams, soon after Fanny dropped him he had begun applying himself solely to getting richer. It rapidly became the one thing that interested him. Absorbed in it, and in the agreeable knowledge that every day he was better off than the day before, he had lost even the recollection that there were such things as love and dreams.

Therefore, when Fanny rang up, he couldn't imagine at first who she was.

It was his practice to go down to the country, where he had a week-end cottage, on Friday evenings, and come up on Sunday evenings so as not to be rushed getting to his work, and he was at breakfast in Montague Square alone, his wife being of those who breakfast in bed, when the call came through.

The parlourmaid—he kept no menservants except the chauffeur, because women didn't drink whisky—appeared and said, "A lady to speak to you on the telephone, Sir Peregrine."

He gazed at her over his black-rimmed pince-nez in surprise that she should imagine he would take any notice. Never did he go to telephones. At his chambers they came to him, in the shape of junior clerks with messages, and at his two private houses they were no concern of his.

"The lady says it's urgent," faltered the parlourmaid, not liking that look over the top of the black-rimmed pince-nez. Servants were apt to falter in his presence. He was the sort of master who asks what has become of the rest of the ham.

"Give a name?" asked Lanks, resuming his reading of *The Times*.

"No, Sir Peregrine."

"Then go and get one."

But before she was through the door he got up, threw down *The Times*, and saying to himself, "This, I suppose, is where a decent wife would come in, if there were such a thing," went himself. It might be a new client—beset as he was with clients, he yet wished for more, owing to the agreeable sensation of growing richer—a wealthy client, who having had no answer from his chambers, where the lazy junior clerks hadn't probably arrived yet, was ringing up his private address.

"Yes? Sir Peregrine Lanks speaking," he therefore said urbanely.

"Oh, Perry, is that you?" urgently answered the voice at the other end.

Perry? Nobody called him Perry. Not to his face, anyhow. When he was a boy people used to, and one or two women later; but nobody had for a long time. His wife called him Dragon. She was so silly that she didn't even know it made him angry. "Now Dragon," she would say, shaking a finger at him, "now Dragon, don't be such a *naughty* Dragon." Lamentable.

"Who is it speaking, please?" he asked, much less urbanely.

"Why, it's Fanny. And I'd be so grateful if——"

"Fanny?" he interrupted, not urbanely at all. "And who, pray, may Fanny be?"

"Oh, Perry—how *can* you ask who, pray, may Fanny be?" cried the voice indignantly. "Are you pretending? Or are you cross because it's so early?"

"Do you mean——" Lanks hesitated, a bleak light dawning on him—"do you mean Lady Fanny Skeffington?"

"Lady Fanny Skeffington!" mocked the voice. "Well, I suppose you've got somebody standing beside you listening to what you're saying. But I haven't, darling——" years since anyone had called him darling, and it seemed to him simply grotesque. "Perry, I'm so *bored*, so limitlessly *bored*. Do come and tell me what to do. As soon as you possibly can. Be an angel and come round directly—before I have to go down and face them."

Face them? Face whom? Had she run through her money, and got bailiffs in the house?

The cautious man, however, wasn't going into that on the telephone. Nor could he really suppose it was bailiffs. Skeffington, he now vaguely remembered hearing, had lost all his money in some wildcat scheme in Mexico, but hadn't he settled a very handsome sum on her after the divorce? It seemed to come back to him that he had. Yes, he was certain of it; and it wasn't possible that she had got through a fortune like that. Therefore he was pretty sure it wasn't bailiffs who were worrying her; but that she was genuinely worried appeared evident, and after all, once upon a time——

Faint memories of that dead *once upon a time* came drifting back to him—rather fragrant, like the scent of roses to nostrils that have long been dry, and rather sweet, like the sound of music to ears growing hard of hearing.

"Very well," he said. "I'll look in on my way to the Temple. In about ten minutes. Charles Street still, I suppose?"

"Yes, Charles Street. Angel——"

But he hung up the receiver.

Annoying, thought Lanks, standing a moment by the silent telephone, pinching his lower lip between his finger and thumb —a characteristic action placed abundantly on record by Low, *Punch,* and similar institutions—annoying, and quite silly, to have to renew acquaintance with Fanny. He had no time for renewals, reminders, resurrections. Dead is dead, and should never again be stirred up. Also, she had been very tiresome at the end, he remembered, his memory getting clearer every moment. Though it was so many years ago, he could remember how tiresome she had been, holding him by her loveliness, once the first worship was over, while at the same time not taking the smallest trouble to be adequately intelligent. A man wants a woman to be intelligent as well as lovely, once the first surprise of headlong adoration is past; and she could have been quite adequately so—see how quick she was, till she got tired of it, at learning chess. Her brains, he remembered thinking, had been definitely good for a woman, if she had chosen to use them; she could have been an almost perfect mate, if she had chosen to be one. But she wouldn't use her brains, and she wouldn't be a mate. He had hung on far longer than was dignified, in the hope that he would be able to influence her—hung on, indeed, till she herself sent him packing, if such a phrase could be applied to a removal so gentle. Too much beauty, she had had; too much of the power beauty gives. She couldn't be bothered to think. Like any harlot, she lived just in the present, and on her looks.

Well, her looks would be gone, and only the tiresomeness left. Women didn't grow less tiresome with age, but more tiresome. Their defects of body and mind, like the stones of a badly-made road, worked gradually through to the surface. He didn't want to see her. It was the last thing he desired. Yet——

Yes; that was it: there was a Yet. For, still standing by the telephone in the gloomy hall, and still pinching his lower lip, he was obliged to acknowledge that there was another side to all this. Didn't he, after all, owe Fanny something? And wasn't it what he once would have called a rather beautiful debt? Because nothing was more certain than that she had brought love into his life for the one and only time, and had brought it in violently. Extraordinary as it now seemed, there was no doubt that he had very violently loved her; and to love violently,. to love with such rapture that one entirely forgets self, does exalt a man, does catch him up to heights infinitely beyond where he had ever been before, or ever will be again. And some words he couldn't immediately place came into his mind from somewhere remote, in connection with that brief period of pure worship, the period before he began to criticize and notice her faults—*Therefore with angels and archangels and all the company of heaven.* . . . Where had he read them? Where had he heard them?

Curious, thought Lanks, pinching his lower lip harder; helped by Fanny, he certainly for a few weeks had dwelt in very high places.

And being a scrupulously fair man, he asked himself whether, then, this being so, he ought to grudge going round to Charles Street for a few minutes in return.

§

He went. Calling for his hat and coat, he got into his waiting car and went; and during the short drive many things came back to him, and he was quite glad, disliking debts as he did, that he was perhaps, by giving her good advice, going to clear off this one.

But when the well-remembered door was opened by a pale, unkempt young man in shirt-sleeves, who seemed to be in the very middle of a bad attack of nerves, his first fear came back to him that she had run through her money, and bailiffs were indeed in the house.

The impulse to do something in return for the angels and archangels received an immediate check, for few things are more disagreeable to a man than for a long-forgotten love to reappear and want to borrow. It degrades her. he will tell himself, accounting in this way for his reluctance to lend; it smirches what might still, in places, be a pleasing memory, with mercenariness.

Lanks felt this so strongly that he would have turned round and gone away again, leaving the dishevelled servant to think what he chose, if the butler—he recognized the butler, distinctly run to seed now and puffy about the eyes—hadn't come hurrying out of the room Lanks knew was the library, pulling on his coat as he came.

"Yes, sir? Oh, good morning, Sir Peregrine," said the butler, startled when he saw who it was. Sir Peregrine had dropped out of the Charles Street life many years before, but he was still quite recognizable. Older, of course. Drier. Grimmer. More imposing. But still quite recognizable.

"I have an appointment with her ladyship," said Lanks stiffly, who considered the butler's puffy appearance and twitchy manner did the house little credit. Bailiffs or no bailiffs, a butler shouldn't lose his nerve.

"Indeed, sir. Oh yes, sir. Yes, Sir Peregrine," said the butler—like the young man in shirt-sleeves, obviously nothing but nervous wreckage.

"Is anything wrong?" asked Lanks, handing over his hat and coat, and looking round the hall for signs of bailiffs.

"Wrong, sir? Oh no, sir. No, Sir Peregrine."

"Is her ladyship in the drawing-room?"

"I haven't seen her ladyship this morning, sir. I believe the maid said she——"

"Then I'll wait in the library, while you send up word I'm here. Pray do so immediately, because I haven't much time."

And before the butler could stop him, Lanks, who knew every inch of the house, had walked across the hall, pushed open the library door, and gone in.

There a sorry sight met his surprised eyes. Hardly ever was he now surprised, but that Fanny should give this sort of party certainly did take him aback. The room, which he remembered so orderly, so austere even, with its beautiful dark panelling and tiers upon tiers of books, was messed over with the remains of what appeared to be a particularly uproarious supper-party. A small troop of anxious-looking servants, maids and men, were trying, in apparently frantic haste, to clear the mess away, and after one alarmed glance at him didn't stop when he came in. On they worked, sweeping up cigarette stubs and ashes, hurrying out with trays of dirty dishes, scrubbing stains from the rugs, gathering together pieces of broken glass, and filling baskets with the trampled remains of crackers.

Crackers? Lanks couldn't believe it, and put on his black pince-nez to have a closer look. Yes, crackers. Impossible, somehow, to connect Fanny with crackers.

The unhappy butler, hovering behind, said nothing. Not for him ever again in that house, he felt, to say anything. His hour was come. He had hoped against hope, trusting in Fanny's mercy; but when he saw Sir Peregrine, now such a celebrated gentleman in the Law Courts, and was told that he was there by appointment, he knew without a doubt that doom was upon him. And, like most husbands, since Adam began it, he told himself it was all his wife's fault.

"Well, I can't wait here," said Lanks, turning away, his thin-cornered mouth drawn down further even than usual. "I'll go up to the drawing-room."

But there again was confusion—at least, in its back half. He stood in the front half, which seemed to have escaped the full blast of the party, and looked on sardonically, his hands in his pockets, while more servants desperately smote cushions into shape and swept carpets.

But why were they all so much frightened and in such a frantic hurry? Had Fanny sunk as low as the sort of party which rouses the attention of the police? This, rather than bailiffs, was the possibility he was now inclined to consider, and he was turning it over in his mind with distaste when Manby appeared in the doorway, and by her mere appearance put it to flight. Manby, grown old; Manby, so quiet and respectable that no suspicion of evil could continue in her presence; Manby, incapable of being the servant of anyone whose conduct was open to question.

He was ashamed of his base thoughts; and when she said, as composedly as if she had seen him last only the day before instead of eighteen—positively, it was eighteen—years ago, "Good morning, Sir Peregrine. Would you kindly——" he interrupted her by going across and warmly shaking her hand, and asking if she were well. His own servants wouldn't have recognized him; but then in Wilton Crescent there had never been even a memory of love.

"Yes, thank you, Sir Peregrine. I hope you are well, too, sir," said Manby politely. "Would you kindly——"

"You still remember me, I see," he interrupted her again, pleased, though he couldn't have told why. Or was it because she went together in his mind with the one period of his life when nothing was of the least account but love? *Therefore with angels and archangels and all the company of heaven.* . . .

"Oh, yes indeed, Sir Peregrine. Would you kindly go up to her ladyship's sitting-room?"

§

The familiar room. He felt that he might presently be going to play chess again by the fire, that face of heavenly loveliness bent over the board close to his. Years dropped off his shoulders. Back he seemed to be walking, straight into his vanished youth, his vanished love. And there was Fanny——

No; that was just it; there wasn't Fanny.

"Good God," thought Lanks, as she turned round.

She came quickly towards him, holding out both hands. She was so glad to see him, so much relieved, that she entirely forgot the eighteen years. And having dressed in a hurry so as not to keep the busy man waiting, besides being too deeply absorbed in her worries to bother, her make-up had been dashed on rather than put on, with the result that even she, if she had had time to look at herself carefully, would have considered it was queer.

"Good God," thought Lanks; and the company of heaven fled in confusion for ever.

"He took both her hands, because when two are offered it is the only thing you can do, but his hold was limp.

"Perry. How kind of you," she said, smiling up at him—immediately, however, adding with a sort of inquiry, as she saw his expression and felt the half-hearted hold on her hands, "Perry?"—as if she suddenly wasn't quite sure of her way, and had to grope a little.

"My dear Fanny, how do you do?" he said.

"Just the same inside," was her quick answer, drawing her hands away. She wasn't accustomed to having them held limply, and didn't care about it.

He took no notice of this answer, because in it he scented

imminent tiresomeness. She might be just the same as ever inside, but without the testimony of a matching outside, of what use was it? He wasn't, however, going to discuss that.

"Please tell me in what way I can be of service to you," he said, looking at his watch.

"You mustn't bother if you are busy," she said, resenting the watch.

"I have a few minutes to spare, and you wished me to come," was his patient reply.

Patient. Still, then, patient. No woman likes it, when a man is being visibly patient. She remembered how visibly patient he had been towards the end of their friendship. Now here he was, patient all over again.

She was annoyed. And she wondered, noticing the thin line of his mouth, whether its corners used to turn down as sardonically in the old days. She couldn't remember their doing that. Indeed, she was sure they usedn't to. And if that was the effect success had on a man, then she didn't think much of it.

And Lanks, reflecting how wise were those who refrain from meeting again once years have separated them, said, "If you will tell me what it is I can do for you——"

"Yes. I'm very much worried. It's the servants," she told him; for now that he was there it seemed silly not to let him help her, in spite of her impulse to ask him to go away, and leave her to manage somehow for herself. And she added unexpectedly, putting out her hand, one hand only this time, to which he behaved as if it weren't there, "Don't let's quarrel, Perry. I feel as if we were rather quarrelling inside."

"The servants?" said Lanks, picking this word out from among the others. He had no wish to go into what she might be feeling they both were doing inside; and if it were only because of servants that she had brought a busy man out of his way, he was severely of the opinion that she had no sense of values. But then, she never had had any. Always the shadows, she had been after, and the substance thrown away. When it came to his turn to be substance, he too had been thrown away. Foolish woman. However, fortunate man.

"Come to the fire, and I'll tell you," she said, going to it herself, and sitting as close to the blaze as possible. She was cold; cold right through—as if the world were full of only ice and strangers. Many and odd were the tricks Time played on helpless human beings, she was discovering these days, but surely quite the oddest was the way it turned one's loves into strangers.

He followed her, but he didn't sit down. He stood leaning against the chimney-piece, pinching his lower lip, waiting for her to explain; and as she looked up at him—being new at the business of growing old, she hadn't yet become aware that a woman who has reached that state should never, from a low position, look up at someone standing above her—he noticed the pouches under her eyes, and wondered if she realized they were there. Not that it interested him. It wasn't of the least consequence, whether she knew about her pouches or not. But once a woman has them, what waste of time for her to assure people she is the same as ever inside. He noted, however, as he scrutinized her, that the ruin wasn't yet quite complete; melancholy vestiges of beauty did still remain—pathetic left-overs, such as the unaltered purity of the line of her nose, and the shape, so potentially intelligent, he used to think, of her brow. These, though, were only regrettable reminders of what her face used to be, and made its present condition only seem worse.

"I wondered if you would send them away for me," she said.

"Your servants? I?" was all he could answer, so great was his surprise.

He stared at her with the same stiff distaste with which he had stared at the puffy butler. That he should have been brought round to Charles Street on such an errand, he, the busiest and most distinguished member of the Bar, really astonished him.

"Or——" faltered Fanny, dashed by his astonishment—"or if you would just stay with me while I do it, Perry? It's so *painful* having to send people away," she explained, leaning forward and looking up at him—those pouches again. "I've never done it before, and when it comes to nearly all of them——"

Never done it before! Seldom amused these days, this, if grimly, did amuse Lanks. Why, she was practised at sending people away. Her hand couldn't have lost its cunning. He dared say it was more disagreeable sending servants away than suitors, because the servants ministered to one's comfort, and the suitors after a time merely gave trouble, but such an adept as Fanny couldn't find it really difficult. Besides, hadn't she a secretary, if she funked it herself?

He asked her if she had, and she said Yes, but the secretary would hate it too.

"Haven't you a——"

He knew, however, that she hadn't a husband. Remote as he lived from the carryings-on of the world, walled in by work and never going out, he yet would have known if she had married again. It would have been mentioned in *The Times*. Turning over its pages on the way to the money-market news, the name would have caught his eye, for, after all, it had once been very much in his life.

And Fanny thought, looking at his mouth, "Hard man, hard man, how you have changed." If she had changed outside, he had changed both outside and in, which made it far more than double as bad. And for an instant a picture of his present inside flashed before her—an inside full of mouths, all turning down at the corners; and she wondered whether it hadn't really always been full of them, only they weren't visible because they were layered over by love.

Love. She looked up at him; he looked down at her. Was it credible, each was thinking, that they had ever loved? And in the expression of his eyes, appraising her so coldly, she saw suddenly for the first time quite clearly how she must now be appearing to other people. A week or two ago she had wept on seeing her face in the glass after a sleepless night and before she was made-up; now, after sleeping, after being made-up, she yet saw in his eyes, and through him in the eyes of the whole world, that her beauty was definitely finished and gone.

"Perry——" she said, forgetting the servants, forgetting why he was there, thinking only of the dark sea of her future across which she had somehow to sail, wave after wave, all by herself, into the gathering night, "Perry—I'm frightened."

"What—of a pack of servants, my dear Fanny?" he said. And he was going on to point out encouragingly, so much did he dislike the idea of perhaps after all having to send them away for her, that a woman of her breeding, of her spirit and character, shouldn't have such feelings, when she interrupted him.

"No, no," she said. "The servants are nothing compared to—compared to——"

Then as he stared at her with that pin-point cold gaze, she began clasping and unclasping her hands, and leaning forward said, "Don't you see—oh, Perry, *don't* you see how awful, how terrifying it is for somebody who has had everything, to be faced suddenly by nothing? For ever and ever nothing? And going to get worse every day?"

He was disagreeably startled. "My dear Fanny, nothing being nothing, it is incapable of getting worse," he said icily; for if her words meant anything, they meant what he had first feared: it was money she wanted. And money, offered and accepted, would disgrace them both, wouldn't it? Of course it would, he told himself firmly. The memory of what was once a great romance must never be debased by a thing like money.

"Oh, but it does, it can," she assured him, twisting her hands about, manifestly a prey to a good deal of emotion. Lamentable when elderly women display emotion, thought Lanks, watching her. Once there are wrinkles, only dignity is possible. And now she was saying the very word he had been dreading. "Bankrupt," she said, twisting her hands. "Bankrupt. More bankrupt every hour."

Now this, to Lanks's ears, was a most unpleasant word, and particularly objectionable in the mouths of friends. "My dear Fanny," he severely explained, "no one can become more bankrupt. A person being bankrupt is bankrupt. There are no degrees."

"Oh, aren't there!" she cried; and told him, with much emphasis, that there were not only degrees but that each degree you got to was worse than the one before. To which, this being more nonsense, all he said was, "My dear Fanny."

He looked at his watch, found he could give her five minutes more, and pinching his lower lip arrived at the conclusion that the supper-party, whose litter was disgracing the house downstairs, had been the last flare-up of improvidence. People, he knew, grew reckless when they were at the end of their tether, and flung away their remaining resources at the very moment when every shilling was precious; after which, as apparently was the case with Fanny, they expected their friends to get them out of their difficulties. Women especially behaved like lunatics with money, when they had no husbands to take it off their hands. If ever, he once again thought, for it was a thought which frequently in the course of his work occurred to him, there was a body of human beings who needed husbands, it was women.

And at the word husbands, a way out of his painful and threatening position illuminated him. "You must ask Skeffington," he said, in the decided voice of one who suddenly sees clearly. "Or, if you like, I will."

Skeffington? She paused in her rocking—during the last minute she had been rocking herself backwards and forwards on her chair—to stare at him.

"Ask Skeffington?" she said, staring. "Do you mean Job? Ask him what?"

"To help you. I understand he is no longer rich, but his advice would be valuable. My dear Fanny, he's the man to go to. You have, of course, no legal claim on him, but perhaps in consideration of having once been your husband—I am quite willing," he went on, as she continued to stare at him in silence, "if you don't wish to write to him yourself, to do it for you. I know it's many years since your divorce, and probably he has long ago formed other ties, but still——"

Fanny got up. Suddenly quiet, she walked to the window, looked out for a moment at the mews below, then walked back. As she turned round, he was taking out his watch.

"Perry——" she began; and stopped.

She had been going to say that the world seemed full of mis-understandings, and tell him how yesterday a woman thought she was a street-walker, and now here he was to-day thinking she wanted him to lend her money; but she stopped, not only because of the watch he kept taking out, but because she was afraid there was little use in words. Words, words; all the words in the world didn't get one a hair's breadth nearer anyone else's understanding, once there was no personal interest, once one had wrinkles, once one had lost one's looks to such an extent that one seemed to be a stranger. Better say good-bye to Perry. Better tidy him up finally, too, out of her life, along with Dwight, Conderley and Miles. But how warming—oh, how *warming* it would have been if, thinking she was in need of money, he had at once gladly wanted to give her some!

Well, never mind. He couldn't help it. He was what life had made him. And some of it was her fault, because, if she had married him, who knew but what the corners of his mouth mightn't be turning up to this day?

Very nearly she smiled at the thought; and he, seeing her expression lighten, felt slightly reassured. Besides, she was quiet, and a quiet woman is always better than a woman who isn't quiet.

He was reassured still more when she said, with that little

look of mockery he remembered, but which, so charming then, sat strangely now on her altered face, "Don't be afraid—I've still got enough to go on with."

"Then why, my dear Fanny, talk of being bankrupt?"

"Because I am. But not over money. I have quite enough of that, thanks to Job's settlements. There are other sorts of bankruptcies, though"—she went on; at which he took out his watch again, fearing further, if different, tiresomeness.

"Oh, Perry, I'm tired of that watch!" she exclaimed. "Don't look at it any more, please. I know you're in a hurry to keep appointments, and it was immensely good of you to come at all. I was an idiot to bother a busy man like you. I can manage perfectly really, with Miss Cartwright—about the servants, I mean. So please don't give it another thought."

She held out her hand. Entirely relieved now, he shook it almost warmly. Such a comfort when people are not, after all, going to make demands on one; and he was rather sorry, now that he knew she didn't need it, that he hadn't shown more readiness to help, instead of recommending Skeffington.

"Well, then, good-bye, my dear Fanny," he said thankfully. "I do happen to be rather specially busy to-day. But if ever you feel——"

"Oh, I shan't feel," she said, going with him to the door. "I shall act."

"Ah, yes. That, of course, is the right way. Quite like old times, isn't it?" he added, looking round him on his way out— almost genial, now that final escape was so close.

"Isn't it," said Fanny.

"Shall we play chess?" he asked jocosely, his eye falling on the chess-table, still in its old place.

"Let's," she smiled, ringing the bell.

At the door he paused. "Seriously, Fanny," he said, "if there's anything I can ever do——"

"Yes. Sweet of you," she thanked him.

Manby appeared.

"Well—good-bye, Fanny."

"Good-bye, Perry."

That was all.

VIII

§

THAT was all.

Staring at the shut door, on the other side of which Lanks
was running down the stairs like a schoolboy off work, she for
the first time suspected that Fate was bent on making a man
of her. Unpleasant, if you weren't a man; but what could these
knock-out blows one after the other mean, except that she was
to be forced to stand on her own feet, and face it like a gentleman that everything, given time, went?

If that really were so, the first thing she had better do was
at once to leave off trying to cling. Straws, they had turned
into, these men who used to be lovers; and deplorable as it was
that lovers should end as straws, it was even more deplorable
to try to cling to them. She wouldn't. She would be a man.
Though it certainly seemed great waste, if one had to end up
as a man, that one should have begun life as the opposite.

Collecting, however, her pride, her grit, her courage, her
spirit—those attributes of hers Lanks had bid her remember,
attributes which she, who longed for cosiness, and the curtains
drawn, and nobody worrying, would so much rather have left
to real men—she crossed to the writing-table, picked up the
telephone, and began her career of virility by getting down to
business.

Her business, at that moment, clearly was the servants.
"Put me through to Miss Cartwright, please——" Something
had to be done about them, and at once. Lanks, she would
leave to God; for there was nothing like leaving people to God,
Fanny knew, who had thus left many in the past, and they
hadn't at all liked it, if you don't wish to waste time feeling
bitter. She was determined not to feel bitter. She even went so
far in the contrary direction, while she waited with the telephone at her ear, as to make an attempt to send a parting
blessing, even if it were only a small one, after him who used to
be her darling Perry and now had become, and for ever would
remain, plain Lanks; but it didn't seem to be able to get under
way—"Oh, Miss Cartwright—what? It isn't Miss Cartwright?
Please find her, then, and ask her to come to the telephone"—
and she had to leave any blessing there might be of him to God
as well.

But if Lanks, and love, and loveliness, and all the rest of what in her present proud mood she called the caboodle, had gone out of her life, she didn't see why the servants should go too. The whole problem of who was to give them notice would be solved by not giving them notice at all. She would forgive them. Long before Miss Cartwright got to the telephone, she had quite decided she would forgive them. First admonish severely, even fiercely; then, having admonished, forgive. So simple, so easy, so pleasant, so, surely, natural, to forgive. Wouldn't she too have been tempted in their place to get up to larks if the old cat—she forced out the horrid word, then amended it, her eye on Fate's intentions, to the old tom—were away? Anyhow, mercy, she was certain, was always best, and nothing would induce her to copy Job's disciplinary methods——

"Hullo, Job—back again?" she interrupted her thoughts to say aloud—the telephone was at her mouth, and down in the office Miss Cartwright had just hurriedly clapped it to her ear—for there he was, or seemed to be, by her side—and looking at her so reproachfully, poor Job, looking at her as much as to say, "But what about the disciplinary methods you applied to me? And since when, my Fanny——" at least he didn't call her his Fanny Wanny—"have you been sure mercy is always best?"

"Well, I can't go into that now," she said; again aloud, and again into the telephone, but not nearly so impatiently as she would have before Lanks's humiliating visit. After Lanks's icy, pin-point eyes, the eyes of a man only wanting to be gone, Job's persistence in turning up seemed to be almost a comfort. He, at least, liked being with her; though he too, she supposed, different as he would always be from the others, and always with a *cachet* peculiarly his own because of being the only one of them she had ever married, would of course be like the rest if he were to see her now——

"Yes, you would, Job," she insisted, on his appearing to protest; again speaking into the telephone.

§

These three remarks, obviously addressed to the ex-master of the house, greatly excited Miss Cartwright, whose imagination, stirred by Manby's pithy if reluctant answers to her

questions, had lately been playing round Mr. Skeffington a
good deal. What—*he* up there? What—Mr. Skeffington
actually in the *house?*

"I beg your pardon, Lady Frances," she said unsteadily,
her heart beating faster, "I didn't quite——"

"Will you send Soames and Mrs. Denton up to my sitting-
room?" her employer's voice came through.

"Oh, *now* they're for it!" Miss Cartwright exulted, flying
to the bell and ringing it so violently that a footman actually
came running. *He* was up there, he, the real master, sent for,
no doubt, in her extremity by his once-upon-a-time wife to put
order into the mess they were in. Manby had told her she
had been telephoning to someone early, before Miss Cartwright,
who spent the week-ends with her aged mother at Ponders
End, had got back. There was going to be an enormous row,
and a complete clear-out of the crowd of idle, insolent servants.
He was here to see about it, and the disgraceful orgy of the
previous night, if it had the effect of bringing *him* back, would
end by being a blessing.

For Miss Cartwright had come to the conclusion from
Manby's answers to her questions, answers always whispered,
always reluctant and having to be dragged out of her, but full
of pith once out, that the late master of the house must have
been exactly the sort of man she, Miss Cartwright, admired.
A just man; a hard man, perhaps—who, though, could be
just without being a little hard?—but a man soft as butter
when it came to women. They, Manby had given her to understand, hardly breathing it, her eyes respectably cast down,
were Mr. Skeffington's undoing. How much Miss Cartwright
liked men who were thus undone! She had never met any,
but was sure they existed; and here, twenty-two years too early
for her, one of them had existed in this very house. Twenty-
two years ago she was quite young. For dead certain she would
have been of those in whose hands Mr. Skeffington was
butter. And perhaps even yet—who knew?

Exulting and excited, she flew to the bell, and could hardly
hide her triumph when she told the footman to send her the
two chief sinners. She would personally give them her
employer's message. She wished to see for herself how they
took it, those two to whom she owed so many grudges. Soames
had always behaved as if he were her equal, and seeing that
she had started life from just about where he had, this naturally

annoyed her. Mrs. Denton, without the shadow of a doubt, left the cooking of her meals to the second, or even the third kitchenmaid, and seeing that in her barren existence the one jolly flesh-joy was food, this naturally annoyed her too.

Now, though, old scores were about to be settled, now the pair of them were for it. "You are both to go upstairs immediately to her ladyship's sitting-room," she sharply informed them; and when they had gone out, or rather quivered out, such pale jelly had they been reduced to, she eagerly prepared everything for their instant dismissal—chequebook open and ready, insurance cards stamped, certificates of length of service filled in, and the original characters they had brought with them, which were now no longer, after what they had done the night before, worth the paper they were written on, taken out of the safe.

Then she sat back and waited; and she waited and waited; and nothing happened. At first there was a silence, a motionlessness in the house, reminding her of Armistice Day, for the staff was holding its breath, expecting judgment to fall on it directly its two heads emerged from the room of Fate upstairs; but long before Miss Cartwright, waiting for her telephone to ring, had started wondering, and from wondering had proceeded to uneasiness, the house began to stir, to make faint movements of thankfully resumed work.

To these accustomed sounds Miss Cartwright listened in growing wonder. Had there been a hitch? Should she herself ring up, and pretend she thought it was her employer who had rung, so as at least to hear what her voice sounded like, so as perhaps to be able to guess from it——?

No, she hadn't quite got the courage to do that; and when at last, thoroughly disturbed, she went out into the hall to see if anybody were about looking as if he or she had been given notice, the first person she saw was Soames himself, in his shirt-sleeves, industrious and absorbed, arranging the morning papers on the usual table. Evident from his whole attitude, was it that here was a man who couldn't do enough; evident, too, was it—only Miss Cartwright found it impossible to believe—that here was a man forgiven.

"Is anyone upstairs with Lady Frances?" she asked uncertainly, not knowing what to think, her voice very different from the one with which she had ordered him into his mistress's presence half an hour before.

"No, Miss. Not that I know of, Miss," said Soames deferentially—pausing in his work to turn round politely.

Then *he* wasn't there, after all. She must have dreamed it. She must be getting Mr. Skeffington on the brain.

Chilled, confused, feeling that somehow there had been a terrible breakdown of justice, she turned away, and seeing Manby through the open dining-room door putting a bowl of roses on the table, she went in.

"What has happened?" she asked, shutting the door quickly and standing with her back against it so that nobody should come in. It couldn't really be true that Soames, that Mrs. Denton, that the whole lot of them, had been let off?

"Happened, Miss?"

Manby turned uncomprehending eyes to her; intentionally uncomprehending, because sometimes lately she hadn't altogether liked being plied with so many questions about her lady's marriage, and wasn't sure that she ought to have answered them.

"Isn't anyone upstairs?"

"Upstairs, Miss?"

"With Lady Frances? I thought I heard a gentleman——"

"That would be Sir Peregrine Lanks, Miss," said Manby, tranquilly adjusting a rose. "He came early, and left some time ago."

"And Soames? And Mrs. Denton? Aren't they going to be turned out?"

"Not this time, Miss. Everything has been overlooked this time," said Manby. "We're saints here," she added, bending over the roses so as to hide the concerned disapproval of her ample, but respectable, lips.

Miss Cartwright stared in silence. Such easy escapes from justice robbed her of speech. And that *he* shouldn't be in the house after all. . . .

"What we need is a man over us," she said, indignant with disappointment, when she could speak.

Manby thought so too. Manby had been thinking so for twenty years. But she wasn't going to say so to Miss Cartwright.

§

And now set in a trying time for Fanny, because it is uncomfortable living in a house full of people one has forgiven.

Only by taking herself firmly in hand, and keeping well before her eyes that it was her duty, by her presence, to prevent further backsliding, she was able to stick it out and resist the temptation to flee back to the irresponsibilities of Claridge's. She was so sorry for the poor pardoned things. She was so secretly apologetic for having come home unexpectedly, and caught them. A mistake, she realized, to come home unexpectedly, putting people in the crushing position of being forgiven. And she wondered how God, who had to forgive nearly everybody, could ever look anyone in the face.

She couldn't. She found herself avoiding eyes. When she gave orders, she evaded Soames's and Mrs. Denton's. She turned her head away when footmen flew, instead of walking, to open doors for her. She blushed at the anxious apologies of the head-housemaid for oversights so tiny that she hadn't even noticed them. Painful, painful it all was; and she lived in a continual acute embarrassment till, from various little signs, it dawned on her towards the end of the second week that they were all recovering, and that she was feeling their situation far more than they were.

And it was true that, after being hang-dog to excess, during the second week the staff, finding it against nature to go on being sorry indefinitely, did begin to brisk up, to the great scandal of Miss Cartwright, who considered this brisking-up altogether premature, and would have had them on their knees for at least a year.

"What *they* want," she said once more to Manby, slightly varying the formula, "is a man over them."

Yes; that was what Soames needed, what they all needed— herself included, Miss Cartwright privately added, irritably jabbing the blotting-paper with her fountain-pen. It wasn't her idea of a really satisfactory job, working for another lady. The other night she had had a wonderful dream, really such a wonderful dream, that a man *was* over her. The comfort of it! And so like Manby's description of Mr. Skeffington——

"Yes, Lady Frances? Is there anything I——?"

She jumped violently, for her employer had just walked in.

§

Her employer seemed now to be always walking in. Not enough to do, Miss Cartwright privately criticized, to whom

such of the idle rich as were women were becoming daily more
distasteful. She didn't mind gentlemen being rich. On the
contrary, she liked it, and would at any time have been happy
to meet a few; but women were never rich through their own
efforts, and always owed their wealth, as in this instance, to
some infatuated, soft-as-butter man. However, on this
occasion there was some reason for her employer's visit.
Usually there didn't appear to be any. Usually she just fidgeted
about, vaguely sketched the contents of a letter or two she
wanted written, glanced at her engagement list, inquired—that
was since the supper-party,—if Miss Cartwright didn't think
she had too many servants for one woman, and when she
received the cautious answer, "It's the house, really," would
look thoughtful, and say nothing. But this time she came in
to tell her to write out a cheque for twenty pounds, and Miss
Cartwright, taken unawares while thinking warm things about
Mr. Skeffington, drew the cheque-book out of the drawer with
hands which weren't quite steady—though why she shouldn't
think as warmly and as often as she chose about Mr.
Skeffington, who long ago had ceased to belong in any way
to her employer, she didn't know.

"What name shall I fill in, Lady Frances?" she asked, as
Fanny said nothing further. There had to be a name filled in.
Useless to write cheques that weren't in favour of somebody.
And she noticed, with some surprise, that a habit of impatience
with her employer was growing on her. Fatal, of course, such
a habit would be if one intended to stay. But she didn't intend
to stay. Directly she could find a nice post under a successful
business man she would be off. Offices, for her. Offices, and
their manifold opportunities.

"Oh yes. Make it out to Miss Hyslup. Miss Muriel Hyslup,"
said Fanny. "I've written a letter to go with it, and I'd like
you to take it round this afternoon."

"Certainly, Lady Frances."

"Only I don't know the address."

Miss Cartwright's pen paused. A man, a man, she thought.

"It's somewhere in Bethnal Green," said Fanny.

Miss Cartwright, doing her best to be patient, waited.

"But I don't know where."

Miss Cartwright resisted an impulse to lay down her pen,
and lean back with resignation in her chair.

"I went to it in the dark. Perhaps by daylight——" Fanny

broke off, struck by the expression on Miss Cartwright's face. Where had she seen it before, that look of impatiently patient resignation? Of course: Lanks. Now Miss Cartwright had got it. Distressing if she, Fanny, were, after all, only the sort of woman who caused resignation in others.

Miss Cartwright, to rouse her, for she appeared to have fallen into an abstraction, suggested that perhaps she could give her some clue as to where in Bethnal Green she might most fruitfully search for the payee, and Fanny, after gazing at her a moment collecting her thoughts, gave her the brother—a priest in a cassock, she said; explaining that everyone was sure to know where he lived, because he stood on chairs in the street and preached.

"You must see Miss Hyslup yourself, and bring back her answer. You could tell her—yes, please tell her that I've very *much* set my heart on its being Yes."

"Certainly, Lady Frances."

"And you had better go in a taxi. Wait a minute—what am I doing this afternoon? Perhaps Griffiths might——"

Miss Cartwright opened the engagement-book. "Mrs. Pontyfridd and Lady Tintagel to lunch," she read.

"Yes. They asked themselves. I don't know why."

"Mr. Pontyfridd at five."

"Yes. He wants to see me about something. I don't know what."

"And to-night——"

But Fanny wasn't interested in to-night; and she was just telling Miss Cartwright that as she would be in all day and wouldn't want the car, Griffiths had better drive her to Bethnal Green, for he knew the way at least to where the chair had been, when the telephone on the table rang, and Miss Cartwright, taking it up, the following brief conversation, of which Fanny only heard the half at her end, took place:

"Yes? Who is it speaking, please?"

"Hullo, darling."

"This is Lady Frances Skeffington's secretary."

"Hullo, then, *little* darling."

"Do you wish to speak to Lady Frances?"

"Clever girl, aren't you?"

"Will you leave a message?"

"What, out already? I'd hoped to find her in bed."

"Will you please give me your name?"

"I say, you're not black, are you?"

"Black?" repeated Miss Cartwright.

"Black?" repeated Fanny. "I don't know anyone called Black. Ring off."

Miss Cartwright, flushed, rang off. "And to-night——" she resumed, turning to the engagement-book again.

But this being Sir Edward Montmorency, K.C.M.G.—he was the one who came chronologically directly after Conderley, and had charmed Fanny by his good looks and irreverence,— arrived that very morning from the hot island he had been governing in the Pacific, it wasn't so easy to ring him off, or rather to keep him rung off.

On this hot island, and on others equally hot, he had been for years successfully and cheerfully governing innumerable blacks; cheerfully, in spite of an intense physical aversion from them, because it was his nature to make the best of things, and successfully, because at heart he was very much like them himself—a simple-minded man, easily disposed to gaiety, to breaking out, for no evident reason, into indications of high spirits, such as humming, whistling, and even *chasséing* along his various verandahs instead of walking. These ways, so like their own, endeared him to the blacks, and what with his popularity, and what with his power, he had got into a fixed habit of being God Almighty.

This is an awkward habit when, having reached the age-limit, a man is retired. At his club in London, they recognized only one God. To waiters, he would from now on merely be the bald gentleman by the window. With taxi-drivers, the future held disrespectful altercations; and no doubt many other troubles lay ahead of Edward. But on this first happy morning of his return, reunited, after twenty years of papayas for breakfast, to that incredibly perfect dish eggs and bacon, he was, to use his own language, as merry and fit as a flea. A bit of all right, little old England was, he had been thinking, taking a few blithe steps about his hotel bedroom while he waited for his Charles Street call to go through. Jolly to have just come in for a real, thorough pea-soup fog. Jolly to be anywhere so bitingly cold. Jolly to be going to see——

"Ah, there she is——" and dashing to the telephone he embarked on that conversation which began with Hullo, darling, and ended by his being rung off.

Unaccustomed to such treatment, unaccustomed, indeed, for

twenty years to any treatment except obsequiousness, Edward asked himself in amazement whether, then, a little scrap of a secretary-girl really imagined she could prevent his speaking to anyone he wanted to, and Miss Cartwright had hardly resumed reading out of the engagement-book when there he was, telephoning again.

"Yes? Who is it speaking, please?"

"The same good-natured fellow as before," said Edward, holding on to himself, because it was his first morning in England, and he didn't want to be cross. "Not changed a bit since we had our last little chat."

"Sorry, but you have the wrong number. There is no one here called Black."

Then Edward's blood got up. Black? Who wanted anybody called Black? Blast the girl, he thought, ringing up a third time; for after years of being God Almighty in hot places, his blood, at the least opposition, got up.

This time Miss Cartwright recognized his voice, and putting her hand over the mouthpiece said, "It's the person who wants Black again. He seems—what do you wish me to do, Lady Frances? Shall I disconnect the phone for a while?"

And Fanny agreeing, the next thing that happened, when the disconnection had had time to sink into Edward's outraged consciousness, was the arrival of a messenger with an enormous bunch of roses, and before she had done hanging over them in wonder at being once more sent flowers, of Edward himself.

For, sweating through the nights of the final months of his exile, he had been making plans for the future, and they included, indeed depended upon, marrying Fanny. Dear, darling Fanny; no longer what she was, of course, but at least white, at least not oily. After the fat native women, oily to the eye, and with a horrible slippery resilience to the touch, like hot snakes, marrying Fanny would have the quality of a cold bath. God, the cool women of England, thought Edward, tossing beneath his mosquito-nets—the cool, clean, fragile, delicate opposites of armfuls! He had come to hate armfuls—so black and big, so slippery. Only just at first they had rather amused him, the unlimitedness of them, the sheer supply; but for years, except in moments of desperation, he had kept clear of them, and could hardly at last wait for the day when, quit of the creatures for ever, he was going home to marry their exact contrary.

Yet no one but an optimist, a man of great natural exuberance, an ignorer of second thoughts, and used, during years of power, to getting what he wanted, would have supposed so easily that he was going to marry Fanny. In the old days she had obstinately refused to let him marry her, but this, though he well remembered it, cut no ice with him now, because those days weren't these days, and a woman will do things at fifty which she wouldn't at thirty, and often be jolly glad to. He had kept careful track of her. He knew all about her—how she had never gone in for any more husbands after her Jew, still lived in Charles Street, still, therefore, was well-off, had lately been so ill that she almost pegged out, and in a few days was going to celebrate her fiftieth birthday. So that by this time, having had lots of rope and presumably done all the silly things she was ever to have a chance of doing, she must be as ripe for settling down as himself. He was sixty. Neither of them had any time to lose. Each had reached an age at which, if one is going to marry, one had better do it at once. He saw no reason why he and she shouldn't. They might even do it on her fiftieth birthday, which would be distinctly *chic;* after which he would take up life with her prepared, for the rest of his days, to love and cherish what there was left to love and cherish, as a good husband, not as young as he was but not, either, as old as he was going to be, should. An admirable plan, Edward considered; a first-rate plan. Both would benefit. She would have someone to take constant and devoted care of her, and he would be able to pay his debts.

Therefore, full of purpose, declining to be obstructed by any secretary, beautifully, too; washed and shaved, as becomes a man who hopes he may soon be kissing, he arrived hard on the heels of his roses, and seeing Soames hovering in the inner hall, pushed past the footman and bore down, beaming, on his old friend. Splendid to see old Soames again. How easily he might have been dead, and a link broken. A bit bulgy, the old boy was, on the downstairs side of his sash, but quite identifiable.

"Hullo, Soames!" he exclaimed, genially advancing, pulling off his coat himself as he advanced so as not to waste a second. "Still with her ladyship?"

Soames, wondering who the jaunty gentleman could be, cautiously said he was.

"Good. Good. Nothing like sticking to the old post. Where

is she?'' And throwing his hat to the footman, which the young man, having been till recently a prominent member of his village eleven, deftly caught, he gave a pull to his waistcoat, a twitch to his tie, wriggled his neck more comfortably into his collar, rubbed his hands, and was ready for anything.

"I doubt if anyone is at home, sir," said Soames, stiffly.

He didn't care about that hat-throwing, nor about the way the new young fellow evidently enjoyed it. Her ladyship's hall wasn't a beer garden. Who could this lively, bald gentleman be?

For if Edward identified Soames, Soames didn't identify Edward. After being baked for years in the oven of the tropics and scorched for years in their pitiless suns, Edward was now as dry as a biscuit and as bald as a coot. Soames had never seen anyone quite so bald, except, sometimes, new-born babies. And knowing, in the way servants know most things, that his lady latterly had come to have a high opinion of hair, he considered it useless for a gentleman without any to try to see her. No good, thought Soames, no good at all, putting on spats and sticking a carnation in your buttonhole if you were a coot. The gentleman should have called sooner, before he had had such losses. Ten years ago, he should have called; perhaps fifteen. Kinder, now, to usher him out before his feelings got hurt, decided Soames; who accordingly began making movements in the direction of the outer hall, signing, at the same time, to the footman.

Edward became peremptory. "I don't want *anyone*. I want her ladyship. Go and find her," he ordered.

Soames, however, unused, since Mr. Skeffington's long-past day, to peremptoriness, ignored the order and merely made more movements and more signs.

Then Edward's blood began to get up, and he strode across the hall, himself pulling open the different doors and looking into the rooms.

Soames was scandalized. How dared the stranger touch her ladyship's doors? "Sir, sir——" he remonstrated, going after him. "Sir, sir——" he remonstrated more urgently, when the gentleman, finding the rooms empty, actually began going up her ladyship's stairs.

Shocked by such behaviour, not sure he oughtn't at once to call in the police, Soames went so far as to make a plunge forward and catch the mounting stranger by the arm—with

the most frightful effect on Edward's blood. What? This
worm? This worm by the merest chance white, instead of
black, and Edward with power of life and death over him,
daring to touch him, daring to try to stop his going up any
stairs he wished?

"Damn and blast you!" he thundered, violently shaking him
off; upon which Soames, who sometimes had rather felt the
absence of a gentleman's hand in that soft, lady-ridden house,
became meek as milk.

"What name shall I say, sir, should I be able to find her
ladyship?" he asked, a little out of breath, but definitely
deferential.

At this Edward, in his turn, was shocked—profoundly; and
hurt as well, feeling it ungrateful, somehow, of Soames, whom
he had spotted at once, not to do the same by him.

He paused. He turned. He stared. "You don't mean to
tell me," he said, "that you don't *recognize* me? You don't
mean to tell me that you don't *know* me, Soames?"

"Well, sir, I can't say——" Soames was beginning, when
the footman, who was new, who was still truthful, who was
kindly, and also who wanted to save his chief from unnecessary
running about, supposing it had slipped his memory stepped
forward and timidly reminded him that they both had seen her
ladyship going into the secretary's office a short time ago; and
before Soames had even begun to glare at the officious young
man Edward was off, straight as a dart down the right passage,
and making unerringly for the right door.

§

There, in the office, sat Fanny. But there sat Miss
Cartwright as well; and the day being dark and the room
darker, only his roses, on the table at an equal distance from
the two women and directly beneath the green-shaded office-
lamp, were lit up. Shadows everywhere else; nothing but
shadows; so that he, looking from one to the other of the figures
sitting opposite each other, was blest if he knew which was
which. One of them was Fanny; but which? Fatal if he made
a mistake. Fatal if he went and kissed—his idea was to begin
by kissing, just as, twenty years before, he had ended by
kissing,—the wrong one.

Therefore he stood uncertain in the door, and said nothing.

The two women gazed at him inquiringly. Neither showed
the slightest sign of ever having seen him before, so he got no
help from that. Fanny thought, judging by his clothes and the
flower in his coat, that he must be somebody's best man, got
into the wrong house and hunting in a hurry for the bridegroom.
Miss Cartwright only knew that he wasn't the man she was
expecting about the dining-room curtains.

Then Edward had a brain-wave. "Fanny *darling!*" he
exclaimed, not moving from the shadow of the door, taking
care to address them impartially, looking at neither in particular
but at both, as it were, on the whole—and how bright of him
this was, he felt, how almost like Solomon, for at once the one
who wasn't Fanny got up, picked up some papers, and
discreetly left the room.

God, what a close shave! thought Edward, drawing a deep
breath. Too awful if he had made for the wrong woman. The
right one would never, could never, have forgiven him. His
shirt quite stuck to him just to think of it. Well, he was all
right so far. The one still sitting at the table must certainly be
Fanny. A bit disappointing she was at a first glance, though
everything, except her hands, being in shadow, it wasn't really
possible to tell. Still, she did seem to have shrunk. Now why
should she have shrunk? he wondered, aggrieved. He hadn't;
quite the contrary. However, he mustn't mind. She was
Fanny, presently to be his Fanny, and he mustn't mind any
little alterations. What he did mind was that, like Soames, she
appeared not to recognize him. She soon would, though, he
told himself; and he went over to her determined and confident,
lifted her unresisting hand, kissed it with all the fervour of
happy reunion, and said with what he felt was immense tact
and presence of mind, "I would have known you *anywhere.*"

Fanny was too much astonished to speak. She stared at the
head bent over her hand. Who was this bald man? Yet, even
as she asked herself this, and while he was still bending, something in the voice, something in the shape of the shoulders,
something in the very feel of his fingers crushing hers, sent her
flying back through the years, and she only just stopped herself
in time from saying, with an incredulousness which would have
been rude, "You *can't* be Edward?"

Unnerved by her narrow escape, she got up—he helped her
solicitously and unnecessarily, but then Edward had never
been tactful,—thinking it better to be on her feet than sitting

down while a bald man she was afraid was Edward kissed her
hand; and the hand being still held tight, she thought the best
thing she could do with his, the most normal thing, was to
shake it.

So she shook it. "How do you do," she said, her eyes fixed
uneasily on the face she was afraid was Edward's. Inadequate,
she knew, such a greeting was to one who was once a dear
friend; but his being so bald did put a barrier between them.
She had had no idea that really all the time, beneath his charming wavy hair, he was so very much like an egg. She must
get over that before she could be natural. And suppose she
found it went further than his head, and he was bald inside
as well?

Alles Vergängliche ist nur ein Gleichniss, her German adorer
used to assure her; and suppose——

"Fanny," he exclaimed, seizing her other hand too, "don't,
don't say How do you do. Don't, don't tell me you've
forgotten me."

"But of course I haven't. You're Edward."

"*Your* Edward," he quickly retorted—again with the nippi-
ness, he felt, of Solomon.

She looked at him uncertain whether to laugh or cry. What
did one do with a man whom she had indeed often called her
Edward—one said so many silly things in one's younger,
warmer moments—and who, after not being her Edward for
innumerable years, turned up again, incredibly changed yet
assuring her that he still was hers? He rather gave the
impression, too, that he was thinking of kissing her. She hoped
he wouldn't do anything so immediately fatal. Not only would
she quite desperately dislike it and be unable to forgive, but her
instinct told her he didn't want to really.

"Yes, *your* Edward," he said, sure he ought to get on with
this quickly, and make hay while the sun shone. Was the sun
shining, though? Of course, affirmed Edward stoutly. "Always
and only yours, in spite of the way you sent me packing——"

"Well, don't scold me for that now," she smiled, trying to
get her hands away. He was holding them tight against his
chest, and she found she objected to his chest. "Besides, you
married quite soon, and lived happily ever after."

"Well, don't scold me for that now," he retorted, snappy
again. "And you can't exactly call it happy ever after, when
she ran away with another fellow."

"Unaccountable," smiled Fanny.

"Look here——" said Edward.

Things weren't going right. Considering he was doing his best, and had come prepared to go on doing his best for the rest of their joint lives, she wasn't helping much. What was the good of saying Unaccountable, in that sort of voice? It didn't help a man, for the woman he meant to marry to start mocking; and mocking him, of all people, who up to six weeks ago had had power of life and death over——

He made a great effort, and successfully choked down the upward tendency of his blood. This was no place and no moment, he knew, for it to do anything but stay quiet. Patience, patience; too much was at stake for him to let himself be put out. Probably the best thing he could do would be at once to kiss her. But he who had arrived determined to begin as he meant to go on, which was kissing, hadn't yet, somehow, got anywhere near it. The way she held her head away from him, so stiffly, so forbiddingly, made it difficult. And it wasn't as if it were the same head, either. No use blinking that; no use trying to fox himself that it was. Even in that badly-lit room he could see that it wasn't. And it put a man off to find a different head——

It put a woman off, too, Fanny was thinking; though she, empty of any plans in regard to him, would have taken his head as she found it if only he would let go her hands and not look as if he were trying to lash himself into love-making. What two elderly people, met again after many years, should do, she considered, was to sit down quietly together and chat—chat about their mutual friends, and who was dead, and why; chat about the climate; chat even, if they wanted to, about the European situation.

Edward, however, had no desire to chat. He was all for activity, for immediate steps in the direction he had set himself; and refusing to be daunted or baulked he pressed the two hands he was holding tighter, shifted them to the left side of his chest, and said, "Feel that? Feel that, you bad girl? Feel it thumping?"

But it wasn't thumping; and, if it had been, how discreditable to them both, she thought. A bald man of sixty, a dilapidated woman of fifty—unbecoming in the highest degree, she felt, that there should be any talk between them of thumping hearts.

"Oh, Edward!" she said—smiling, to hide how much concerned she was for both their dignities.

"Well, it is," he insisted. "And all because of you."

"Oh, Edward," she said again, not able this time to smile.

He must be stopped. Too unseemly such talk was. And worse than the talk was a look in his eye suggesting he was going to propose. Certainly he must be stopped. Nothing in the world, she well knew, could be more deeply insulting, sometimes, than a proposal. Did he then think she had fallen so low, was so entirely bereft of other interests and resources, let alone of decent pride, that she would accept anybody?

"Now listen, my girl," he said—how profoundly she objected to being called my girl, or bad girl, or any sort of girl,—"you usedn't to keep on saying Oh, Edward. What has come over you?"

"Age," said Fanny firmly.

"Age!" scoffed Edward, loosening her hands, but only to take her by the shoulders. He actually gave them a shake; and the depth of her objection to this was positively unplumbable. "Age? What rot! I would have known you——"

"Anywhere," nodded Fanny, very stiff in his grasp, her head held as far back as it would go. "I know. You told me so."

"And what about me, then? If you get talking about age, what about mine?"

"Ten years more of it," she said.

Then Edward again had to do what he could in regard to his blood. She usedn't to be like this. She used to be the greatest fun, besides being so lovely that you wanted to cry. In the old days there was none of this straining-away nonsense. She had been very fond of him, he could swear; and no wonder, after having had that chap-fallen old geyser Conderley hanging round so long. She had laughed and laughed, at all his jokes, at everything he said, and had nicknamed him her A.D.C. —which stood, she explained, for Adorable Darling Clown. Oh yes, she had. Adorable Darling Clown, she had called him. Should he remind her? By God, he would; he would remind her of everything.

"Let's get this clear," he said.

"I'd like to."

"You and I are both in the prime of life——"

"Oh, Edward!"

"You can say Oh, Edward as often as you like, but it's the fact. Don't you make any mistake about it."

"I suppose you want to cheer me up?"

"I don't want to cheer you up—I want to marry you," he burst out, gripping her shoulders and looking so fierce, for his blood refused to stay down an instant longer, that again she didn't know whether to laugh or cry.

Better laugh. Safest, always, to laugh. And poor Edward would really be too much crushed if she were to cry over him, and he began to guess the reason.

"What a thing to want to do," she therefore smiled, choosing laughter, while he, gripping her shoulders, got quite a turn, they were so thin. "My God," he thought, "there's nothing there to marry."

Then Soames came in—an angel of succour, was Fanny's view; blast him, was Edward's,—and after a slight hesitation, because for months past no door opened by him had opened on proximities, and he was taken aback that it should be the bald gentleman who had managed to get into one, said, recovering his balance, "Lady Tintagel and Mrs. Pontyfridd in the library, m'lady."

"Blast him," thought Edward, who had jumped away from Fanny just as if he had a bad conscience. Fanny, who never had a bad conscience, didn't move, except her head, which she turned to Soames. Throughout her life she had refused to be flustered by interruptions. Whatever she happened to be doing when a servant came into the room, she went on doing it; and the practice had invested her behaviour on these occasions, on these sometimes rather startling occasions, with a curious dignity, an air of rightness, of inevitableness, and therefore of propriety, which silenced conjecture.

"Very well," she said, dismissing Soames; and only after he had gone and shut the door, moving from where she had been standing.

What a relief to have got away from Edward. She went over to the looking-glass in front of which Miss Cartwright was accustomed to titivate, to see how her hair was getting on after the shake he had given her, tucking, as she went, a straying curl behind her ear. Always a little anxious now when a curl started straying, in case it should be one of Antoine's and end by dropping off on to the carpet, it was her habit to give the strayer a slight pull, and if the pull hurt to feel reassured;

but this time she didn't pull, because of Edward. Yet, on second thoughts, wasn't it rather because of Edward that she ought to pull? Face him with facts? Cure him of wanting, or pretending to want—which was so much worse,—to make love to her?

A heroic remedy, though; almost beyond her strength, she was afraid; for being comparatively new at these miserable substitutes, she was excessively sensitive about them. That being so, all the greater would be her heroism. But could she? Could she really bring herself to do anything so terribly humiliating? It would finish Edward, of course; rid her of him for good and all; but—could she?

"Fanny——" he began again, greatly cramped, this time, by the knowledge that he would have to be quick because of those women in the library, "Fanny——"

"Two of my cousins are lunching with me," she said, arranging her curl in front of the glass. "Will you stay?"

"Stay?" echoed Edward, amazed at such coolness. Hadn't he just told her he wanted to marry her? Hadn't she heard?

"Yes. And lunch," said Fanny.

The curl seemed to be hanging on only by a single hair. Should she rise to incredible heights of valour, give it a tiny tug, and let it drop off? It would glisten on the carpet; he was bound to see it. The other curls seemed to be very loose too. Of course, after being shaken. No woman whose hair is pinned on instead of growing on, should ever be shaken—not, anyhow, without notice, not without being given time to make provision against vehemence by extra hairpins. She was ashamed of Edward, at sixty, shaking her, Fanny, at fifty. Such boy-and-girlishness made her blush for him. He should look at himself in the glass. He should look at both of them, side by side, in the glass.

"Stay?" he repeated indignantly. "When I've just asked you to marry me, and haven't had an answer yet? Stay, and talk to a lot of cousins?"

"Two," said Fanny, busy with her curl.

"I'll be damned if I will," said Edward.

"That's a good way of refusing an invitation," she smiled into the glass.

"Yes, and now you show me a good way of accepting an invitation," he retorted, advancing on her from behind almost threateningly.

"Can I do better than copy you, and say I'll be damned if I will?" she smiled again.

"Fanny!"

He came up close, and seized her round the waist. She put her hand up quickly to her ear and gave a tug, then reached out and switched on all the lights.

The room blazed. Every nook and cranny in it was suddenly visible; every nook and cranny, too, in their faces, and the shining dome, like polished pink ivory, of his head. "Look," said Fanny, pointing at their reflections. "Do just *look*, Edward."

He wouldn't look. He didn't look. Why look? What was the good of looking? He knew what he would see, and had no wish to see it. "Fanny," he said, his arms round her, his face hidden in her hair—she could only wait now, holding her breath, for the shock to him if and when it began to fall off— "you shan't say horrid words like age and old about us; you shan't get into your head that you and I are anything but just beginning the best part of our lives. We'll have the most glorious time. We'll be happy and jolly. We'll go off to Monte Carlo—God, how I've ached for Monte Carlo, stuck away up to my neck in niggers! Bad girl. Naughty girl. It's high time your A.D.C. came and took you in hand——"

She winced and shuddered. She tried to shake him off. This stranger, this bald stranger, daring to touch her, daring to remind her of what, in her foolishness, she used once to call a good-looking young man. How infinitely more dreadful than curses was love-talk coming home to roost.

"Oh, Edward," she begged, "do stop talking nonsense, do look at us both—do just *look!*"

And he, before this insistence, gave way and raised his head and did look; and after the briefest glance, not at all liking what he saw, looked somewhere else, and the somewhere else happened to be an object, shining even more brightly than his head, on the carpet at his feet.

He stared down at it. Could it be——? Was it——?

Still holding Fanny with one hand he stooped, and with the other picked up the bright little thing.

"Yes," said Fanny, watching him in the glass. "My curl. Give it to me, please."

"Do you mean to say——" began Edward slowly, staring at the frisky, golden thing on his palm. But he broke off, too much dumbfounded to go on.

"Yes," nodded Fanny at his reflection. "I get all my hair at Harrods."

There was a silence. She had substituted Harrods for Antoine as more likely to be a place a man long buried in islands would have heard of, and stood watching the effect of her words.

He, well aware that he had got to a highly critical moment in his wooing, felt that nothing but a brain-wave now would save him. And sure enough, as he stood staring at the curl and she stood staring at his reflection, he had one; another one; in the nick of time. When first he got into that room, and things seemed touch and go, he had had one, and now when they were more touch and go than ever, he had another. After all, what could one expect at her age? Many a husband had had worse shocks than a curl coming off. A man didn't marry a woman of fifty for her hair. Only a fool, or a boy, would expect her by that time still to be all of a piece.

Gazing, therefore, at the curl lying in his hand, he screwed his lips into the shape and sound of a kiss, and then said with what even Solomon, he felt, would have admitted was immense tact and presence of mind, "Pretty."

She stared.

"Ah, pretty—*very* pretty," he said, gazing fondly at the curl. "Let me stick it on for you, darling. Have you got a spare hairpin?"

She couldn't speak.

Extracting one himself from another curl, which immediately fell to the floor—"Lively little lot, aren't they," was his admiringly affectionate comment—he began to get busy.

She stood like stone.

"Luncheon is served, m'lady," said Soames at the door, after another slight hesitation.

"Now don't move—don't move, Fanny," Edward cried, the hairpin between his lips while his hands busily adjusted and arranged. "This is a very delicate operation, you know. I can't have your cousins seeing you till—now *don't* move——"

She had been outwitted.

IX

§

THIS was the fifth of March. There was only one week more
before Fanny's birthday, and her two cousins, Martha Tintagel
and Nigella Pontyfridd, aware of this, after putting their heads
together had decided that something must be done to help her
not mind it. Being cousins, they knew exactly which birthday
it was; being women, they knew it would be painful.

So they thought, since nowadays she never went to see them,
they would ask themselves to lunch with her, and feel about
tactfully till they hit on what might give her pleasure. They
were inspired, they felt, by the purest motives. Their impulses,
they felt, were wholly laudable. In no way did they deserve
not to enjoy themselves.

Martha's idea was that it would be nicest to have a tiny
party down at Tintagel, where in strict privacy poor Fanny,
who of course didn't want now to be looked at much, could
be made to realize how little faces really mattered as long as
one's relations loved one. Nigella thought her own house in
Surrey would be better, because of being nearer and smaller;
you wanted something small, said Nigella, for an affectionate
party, and you wanted something near, so that when it was
over you could get away quickly. Both cousins wished to do
what they could to help Fanny; both acutely felt for her on
reaching a date so dreadful for one who has been beautiful——

"And I dare say thinks she still is," said Nigella.

"Perhaps," said Martha.

——as the beginning of the second half of a century. They
themselves, each in the quite early forties, had never been
beautiful, but merely manageably pretty women, yet they could
well picture what it must be like, this definite good-bye to
beauty, this stepping across, for good and all, into the ranks
of the Have Beens.

"And I'm afraid the poor darling *looks* rather like fifty, too,"
said Martha, sighing.

Nigella said she thought she looked more.

"Perhaps," said Martha.

Sad for one who had lived so radiantly, outdoing everybody
in loveliness, rolling in money—the Tintagels, owning a number

of unprofitable acres, had never been within measurable distance of anything of the sort,—and able at any time to play havoc with people's husbands,—the Pontyfridds, right up to Fanny's illness, had been apt to have words about her, Nigella finding it difficult to believe she wasn't still trailing George after her in her long, her densely populated, her for-ever-being-added-to train,—sad for such a one to have lost everything except the money, and now have nothing at all.

"You mean no children," said Martha; for it was Nigella who had thus been reflecting. Martha was the happy mother of the precise number of children the poorer peers prefer, two boys and a girl, and was wrapped up in them. Therefore, to her, the worst of Fanny's misfortunes was being childless.

"I was really thinking no husband," said Nigella, who was without children, but didn't mind because her heart was full to the brim of George. Therefore, to her, the worst of Fanny's misfortunes was being husbandless; and this was the worst of other women's misfortunes too, for a husband might (possibly) have kept her in order.

"I never understood why she didn't marry again," mused Martha.

"She used to say she didn't want to be tied up," said Nigella.

"Then," said Martha.

"Yes," agreed Nigella, "then. I dare say she's sorry now."

And Martha, who loved being tied up, and was sure she couldn't have stood five minutes on her own feet unassisted, sighed again, and said, "Poor Fanny."

Yet, though sure they were devoted to her, especially since her illness, and really concerned by the rapid disintegration, spiritual as well as physical, which seemed to have set in—for was not her behaviour lately, not wanting to see her cousins, shutting herself up at Claridge's of all places, very odd?—they couldn't help, deep down inside, feeling that here, somehow, was justice, here was payment at last being demanded for the rare and valuable goods handed over to her so lavishly, and now all consumed.

It was in Nigella's car, which had picked up Martha at Claridge's on the way to Charles Street, that the above short conversation took place. After it they fell silent, each wondering, in spite of herself wistfully, what it could have been like being so very beautiful, and each taking comfort by deciding that, on the whole, those who weren't were better off.

"In the long run," said Nigella aloud, having come to her conclusion.

"Yes. In the long run," said Martha, having come to hers.

No need to explain. Both knew exactly what the other meant. Strange how frequently now, in connection with Fanny, women used these words.

§

Filled, then, with warm intentions, with affection and with pity, the cousin by blood and the cousin by marriage arrived, only to find the cousin they had come to benefit intractable.

Nothing at all to be done with Fanny. From the first mention of her birthday she visibly shied, and from the suggestion of celebrating it in the family circle, either at Tintagel or at George's and Nigella's, she turned with such ill-concealed aversion that it was positively rude.

They didn't get to the birthday for some time because of Soames and his crowd, but even before that Fanny seemed to be having an attack, Nigella considered, of very bad manners. She came into the library, where they had been kicking their heels for ages, already in the grips of it, not saying a word about being sorry to have kept them waiting, and kissing them with unflattering abstractedness. She looked untidy too; her hair was all at sixes and sevens, and for the first time Nigella doubted its authenticity. Also, she hardly spoke. Conversation was most difficult, and was left chiefly, which was extremely wrong, to the two guests. To add to everything, when at last they had been given coffee and left to themselves, and Martha began explaining why they had come —very nicely and kindly, and taking great pains not to show anything like sympathy,—she instantly became obstructive.

"Please, Martha——" she exclaimed quickly, putting out her hand as though to stop her.

"But my sweet, how you must try to look at it is that it's wonderful to have lived so long," said Nigella.

"It isn't. It's bloody," said Fanny.

"*Darling*," murmured Martha.

"My *poor* sweet," murmured Nigella; and whether these murmurs were of sympathy, or of rebuke for such a nasty word, no one could have told.

This wasn't a good beginning. The visiting cousins felt it

wasn't, yet weren't going to let themselves be daunted so soon.
The receiving cousin knew it wasn't, but then she had just had
a series of shocks. Shocks or no shocks, though, Fanny didn't
like being Nigella's poor sweet; nor, very much, the way
Martha had said *Darling*, as if apologizing to her for her own
word. She dared say she did seem nothing to them now but
a poor sweet, but they needn't tell her so. As for bloody, she
stuck to it. What could possibly be more awful for a woman
who had walked in beauty, as Jim used to say, than to be
fifty, a wreck, and still in the same world as all the people
who used to know her in the days of her perfection? In the
same world, too, as Edward; as that Edward who then, on parting from her, had cried, and now, on parting from her, had
winked.

She shuddered at the awful recollection. She shuddered at
the narrowness of her escape from his blandishments. Almost
she had been touched by his attitude about the curls into
believing he really did love her for what she persistently, and
vaguely, called herself—a clownish, an incurably facetious love,
but still quite genuine. And as she crossed the hall to the library
door being held open for her by Soames, with Edward following
her in silence on his way out—she had marched out of the office
without a word or look, and he, feeling he had done very well
so far, was quite content to bide his time,—she wondered
whether perhaps he wouldn't be better than loneliness. Not a
very good alternative, but better than nothing if he really loved
her too sincerely to mind all those changes in her which she
minded so profoundly herself. At least she might think it over.
No harm in thinking it over.

And moved by an impulse of compunction for having walked
off so haughtily—one of those impulses which so often, in her
life, had ultimately made things worse for the other person,—
she turned her head to nod a grave good-bye, and caught him
winking at Soames.

Edward. Winking. Because of her. At her servant.

Both Edward and Soames saw that she had seen. Soames
stood petrified, looking down his nose, shocked beyond
measure, a man turned to stone. Edward was instantly aware
that he was done for. No woman could be expected to forgive
that. His high spirits, throughout his life apt to get the upper
hand, had got it now at a fatally wrong moment. Of all the
blasted fools——

"You don't *know* what humiliations are," Fanny said to her cousins with sudden vehemence, hot at the recollection of this scene. "You simply don't *know*——"

And Martha, who couldn't think what she meant, again said, *Darling,* and Nigella, who couldn't think either, said, My *poor* sweet.

Then Fanny made a great effort to thrust Edward and his wink out of her mind, for else she would never get through this business decently of lunching with her cousins; and sitting very straight and stiff in her high-backed chair, opposite that other high-backed chair, empty at the moment but liable, at the slightest thought of him, to become full of Job, she tried to say something about her birthday, which appeared to be what her cousins had come about, and behold instead she heard herself asking, so full was she of him and his wink, so desperately smarting, "Do you remember Edward Montmorency?"

They looked at her in surprise. Indeed they remembered Edward Montmorency. Nobody who had watched Fanny's career could have missed him. They themselves had watched it with bated breath—adoringly to begin with, and less adoringly later because of their husbands, but still with bated breath. From childhood they had been witnesses of the comings and goings in Charles Street, and in due season had therefore also witnessed the coming, and presently the going, of Edward Montmorency. A noisy man; conspicuous for his extreme good looks, and appearing to be in a perpetual condition of overpowering spirits. Not out of the top drawer. Hairy-heeled. Causing infinite astonishment to Fanny's friends that she should be able to endure him hanging round.

"I saw in *The Times* he was back," said Martha, mild but uncomfortable, for she couldn't see what he had to do with anything.

"Up to his ears in debt, they said," said Nigella.

"Oh?" said Fanny, turning to her quickly. And after a pause she said a second time, in the voice of one to whom much is made suddenly clear, "Oh."

"But what has that got to do with your birthday, darling?" Martha asked timidly; and Nigella thought, Surely poor Fanny couldn't be thinking of going in for another bout of Edward Montmorency?

"Nothing, except that he and it should both be ignored," Fanny answered, with what seemed irrelevant haughtiness.

"Well, you dragged him in, my sweet," said Nigella.

"I'm all for ignoring Sir Edward," said Martha, "but not your birthday. Such a birthday of birthdays, darling."

"You talk as if I were going to be eighty," snapped Fanny—Fanny, who in her life had hardly ever snapped. But then Edward . . . so nearly making a fool of her . . . She had been saved by a wink. And shattered by the realization of how deeply humiliating that saving was, was it to be wondered at that she snapped?

"No, my sweet, but you *are* going to be half a hundred, aren't you," said Nigella.

Half a hundred. It sounded so much worse than fifty. And Martha, sorry that Nigella should have let herself sound unkind, when at heart she was often quite a dear, began hurriedly to unfold their plan in more detail. What with Niggs sounding unkind when she wasn't, and Fanny saying a nasty word when she shouldn't—one of those nasty words beginning with b, which Martha kept carefully from her two boys and girl, but which somehow they seemed to know about,—and what with that horrid Edward Montmorency getting into the conversation, she felt her hands, never much good, she was afraid, were full.

"Above everything, darling," she said, anxious and earnest, "we would love to have you to ourselves on your birthday, alone with just your *own* people. So do come to Tintagel—or to George's and Niggs's. We feel that on such a very—such a very——"

She faltered, because of Fanny's expression. Nigella helped. "Special day," said Nigella.

"Yes. Special day. You've hardly ever spent a birthday with your *own* people, have you, darling, and of course we've always quite realized it would be dull for you, but now——"

She faltered again, again because of Fanny's expression. Nigella helped. "Yes. Now that you are——" began Nigella.

"Down and out?" suggested Fanny.

"That's not what I was going to say," said Nigella, offended.

"We've come here only because we love you," said Martha, hurt.

"Darlings," said Fanny, sorry.

There was a pause. Martha, gentle, sweet-eyed, whose one wish had been that poor Fanny shouldn't hate her birthday too much, shrank back into her shell. She felt she was no match for Fanny, and no match, either, for any of the other wide-awake people in London. The only thing she was a match for, and that doubtfully, was her quiet country life at Tintagel. How much she wished she were there at that moment, with her children, and kind Zellie, and old James handing round the boiled potatoes.

Nigella, made of sterner stuff, regarded Fanny's remark as yet another proof of the rate at which she was disintegrating. Positively cynical, Fanny had become—Fanny, who used to be such friends with life, so wholeheartedly uncritical of everybody and everything. Soon there'd be nothing left of the original Fanny except snappishness, thought Nigella, watching, with narrowed eyes, what she could see of the face turned to Martha —for Fanny, sorry for what she had said, was assuring Martha she was an angel. If she had been born ugly, thought Nigella, watching her, she would, quite possibly, from the beginning have been snappy. Who knew but what it wasn't her real nature to snap? And she only hadn't till now because all the flattery, and all the spoiling, and all the being fussed over, had been like a hand laid over her mouth——

"Angel," said Fanny, turning to her suddenly at this point, mindful that Nigella too had come round full of good intentions and anxious not to be cross to the two kind little things.

Perhaps one should never turn suddenly to somebody. Indications should be given that one is going to. Room should be allowed for readjustment. As things were, Nigella couldn't quickly enough change the expression in her narrowed eyes, and Fanny saw it. Why, Niggs was looking at her as if——

There was another pause. Then she said it again. "Angel?" said Fanny again; but this time hesitatingly, and with an inquiry at the end.

Naturally Nigella couldn't be expected to like that.

§

For a moment, after this, there was estrangement, expressed by silence, between the cousins.

"If she imagines I *care*," thought Nigella, fixing another cigarette in her long jade holder, and lighting it impassively.

"If they knew what I've just been *through*,—" thought Fanny, trying to justify herself.

"How I wish people would just simply *love* each other,"

thought Martha, who hadn't seen Nigella's narrowed look, and wondered that Fanny should be so cross and unkind to Niggs, who was often such a dear really.

Fanny rather wondered at it herself. Why, because Edward had winked, because Edward had succeeded in making her almost believe he loved her for herself, be unkind to two innocents? And what did it matter if Niggs eyed one with hostility? In dealing with Niggs, one should always remember how constantly she was forced, because of the state of her inside, to go to that man Byles, an activity enough to upset anybody's disposition. And wanting to make up for her uncalled-for query and break the reproachful silence, she plunged into unfolding a plan of her own for her birthday, that minute entered her head.

This plan, unthought of a minute before, much surprised Fanny. How suddenly it had sprung into life! How excellent it was! Almost an inspiration. In the same category as the impulse which had made her turn her head in the hall at the exact right moment for seeing Edward wink. Not only would it remove her well out of his reach, if he should dare try to come near her again, but it would protect her from her cousins' invitations, and prevent her refusals from seeming ungrateful.

"Listen, darlings," she said, stretching out a placating hand to each, which neither took, "listen——"

And she told them that, long ago, she had made up her mind —actually she was making it up as she spoke,—to spend this particular birthday, which she agreed was an unusual one, in retirement. Strict retirement. At Stokes—Stokes being her cottage at the foot of the South Downs,—considering, undisturbed, what she was going to do next.

"You do see, don't you," she said, looking from one to the other, but not able to catch their eyes, "you do see that what a woman does after fifty can't be quite what she does before it. She may dribble on looking much the same for a bit, in ordinary cases, but not if she's me, suddenly shorn by illness of—well, most of her attractions."

"Of all of them," thought Nigella.

"Poor love, she doesn't a bit realize," thought Martha.

"I notice you've observed how closely shorn I am," said Fanny, watching their expressions.

"*Darling*," protested Martha, raising her eyes and turning red.

"And I feel it's important, now that I'm obliged to begin and be old——"

"Darling, not *old*——" protested the kind Martha, never able to stay hurt in her shell for long.

"—to get to grips with things, and think them out."

"What things?" inquired Nigella, taking her jade holder out of her mouth an instant, and immediately putting it back.

"Oh—Life, Death. All the things," said Fanny, airily.

"Darling, not *Death*," protested Martha.

Nigella again took her holder out of her mouth. "Of course," she said, "if you *prefer* to be by yourself at Stokes instead of with us——"

"How embarrassingly you put it," smiled Fanny—her first smile since they arrived, Nigella noted.

"And won't you be miserably lonely, darling?" asked Martha. "You were so ill there. Won't that rather haunt you?"

"Oh, I'm used to being haunted," said Fanny, thinking of Job—indeed, finding she was looking at Job, for there at once he was, in his usual place at the foot of the table. It was like pressing a button, she thought, to think of Job; like switching on light. Light? Surely not light? Job didn't in any way resemble light?

Her cousins followed her look, and thought it queer. Queer to stare like that at an empty chair, and queer, too, to say she was haunted. Martha couldn't make head or tail of a remark like that. Nigella took it to mean that she was haunted by remorse—as well she might be, considering the many heartaches she had given people's wives and mothers.

Often and often Nigella had wondered how far Fanny had really *gone*. She was so skilful at covering up her tracks, she went about looking so innocent and carefree, that nobody had ever been able to discover how far she really had *gone*. Now Nigella began to be afraid she had gone farther than she should —with George, for instance, with Nigella's own precious George. Else, why be haunted? The good weren't haunted. Thank God, thought Nigella, that she's finished at last.

"And I won't be lonely," Fanny went on to explain, turning her head away with what seemed to be a jerk of impatience, Job not having joined her before in company, and she was feeling this new departure wasn't playing the game,—"because this very day I wrote inviting a friend to come and stay with me. Do you remember little Mr. Hyslup?"

They looked at her in surprise. Indeed they remembered little Mr. Hyslup. Nobody who had watched Fanny's career could have missed him. Even as they had witnessed the coming, and presently the going, of Edward Montmorency, so in the fullness of time they had witnessed the coming, and presently the going, of little Mr. Hyslup. A clergyman. An ordinary, curate-sort of young clergyman. No gaiters nor apron, nor anything of that sort. Just a clergyman, and conspicuous for that reason in Fanny's crowd. Conspicuous, really, in any crowd, because of his evident, his excessive and his entirely speechless love. Could it be possible that she was going in for another bout of little Mr. Hyslup? wondered Nigella. And if so, oughtn't she to be got as quickly as possible into a Home for Incurables? For old ones?

Even Martha doubted if it were a good thing to stir up little Mr. Hyslup and bring him out of his decent obscurity; and Nigella being quite sure it wasn't, both ought to have been glad when Fanny said, "Well, I've invited his sister to come to Stokes,"—instead of which they both felt let down.

"Oh, his *sister*, darling," said Martha, flatly.

"For a moment I thought you were actually still——" began Nigella.

"Carrying on?" suggested Fanny.

"How embarrassingly you put it," said Nigella.

"*Touchée*," smiled Fanny; and Martha, in spite of the smile, was afraid they weren't being very nice to each other.

"Aren't we going up to the drawing-room, darling?" she hastily asked, to distract their attention; for there they were, luncheon long finished, just sitting and rapping out things. "I love that room," she explained, feeling her sudden wish to go up to it needed explaining.

"Is it worth while going up, when we've got to come down again?" inquired Nigella.

"You might say that of everything," said Fanny.

"I might," agreed Nigella. "And I do."

No, they weren't being nice to each other, Martha was afraid, anxiously trying to think of something really clever as an excuse for getting Nigella to leave.

But before her slow mind had hit on something plausible, Fanny, still keeping them sitting there, said, "His sister is a child of God."

"Oh," said Martha. And murmured, "Darling, how nice."

The information made her feel uncomfortable. Of course there were such things, she knew, as children of God, especially in the Catechism, but did one talk about them in dining-rooms? Queer that Fanny should—Fanny, of all people. Never in her life had Martha heard her mention God, unless joined with either Good or My, and she was afraid Nigella, who was often such a dear really, might scoff.

She glanced uneasily at her, but Nigella sat quite quiet, smoking in silence.

"A creature of the most complete self-sacrifice," continued Fanny, the cold beetroot and sardines vivid before her eyes.

"Darling," murmured Martha, now definitely soothing.

"So I thought——" said Fanny.

Surprised, she broke off; for till that minute she hadn't thought of it at all, nor, for that matter, had she invited Muriel in her letter to Stokes, but only to lunch in Charles Street. Funny, the way things became real, became inevitable, just by talking about them. Here was her immediate future being fixed for her, just by some words she had used so as to get out of spending her birthday with relations. Stokes, unthought of till then, just through talking had become the certain background of that birthday, and Muriel Hyslup, just through talking, was going to stay there instead of only coming to lunch. No one could tell what the result of her visit might be. Shut up in the country, on such a serious occasion as her fiftieth birthday, alone with a child of God, wasn't it at least possible that she might be helped to see what her next step should be? And helped, too, which was the most important, the vital need, not to mind it?

"So I thought——" she began again; and again hesitated; and then went on quickly, "Well, you see, I thought that as life has suddenly become different and difficult, and Muriel Hyslup is so good, she would be able to tell me what I must do to be——"

But this time she broke off to look at them in a kind of wonder, for up to that instant she hadn't thought of this either. All she had intended was to be kind to poor Muriel for an hour or two, give her a good meal, let her rest in the flowery comfort and warmth of the library, assure her she was her friend, and send her back to her sacrifices refreshed and strengthened.

There was a silence. Martha knew the word that was to have finished the sentence, because of having to go to church every

Sunday at Tintagel. It was *saved*. It came out of the Bible.
A rich young man had asked what he must do to be saved, and
hadn't liked the answer, and had gone sorrowfully away. But
fancy Fanny! How funny of her to begin talking like him.
Extraordinary, really; even more extraordinary than going to
Claridge's. For only the wicked needed saving, and Martha was
sure Fanny had always been nothing but an angel. Martha
could remember an infinitude of angelically kind things she had
done for her young cousins, till they grew up and their husbands
rather took her over. No one who was so sweetly kind to two
quite ordinary, dull little girls could possibly, Martha was sure,
need saving.

"*Darling*," she said, laying her hand on Fanny's, and full of
loving concern that she should have such ideas.

But Fanny wasn't looking at her. Her attention seemed to
have been caught again by that empty chair. Really it made
one feel quite creepy the way she stared at the chair—so intently,
and this time with a sort of questioning.

"Do tell me what's the matter with that chair," said Nigella
impatiently; Martha, for some reason, was sorry that she asked.

"Do you remember Job?" asked Fanny.

"Job?" repeated Nigella.

What a question. As if they didn't. Why, she and Martha
had been his bridesmaids, or rather Fanny's, and he had given
them the most extravagantly inappropriate diamond bangles.
Two children, with diamond bangles. Their mothers had taken
them away and worn them themselves. Could it be possible,
Nigella wondered, that poor Fanny was going in for a second
bout of Job?

"That was the one you married, wasn't it, darling," said
Martha.

Nigella gave her a quick glance; but no—Martha was quite
without guile.

"Of course we remember Mr. Skeffington," Nigella said,
shortly. "What about him?"

"Only that that was his chair, and still is," said Fanny.

At this Nigella got up, swept her gloves and cigarettes and
bag together, and announced that they must go. She had an
appointment in Dover Street. She was late already. She would
send Martha on to Claridge's in the car.

Then she turned to Fanny, who still was sitting at the table,
leaning on her elbows. Something must be done about Fanny.

She was her cousin, if only by marriage, and as such should be, if possible, helped and guided. "You don't mean to tell me," she said, "that you are still hankering after Mr. Skeffington?"

"What a word," smiled Fanny, looking up at her, her chin cupped in her hand. "I can't remember ever hankering after anybody in my life."

"I dare say, but things are different now."

"You mean, I'm different. I still, though, don't hanker. And for some time I've had an impression that it's Job who is hankering after me."

Well, one could only pity poor Fanny, decided Nigella. "You should go and see Sir Stilton Byles," she said, after a moment, during which she stared down at her unhappy cousin. "He's the person to help you. I'll give you his address. And do remember, my sweet——" she actually laid her hand on Fanny's shoulder, who actually managed not to mind——"do remember, when it comes to fancying people are hankering after you, that both you and Mr. Skeffington are a quarter of a century older than you used to be."

"How you deal in centuries," was all Fanny answered, with another smile.

§

In the car on the way to Dover Street, Nigella said:

"We needn't bother about her birthday. You'll see if she doesn't spend it in a Home. I shall speak to Sir Stilton about her, and find out whether he knows of a nice one. If ever a woman was heading for a nervous breakdown, it's Fanny."

"Or——" Martha hesitated. "Or for just the opposite," she got out.

"I don't know what you mean by just the opposite," said Nigella, turning to look at her.

"I don't think I do either," said Martha, with hasty meekness. "It just—it happened to come into my head."

X

§

Now there was George to be got through.

Fanny had had enough of everybody for one day, but there was still George to get through. Slowly she went upstairs, after her cousins had gone, to have her desecrated curls washed clean by Manby of the feel of Edward's fingers, and while they were being washed—there were advantages sometimes in not having to be in the same room as one's hair,—she would have a bath, change her clothes even to her very shoes, and rid herself of the smallest trace of how close he had been.

Climbing the great staircase, the great, becoming staircase, down which she had come a thousand times in the days of her loveliness, her progress watched from below by bewitched adorers, a horrid tale someone told her once came into her mind, a tale of young men who danced, for their own discreditable reasons, with elderly women, and while they danced winked at their friends over the poor old things' trustful shoulders. A very horrid tale. It had infinitely shocked her. Now here she was, in her turn become the subject of a wink. Dreadful; dreadful. Edward, at sixty, behaving as if he were one of those young men, and she were one of those old women. Worse: it wasn't at his friends he had winked, but at her own servant. And the very badness of such behaviour made it quite impossible to do anything, really, but forget it.

Indeed, that was what one must do with Edward—forget him. She wouldn't even pay him the compliment of being angry. She had been angry almost beyond speech during the first part of luncheon, and now that was enough. Good-bye, Edward. Without fuss, or big words like humiliation and shame, but quietly, nicely, and with nothing vindictive about it, she would leave him to God.

That made one more of them; one more of her past loves left in this situation, place, condition, or whatever one might call it. Congestion up there? Perhaps. She paused at the turn of the staircase to get her breath, and was glad to find she could already smile about Edward; and catching sight of Manby crossing the hall below with his roses in her arms, she leaned over the balustrade and called "Manby!"—not, though, to tell her to throw the things away, because neither Edward's roses nor his wink, once he had been left to God, were any longer of the least consequence, but to ask her to come up to her room, because she wanted to have a bath.

"Mr. Pontyfridd will be here at five," said Fanny over the balustrade; and if Manby wondered what connection there could be between Mr. Pontyfridd and a bath, she showed no sign of it.

Mr. Pontyfridd; Mr. Pontyfridd; bother Mr. Pontyfridd, Fanny thought, going on up the stairs. These relations. There seemed that day to be no end to them. What did he want of her? She hadn't seen him since they met in the train, when he had so much annoyed her. She hoped he wasn't going to annoy her again, she had had enough of that for one day. And it wasn't as if he were someone, if he did, who could be left to God and done with, for he was her dear cousin, the cousin she loved, her faithful and devoted friend, with the all-important addition of being a gentleman. After Edward, Fanny would have liked, positively, to wash in gentlemen; and she thought, as she climbed, of the silly Niggs, who having by God's grace got such a treasure of a husband, spoiled his and her own happiness by jealousy and suspicions, when heaven knew——

Out of breath, Fanny arrived in her bedroom, and according to the immemorial habit of women arriving in their bedrooms, went straight to the looking-glass. There she stood staring at herself, honestly surprised that Niggs should still mind her enough to want to stick pins into her in the way she had been doing during the whole time at luncheon. Surely she couldn't think that a thing so lean and hollow-cheeked, so evidently desperately tired as the creature in the glass, could be a danger to her George?

An agèd man—or woman, it didn't matter which—*is but a paltry thing,* she had read that very morning, turning over a book of poems she kept on her dressing-table, to read while Manby was doing her hair.

How did it go on? She picked up the book, and searched. Yes; here it was:

> *—a paltry thing,*
> *A tattered coat upon a stick, unless*
> *Soul clap its hands and sing, and louder sing*
> *For every tatter in its mortal dress.*

Well, wasn't it plain enough, she thought, raising her eyes from the book to examine her reflection, that the lady in the glass, though in years not yet an aged woman, was heading at a great rate towards the stick stage? And that when she reached it she would either have to sing or go under? Base, though, to go under. Base to let oneself be buffeted into giving up. The alternative was somehow to sing. But sing what? She didn't know. That was the worst of being uneducated: one wasn't able, when things got past a joke, to find comfort and satisfaction, as the agèd man found it, by studying monuments of one's soul's magnificence. She must find something humbler. She must chirp on a lower level. He went to Byzantium; she would go to Stokes. And there, with only sheep looking at her, and Muriel Hyslup, she hoped, to give her a helping hand, she would grope till she found something decent to do with the rest of her life, so that at least she needn't die blushing. Oh, she didn't want to die blushing; and she would, she would, she knew she would, if she went drifting along, and made no attempt to leave off mopping and mowing, and didn't get busy paying back something, at least, of the debt she owed for her creation, preservation, and all the blessings of her life. Such blessings. She thought of them now with wonder. And if, Jim not being there to point out and explain, she wouldn't be able to clap her hands and sing over the more obvious magnificences, such as, say, Westminster Abbey or Shakespeare, she could surely clap a little each morning in gratitude for having been safely brought to the beginning of another day. Days, after all, were precious—even one's older days, if one approached them in the proper spirit. The supply wouldn't last for ever——

"Mr. Pontyfridd has rung up, m'lady," interrupted Manby, coming in, "to say he hopes your ladyship will see him in your sitting-room."

"See him in my sitting-room?" echoed Fanny, turning her head in surprise. "I wonder why he says that."

Manby, who had no opinion to offer, merely asked if she should get the bath ready.

"Yes. Tell Soames we'll have tea there," said Fanny. "In the sitting-room, I mean," she explained, observing Manby's face. "Bless you, Manby," she smiled; and pulling off all Antoine's curls, laid them in a neat row on the table, and bade her wash them.

§

By this time it was nearly four. George would be sure to be punctual, and if she wanted to rest a little, after her bath before he arrived, she must be quick.

Funny of him to ring up about the sitting-room. She wondered again why he was coming, why he had been so insistent that she should be alone. Niggs, of course, would read the most

sinister intentions into it. Fanny could only suppose he too had
got some well-meant plan for her birthday, though why it
should have to be talked about so privately——

"Miss Cartwright has sent up this letter, m'lady," said
Manby, meeting her when she went back into the bedroom after
her bath.

It wasn't from Muriel, but from Miles. He thanked her for
the cheque, he said he would lay it out only on strictly deserving
cases, and he regretted that his sister could not lunch. *My sister
does not go out*, said the letter briefly.

"So that's that," said Fanny, laying it down. No Stokes,
then, with Muriel; no being helped. She was, once more, to be
forced to stand on her own feet, she was to manage by herself.

Staring thoughtfully at Manby, she remembered how it was
at Stokes, during her convalescence, that Job had first begun
to dog her, and said, "Then there won't be anybody with me
on my birthday but Mr. Skeffington,"—a remark which upset
Manby's decent calm to the extent, as she afterwards told Miss
Cartwright, of feeling ready to drop.

§

It was a thoughtful Fanny who left her bedroom, soon after
five, to go and greet George in the sitting-room; a Fanny inclined
to think Fate was being unduly hard on her. The instant, however, that she went into the passage joining the two rooms, she
forgot this; and she forgot it because there was something queer
about the feel of the house. Arrestingly queer. Quite different
from what it felt like before.

She stopped, her ear cocked, her head on one side, listening.

Dead silence; a sort of holding of the breath, as if the house
itself, and everybody in it, were waiting, in passionate yet fear-
ful curiosity, for what would happen next. Odd, thought
Fanny; extremely odd; and turned inquiringly to Soames.

He was waiting to open the sitting-room door for her. He
looked shattered; but this, she explained to herself, was because
he hadn't yet recovered from Edward's wink. She could understand that. An awful position for poor Soames to find himself,
and so innocently, in, and made more awful, if he only knew it,
by her extreme reluctance, as a result of it, to have him anywhere about her. She had got over his party, but could she
get over the wink? A shared wink; shared with Soames; the

very raw of her vanity and dignity got at. No, it was intolerable, and she was afraid he would have to go.

"Is anything the matter?" she asked, while he, avoiding her inquiring eye, bent over the door-handle with the anxious assiduousness of one who wishes quickly to usher in and then escape.

"Matter, m'lady?" was all he found he could say, while his legs felt as if they were giving way at the knees.

Fortunately for him the door was pulled open from the other side, and George appeared. He too seemed different, thought Fanny, scrutinizing him curiously—flushed, and very much, though this was a strange thing for George to be, embarrassed.

"There you are, darling," he exclaimed with nervous heartiness—surely the heartiness was nervous?—putting his arm round her, and quickly drawing her into the room. "I *am* glad to see you. I thought—well, you were rather long, weren't you." And he glanced over his shoulder at Soames, who immediately shut the door and went.

Fanny dropped, as if she were tired, into her usual low chair by the fire. "I don't know what you've come about," she said, looking up at him, "but I beg you to be kind to me. I've had a trying day."

This made him more nervous—obviously more nervous; his hand was quite unsteady as he lit a cigarette.

Startled by its behaviour, she asked, staring at it, "Why is your hand shaking?"

"It isn't," he said.

"Well, well," she smiled, lifting her eyebrows—but only half a smile, because really George, and Soames, and the house generally, were behaving too mysteriously for comfort. If it were more money George wanted for his charities, so soon after what she gave him a month ago, that might explain his embarrassment; but it wouldn't explain why Soames looked as if he were seeing ghosts, nor why the house was hushed in a kind of alarmed expectancy. Fanny was extremely sensitive to atmospheres. She hadn't felt this particular atmosphere in Charles Street since—she cast back her mind through the years, and found, to her great surprise, that she hadn't felt it for twenty-two years, not since the time when Job was last there.

"Let's have tea," said George abruptly.

He felt deeply uncomfortable. It was all very well not being able to see suffering and injustice without instantly determining to do away with it, but considering it was only Fanny who could do away with it in this case, and not he himself, wasn't he being generous at someone else's expense? And suppose she didn't come up to scratch, and turned out to be pure undifferentiated female—grievance-nursing, grasping, selfish, without imagination? Women, he had sometimes uneasily suspected, when listening to Niggs's tirades, weren't gentlemen; justice and fairness didn't seem to mean much to them. Older women especially, having grabbed, were inclined to clutch. Fanny was now an older woman. Her beauty was gone, but her money remained. Suppose, having years ago got off neatly with the Skeffington swag, she refused to disgorge any of it? Then the second and only remaining string to his bow would come in, and he would appeal to her pity; and if that was no good, seeing that he was of those who can't love if they don't respect, he would have lost her. Lost his darling cousin, he thought, frowning with anxiety; the cousin who for so many years had made the world a more beautiful place, simply by being in it.

"It's not hot, you know," she remarked, watching him wiping beads off his forehead; and, as he didn't answer, she took up the teapot. "There's nothing else you'd like better?" she asked, holding it suspended.

"No. Tea, please."

He crammed his handkerchief into his pocket, snatched a cushion off the nearest sofa, threw it on the floor on the other side of the short-legged tea-table, sat on it, and glanced uneasily across, not so much at her as at the chair she was sunk in.

It seemed to have grown. Always big enough for two, as no one knew better than he, it now seemed big enough for three. When last he saw her, muffled up in fur, he hadn't realized how little of her there was left. "Was it fair," he asked himself, more beads coming out on his forehead, so that he had to pull his handkerchief out again, while again she watched him, her head on one side,—"was it fair to give anyone who looked so exactly like an invalid a shock? Hadn't he better wait till she fattened up a bit? Or at least till she didn't just happen to have had what she told him was a trying day?"

No, what he had come for couldn't wait; what he was doing was, anyhow, so outrageous that there was nothing for it but to plunge ahead and see it through. "Now we can talk," he said, taking his cup from her—taking it with both hands, so as to prevent its rattling in the saucer.

"Yes. What about?"

"First, tea."

He drank as if he were thirsty, gulping it down, and immediately held out the cup for more. "I'm worried," he said, while she refilled it.

"Niggs?"

"No. You."

"Me?"

She put down the teapot, and looked at him uncertainly. "If it's about my birthday——" she began; but he interrupted her, and said it was more serious than that.

She asked, with a small grimace, whether anything could be more serious.

He bade her, almost sternly, not be silly; and then, brushing birthday nonsense aside, told her he was so fond of her that he was in a mortal funk.

"Promise me, promise me," begged George, "that you're not going to fail me. Really I couldn't bear to lose you. But you flounced off that evening at Paddington in such a huff because I began talking about Skeffington, that you may flounce off again."

"Are you going to talk about him?" she asked.

"It's what I've come for," he said. Whereupon she remarked, with unexpected tranquillity, "How that man keeps on cropping up."

George stared. Her hands were busy among the cups, her head was bent over the tea-table. "What do you mean—keeps on cropping up?" he asked.

"Well, he does," she said.

She turned, and looked over her shoulder round the room. She looked carefully, with a kind of gingerliness, as if reluctant to see what she was searching for. He watched her, completely puzzled.

"Funny," she said, after craning her neck to peer, peering so thoroughly that it even included behind the writing-table. "He isn't here."

"Who isn't?" asked George.

"Job."

Then George felt that sensation down his spine which is called the creeps. It was the way she peered round behind the writing-table, where there was hardly room for a flat cat to lurk, which made him creep most. "Did you expect him to be?" he asked, suppressing a shiver and managing to take on the gentle, humouring manner of one dealing with a beloved but illusion-ridden patient.

"He usually is," she said. "Since my illness, he hangs about a good deal. But you know," she added with a shrug, "one gets used to everything."

For an instant, bewildered, he thought Skeffington had double-crossed him, but light quickly dawned on him. She was being haunted. She had Skeffington on her conscience. She couldn't get him out of her mind because of doubts, and thoroughly well-founded ones, in George's opinion, as to whether she hadn't been too hard on him once upon a time. So she had been, and for entirely discreditable reasons. It wasn't, George was sure, from any strictness of principle or wounded love that she had divorced him, but simply because the opportunity was too good to be missed for getting rid of her little Jew. Now she was being punished. Now her conscience, awake at last in a life grown suddenly empty, was gnawing at her. Nobody who was hard had a conscience which gnawed. As far as that went, then, she was still his darling cousin. And he got up, went round the tea-table to her chair, sat on the edge of it, put his arm round her, and said gently, "My poor little one."

"Yes," nodded Fanny. It was what she had been thinking at intervals lately herself. After each fresh blow she had thought it, before pulling herself together and holding her head up again.

"Have you seen a doctor?"

"But I told you the day I met you at Paddington that I had just been to Byles. And all I got out of him was insults, and that I'd better ask him to dinner."

"Ask Byles to dinner?"

"No, Job."

George bent down and kissed the top of her head. This was not only to show he loved her and sympathized with her, but also so that he might have a second or two to think what he ought to say next. George was in great stress of mind. That Byles should come to his help in the difficult, the really appalling job his impulsiveness had landed him in was the last thing he had expected. Byles was certainly, from what he had heard and from the size of his bills, a highly unpleasant person, but equally certainly he had broken the ground by that suggestion about dinner, and all he, George, had to do was to feel his way along those same lines with tact and prudence. Still, when he thought of what he had done, and where Skeffington was at that moment, tact and prudence seemed poor things compared with courage, and out kept coming those damned beads on his forehead.

"*I've* been seeing him *really*," he said, taking the plunge.

"Who? Byles?"

"No, Job."

"You have?"

She drew herself away to stare, astonished, at him. Nobody she knew had ever seen Job since the divorce. He had disappeared. Gone abroad. Gone, the rumour went, to Mexico, and stayed there. Was George, it occurred to her, being of the same blood as herself, perhaps seeing things too which weren't really there? He certainly seemed to be perspiring a good deal.

"You can't have," she said with decision. "He's in Mexico."

"He isn't. He's——"

But George had to stop, in order to swallow. His throat felt all dry and choky. He stretched across the table, seized the teapot, and poured himself out some more tea. What he had done seemed to him now, alone with the unconscious Fanny, wholly unpardonable. But then, when he thought of Skeffington——

Having gulped down the tea, watched by her curiously while he gulped, he went on quickly, "The fact is, darling, I ran into him yesterday, in Battersea Park."

She could only repeat, her eyes on his face, her body quite still, "Yesterday, in Battersea Park."

"I was walking across it, and he was on a seat, sunning himself."

Again she could only repeat: "Sunning himself."

Job, sunning himself. Job, having leisure to sit and sun himself. Job, *wanting* to sun himself. This indeed was strange, that Job, a man of offices, of board-meetings, of a thousand irons in the fire, of power, importance and ceaseless activities, should *want* to sit and sun himself.

Incredulous, she remarked that it was very unlike him.

George agreed. "Completely," he said. "So is everything else. Just listen. At first I didn't notice him, because I was looking at the dog——"

"What dog?"

"His."

"He couldn't have had a dog," she objected, again with decision. "He didn't like them."

"He liked this one all right," said George. And added, after hesitating a little, "One must have something, you know."

"Yes; one must have something. Who in the world realized that more clearly now than herself? Still, a dog did seem about the last form of companionship Job would go in for. And she fell to wondering if she too, perhaps, would end up with a dog, and for a moment *rêverie* overtook her, and she saw pictures of herself and Job at the last, each somewhere where the other wasn't, alone with a dog. The final summing-up of their brilliantly spectacular lives: One dog.

"He was such an enchanting dog," George went on, "such an obviously proud and responsible dog——"

"Responsible?" said Fanny. The unusual word roused her from her *rêverie*.

"Well, you know how dogs look," said George hurriedly.

Fanny said she didn't, and he went on quickly, "Well, anyhow I couldn't help stopping and patting him. And then I saw that the man he had in tow—I mean," he amended hastily, "I saw it was Skeffington he belonged to. A good deal changed, of course—shrivelled and so on, but there was never any mistaking that fellow's strongly marked features, and I'd have known him anywhere."

Her eyes wandered from George's face to the fire. Shrivelled, she was thinking. The Job she saw so often was just as she remembered him after the divorce, an agile, sinewy, small man in the very prime of life, and she tried hard to imagine the change. There must, she knew, be a change, but it gave her a curious stab that Job, too, should have had to submit to one. That live-wire, that over-rider of any and every obstacle, now sitting shrivelled on a seat in Battersea Park, doing nothing. One more of her past worshippers gone to pieces, one more of them turned into an old, tired man. And this time it was her husband. Say what you will, Fanny reflected, going to sleep every night with somebody, as she had dutifully done with Job till the typists started trouble, does make—well, a link.

"Seventy-two, he told me," was the next thing she heard George say.

"Yes," she assented, after a pause during which, her eyes still fixed on the fire, she appeared to be counting. "Seventy-two."

"I had great difficulty in getting him to talk, but bit by bit——"

"Must I hear about it?" she asked, shifting a little in the chair.

"Who else, if not you?"

"Why me?" Yes, indeed, she asked herself—why her? What had become of all those——?

He read the question in her eyes. "Surely you're not going to bring up the typists again?" he rebuked. "You know, there does come a close time for that sort of thing in a man's life, and I've just told you he's broken up."

"You didn't tell me he's broken up," she said, looking up at him quickly.

"Well, he is. And I'm really surprised at you, Fanny, that you should still go on about——"

His arm round her shoulders relaxed its hold, and she, feeling the withdrawal, put up her hand and caught hold of his coat.

"Don't do that. Stay close," she begged. "It's only that I can't picture Job without women in his life, and—broken up. Oh, but how cruel, how utterly *beastly*," she burst out in a sudden flame of indignation, which filled George with hope, "to leave him when he's broken up!"

"And poor," said George, making the most of his opportunity. "That sets them off running quicker than anything, you know."

"Poor?"

At this she herself put away his arm, and sat up straight, looking at him incredulously. He had hinted at this before, but uncertainly. Now he seemed sure. Job, poor? Job, that expert in millions? Really, she couldn't believe it. He might be relatively poor, compared with what he used to be, but not actually—not poor in the way Miles and Muriel were poor, or the women at Paddington, or the people at street corners to whom she gave half-crowns, whenever they looked as if they'd like some.

"*Actually* poor," said George, as if he could hear her thinking. "Stranded. On the rocks, if ever a man was."

Silence. She, trying to believe it. She, struggling with a thought which, if she did believe it, would have an instant effect on her own future. George wouldn't lie. Then, that being so, it must be true that Job was in a bad way.

She sat trying to take it in. Job on the rocks, and she with power to rescue him. Rescuing, she would herself be rescued. No need now for Muriel Hyslup to help her find what her next step should be—Job was doing it; Job himself was her next step; Job, turned miraculously into an instrument of salvation.

"But then——" she began.

"Yes, darling?" he said eagerly, bending down.

She didn't, though, go on. She was too much dazzled by the light thrown on what she must do next, and sat staring at him speechlessly. Miserable, of course, for poor Job to have to be broken up before he could become the instrument of her salvation, but at least his misery wasn't going to last. He should have everything. She couldn't give him back his vigour and wholeness, but she could and would give him the means of having himself cared for and mended. Give him? No, not give; restore what had always really been his. Everything should go back to him. She would only ask for just enough to live on, hidden away somewhere in the country, where no one who used to know her would see her, and where she could, at long last, apply herself to that wisdom and that getting of understanding which Lanks, in the days of his waning devotion, used to recommend as desirable. The great, resounding house should go back, complete with its contents. Except for Manby, the servants should go back too, including Soames. Truly the ways of Providence were admirable, thought Fanny, struck by its thoroughness, by its attention to the smallest detail— here, for instance, was Soames going to be removed from her life legitimately, smoothly, and happily. One should trust more, she said to herself. One shouldn't, as she had been doing lately, be in such a hurry to despair.

But astonished as she was at the ways of Providence, she was very nearly as much astonished at the ways of George. Who would have thought, she asked herself, that he could doubt her decency to the point of being in what he called a blue funk? He had positively perspired with fear lest she should fail him. How on earth had he managed to be so fond of her all these years if the whole time, in his heart, he had never been sure she would behave honourably when put to the test?

Doubly astonished, her breath quite taken away by these sudden revelations, she sat looking at him, unable to say a word, listening in a silence he took as boding no good to what he began telling her about Job.

"I had the greatest difficulty in getting anything out of him,"
said George. "I had to keep on assuring him no one was listening"—and he went on to tell her how poor Skeffington, as
he persistently called him, had first begun losing money in
Mexico, where he got mixed up in politics, and revolutions,
and God knew what, and when things got too hot for him there
he had come back to Europe, and gone to Vienna and started
again, and with his usual skill had managed to get richer than
ever when the Nazis walked in. Vienna wasn't exactly a
healthy place for a Jew, and he was soon in serious trouble—
for a moment George didn't seem able to go on, seemed to be
staring, with horror in his eyes, at something he could hardly
credit,—such serious trouble that he was lucky to get away
with bare life, if bare life, said George, his eyes full of that
incredulous horror, could be called lucky, and was now in
London, and on the rocks.

"And you think I ought to get him off them," said Fanny
as he paused, in the chilly voice natural to one whose decency
is doubted.

The chill annoyed George. "There's no *ought* about it, my
dear," he said; and that he should address her as my dear showed
her how much annoyed he was. But then, so was she—and
most justly, considered Fanny. "You have no duty. He has
no claim. I think, though, you should remember that every
bit of all this——" and he looked round the flower-filled room,
and at the extravagantly wasteful amount of stuff to eat,
untouched by either, of them, on the tea-table, and at Fanny
herself, sunk in softness, wrapped in probably wickedly
expensive garments for all their air of simplicity, with an eye
made hostile by its inner vision of the shabby, patient figure
on the seat in Battersea Park—"everything in this house, every
stitch on your back, is yours because of his generosity."

"Yes," agreed Fanny, "he was very generous. But it's
easy," she added, going on being extremely chilly with George,
"to be generous when you're so rich."

Well, George didn't want to sit close to a woman who talked
like that, and he got up and stood with his back to the fire,
glancing, with a swift upward jerk of his wrist, at his watch.
Awful not to be getting on with this better, when speed was
so vital. At any moment someone distraught might burst in,
wanting further instructions——

"Are you in a hurry?" asked Fanny, even more coldly than

before, for she had had enough of men who looked at their watches.

He glared down at her. He ignored her question. He was asking himself if this were really his Fanny, this cold thing, and whether her heart had grown as fleshless as the rest of her. "Let me tell you," he said, glaring, "that you only had a legal right to a fraction of what he insisted should be settled on you."

"I know."

"And now——"

"Now that he's poor, and I still go on being odiously and unfairly well-off—say it, George, say it. You're simply dying to."

"Exactly. It *is* odious. It *is* unfair," he said, beginning to stride up and down the room, "when things are so wretchedly different for him. My God, yes," he broke off, stopping suddenly, as though overcome by what he knew.

"And you suggest——?"

"I suggest——"

He came back and stood over her, a man flushed with agitation, with the necessity for persuading her quickly to do the right, the only thing.

"Yes?" she encouraged.

"I suggest that you should talk over how much you would like to give him back."

"Well, but of course, my dear——" she, now, was calling him her dear, always a symptom of at least temporary dislike. "What do you suppose? I'll send for my lawyer the first thing to-morrow morning, and talk it over." But, struck by something in his face, she leaned forward in her chair, and inquired, "Talk over with whom?"

"With Skeffington, Fanny. No earthly need for lawyers. Make it a *kind* thing. Make it a *warm* thing," said George, almost implored George.

"You mean——"

She stared up at him as one unable to believe her ears. "You mean—let Job come and see me?"

"Come, anyhow," George said, after hesitation, as if he were picking his way carefully among words; and then waited, his heart in his mouth, for her answer.

He hadn't long to wait. Almost at once she said, briefly and firmly, "Never."

§

For a moment they gazed at each other, without speaking.

So this was Fanny, he was thinking. This was what she was really like, must always have been like, beneath the wonder of her beauty. All that radiant sympathy and eagerness to do kind things—had it, then, been nothing but the effect of perfect health, and perfect contentment with her lot? Was it possible? Yet how final, how flint-like was that *Never*. At fifty, Fanny revealing herself as a flint. So old and so untender, he said to himself, staring at her as though he were seeing her for the first time.

And she was thinking, "He's hating me. I've shocked him beyond recovery unless I do something quickly. I can't let him go. I can't lose George. I shall have to tell him why I won't see Job. One humiliation more or less doesn't really matter. I'd rather he knew what a fool I am than think me hateful and hard.

She tried to get out of the deep chair, feeling she would be able to say what she had to say better on her feet, but it was too low, and she held out her hands for him to pull her up. He, extremely reluctant to take hold of hands he felt he never wanted to touch again, was obliged to help her; and when she was on her feet, standing quite close to him, rather like a little girl forced to say a difficult lesson not yet really learned, to a judge she knows will be severe, he informed her that if this was her last word, this detestable, unchristian *Never*, then he thought he had better go away. "And not come back," said George, glowering at her from beneath drawn-together eyebrows.

"But it isn't my last word," she hurriedly explained. No, she couldn't lose George; even if he had been misjudging her, she couldn't. He was the only one of her old adorers left— unless one counted Job.

"I'll at least thank God for that," he answered, his brows a little relaxing.

"There are several more——"

Did he hear something very like a bark in the lower regions of the house? Anxiously he glanced, first at the door, and then at her; but she seemed not to have noticed it, or else supposed it was outside, in the dog-populous mews. Besides, he knew by the way she was pressing her hands together—a trick familiar to him whenever she was in difficulties,—that she was absorbed in what she was trying to say.

"And if," she went on, after taking a deep breath, "you look at me carefully, you ought to guess what they are. I mean, if you look carefully at what is left of my face."

He melted at once. A man who readily melted before any kind of distress, the distress she was evidently feeling at having to say this, left him wholly tender and sympathetic. Niggs had assured him that Fanny was unconscious of the change in her face, that women never did know when their beauty left them, that it was a great pity, and that someone ought to tell her about it; and he had believed her, and taken comfort in the belief that his darling cousin was at least spared what must, to any woman once so beautiful, be a torment. Now it appeared that she hadn't been spared, and that she was perfectly aware of what had happened to her.

Pity washed away the last traces of his anger. "I know all about your darling face, my Fanny," he said gently, taking it in both his hands and kissing her forehead.

"Then need I go on? Job hasn't seen it for nearly twenty-five years, remember."

"That doesn't matter," he said.

"Not matter? Why, but George——"

She drew away from him. Was this her understanding cousin? Had he been married for years to Niggs without getting an inkling of what a woman's vanity could be, how it could seep through her whole character, drowning every good impulse on the way? She *wanted* to be kind, and warm, and personal with poor shipwrecked Job, and she couldn't, she couldn't, because it was unbearable to her that he, who had so abjectly worshipped her beauty, should see her as she was now.

"I assure you," said George earnestly, "that you'll always seem the same to Skeffington."

"Do you take me for a fool?" she protested—and again he thought he heard a distant bark, and again he started nervously, and again she didn't seem to have noticed. "Job loved me agonizingly, you know."

"And I'm certain still does," said George; though was he certain? That apathetic figure on the seat in Battersea Park, rousing only at a sudden noise or movement behind him; that patient, unarguing listener to his impetuous proposals; that obedient follower wherever he led, even if it were into Fanny's own house; could such a positive emotion as love still be expected of him? And agonizing love, too. Poor Skeffington. He had had enough of every sort of agonizing.

"Unfortunately he only loved what I looked like," she said. "Not me at all. And I'm not going to give him a shock."

"But you wouldn't," said George.

Then Fanny was really angry. "Oh, stop treating me as if I were a mental deficient!" she cried. "I've been seeing some of the others lately, some of the ones who used to think they loved me agonizingly too, and they one and all recoiled. Every man-jack of them. I've had enough of recoilers. I'm not going to add poor Job to them. After all, he was the only one who was my husband, and deserves a little extra consideration." And she indignantly turned her back on him.

He took a quick step forward, caught her by the wrist, and twisted her round again. "Do you mean to tell me," he said, his eyes very bright and strange, "that the only reason you won't see Skeffington——"

"Yes," she interrupted, looking at him defiantly. "That's why. Simply because, if I saw him, he would at the same time see me. Now despise me. You didn't guess, did you, what a poor, vain thing you've been fond of all your life, what an absurd——"

"But—is that all, Fanny?" he cut her short.

"All? Why, but it's contemptible. I've no words——"

"Listen," he again cut her short, holding her wrist very tight, "you don't want any words. What you've got to do now is to listen to a few of mine——"

But she was never to hear them, for at that moment the door opened, and Soames appeared.

George turned on him with extraordinary violence. "Didn't I give you the strictest orders not to come in?" he cried.

Fanny was astonished. So much violence about so small a thing. Why shouldn't Soames come in? The poor man, still obviously in a state of inner turmoil, which she still put down to Edward's wink, only wanted to take away the tea. George was her cousin and all that, but the strict orders and the violence did seem rather overstepping the bounds of what he might and might not do. Funny, everybody and everything were that day. Nothing, since she left her bedroom, had been in the least what she was accustomed to.

Puzzled and frowning, she stood, her wrist still held by George, while Soames, met by this outburst, hesitated on the threshold. Yes, he had been told not to come in, but after a while he had found it impossible to stay out. He was much too frightened. The silence, the death-like silence downstairs, had frightened him enough to begin with, but it was nothing to the fright which overwhelmed him when that dog started barking. What business had the secretary to go into the library and upset the dog? It had been as quiet as—as the other contents of the room till Miss Cartwright went pushing herself forward, and the noise it made had sent him hurrying upstairs, followed by two of his footmen, to take cover with Mr. Pontyfridd and her ladyship on the pretext of clearing away the tea. He had lost his nerve. He couldn't be left downstairs, without guidance or protection, when anything might happen. So there he was, the door, blocked by the footmen with trays, wide open behind him, and at that very moment there was another bark, loud and distinct this time, echoing through the resounding hall, up the great staircase, and along the passage to the sitting-room.

"Is there a dog in the house?" asked Fanny, more surprised by the way they all started than by the bark.

"Dog, m'lady?" stammered Soames. Why had Mr. Pontyfridd done this? Why had he put them in such a position, after years of getting on very well as they were? Soames pitied misfortune as much as any man, but it oughtn't to be brought indoors.

A second bark, a succession of barks, a whole volley of them, made any further answer unnecessary, and Fanny, looking from one to the other, from the white-gilled Soames to the red-gilled footmen, and from the red-gilled footmen to the beaded George, said, "I don't know what's the matter with you all, but as you're so mysterious and absurd I'm going to find out for myself——" and moved, with determination, towards the door.

George went after her. "Fanny, you've got to forgive me," he said eagerly, laying his hand on her shoulder. "I brought the dog in. You'll find it in the library."

"Well, really, I don't see why you shouldn't bring your dog in if you want to," she said, for an instant not sure she would bother to go downstairs, only to find George's dog in the library.

But there, meeting her through the open door, again flooded the peculiar atmosphere she had noticed when she came out

of her bedroom, the peculiar feeling that the whole house was
holding its breath, waiting for something to happen, and afraid.
It had got even into her bedroom, for she saw Manby peeping
out, sniffing inquiringly. Really, she must go and find out what
was happening. Till she handed everything over to Job she
still, after all, was mistress here, she couldn't just stand frowning and not doing anything. Besides, George's hand on her
shoulder seemed to be urging her along. He wanted her, she
felt, to go down and investigate. Not that that would have made
her go, but dignity demanded that she shouldn't put up with
mystifications.

"It isn't my dog, you know," said George, his voice very
strange.

"Not your dog?"

She turned her head and looked at him; and, as she looked,
the inquiry in her eyes changed first into incredulousness, and
then into a horrified certainty.

"*George?*" she said under her breath, as if quite unable to
believe it was he who had done this thing.

He began stroking her shoulder with quick, nervous, eager
movements. "It'll be all right," he assured her, jerking out
the words in time with his strokings. "You'll see—you'll understand—there are some things that can't be allowed to go on—
I was just going to tell you—I had meant to explain—don't
mind, darling—don't mind too much—go down—face it——"

"Of course I'm going to face it," she said, and withdraw-
ing her shoulder, walked out of the room.

George wiped his forehead. Soames, with his back turned,
furtively wiped his. The footmen would have liked to wipe
theirs, but couldn't because of the trays; besides, footmen don't.

Yes, it would be all right, it must be all right, it couldn't
help being all right, George assured himself, watching Fanny,
haughty indignation in every line of her body, going along the
passage and disappearing down the stairs. As for him, there
was nothing more he could do except pray for the salvation of
the Skeffingtons—of both the Skeffingtons, for surely his Fanny
needed saving from her blank future as much as the unhappy
Job from the memory of his frightful immediate past?

With all his heart, George prayed; but Soames, who couldn't
know that he was praying, except that he looked worried,
interrupted him. "If you'll excuse me mentioning it, sir,"
Soames whispered fearfully, under cover of the clatter the foot-

men's unsteady hands were making collecting the cups, "isn't the—the encounter likely to give her ladyship a terrible shock?"

"Devils, *devils*," was George's unexpected answer, clenching his fists and going suddenly as red in the face as the footmen.

It wasn't, though, of the Skeffingtons that he was thinking.

XI

§

AND now here was Fanny, going down all alone to meet her fate. Her head was high, and her spirit up in arms. This, if you like, was an outrage, she said to herself. How dared George. But, a thousand times more inexplicable, how dared Job. Worse, infinitely worse, than George's bringing Job into the house was it that Job should have let himself be brought. It had been bad enough for his figment to pervade it, upsetting her nerves almost into fits, but what was a figment compared to an actual body? The decent impulse she had had of restitution, of wholesale giving back, went curdled within her. Like the Kingdom of Heaven, she wasn't going to be taken by violence. So justly angry was she, so rightly revolted, that as she hurried downstairs she actually forgot her determination that Job should never see her in her decay. Not till she reached the last step did she remember that she couldn't possibly show herself to him as she was now, and pulling up short was on the point of turning round and going upstairs again to George, tell him to collect his friend, leave the house, and never let her set eyes on him again, when the library door opened, and Miss Cartwright, pursued by barks, hurriedly came out of it.

Now how strange, thought Fanny, stopping dead. What had she been doing in there? And how very intelligent of the dog to chase her out.

She had no time, however, to disentangle what her secretary's probable motives could have been in going into a room where she had no business, though she felt in her bones that they were bad, and only said inquiringly, standing on the last stair, looking down at her, "Yes?"

"Oh, Lady Frances, I beg your pardon, I'm sure," stammered Miss Cartwright, in quite extraordinary confusion. "I

thought—I thought you were in the library, and I wanted—I
just wanted——"

Her voice died away. Any voice would have, before Fanny's
look.

"There's nothing more I want to-day,", was, all she said,
coming down the last stair.

No turning back now. Miss Cartwright was obliging her to
go into the library. And remarking, in case the secretary should
imagine she didn't know whom she would find there, "I'm
afraid you have upset Mr. Skeffington's dog," she opened the
door, went in, and shut it behind her.

§

Yes; there was Job, just as George had described him, white-
haired and shrivelled, sitting under the lamp at the other end
of the long room, and the dog, no longer barking but watching
her with bright eyes, upright on its haunches beside him.

How still the room was. A curious quiet seemed settling on
it, now that only she and Job were there—like dust falling softly
on ancient, finished things. She stood just inside the shut door,
not moving, feeling as if she were looking into a picture. Job,
in his distant chair, didn't move either. And the dog, upright
on its haunches, stared at her in bright-eyed silence.

An old man, with hands folded on a stick. An old man, so
entirely unlike the Job she remembered and the Job of the
hauntings that her wrath all died away. How could anybody
be angry with a pitiful stranger? And those dark glasses—
George hadn't told her about the dark glasses; there never used
to be glasses; Job's eyes, except when gazing at her and they
became wet with worship, had been as keen as a hawk's. Now
they were hidden, and she couldn't tell, though his head was
turned towards her, whether he were looking at her or not.

But he must be looking at her; he couldn't help it, with his
head turned that way. Was it possible—she caught her breath—
that he didn't know who she was? That he, of them all, hadn't
an idea?

Shaken by this dreadful suspicion, instead of asking him to
explain his unpardonable invasion of her house, all she found
she could do was to falter, "Job——?" and after a silence
which seemed to last for ever, the voice she hadn't heard for

twenty-two years answered, very slowly and gently, as though groping its way down the long room, "Is it Fanny?"

Is it Fanny? For a moment she couldn't speak. The others, every one of them, had at least recognized her, even if with evident shock, but here was Job, not recognizing her at all.

"You don't—know me again?" she asked, swallowing.

He said slowly, after another silence, "The voice is Fanny's."

Stricken, she stood motionless, leaning against the door, pressed for support against the door. Her voice. Nothing left of her now, for Job, but a voice.

He began getting up. The dog, shaking itself, immediately got up too. It was fastened, she saw, by a loop to its master's arm. Was he afraid that it, too, as she had, and her successors had when he grew old and poor, would run away and leave him?

He seemed to have difficulty in getting up. He fumbled, feeling his way along the arm of the chair with the hand that wasn't holding the stick. And she thought, watching him, defending herself against the appeal of his helplessness, "It's not fair. I'm being got at unfairly. This isn't the way to—I won't be caught by——"

But when he tripped on the rug, and the stick was jerked out of his grasp, and he would have fallen if it hadn't been for the dog pulling him back into the chair, instinct was too much for her and she flew to him, holding out her hands.

He took no notice of them—she, Fanny, holding out her hands to Job, and he taking no notice of them,—while his face, upward turned to hers, had the same queer, blank, listening look she had noticed when he heard the door open.

Something in it, now that she saw it close, something behind the thick, dark glasses, invisible but felt, froze her. "Job," she whispered, hardly able to breathe, "you're not—they didn't —you can't be——"

But the word wouldn't come out, and he said it for her. "Yes," he said, bowing his head, speaking very gently, as if anxious to avoid the smallest appearance of complaint, or even of criticism. "Blind."

"Not the——?"

But terror came into the room, into the quiet, safe, Charles Street room, at the bare approach of the word she was going to say if he hadn't stopped her. "Hush, hush——" he whispered in quick panic, showing his first real sign of life, fearfully turning his head, as if to see if anyone were hiding behind his chair, his body suddenly going tense, instinctively getting ready to be hurt.

She stared down at him, struck to stone by the terrible implications of his movement. This, then, was life, beneath the smiles. While she, in the sun of its surface, was wasting months in shamefully selfish, childish misery over the loss of her beauty, Job was being broken up into a sort of frightened animal. How could one live, while such things were going on? How could one endure consciousness, except by giving oneself up wholly and for ever to helping, and comforting, and at last, at last, perhaps healing?

There was a noise outside the door, quite an ordinary, everyday little noise, a noise Fanny wouldn't even have noticed, but it was enough to make Job start and clutch the sides of the chair; and this second movement, again appalling in its implications, brought her to her knees.

Flooded by a passionate tenderness, she knelt down and gathered him to her heart. "No, no," she assured him, holding him close, almost rocking him, as though he were the baby she had never had, "they shan't—they never, never shall again —you're safe—you've come home——"

He said nothing. He was listening intently; but not to her. His head was turned towards the door, while she, overwhelmed by an agonizing pity, held him to her, protecting him, daring anyone to harm him, incoherently whispering words of love he would have given his life to hear a quarter of a century ago.

Now he said nothing. He was listening; but not to her. And the dog, upright and alert, watched them both in bright-eyed silence.

§

Manby found them like that. It was she who, to her great vexation unable quite to control her hands, had bumped the tray she was carrying against the door.

Long ago she had discovered that the only way to approach the varied situations in which her lady so easily became involved, was to behave as if nothing were happening. A single glance at Fanny's face, as she peeped through the door at her walking along the passage to the stairs, had convinced her that

yet one more of these situations was upon them, and hurrying
back into the bedroom she telephoned down to Miss Cartwright,
and asked her if she knew what it was.

The answer she got made her first hold on to the table,
because her legs gave way, and then, recovering her breath and
her courage, immediately rise to the occasion. Now indeed her
mistress must be helped.

To Manby, the only husband her mistress had ever had was
still the master. She slid over that long-past lapse into the Law
Courts, being unshakably of the opinion that once God had
joined people together, no amount of talk by gentlemen in wigs
could put them asunder. The master had behaved in a way
he shouldn't, but gentlemen weren't ladies, and ought to be
forgiven. By this time her mistress ought really to be able to
forgive. Therefore, her mouth tight with determination, the
thumping of her heart sternly suppressed, as a preliminary to
steadying and helping she began measuring medicine into a
small glass.

Her ladyship's tonic. Dr. Clark's Blood Mxture. Recommended by Manby herself, and administered every evening at
seven o'clock. It was now seven o'clock. Habits, in her
experience, if punctually kept to, were invaluable as reminders
that there were other things in life besides shocks. Look at
breakfast, for instance; look at brushing one's teeth. And
having measured, she put the glass on a tray, took it down to
the library, advanced, after that single moment's bungling at
the door, with the composed tread and impassive countenance
of one performing a daily duty at the appointed hour, and said,
her eyelids respectfully lowered, "Your drops, m'lady."

"You see—it was only Manby," her mistress anxiously
assured the poor master, just as if he were a frightened child
being coaxed to believe that there was nothing to be afraid of.

"Yes, sir. And very glad to see you, sir," said Manby, taking
one shocked glance. "I hope you are——" she was going to
say keeping well, but how could a poor gentleman be keeping
well who was so old, such a skeleton, and, worst of all afflictions,
blind?

Fanny sat back on her heels, and looked up at her through
wet eyelashes. Her face was the face of grief itself, but grief
shone through with hope and resolve. No need for help here,
thought Manby, suddenly aglow with pride; her lady was going
to do the right thing, and she was more beautiful to Manby

at that moment than she had ever been in the days of her glory.

"Mr. Skeffington has come home," she said.

"Yes, m'lady. Should I——" a small pause, while Manby struggled with, and triumphed over, an inconvenient and unseemly feeling in her throat which easily might have ended as a sob—"should I tell the housekeeper to prepare a room?"

"His own room," said Fanny.

"Yes, m'lady. And will your ladyship wear——" another small pause, during which, with an almost superhuman effort, she recovered her usual respectful impassiveness—"should I put out the pink velvet, or the new white lace?"

For an instant Fanny's head drooped; for an instant she made odd, uncertain movements with her hand, trailing it backwards and forwards on the rug, her face hidden.

Then she looked up and said, "But of *course,* the new white lace."

THE END

Also by Elizabeth von Arnim,
available from Virago

ELIZABETH AND HER GERMAN GARDEN

In this, her most famous novel, Elizabeth von Arnim wonderfully evokes the seasons and their events, immortalising her garden with her uniquely witty pen.

THE SOLITARY SUMMER

With the pleasing astringency for which she is noted Elizabeth von Arnim returns to her famous heroine and garden. A witty, lyrical account of a rejuvenating summer, this is the delightful companion to *Elizabeth and her German Garden*.

THE PASTOR'S WIFE

The experiences of Ingeborg – a pastor's wife in East Prussia – are recounted with subtlety and humour. Yet beneath Elizabeth von Arnim's characteristic wit is her recurrent theme: the bondage of women as daughters and wives, never more deftly explored than in this accomplished novel.

THE CARAVANERS

England presents more than just a contrast of scenery to one German couple: amongst English companions on a caravanning holiday in Southern England, Edelgard proves to be less biddable than her upright husband the Major had believed . . . Originally published in 1909, *The Caravaners* reveals once again the incisive humour for which Elizabeth von Arnim is acclaimed.

THE ENCHANTED APRIL

Recently dramatised on screen and for the BBC

A discreet advertisement in *The Times* addressed to "those who Appreciate Wistaria and Sunshine . . .", is the prelude to a revelatory month for four very different women. This delightful novel is imbued with the descriptive power and light-hearted irreverence for which Elizabeth von Arnim is so popular.

LOVE

Beneath the humour of this engaging novel lies a sharper note, as Elizabeth von Arnim uncovers the hypocrisy of society and the codes it forces women to ascribe to in the name of 'love'.

THE ADVENTURES OF ELIZABETH IN RÜGEN

When a drought threatens Elizabeth's beloved garden, she is tempted to explore the island of Rügen, off Germany's Baltic coast. And as she immortalised her Pomeranian wilderness, she now writes enticingly of this remote and attractive island.

VERA

First published in 1921, this is Elizabeth von Arnim's masterpiece – a forceful study of the power of men in marriage, and the weakness of women when they love.